The Butcher Boys

Chris Gill

Joyce Gill Deeger

Fisher King Publishing

THE BUTCHER BOYS

Published by
Fisher King Publishing
fisherkingpublishing.co.uk

For my son, Archie, and my best friend, David.

And for Mum, Jo, Karen and Christine.

SUMMER 1976

CHAPTER ONE

Jack fancied a crack at The One-Handed Leap-Frog. Michael was squatting at the edge of the river, short and stocky in his white school PE kit, filling an old Fairy Liquid bottle so he could use it as a water pistol. Jack scurried down the riverbank in his shorts, scuffing up powdery dirt with his pumps, trying not to piss himself laughing. He had hold of a squeezy bottle water pistol too, fully loaded. That left one hand spare to pull off his daring stunt. He came up fast and quiet, planted his palm between Michael's shoulders and leapt through the hot air.

"Geronimo-o-o-o-o-o!"

Jack was usually right good at PE, he'd fairly flown over that pommel horse at school sports day this afternoon, but he'd got too much speed up this time in his daftness. If he'd done the job right, he'd have landed in the water on his feet. But now he'd spun half a somersault. His bare back slapped into the river. Frigging hell, what a stinger! Lying in the shallow water on the stony riverbed, he squinted at the blue sky. Then he shielded his eyes from that boiling sun so he could make out Michael, who was standing over him now, staring at him with a sweaty upside-down face.

Michael could tell Jack were in pain. He had a grimace on, not a smile. But the lad was the hardest kid in their school year, crazy like a mad allik and as tough as one of them film heroes of his, Dirty Harry. Michael screwed the red nozzle back onto his plastic bottle, like it were akin to a silencer on a gun, and aimed the weapon straight at Jack's head.

"Do yer feel lucky?" he said.

"Give over tekin' t' piss," said Jack, gritting his teeth. "My back's killin'!"

"Well, do yer, punk?"

But then Michael was caught unawares. Jack suddenly flipped over like a salmon, tugged at his ankles, put him on his arse, dragged him into the river. Michael were pretty decent at handling himself too, mind. He kicked free and stood knee deep. Feeling his drenched T-shirt sucking coldly on his skin, he watched Jack get up to face him. Flipping heck, the lad was a long streak of piss nowadays. 'Lanky,' the nickname Michael had for him, was just right. He could tell Lanky wanted to laugh, even though he were trying summat rotten to look mean, like Clint Eastwood in his Westerns. Jack might have only been twelve, the same as Michael, but his dad had let him stay up late to watch 'The Good, the Bad and the Ugly', because that's how he reckoned real men should be.

As the boys moved well away from each other, wading heavy backward steps in the shallow waters near the river's edge, slowly lowering their water guns to where a holster might hang, Jack was picturing his favourite Clint gunfights. They were locked in the glare of hard men. The still heat beat from a clear sky. At last, they stopped. Jack raised a fist, uncurled one finger...Two fingers...Three.

"Chaaaarrge!" they cried, shooting from the hip, surging toward one another.

Jack kicked his long legs up high, as if the riverbed's mossy stones were white hot.

"Pile in, then, Micky!" he said.

Jack thought it was a right laugh watching his best mate Michael plough through the water rhino-style, his fat little legs going ten to the dozen. As the gap between them narrowed, Jack cracked up. This newest game of theirs was such ace fun! Rugby River Scrum only had two rules. One, it was against the law to play it downstream from the village, because that was 'down south' and Rugby River Scrum wasn't for southerners. And two, only Jack and Michael were allowed to play it, anyway. Well, they'd invented it.

"Watch yer bones, Lanky!" said Michael, head down for use as a battering ram.

Each time the collision came, it put Michael in mind of them Tom and Jerry cartoons everyone watched on telly, when Tom the cat ran into an anvil or summat. Or got whacked so hard with a frying pan that the shape of his face came through the bottom. The boys clattered together, squeezy bottles flying. It hurt Michael every flipping time, but it were proper funny. They went under, clinging to one another, rolling in the silty currents, roughing up the riverbed. Then Michael managed to break free. They stood again, circling each other, crouching akin to Saturday afternoon wrestlers looking for an opening. Michael knew he'd need all his powers to pull off his big move, but, even then, Jack were so strong for a streaky sod. Might have been down to all them floppy pig carcasses they got shipped in from town, which his old man got him to carry on his shoulders from the slaughterhouse wagon into their shop. Jack was chopping at the river with a flat hand now, skimming water into Michael's face. Michael had to get revenge, so he cupped his hands and started scooping up water superfast.

"That t' best ya can do, ya great lummox?" said Jack. "Rat-a-tat-a-rat-a-tat-a-tat-tat-tat!" he continued, doing his machine gun impression, hitting Michael with loads more water bullets.

Michael knew the lad were only teasing. Nowt nasty in it. Jack found it so easy to take the piss, mind, and that did wind Michael up sometimes. He tried thinking of sharp replies, and they did come to him, but nearly always too late. After they'd been playing out. When he was by himself again.

When he was walking home through the fields, whacking heads off clockwork dandelions with a stick. He had thought of a brilliant one now, though. He opened his mouth to say it, but Jack immediately fired in a slug of gritty river water. Michael's gob spluttered. And there was his best mate, near as damn it wetting himself!

"Soz," said Jack, sticking his hands up like he meant it. "Sorry."

When Michael had given over coughing, they started circling one another again. Michael set his jaw so it felt as hard as Yorkshire Dales limestone.

"You've got the look o' Desperate Dan, Micky. Dyin' for a cow pie!" said Jack, pretending to be a huge pie with horns poking through the pastry, like the one Desperate Dan always tucked into at the end of his comic strip. "Mooooooooo!" he bellowed.

Jack might have been mucking about, but there was summat in that stupid cow noise which riled Michael. What did the lad think, that he were gormless? An idiot? Folk were being so kind to Michael nowadays, after what had happened. Asking if he was all right. Patting him on the head. But did they do that because they had him down as thick too? Sometimes he just wanted to be let alone. Definitely time for his big move now. He suddenly bulldozed forward and crushed his skull into Jack's guts.

Jack could feel that one knocking the wind out of his sails! And, with the force of it, Michael had lifted him clean out of the water. Frigging hell, the lad was ten times stronger when he got a bee in his bonnet. They fell back into the river, Michael crashing down on top of Jack with all his weight and clinging on like a croc in a death roll, excepting there was nowt cold-blooded about it. Jack could feel the hot anger squeezing his body. It was making him breathless. He tried slipping out of the hold, pushing down on Michael's shoulders, but that grip was too tight. Michael raised him from the water again and he somehow managed to dredge up a few words.

"Micky, I'm on...Your...Side..."

They plunged back under. Maybe Jack would have to start wringing his friend's neck. But then he sensed his words might just have got through, so he held Michael's head to his chest. Then he felt that grip loosening. They emerged from the water and stood opposite one another, hands on knees, slowly gaining breath.

"Fuckin' hell, you've got a fair grip on ya," said Jack, at last.

"I know we were only laikin', but..."

Michael broke off. His cheeks were usually right rosy, proper butcher's cheeks they were, but now Jack clocked them looking hellish red. He watched Michael pinch his chin with his sausage fingers. Looked like he was after stopping it trembling.

"Come on, Micky, you'll be reet."

Jack had a gander up and down the parched riverbanks and surrounding bone-dry dale, making sure there was no-one about. He couldn't see anybody, so he reached out to Michael and hugged him. With pats on the back, mind, so they were clear this was no sissy embrace.

"Let's reload and get up that tree," said Jack. "Someone's gonna be walkin' past soon, on a beltin' day like this."

After they'd refilled their bottles, Jack led the way as they waded back to the bank. The best tree for camouflage was a few yards upstream, right at the edge of the riverside path. A massive ancient sycamore with thick, leafy branches. Proper good for ambushing, it was, because one bough spanned over the path and out above the river a fair way, letting them attack from both sides as their victims strolled along. Jack tucked his water bottle under the elastic of his shorts, reached up to grip the bough, swung his long legs onto it.

Michael did the same with his water bottle and followed, taking a running jump to reach the bough and hoist himself up. A magpie made a racket and scarpered. Flipping heck, how he'd just been with Jack had scared him. You've got to give over letting your anger get the better of you like that. Does you no good. He balanced his way along the bough, out to his favourite spot overhanging the river. By the time he'd reached his position, crouching in wait, he could see Jack near as damn it halfway up the other side of the tree already.

"Careful, Lanky! You're not an orang-utan."

"Ooo ooo ooo ooooo!" came the idiot call from above.

"Stop swingin' off one hand, yer psycho!"

Jack swung back onto two, laughing his head off. Michael watched him climbing again. He didn't like it when Jack were reckless, when he seemed not to give a toss about owt. At least as he reached the higher, thinner branches you could make out them feet in white pumps stepping more carefully between the leaves.

"Just take it steady," said Michael.

"Ya worry too much, Micky, lad," said Jack.

Michael did worry too much. And that worried him. Best concentrate on his water pistol. He cleaned it on his soaked PE shirt a while, trying to imagine he was someone else. A baddie getting ready for a gunfight.

"Arrgghh!"

That were Jack. Michael snapped out of it, standing from his crouch and stretching his neck to look for him between the greenery and broken sunlight.

"You all reet, Lanky?"

"I'm right, mate," said Jack. "Just scraped me sen on a knobbly bit. Owwwah!"

Michael caught sight of him lowering his shorts to have a gander at where it hurt. Now there was one bare arse staring down from up high.

"Full moon today?" said Michael.

"Ya what?"

"We're not usin' our backsides to fire on folk."

"Give over...Gi' o'er, can't ya?" said Jack, in fits. "You're crackin' me up."

"I can see up yer crack from here!"

If they'd not held on tighter, their laughing might have shaken them from the tree like coconuts. But having a good laugh felt better than owt else to Michael nowadays, so he kept glancing at 'the moon.' Then he caught sight of a big bruise across them buttocks.

"Flippin' heck, that's come on quick!" he said.

"Eh?" said Jack.

"Thee's got a fair bruiser already. All t' way across yer arse, it is."

Jack's laughing had dried up.

"Oh, that. Got it slippin' on t' shop floor, Saturday."

"Serious?" said Michael.

"Molly the Mop's doin'. Know Molly, don't ya?"

"Aye."

"Wanna see me new war wound, then?" said Jack.

Before Michael could say owt else, Jack had spun round, shorts still low, and there was a bloody graze scarring the inside of his thigh.

"Nasty one," said Michael. "Reet, can yer pull yer kegs up now? Don't fancy an eyeful o' yer todger an all."

Crouching again at the end of the bough, half out of the shade, Michael got back to cleaning his water gun, its plastic gleaming in the hot sun.

Jack hitched up his shorts and said he'd keep spying for anyone coming along the path. He reckoned he was fifty foot up now, no bother, sitting on a branch as lookout. He flicked his coal-black fringe, which was so long it touched his eyebrows. Loads of folk had their hair long these days, but he'd likely be forced to get it cut soon. There had already been grumblings from that front room armchair, mixing with the smell of St Bruno pipe smoke. Once or twice lately, when the armchair was empty, he'd had a sneaky few minutes watching Top of the Pops. And he didn't want his frigging hair cut at all. He wanted to grow it to his shoulders, like Slade. He'd heard that a few years since that band had performed in big top hats with fancy mirrors all over them. He loved imagining wearing one of those on Fowlbeck village High Street, so people could walk toward him and look at their own miserable faces gawping back in shock. Doubtless they'd just have a good laugh at him, though. As if it would ever happen, anyway.

His eyes strayed from the riverside path, across the brownish river and straw-coloured fields, shaped by dry limestone walls and dotted with sheep and hay bales, toward the darker moors. There it was, the highest hill for miles around: Fowlbeck Beacon. In a month or so, when its acres of heather turned purple, it would look right pretty. Jack knew there was more to it than that, mind. Because you could easily trip on the heather's roots, or sink into a boggy patch when it pissed it down, or twist your ankle on a jagged rock. But the danger was what made it such an ace adventure. He'd been there with Micky eleven times now. It was definitely eleven, because they kept a logbook by way of proof. The lot was in there. Dates, wildlife spotted, weather conditions encountered, secret maps, fingerprint 'signatures' hardened in their very own blood. They'd been blood brothers a fair while now, albeit they'd only used a poxy penknife for the purpose, so blood fingerprints had to go in.

Jack gazed at The Beacon's summit, thinking on what it felt like looking over into the next valley and beyond. Every time he stood up there, he imagined being Clint riding to a new horizon. Wouldn't it be fine and dandy, being Clint? Then you could just fuck off somewhere else whenever you fancied.

He was only reminded of his lookout duties when summat as smooth and shiny as an otter caught his eye. A Brylcreem hairdo looked to be bobbing across the top of that nearby drystone wall, moving toward them.

"Rocker Billy's comin'!"

"You're jokin'," said Michael.

"Headin' this way. All slicked back like a duck's arse."

"He'll go nuts."

"Your turn for t' openin' shot, Micky. Aim for the hair! Aim for the hair!"

Jack slunk back further among the dusty-smelling leaves, sighting along his poised plastic weapon. Still, like a hunter in tall grass, he waited. Rocker Billy was two years older than him and Michael, a teenager, and all he seemed to give a shite about was how he looked. Black leather jacket, bouncy soles on his shoes, tight-arse trousers, greased hair whipped up into a big curl on top. He took some stick in the village, but it seemed no bother to him. Jack wasn't right sure what to make of Rocker Billy.

A minute or so later, he got to staring down at him through his favourite gap, as he was about to strut on under the tree. But now The Rocker had stopped. He was touching his hairdo, then gawping at his fingers. Micky must have fired in the early one! They always held back after the first hit, before the victim made their next move, before it got to all guns blazing time. If the person just walked on, they'd still get blasted. But the best ones were when they realised they'd been squirted from above and looked up. Then they'd get soaked in the face, which was always a belter. Rocker Billy looked up. The jets hit their target. Some water must have got in his gob and up and round into his nose because, between his coughing and hacking, Jack saw him press a finger to each nostril and shoot watery greenies into the dust. And, now he was properly open, the ambushers squeezed their water guns dead hard, giving the lad's sculpted hair the full treatment, soaking it with all the ammunition they had left. When it was over, Rocker Billy, hair all stringy, raised his sodden head. Now he had them spotted. Jack reckoned he didn't look too chuffed either.

"Butcher boys!" he shouted. "Bastard butcher boys!"

Michael was crapping it. And, looking up through the branches, he even thought Jack seemed edgy. They knew Rocker Billy could handle himself, and now he had a proper strop on. This were still the funniest bit, mind, seeing someone get riled after being soaked.

"Come off it, Rocker Man," said Jack. "We're just havin' a laugh."

"Aye, Rockin' Man," said Michael. "No hard feelings, eh?"

"Cocky bastards," said Rocker Billy, looking right sulky now, bowing his head.

Michael watched him scuff his thick rubber soles about in the dry earth.

"We were just havin' fun, Billy," he said. "Soz if we made yer feel bad."

"Cocky bastards!"

Rocker Billy ran at the tree and was onto the bough so

quick that Michael wondered if he'd used his rubbery shoes to bounce up. Then he were standing there in his shiny leather jacket, leaning against the trunk, watching him from a few yards away with right still eyes.

"Where is he, Micky?" said Jack. "What's he up to? Can't see him from here now."

Michael's mouth felt akin to the dry summer, as he watched Rocker Billy clench and raise a fist. And when The Rocker Man started moving slowly toward him along the bough, he watched the chunky rings on each tight finger, silver glimmering in the sunlight sliding between the leaves. He didn't want to gawp at the anchor, the skull, the word 'LOVE,' the crucifix, but he couldn't help it.

"I can see him!" said Jack. "Jump in t' river, Micky!"

Michael had a struggle concentrating on Jack's words, though, as anchor, skull, 'LOVE,' crucifix loomed closer.

"He won't wanna ruin his fancy clobber. Just jump, mate!"

Anchor... Skull...'LOVE'...Crucifix...

"Leave off him, Rocker Billy! Touch him and I'll fuckin' brain ya!"

"Got any more belters, Jack Hargraves?" said Rocker Billy, stopping a couple of feet from Michael. "I'll piss me sen in a minute."

"Yeah, Rock-A-Bye-Baby," said Jack. "I reckon you will. Not such a big man, are ya? Were you cryin' a minute since, when ya went reet quiet? Just a cry-baby under your pretty Elvis clothes, aren't ya? Cry-baby, cry-baby, cry-baby!"

Michael saw Rocker Billy tense up at that, then lower his heavy fist, then crane his neck to look for Lanky. At last, Michael realised what he should be doing. He jumped off the bough and splashed into the river. He watched Rocker Billy turn to see him squatting there like a hippo, water level just below his nose. Flipping heck, that were close!

"You comin' up to get me now then, Rocker Baby?" said Jack.

Michael stared at Rocker Billy climbing. You couldn't see any fear holding him back. More like rage shifting him up that tree. Red rag to a bull time! Why did Jack have to rile him even more, when he was already so narked? Because he'd been pushed into one of his 'I don't give a shit' moods again. Why did he have to do it, though? Scrapping on the ground were one thing, but high up a tree? He really was a mad allik, no mistake. Michael stood, the cool river water lapping at his bare legs.

"Don't be daft, you two!" he shouted. "Yer can't fight up there. What if yer fall?"

Where was Jack now, anyhow?

"Micky, find the deep bit!"

There he was. Made his way out to stand on a branch overhanging the river. How far up had he got? Eighty foot?

"Yer what?" said Michael.

"The deep bit! Quick, find it! He'll be here any sec!"

"You're not gonna jump?"

"I'm jumping!" said Jack.

"You'd just as well fall in The Surge!"

"It's nowt like The Surge. Just find that deep part, will ya?"

Michael knew the flipping barmpot were serious too. Bloody hell, where's that deep bit? Further out for sure. Near where them stones underfoot got bigger. Then it went sandier somewhere, didn't it? He waded out a few steps further.

"I think that's far enough out!" said Jack.

"Left or right, then?" said Michael, stopping, looking up at him.

"Your left, I reckon."

"Goes sandy near there, dun't it?"

"Aye," said Jack. "Then it just drops straight down, sharpish."

"Flippin' heck, you're not jumpin'!" said Michael, moving to his left.

"I'm jumping! Ya must be close to it now. Oy, Rocker Billy?"

"Don't get his dander up any more, Lanky!"

Jack could hear Rocker Billy climbing now, brushing against the leaves and branches, and he kept catching glimpses of the sheen on top of his flattened hair. He was dead near.

"You not speaking to me, Rocker Baby? Not cryin' again, are ya?"

"Found it!" yelled Michael.

"Right, Micky, tread water there, then!" said Jack. "So I know where I'm jumpin'! Then, soon as ya see me fly, swim like hell! Don't wanna land on ya bonce!"

Jack thought Michael was doing a good job, staying afloat in one spot, all the time looking up high into the tree, waiting.

"Be careful!" said Michael.

Then Rocker Billy's ringed hand grabbed the branch Jack was on, making it creak. Now you could smell his frigging Brylcreem.

"Too late, Rock-A-Bye. Bye bye, Baby!" said Jack, springing like a long-legged frog, up and away, clearing the branches. "I'll be seein' yaaaaaaaaahhhh!"

Michael gave it a split second so Jack was certain where he needed to land, then went flailing into the backstroke, looking up at the boy with bicycle legs and windmill arms steering through the sky.

"Please hit the deep bit," he whispered. "Please hit the

deep bit."

Jack fell faster, faster, faster and plunged with a giant splash.

"He hit it! He hit it!" cried Michael. "Geronimo! He hit it! Geronimo! Geronimo!"

Moments later, Jack's grinning head appeared above the surface.

"Geronimo, Micky!" he said, swimming toward him. "How about that for a leap?"

"Geronimo! Geronimo! Geronimo!" they shouted, hugging each other, laughing like loons.

Now Rocker Billy looked to have had enough. He seemed knackered after he'd climbed down, and he wasn't about to get his precious clobber wet for anyone. Michael and Jack watched him from the river as he swore revenge and sloped off under the trees.

"You're a proper nutjob, you, Lanky," said Michael.

"Gotta keep things lively, lad," said Jack.

Michael gazed at the water still rippling from Jack's jump.

"Did yer see his rings?" he said. "Anchor...Crucifix...Skull...'LOVE'..."

"You all reet, Micky?"

But Michael couldn't stop staring at the ripples.

"Micky?" said Jack, after a few seconds.

"What?"

"I wish it was my dad who died."

CHAPTER TWO

Acouple of days later, in the front room of his house near the top of Fowlbeck High Street, Michael was standing face to face with his mum beside the oak Yorkshire dresser and its display of blue-patterned china. They were nearly ready to go to Grandad's house for Sunday dinner, but Mum were after straightening his shirt collar first. He hated it summat rotten when she mothered him.

"Now, let's have a good look at you, Michael Bowers," she said, smoothing out his paisley lapels, taking a step back.

"Mu-um," moaned Michael.

"Very smart."

"We off or what?"

"Still my smashing little boy, aren't you?" said Mum, gently squeezing his cheek.

"Give o'er," said Michael, shaking his head.

Mum picked up her cream handbag from the worn leather settee.

"My one and only," she said, eyes watery.

"Mu-um, don't."

When they'd stepped out of the front door onto the village High Street, Michael stayed a couple of yards ahead of her as they moved down the sloping road's flagstone pavement in the sunshine. Well, he didn't want all and sundry seeing him as a mummy's boy, did he? He tugged at his collar. Flipping heck, it were boiling this drought summer! You could see the midday heat shimmering above the tarmac, as a day tripper's Datsun coughed up oily-smelling fumes on its way past. Tourists, or 'off-cum-dens' as Grandad called them, easily outnumbered locals on sunny weekends. Grandad knew that Bowers' Family Butchers needed off-cum-dens, but he couldn't bide the ones arriving in Datsuns. Michael hoped he didn't blither on about it today: 'Why do they allus arrive in them cars?' he'd say. 'Who wants a Datsun, any road? Tin cans! Don't last five minutes. And what about all t' bother at British Leyland? Foreigners caused that, yer know. Bloody Japs tryin' to take o'er t' world agin! Cheap imports. Do you blame our boys for striking? Not that I'm a union man, but...' Michael wished he didn't have to do this family thing every blooming Sunday. Now there were only three of them, anyhow. He wanted to be dossing about with Jack, playing Rugby River Scrum. It didn't hurt as much.

"Michael!" called Mum.

"What?" he said, stopping, turning round.

"Wait on for me, eh, love?"

She was about twenty yards back now. Only, now, she'd stopped to chat with Eddie Weir, general builder and all-round ladies' man. He'd likely spotted her from The Dog and Gun, which they'd just passed. In there every Sunday, he was. As soon as them doors opened, sitting in that bay window, supping his pint of ale, keeping an eye out for passing 'crumpet'. Michael reckoned he were a knobhead. Especially now it looked like Mum was the crumpet. The vultures were out already.

"Mum, we're gonna be late."

"I'm just talking to Eddie."

"Eh up, Michael," said Eddie, waving at him. "You look smart, Son."

Michael leant his back against a shop window and tried taking his mind off them. He looked down the High Street and set to thinking on some of the stuff Dad had told him about their big village in the middle of nowhere. These limestone shops and terraced houses, lining either side of this steep, straight road, had been turned a bit black by all the mucky soot floating down from the chimney pots...Tractors, hay lorries, meat wagons had been squeezing between these buildings for donkey's years...That undertaker's sign had swung on its rusty hooks for nearly as long as Michael's family had owned Bowers' Butchers...Jack's family's butcher's shop, a few yards down from here on the opposite side of the street, modern refit near as damn it complete, used to be a... Oh, it were useless! Where does Eddie Weir get off calling you 'Son', anyhow? Look at him, chatting up Mum. Fancying himself in his Sunday best shirt and mutton chop sideburns. He was a cocky git and no mistake.

Everyone had seen him up the scaffold with no top on, even in February, shouting down at women so they'd see his muscles. Hold up, he's got his hand on Mum's bare arm now, trying to show how kind he can be. Folk might reckon Michael wasn't the sharpest, just because he wasn't right good at quick comments like Jack, because he were quieter, but he thought he knew fairish about people. He always watched them, worked them out. And he'd cottoned on to what Eddie Weir really wanted to do with his hands.

Michael watched Mum a minute. She had her favourite tartan dress on. He knew loads of blokes fancied her. Old John Dent used to come into the shop of a Saturday morning for his tongue and liver, and every time he'd say: 'Nay, lass, thee's too bonnie for a butcher's wife.' And once, when some teenagers were supping dandelion and burdock by the village war memorial, Michael had heard them say how 'fit' she was. He wouldn't have minded right much, but a couple of them had made mucky gestures too. You could see Mum trying to move away from Eddie now. She wasn't giving him the wide smile back, or returning the long look into the eyes. You could hear her thanking him for his 'kindness', but there were no flirting going on. Tough shit, Eddie! Go and pick up one of your tarts from The Dog and Gun. My mum's not like that. Michael knew she wasn't like that. She'd only loved Dad. She still only loved Dad.

"Look after yer sen, Carol," said Eddie, eyeing her as she walked off.

"You too, Eddie," said Mum.

"See yer soon, Michael."

Eddie Weir disappeared back into the pub. Mum caught up with Michael and put an arm round him.

"You all right, love?"

Michael pulled away from her arm, but for some reason he wanted to stay by her side now, as they carried on down the hill. Best forget about Eddie Weir. No point getting wound up over a pillock like that. And Fowlbeck were ripe for people watching today. All these Yorkshire Dales visitors traipsing about, sweat patches on their shirts, drips on the tips of their noses. It might have been Sunday Closing, but folk had still come for a gander at the shops, shielding their eyes from the sun, peering through windows at second-hand books and clothes and jars of boiled sweets.

They met a couple more locals on their way to Grandad's house. Michael remembered that, for a while after the accident, some folk had crossed the street to avoid them. It was just too horrible to face. That riled Mum at first. Weren't she and her son the ones who really knew how horrible it was? Then she decided to take control of matters. Every time somebody crossed the road, she crossed too and gave them a proper lovely smile. Their only escape was to cross back over, but that would have been more awkward than facing what they'd set out to dodge. Oh yeah, Mum put a stop to the avoiding all right.

The last person they bumped into, just after Bowers' Family Butcher's shop near the corner at the bottom of the

High Street, was Joe Thursby. Or, as Mum called him, 'Big Bear'. Retired, round, corduroys up to his armpits, and mad about the regional 'In Bloom' competition, he was tending to one of his roadside flowerbeds. Joe had been a street crosser and Michael reckoned he still felt bad about it. But, since Mum had faced him down, whenever she saw him she just went in for the massive hugs. Joe flipping loved her for it. He always held on tight. You couldn't take your eyes off her now, as she got the cuddle going with him. Sometimes she were a pain in the arse, she mothered Michael too much, but he had to admit she was the best, his mum.

"Your flowers are looking grand again this year, Big Bear," she said, letting go of him. "Smelling lovely too."

"Comin' from you, lass, that's first prize already!" said Joe, straightening his braces.

"Aww, Big Bear, you're a rum one, you are."

"Could do wi' out this hosepipe ban, mind."

"Who's checking up out here?" said Mum. "Miles away from everywhere?"

"How about PC Plod?"

"Trevor? He's drunk half the time."

"I'll let you two into a little secret. Come closer, come closer," said Joe, lowering his voice, beckoning them in. "I sneak out of a night-time for a quick sprinkle."

"Big Bear!" said Mum.

"Surprised they've not wilted," said Michael, dry as the drought.

Mum and Joe got off laughing at that one, turning the heads of a group of passing off-cum-dens. When they'd settled down, and it really was time to get to Grandad's, Michael watched Joe give Mum a gentler hug, one which said everything it needed to. She came out of it with them watery eyes again. Michael stared at the flowerbed.

When they got to Grandad's, just off the High Street, Michael knocked on the front door of his little terraced house and Grandad answered. He was wearing his navy blue apron with white pinstripes, and his shirtsleeves were rolled up, likely to stop them dipping in the gravy he always made with the meat juice. Short and old he might have been, but you could see he were still strong. Michael looked at them thick forearms and wondered how much chopping on the block he'd have to do to get muscles like that.

"Now then, who's ready for a juicy slice o' topside?" said Grandad, after they'd said their 'hellos', shutting the door behind them as they stepped into the dining room.

"Best beef in Yorkshire?" said Mum. "What do you think, Dad?"

"I think it's smashin' when you call me Dad."

Mum had told Michael how it felt being in these rooms when she was sixteen, meeting her new boyfriend's parents: 'Like Alice in Wonderland. If I'd been a couple of inches taller, my head would have been bumping against that ceiling.' Michael knew what she meant. As he grew taller, the house did seem to shrink. And this dining room were a right squeeze. The big oak table in the middle took up near as damn it half the space, and there wasn't much room left for the dark furniture standing either side of the fireplace. Michael watched Mum and Grandad edge past the dining chairs toward the kitchen. For now, his part in the routine was to do nowt until Grandad brought him the beef through on the carving dish, so he could practise his carving. He sat in his place at the table, closed his eyes, breathed in through his nose. The hot air was filled with the smell of bloodied meat. Flipping heck, why did they have to keep up this Sunday roast at Grandad's tradition even when the weather were proper scorching?

Michael loosened his paisley collar, trying to let in happy memories of his dad. But that meaty smell seemed to be getting thicker. Felt like it were clinging to the inside of his throat. Not more thinking on the accident. He didn't want to think any more about the accident. Best listen to them familiar sounds coming from the kitchen. They had their set jobs. He knew they needed their set jobs more than owt nowadays. Mum was being noisy with the cutlery. Grandad kept opening the creaky oven door, letting out a crispy smell of roast potatoes that drifted into the dining room. That smell were akin to summat. Brought on memories of a camp-fire. It made Michael think of last summer, a scorcher too, when Dad had taken him and Jack on a camping trip up the dale.

They'd pitched the tent and Dad had swung his long-handled axe into a thick, fallen tree trunk, chopping three pieces off it. A seat each. You could still hear the t*hunk thunk thunk* noise of the axe sinking into the wood, sending big wedges flying through the air. They'd had to roll their seats uphill a fair way to get them to the middle of camp, and Dad wasn't a bit out of breath, even after all his chopping. When the boys had a breather at the top of the hill, Michael told Jack he bet Dad could have lined up all three and pushed them up in one go, no problem. Jack turned on him and told him to give over showing off.

A bit later, Dad taught them how to make an oven out of mud, with its very own chimney and a fire pit underneath. They let it bake in the sun until it were dry enough to use. In the evening, they chucked potatoes in, with a few Bowers' Famous Sausages of course, and kept the fire stoked with broken branches they'd collected from the surrounding woods. It was getting dark and the first stars were out when they got to tucking in around the mud oven, but them were the best roast spuds and sausages ever!

Clatter went the cutlery, as Mum put a pile on the dining room table.

"Let's get ready for dinner, then," she said, moving sharpish between the chairs, setting out the bone-handle knives and forks and foxhunting place mats.

Michael wondered how she could be so lively all the time. There were no point asking her anymore, because she'd say what she always said: 'What's the other option? Sit around moping?'

"I'll set t' table, Mum," said Michael.

"Now you have a rest, love. It's so hot today. Anyhow, you'll be doing the most important job in a minute."

"Aye, Mum."

"*Carving.*"

Nowadays, she said that word as if it was a kind of secret, akin to summat the Fowlbeck Freemasons kept to themselves behind the walls of that barmpot lodge of theirs. In a moment or two, she was back in the kitchen, nattering away with Grandad, asking if the vegetables were ready for draining and whether he wanted more pepper in the pepper-pot. Michael found himself gazing at the fireplace's shiny beige tiles. There were still a bit of ash left over from winter in the grate. He leant closer. Smelt dry and dead. Set him off thinking on last year's camp in the woods again.

When Michael, Jack and Dad had eaten, it was dark, save for the moon and stars. The moon looked bright and massive. Sitting there on them hard tree trunk seats felt flipping cold by that time too. Dad ducked into the tent, pulled out a thick tartan blanket and draped it over Michael and Jack, who'd pushed their log seats together. They watched him as he raked the embers from under the mud oven out into the open with his axe. He gave the embers a right good kick with his boots to spark them up, afore dropping on some brushwood and a big handful of sticks.

"Whoosh!" said Jack, as the fire suddenly blazed.

"Fairly handy at that, aren't yer, Dad?" said Michael.

"Aye, lad," said Dad, making a pyramid over the flames with three chunky bits of firewood. "Only practise, mind. You two will do it just as well as me afore long. And you can start practising tomorrow. I'm puttin' you tykes in charge o' t' fire."

"Brilliant, Dad!"

"Fuckin' ace!"

"Language, Jack."

"Soz, Mr Bowers."

"It's reet. There's only thee lads and me listenin' out here, any road. Except the owls and that wild boar everyone's trying to catch."

"Wild boar?" said Michael and Jack.

"Shhhh!" said Dad, a finger to his lips.

Michael and Jack froze. But hold up, why were Dad smiling?

"Aww, Da–ad."

"Mr Bowers."

"Watch out for t' wild boar, boys!"

Then Dad had done a daft boar run to his seat to get them off laughing. They talked about butchery a while and he gave them some tips on how to cut up a carcass, chopping his hefty hand through the smoky air by way of demonstration. Michael watched every 'cut', listened to every word, as the flames made Dad's face glow. But he turned to Jack at one point to make sure he was all right, and every bit of his friend's attention was fixed on Dad as well. It looked like he were in a trance, but Michael knew that didn't come from a love of butchery, so he reckoned he'd best put his arm round his shoulder.

A beefy smell reached Michael's nose and he remembered he was in the cramped dining room.

"Reet, Michael," said Grandad, apron off now, carrying the meat in on his china carving dish like it were as important as communion wine. "Let's see you carve this champion topside joint."

Grandad carefully placed the beef in front of Michael, then sat at the head of the table. As Michael looked down at the long-pronged fork and proper sharp knife glinting in the sunshine slanting through the window, he could feel Grandad's old eyes on him. He picked up the fork and knife and, gripping his tongue with his teeth, started carving. As he sliced through the meat, watching the red juices ooze, he heard Mum in and out of the kitchen, busy round the table, laying plates and setting down dishes of vegetables. She kept putting him off with her dashing about.

"Steady, boy," said Grandad. "It's not a tree. Don't saw at it. Slice, remember. Slice ...Slice...Slice."

"Sorry, Grandad," said Michael.

"That's the job. You can do it. You can do it."

"He's a natural, isn't he, Grandad?" said Mum, planting a serving spoon in the carrots.

"He's a Bowers. Course he's a natural."

"Naturally."

"Slice...Slice...Slice...Slice...Slice..."

When they'd piled their plates with hot food, they settled down more quietly to eat. Michael noticed a drop of gravy on Grandad's chin, but thought he'd best not mention it, as he were grinning fairish and seemed to be enjoying what he'd cooked. Grandad and Mum kept smiling and nodding, and saying stuff like 'mmm, lovely,' even though there were a photo of Dad looking at them from the chimney breast. Michael reckoned it might have been because there was a picture of Dad that they were doing that. When Grandad smiled, you could see where his gums had shrunk back from his nicotine-stained teeth. Half the roots were showing on them gnashers. And under the skin on his nose were a hundred burst blood vessels, which put Michael in mind of the tadpoles he caught with Jack when they were playing about in the streams around Fowlbeck. Folk in the village might have said Grandad had a face well lived in, but he'd earned the right to live a bit, to sup his ale in The Dog and Gun, to take hard drags on his roll-ups. He'd worked his flipping guts out for his family in that butcher's shop, no mistake. Slogged away at the chopping block all his life. Michael wouldn't mind having them little swimming blood vessels, or even the scary teeth, as long as he could do a job like Grandad had for Bowers' Family Butchers. As long as he could. Now he noticed Grandad looking at the photograph of Dad. He thought it made his face drop somehow, as if that saggy skin suddenly had weights hanging off it. Then Grandad saw him gawping and brought out the big toothy grin again.

"Summer holidays soon, boy?" he said.

"Aye, Grandad," said Michael, pushing peas onto his fork. "School finishes on Friday."

"Be puttin' a few more hours in at t' shop, will yer?"

"Yes, Grandad."

"Good lad. We'll make a proper butcher o' thee afore we're done. You want to learn, don't you?"

"Dad taught me a lot."

Mum took the napkin from her lap and dabbed at her sweaty forehead.

"Aye," sighed Grandad, looking at the photo on the chimney breast again. "He were a good teacher, my son."

Michael watched Mum put the napkin back on her lap,

then sort her food dead neatly onto her fork. She looked to be really concentrating, chewing right slow, like this were her final meal and she had to savour every mouthful.

"I worked three days a week in our shop when I were your age, Michael," said Grandad, cutting a corner off a slice of beef on his plate. "Young 'uns were supposed to be at school every day, even in them times, but when you were born into a family of butchers like ours? When you were part of summat so important to t' community like we were, and still are don't forget, nobody fretted o'er me learning t' trade at me father's shoulder. They saw the need for me to be schooled in butchery. Well, they knew it were my responsibility to take o'er that shop one day. And Fowlbeck has allus needed a *proper* butchers. Still does. Despite supermarkets. What do they know about real butchery, any road? They might think they'll push us out o' business one day, but that'll never happen. This village still needs that special person, Michael, wi' all the traditional skills and knowledge of a top-class butcher. And you can only gain that when generation after generation work in t' business. I've no time for these so-called modern family butchers wi' nowt but a couple o' years under their belts. Like that one your mate's dad's makin' a pig's ear of up t' road. I were full-time in 1918. The end of The Great War. That's a long time sin, in't it? And my grandad established the business o'er forty year afore that. Nearly a century ago. It'll be our centenary next year. Now there's summat to be proud of, lad."

"Yes, I know that," said Michael, puffing out his red hot cheeks.

"Makes yer think, dun't it?"

"Can I open t' window, please?"

"Aye, go on, go on," said Grandad.

Michael needed some fresh air to calm him down. Right

proud of the shop, he was, but it worried him when Grandad blithered on about it too much. He reached back from his chair, lifted the iron fastener on the little lattice window, pushed it open.

"Don't lean back on that chair," said Mum, barely looking up from her plate.

"I wasn't, Mum."

"It's got four legs, not two."

"I wasn't," said Michael.

"Well don't."

"I won't."

"No fridges to preserve stock in them days o' course," said Grandad, waving his fork about. "We had to salt the meat when we hung it. And you'd only slaughter a beast if you knew you'd be sellin' it all a fortnight after ageing it. Had to have good judgement in them days. Our little slaughterhouse were even more important back then. Meant supply and demand were not so much an issue. No waste, that were t' main job to surviving. Do you know, your grandma, God rest her soul, used to render all t' spare fat down in a big vat? What a rotten, stinkin' job that were! But she never once complained. We sold it separate in jars. Look, Michael, all as I'm saying is that Bowers' Family Butchers has a long, distinguished past. And you're an only child. There's only you now who can become custodian of all that history."

Mum put down her knife and fork and glared at Grandad. Michael saw that sweat had stuck her black hair to her temples, and he noticed the dark brown of her eyes.

"Why are you pressuring him?" she said. "He's only twelve."

"I din't mean any bother to t' lad," said Grandad.

"He's not finished being a child yet."

"I know, love. I'm sorry. I were only thinkin' on his

future."

"We've got all the time in the world to think about his future. All the time in the world to...Oh God…"

Mum picked up the napkin and buried her face in it. Michael went to her, bent down and hugged her. They were both crying.

"I miss him so much, I miss him so much, I miss him…" came the muffled, broken words through the napkin.

Then there was a quiet knock on the front door. Michael stood up straight, tried wiping away his tears.

"Shall I answer it, Mum?" he said.

"I'll be all right," said Mum, breathing deeply. "Don't worry about me. Answer it."

Michael opened the door. Standing there was Elsa, a lass in his class at school. Mum liked her, she was always polite, but she felt sorry for her because she came from a poor family on the council estate and never looked right well fed. Most of what she wore seemed to have holes in it too. Today she were in threadbare polka dot. Mum always said it was a pity she had to wear them milk-bottle specs, because she actually had a pretty face.

"All reet, Michael?" said Elsa, staring at the doorstep. "Thought you'd be at your grandad's. Hello, Mr Bowers. Hello, Mrs Bowers."

"Hello, Elsa," said Mum.

"Oh, sorry, you've not finished your food," said Elsa, managing to look up. "Appen I'll see you later, Michael? Everyone's playin' at t' river. Jack's there...Eh, you look like you've been cryin'."

Now she seemed to forget her shyness and reached out to touch his face.

"Why don't you come in and eat something, Elsa,?" said Mum. "There's plenty."

"No, thank you, Mrs Bowers. Me Mam sez not to take folks' charity."

"It's not charity, Elsa," said Grandad. "It's friendliness."

"I am sorry about everythin', Michael," said Elsa, looking into his blurry eyes. "About your dad... Mrs Bowers, Mr Bowers, I am sorry about what's happened to you all."

Michael watched a tear slip down Elsa's cheek. Then she ran away. He closed the door and turned to Mum and Grandad. At last, Mum spoke.

"What a nice girl. I think she's sweet on you, love."

"Mu – um," said Michael.

CHAPTER THREE

It was twenty to nine on the following Saturday morning and Jack wanted to be dossing about in the hot July sunshine with Michael and the rest of his mates, not working in the cooler air of the shop with its cold smelling meat and gleaming white fridges. School had only broken up for summer holidays yesterday, but today was Grand Opening Day. At nine o'clock, The OB (Old Bastard), as Jack secretly called his dad, would be as proud as owt. He'd raise the metal Venetian blinds on the shop window and freshly painted red door, click back the latch and let the punters in to traipse all over his new chessboard floor. After a proper modern refit, *stack 'em high, sell 'em cheap* Hargraves' Butchers was reopening for business.

The OB was on the customers' side of his brand new pride and joy, the very latest glass meat cabinet. It near as damn it spanned the length of the shop, all the way from the front window display to a couple of feet from the back wall, where it stopped, leaving a gap for access. The Old Bastard was giving it a final polish with Mr Sheen. Jack was on the serving side, kitted out in the same clobber as Father, blue pinstripe apron over butcher's whites, setting out the oblong trays of raw meat with their plastic tags and black ink bargain prices. He glanced at The OB a time or two when he sensed he wasn't looking. You could see his bald head shining through that right greasy sweep over hair as he worked away at his precious cabinet. He might have been grooming a horse for a crack at a rosette. Jack had never seen him show such love.

Molly the Mop was in too, sliding sharp-smelling disinfectant over the chessboard floor tiles. She was in her sixties now, big-boned, with a fat face and a giant laugh. If anyone seemed like a proper butcher in Hargraves' shop, Jack reckoned Molly did. She'd likely say she'd earned it, mind, having been butchering up and down the dale most of her born days. It made Jack chuffed if she was working when he did a shift, because she was usually right good at taking the edge off The OB.

"Shape yer sen, Rodney," she said, giving it some elbow grease with the mop. "I'll be outshinin' thee again."

"Molly, do I pay you to extract the Michael?" said The OB, doubtless reckoning he was funny.

"Pay me? Is that what yer call a few weekly farthings?"

"We're decimalised now, dear. We're not stick-in-the-muds like the Bowers at t' bottom o' t' street. 'Stick-in-the-muds'. They should shove that above their shop. They likely still tek farthings. Still have sawdust on their shop floor. Ruddy sawdust. I mean, good heavens!"

Jack hated the way Father talked northern one second and posh the next. He really was up his own arse. It was a laugh when he didn't know which way to go, mind. 'Butter' and 'London' were best. Or was it 'Batter' and 'Landon'?

"What's wrong wi' usin' sawdust, Dad?" said Jack, trying to be matter of fact, mutter of fuct.

"Oh, I am sorry, lad," said The OB, stepping back from the cabinet to make sure Jack was doing as he'd been told with the sirloin and chump. "Don't be upset. God forbid if I've uttered summat offensive about your little chum, Michael Bowers. I don't give a toss, to be honest. If they're content rollin' around in sawdust, that's their business. We've got a new cabinet to fill. Wait on, why have you put t' mince there? What's special about our mince, boy?"

"Erm... "

"It's our best seller, gormless! Now put it at t' front. And those trays are nowt like straight. Out the way! Out the way!"

The OB strode round to the serving side of the cabinet, his face now as pink as that baldy head. Jack was kakking it, but he wasn't going to shift for him at first. He didn't move right up until the moment he could see he was about to be shoved aside, either that or be given another thick ear. When The OB was bearing down on him from that great height of his. When that craggy old face was drawing up close and those eyes looked to be bulging even more than usual. Only then, and still not flinching, did Jack step back.

The OB bent down and put his head in the cabinet. Beside the other similarly coloured meat on bone, it looked like it belonged there. He busily started rearranging the meat with his long, scraggy fingers. Jack reckoned they were more like a keyboardist's fingers than a butcher's. A picture of the old man playing on Top of the Pops with Slade in a mirrored top hat and a white butcher's smock came to mind. He had to put his hand over his gob to stop himself cracking up at that one. Perhaps that's what kept putting his dad in such a shite mood. Maybe he was in the wrong job. Molly stopped her work a moment and gave Jack a smile over the top of the sparkling glass. One which said: 'I know, love. He can be a silly bugger sometimes, your father.' He wished she was his big sister, then she might be able to take the sting out of things at home as well.

"Look how neat Jack sets his cuts out on t' trays, Rodney," said Molly, gliding the mop across the floor again. "The lad's certainly showin' skill and pride in his work."

"So he should," said The OB.

"Gi' o'er bein' a Scrooge."

"He is going to be runnin' this place before he knows it, Molly."

"I'm what?" said Jack.

The OB withdrew his head from the cabinet and looked down at his son from six foot three. A fly buzzed over their heads, then whizzed between them. Jack clocked the lines above The OB's eyebrows getting deeper as he crumpled up his forehead. He seemed right serious, but at least it wasn't one of his scowling faces.

"Listen, Son," he said, almost softly. "Okey dokey, I can see you're a hard working boy. You shape your sen reet enough. And I'm... I'm... Well, that pleases me."

Did he nearly say he was proud of him then? Jack watched him struggle to find his words, praying he'd come out with the ones he longed for. That forehead had a look of corrugated iron now.

"Nobody could pull you up for flaggin', lad... "

Go on, Dad.

"That's all I'm saying... "

Go on, Dad!

"But..."

Oh no.

"But..."

Oh fuck.

"Your problem is you don't listen half o t' time," said The OB, his crumpled brow turning flatter now, his voice sounding harsh again. "You've got to start taking more responsibility. I don't want to be allus playin' pop wi' you. But wake up, lad! This shop is your future. That's why you need to learn how to manage the cabinet properly. And look at our place. Can't you see it? Are you dumb? Just look at our shop now."

He held out his arms like he was after hugging all the new equipment. Then he stretched even taller, as if to hammer home the point he wanted to make. Looking up into those eyes, Jack reckoned they were fairly pulsing, they were bulging that much.

"What a marvellous opportunity for a young 'un. I am putting *one hell* of a lot of trust in you, Jack."

Jack listened to that sentence as it echoed around inside his head. He searched for his father's approval. His pride. His love. And, if those words had been kindly spoken, they could have meant: 'I know you can do it, because I believe in you.' But, as he turned them over and over, all he could hear was: 'Muck this up for me and you're dead meat!'

The next thing Jack saw was The OB's eyes nearly popping out of their sockets. He was gawping at the time on the clock with roman numerals above the shop door. The one he'd bought because he reckoned it added class to the establishment.

"Bollocks!" he said. "We're openin' in fifteen minutes! There's already a queue outside. Everyone knows we're reopening. We've had a big build up. I've done that interview in t' Gazette." He pointed a scraggy finger at the framed article and photo of himself on the wall opposite the cabinet. "Their photographer's comin' back to snap this. It's our reputation on t' line here!"

"Don't panic, Mr Mainwaring," said Molly, a big fat smile on her face.

The Old Bastard really had taken to darting about behind the cabinet like Corporal Jones in Dad's Army. Jack thought this frigging racket was Dad's army all right. He knew father had fought in the Second World War, he was always blithering on about it, but this was a load of shite.

"Molly, clear that mop and bucket away now," said The OB.

"There's just this last wet bit needs... "

"Now!"

Molly was tough, but Jack knew she wasn't stupid. She'd

seen how Rodney Hargraves could fly off the handle before. She did as she was told.

"Dump your mop," said The OB, moving toward the prep room. "Then help those two wi' t' pork pies and sausage rolls. They're out o' t' oven. I can smell 'em. Why haven't they brought them out here yet?"

Covering the opening to the prep room were vertical plastic strips which made a big Union Jack when they were settled. The OB yanked them to one side and peered into the room. Then he yelled at Jack's mum, who was working in there with his little seven-year-old sister, Tracy.

"Judy!"

"Yes, sweetheart?" squeaked Mum's mousy voice from the prep room.

"I want those pies and rolls on top o' this cabinet in two minutes!"

"We're just letting 'em cool a bit, aren't we, Tracy?"

"We're just letting 'em cool a bit, Daddy," said Tracy.

"All right, darling," said The OB, after a moment. "Are you doing a grand job for Daddy?"

"A very grand job."

"Good girl."

Jack watched Molly squeeze past the end of the cabinet toward The OB, the mop sloshing about in the galvanised metal bucket she was lugging with one chubby hand, the bucket creaking as it swung on its handle. She tapped the old man's shoulder with her spare fingers.

"Room for a big 'un, Rodney?" she said.

"Go on," he said, letting her through the prep room opening. "Eh, what's that spare lintel still doin' there?"

"What's that, sweetheart?" said Mum's mousy voice.

"The lintel tucked away in t' corner behind that box!" said The OB, pointing into the prep room. "I told Eddie Weir

I wanted it shiftin' after he put this new doorway in. Why the hell he forgot to do it... I thought he'd already... He knows we're opening again today!"

"Do you want me to phone him, sweetheart?"

"Not now, woman! Just concentrate on your job."

The OB released the red, white and blue strips so they settled back across the opening. Then he turned to Jack, who was staring into his pink face now, trying to read it. What was he? A proper bastard? Or did he care? Sometimes he showed he cared, didn't he? Like with Tracy. With Tracy he showed he cared.

"What are you gawpin' at?"

"I'm just lookin' at ya, Dad."

He didn't know why, but it felt like those were the hardest words he'd ever had to say to him. The bulging in his dad's eyes seemed to shrink for a second. But then he was rummaging about in his apron pocket, pulling out his pipe and St Bruno tobacco.

"I'll be back in a few minutes, lad," he said. "To make sure this cabinet's perfect."

"Yes, Dad."

"So think on."

"Aye, Dad."

"I need a smoke."

Then he was away through the opening. Jack was left listening to the swishing strips as they settled again. He gazed down at the dark slabs of red meat in the cabinet. Waist deep in the stuff, he was. Under fluorescent lighting, it looked as glossy as the walls, which had just been painted red. Bloody red! The OB loved that colour summat rotten. Even the pale skin on the tucked up chickens looked reddish, surrounded by so much of it. Jack tried to imagine living out his days working here. He knew when The OB packed in his plumbing business and bought the shop three years since that he was being lined up. But just now, when he said he'd be running the place *before he knew it?* What the fuck did that mean? In a few years when he left school? The old man would be nearly sixty by then. Perhaps he wanted to retire at sixty. Jack would have to start deciding what he really wanted. Frigging hell, what was he going to do?

He caught the faint smell of the uncooked meat in the cabinet and the whiff of polish on shiny glass. Did he really fancy chopping up cows and scrubbing down till he was six foot under? But how did you get to be a pop star or a cowboy? It was just daft, folk in Fowlbeck, back of beyond, even asking that question. Jack always questioned things, mind. Sometimes he wondered if it started when he got his first slap: 'Why does he hate me so much?' He did want something better. To follow his own dreams. Away from Fowlbeck and Hargraves' Butchers. Fat chance of it, but he couldn't give over asking the questions: 'One day? Maybe one day?' He'd tried talking to Michael about it, because he usually had no bother being a good listener. Apart from messing about and having a laugh, sharing what nattered them was what made them such ace mates. Except good old Micky clammed up at any talk of Jack wanting to do summat other than take over his family's butchers. Couldn't make head nor tail of it. Completely off his radar. Michael would have taken a guillotine on the butcher's block for his family's business. At least the lad had a shot at being happy running Bowers' shop, mind. What chance did Jack have with The OB around? Maybe if they could just be mates, like Micky had been with his dad, it might make a difference.

He tried getting his head round all the latest modern equipment. Weighing scales, fridges, knives, cleavers, bacon slicer, cash till. Must have cost a fucking packet. It was right there, clean white or silvery grey, twinkling at him, mapping out his future. The OB had likely done it all for himself, inviting the whole of Fowlbeck to The Grand Opening so they could see what a champion businessman he was. But wasn't it for his son too? Didn't that at least show he cared? That he did love him? If you can only please him more it could make the difference. You could have a good crack working together. You might be happier at Hargraves' Butchers. Perhaps you just have to work a bit harder. Didn't Dad say your hard work pleased him?

Jack heard a short electric zap behind him as The OB's favourite new toy, his blue neon insect killer, frazzled another fly. Better crack on with the cabinet. He made sure everything was lined up to the millimetre, checking the labelling and that each cut of meat was in the right place, doing his best to make it all fine and dandy. Then he went to the customers' side of the cabinet, moving slowly along the whole display to see if he'd missed owt. As he got nearer the shop door, from beyond the closed Venetian blinds, he listened to bits of chin-wagging in the queue outside.

"Apparently, they've made a grand job."

"Eck, it's already warm!"

"You can bet Bowers'll see it as a threat."

"Gonna be swelterin' again today."

"West Indies cricket team must think they're playing at home."

"Did you see Rodney Hargraves in t' paper, all dressed up in his best bib and tucker?"

"No wonder England's gettin' stuffed."

"Bit of a fancy dan, that one."

"Richards, Holding, Kallicharan, Roberts? That lot'd stuff our eleven in t' Antarctic."

"Aye, them four and seven penguins."

"You barmpot!"

Then Jack could hear a van pulling up and soon there was a knock at the door. Turning the latch, he opened it, felt the sunny heat on his face. Mutton chops Eddie Weir, in summer vest, shorts, dirty builder's boots, was standing on the top step of the three which led up to the shop from the High Street.

"All reet, Jack?" he said, keeping his voice down. "Your dad about?"

"Aye, he's out back havin' a smoke. I'll collar him for ya... " said Jack, turning on his heels.

"Hold up," said Eddie, grabbing him by the arm. "What mood's he in?"

"Summat between simmerin' and steamin'."

"Oh. Think I'd best gi' it a miss, then. I was gonna tek that spare lintel away for him. He's been naggin' me to do it afore you open again, but if he's that way out. He's ratty wi' me, any road. And I've got a bangin' headache."

"Too much loopy juice last neet?"

"Aye."

"Ya might as well tek it now you're here," said Jack, thinking about the brownie points he was going to get for sorting this one out. "My dad'll be chuffed if ya shift it. It's just inside t' prep room. If ya don't wanna see him, I'll check the coast's clear while you come and grab it."

"Seen his shiny new floor, though?" said Eddie, setting off back down the steps and toward his van. "Not walkin' on that in these mucky boots. Value me balls too much. Pardon my French, folks."

Standing in the shop doorway, Jack clocked the flared trousers and piled up hairdos in the queue. All their regular locals were back. Beaky Susan from Susan's Antiques, opposite. Grumpy George, landlord at The Dog and Gun.

A few sweaty fogies. Couple of sunburnt tourists too. Dad would be well happy. The photographer from The Gazette was there, the strap of his heavy silver and black camera digging into his pockmarked neck. Even Rocker Billy had showed up, all leathers and quiff, trying to stare Jack out. What's he doing with his top lip? Curling it up like Elvis to look hard or summat? Twat. Now that Eddie had moved, folk peered in at the door, passing comment.

"Looks smashin', lad."

"Bet your father's over t' moon."

Eddie's hangover must have got to slowing him down, because he'd only just opened his van door. About to jump in, he was. No sign of Dad yet, and Jack really did want to get that stone lintel shifted for him.

"Eddie?" he said.

"What?" said Eddie, one foot in the van.

"I'll lug that lintel through for ya."

"Sure you can manage? It's short enough, but there's fairish weight in it."

"Sure you can manage, butcher boy?" said Rocker Billy, sneering from the queue.

"Belt up, Billy," said one of the locals. "Need a hand, Jack?"

"No ta, Mr Coates. Rocker Baby knows I can handle me sen."

"Get movin', then," said Eddie, walking back toward the shop. "I'd prefer not seeing your father. No offence."

Jack strode across the shop, down the side of the cabinet, through the Union Jack opening into the prep room. The door to out back was open. He caught the smell of pipe tobacco drifting in. It made him think of wood burning under a mud oven. Bending down, gritting his teeth, he picked up the stone lintel. Molly said she'd give him a lift. But he said he could manage. Mum told him to be careful.

Feeling the strain in his arms and legs, he walked back into the shop through the strips of red, white and blue. With proper heavy feet, he made it to the cleaned chessboard floor where punters would soon be standing. He was right near the cabinet. He nearly stuttered beneath the lintel's weight. But he could see Eddie and the front of the queue gawping at him through the shop doorway. He carried on alongside the cabinet toward them. He was nowt but halfway when, like a pawn, he made the move onto that white square. Must have been one that was still a bit wet because Molly had been told to clear up too soon. His rubber sole squeaked as it slid, his foot shot from under him, he squealed like a pig being slaughtered and, as he fell flat on his back, one end of the lintel crashed through the glass. Folk outside at the front of the queue gasped. As Jack stared up at the lintel poking from the wrecked cabinet, he pictured sharp shards scattered over the meat, embedding themselves like diamonds.

Then everyone was there. A worried little crowd looking down at him, asking if he was all right, saying thank goodness he'd not been cut. Mum squatting beside him, stroking his hair. Poor little Tracy crying. Eddie carefully pulling the lintel from the cabinet. Rocker Billy with a smirk on his chops. The photographer snapping a couple of sneaky pictures before... Before he arrived.

Jack heard a murmur from the crowd, saw a nudge or two, people standing back to let someone coming from the direction of the prep room through. Then there he stood, at Jack's feet. He seemed massive from the floor. But why wasn't he looking as angry as he should? His eyes didn't even look to be bulging that much. Summat cold about them now. Like they belonged to a robot. Or a bounty-hunter. They were the only bits of him that moved. First they stared down at the smashed cabinet and what must have been glassed meat. Then they took in all the punters, all those folk who'd turned out especially for Rodney Hargraves' glorious day. Then they found Jack and slowly went right narrow. Like they'd recognised something. Like they'd found what they were looking for.

That night, Jack was under the covers pretending to be asleep when The OB walked into his room and whispered that, if he made too much noise and woke his little sister in the room opposite, he'd be getting a pair of smashed kneecaps to go with what else he'd got coming. By the time he'd finished laying into him with his fists and left him there, cowering, shivering despite the hot night, Jack had a non-stop ringing in his ears, a bust lip and what felt like slit eggs for eyes. It wasn't just for more punishment that The OB grounded him, kept him shut away, hidden in his room for the next month. The Old Bastard abandoned him to his mousy mum, who scurried about, scratching around, trying to build up his strength with boiled vegetables and soup. Jack really did feel like he was Clint Eastwood during those weeks. Not in the heroic gunfights, mind. In the desert, when his face is all crusted over and he's been left for dead.

CHAPTER FOUR

On the sweltering morning of the last Wednesday in August, Michael, in brown shorts and a green T-shirt mucky with grease, was trying to straighten a wheel axle with a hammer in the little flag-stoned yard behind his house. At one o'clock this afternoon, after the shops had shut for half-day closing, it would be Fowlbeck Children's Bogie Race. He should have been right excited, because him and Jack were defending champions. Except Jack wasn't about, was he? He stopped clanking with his hammer and stared at the ancient looking shed in a corner next to the limestone walls, where their championship winning bogie was still locked up. Jack had been locked up for a month now. Michael hoped he were all right. Flipping heck, he missed him. He'd likely see him back at school in nowt but a few days, but summer holidays were near as damn it over and they'd not had any fun. That Rodney Hargraves didn't deserve a son.

He'd best get this axle sorted, anyhow. Shame Elsa had crashed into that drystone wall when they were practising yesterday. She'd needed some practise runs, mind, what with her taking Jack's place in the race today. Thank God she'd not been hurt. She'd done a grand job painting their racing machine, hadn't she? Lanky would like it, wouldn't he? Even if they had done it without asking him. Give over fretting. You've just got to hope Elsa can hold the old girl steady down that High Street slope. You know you've got to be the pusher to get some speed up. She'll be here soon. Get a shift on, then.

Michael bent over the wheel axle again and started hammering away at it against the flagstones. But, moments later, someone grabbed his ears from behind and gave them a tug.

"Ahhhhhh!" he yelled, as he cracked the hammer into his thumb.

"Oh sorry, Micky. Soz, lad. Oh shite."

"Ahhhhh! Ahhhhh! Ahhhhh! Ahhhhhhhhhhhhhhh!"

Nursing his injury, Michael leapt up and down all over the yard, like a frog with its feet on fire. When he came to settle on the back doorstep, sitting there whimpering, he kept sucking his thumb and narrowed his eyes at Jack, who was standing over him now, wearing a white T-shirt and cut-off jeans with sown on motorbike badges.

"Where the flippin' heck did you come from?"

"Jumped o'er t' wall, didn't I?" said Jack. "How ya doin'?"

"What you reckon? Just brayed me sen, thanks to thee."

"Gi' us a butcher's."

Jack nodded for Michael to show him his thumb. Michael raised it toward the sun in the cloudless sky. Jack moved closer to inspect it, then got hold of his mate's hand and started blowing where the thumb had gone right red.

"What yer doin', yer daft prannock?" said Michael, shaking his head.

"Dunno... I was just..."

They watched one another a moment. Then the smiles cracked open and the chuckling started. They were soon laughing their heads off, going in for manly bear hugs and lolloping round the back yard like idiots.

When they stopped, they were out of breath, their throats were proper dry and they needed a drink. While Jack took his turn at knocking the axle into shape, metal on metal ringing through the warm air, Michael went into the kitchen and filled two Tupperware beakers with cool American cream soda from the fridge.

"Drink, Lanky!" he said, as he came back outside, raising his voice above the hammer, smelling the sweet, fizzing cream soda under his nose.

They sat opposite each other on a couple of ancient millstones which Michael's dad had been going to make into a stone table. Blooming heck, he wished Dad was sitting here with them, supping a cold drink, teaching them butchery. But it were brilliant seeing Jack again. You couldn't help noticing a bulge in his bottom lip when he smiled, though. That weren't there afore. Michael knew what had been going on. He wasn't thick. It should have been *Lanky's* dad who was dead.

"You all reet, Jack?"

"Suppose."

Jack rested his top teeth on his bottom lip and nipped down on it. Michael gawped at the little bulge slowly squeezing itself back out into the bright daylight.

"Wanna talk?" he said.

"What happened to t' axle?" said Jack.

"Little accident on a practise run. Summat and nowt."

Jack drummed his fingers on his beaker, stared into his drink a moment.

"Old Bastard's as happy as a lamb now, ya know."

"Oh aye?" said Michael.

"Now his precious cabinet's mended and his business is back in *rude health*."

"How come he let you out today?"

"I reckon customers have been badgerin' him about t' bogie race."

"Yer sure everything's...?"

"Let's go up to The Waterfall Den and The Beacon again soon," said Jack.

"If yer like, mate."

"I've missed you, Micky."

"You an all, Lanky."

Jack put his drink on the millstone, reached for the nearly straightened wheel axle that he'd left on the ground, started turning it in his hands.

"Where's ya mum?" he said.

"Where'd yer think, barmpot?"

"Fuck off, fat bastard."

"Long streak o' piss," said Michael.

"Is t' auld lass fettlin' darn at t'shop?"

"Aye, lad. Yon butchers wain't run its sen!"

"What's the crack, then?" said Jack, spinning the axle in the air and catching it.

"Well, today's Green Bogie Day, in't it?"

"And who's champions?"

"Thee and me," said Michael, looking into the bottom of his empty beaker, running his finger round its rim.

"What's up?" said Jack.

Michael had thought it were a good idea at the time. Now he wasn't right sure.

"Come off it, Micky. You're allus sayin' we can talk about owt."

Might as well take the plunge, then.

"Yer know we painted the old girl green?" said Michael.

"Yeah."

"Cos bogies up yer nose are green and it's dead funny?"

"Aye."

"Well...Erm..."

"Friggin' hell, just tell us." said Jack.

"It's not green anymore."

"Ya what?"

Jack got off the millstone, started pacing about, huffing,

scuffing his trainers against the flagstones, pulling at his cut-off jeans. Then he stopped and glared at Michael, pointing at him with the axle.

"Go on, then," he said. "What colour ya done it?"

"Yer know Elsa's brilliant in art class at school?" said Michael.

"Elsa?"

"Aye, Elsa."

"What's it got to do wi' her?"

Michael knew Jack reckoned himself above Elsa, because she lived on the council estate or summat. He could think what he wanted, but he didn't like the way he'd said that.

"Now hold up a minute..."

"Not painted it girly pink, has she?"

"It's Starsky and Hutch colour, if yer wanna know. She's done it like Starsky's car."

"The Torino?" said Jack, sitting on the millstone again.

"Yeah. She finished it last neet. Bright red wi' fancy white stripes down t' sides."

"Same as Starsky's, eh?"

"We knew yer liked it, see," said Michael. "And we thought it'd be a good surprise for yer. You know, for when he let you out. It were Elsa's idea."

"It's fuckin' ace, that motor," said Jack, starting to grin.

"We hoped he'd let you out for t' race. Din't reckon he would, mind. Elsa were gonna take your place, but now you're here... Eh, this is brilliant, we might win it twice!"

Michael was happy Jack had got to smiling again, even if he did have that bulge in his bottom lip.

When they'd pulled their newly painted racing machine from the shed, properly straightened the wheel axle, bolted it back on the front of the bogie with old pram wheels on each end, they spent the rest of the morning fine-tuning and doing dry runs down the backstreet slopes of Fowlbeck. Michael was chuffed when Elsa turned up just afore they set off to practise and said she'd time them with her Mickey Mouse watch. It riled him when Jack took the piss out of her. But, even if she were shy, she could stand her ground, could Elsa.

"You're jokin' me!" said Jack, after one dry run. "That was well quick. Sure ya can see that watch through those milk-bottle specs?"

"I can see your ugly mug, I know that."

At one o'clock, the defending champions, with their fantastic red bogie with its superfast white stripes, were 'revved up' in the middle of the start line at the top of the High Street. The pavements were right noisy with chatty folk, three or four deep, dressed in summery clothes, waiting for the race to begin. On each side of Michael and Jack were two other bogie teams, made up of higgledy-piggledy wood and nail contraptions and two sweaty lads. If it weren't such a boiling day, it could have near as damn it been a bobsleigh race: One kid from each team sitting up front, crouching low, using a piece of rope like reins to steer with. The other standing behind, pushing like billio at the start, then jumping on the makeshift tailboard when they'd got some speed up. Jack always did the pushing. He were as fast as an East German in PE.

Michael was ready at the front, tightly coiled. Knees up to his chin, forearms resting on his bare thighs, rope properly gripped. He wanted to make a good job of steering and win this one for Jack. They'd show his evil old man that he'd not beaten him just because he'd beaten him up. He looked straight down the street between the two rows of limestone shops and terraced houses, trying hard to focus on the sticky-smelling tarmac, thinking about how much of it they had to eat up before the others to win the race.

"Stay low," he whispered to himself. "Steer straight. As far as yer dare afore t' corner at t' bottom. Like James Hunt. Straight till t' last second. Then turn it. But not too sharp. Don't want to muck it up. Don't want to tip her o'er. Don't want to crash."

He tried his best not to take his eyes off the shiny black tarmac. If he did, perhaps he'd not be concentrating when Mr Roe, the baker, chucked his apron in the air and bellowed 'Get set, go!' There were summat else shiny in the corner of his eye now, mind, coming from the crowd to his left. Something glinting. Bloody hell, he couldn't hack it. He had to look. Rocker Billy's rings! The sun meant he couldn't make them out properly, but he knew what they were, no mistake. Anchor... Crucifix...'LOVE'... Skull. He didn't need to see them right well. Since that day at the river, it was like they were burning and sunk in his brain. The skull woke him up at night. Always the skull. What's The Rocker Man playing at? Trying to blind him so they'd lose? Was he still wound up? Hadn't it been enough for him that Jack had been locked away and battered by his father? He must have known. The old folk chattered about it every day at the bus stops. Somehow, everyone knew. But nobody had the balls to do owt about it. Half of them still shopped at Hargraves' for God's sake. People saw it as a family matter because that were easiest. Hold up, what's Rocker Billy doing now? Bouncing out of the crowd in his rubbery shoes, heading this way. Not after a scrap again, is he? With all of Fowlbeck watching?

"Billy?" said Michael, as he watched him walk straight past and stand at the back of the bogie, right next to Jack. "Come off it, please don't."

Michael kept his neck twisted so he could see what was going on. Jack was staring into Rocker Billy's mug, but his eyes looked a bit shaky. And when the heavy ringed hand got raised he flinched, like he were waiting for the punch. A few weeks since, Lanky wouldn't have been waiting or flinching. He'd have been cracking his fist into the other lad's jaw afore he had chance to swing.

"Billy!" said Michael, half standing.

But the hand wasn't making a fist. And now it settled on Jack's shoulder, the rings sparkling in the sunshine. What the flipping heck's this? Michael sat back on the bogie.

"Don't let any bastard drag you down, Hargraves," said Rocker Billy. "Never let 'em drag you into the shit where they choose to dwell. You're better than that."

"Thanks, Billy," said Jack, eyes turning watery like Michael's mum's.

"You *are* better than that, kid."

Then Rocker Billy turned on his rubber soles, bounced back into the crowd and walked off down the street. Michael, gob wide open, kept catching glimpses of that slick, oily hair moving among the spectators' red and puffy faces. Who'd have reckoned on him saying that to Jack? Grandad would be hugging foreigners next!

"How yer doin' back there, Lanky?" said Michael, twisting his neck to look at him.

"I'm right, mate...I'll be reet...Ya ready for it, Micky?"

"Aye, I'm ready."

"Let's win this thing!" said Jack, raising his voice, looking round at their rivals. "We'll tonk this lot of no-hopers into t' middle o' next week!"

Michael could see Jack hunched over the back of the bogie now, tightly gripping the two pieces of cut up broomstick they'd screwed to the frame to use as push handles. As Jack took some shit off Smithy and Stubbsy, race rivals to their right, for that last comment, his teeth nibbled at the bulge in his bottom lip. Michael watched them gnashers grit together. The lad's got his mad dog face on now. You'd best hold the old girl steady, with the burst of speed she's about to get from behind.

A few yards away, on the flagstone pavement, stood Mr Roe, his bushy moustache dusty with flour. Michael turned to see him lift his apron over his head, the white material brushing past the black hair sprouting from his ears. Nearly time.

Gripping the rough steering rope with one hand, Michael held the handbrake him and Jack had nicked from a conked out old car, left to rot in a field after the war, with the other, getting ready to release it the moment Mr Roe said 'Go!' Dad had told him he used to muck about in that rust bucket motor when he were a nipper. Reckoning to escape from the Nazis, pretending to screech round corners at full pelt. He must have held this handbrake as well. No, you couldn't be thinking on that. Got to frame yourself and focus on the High Street. Got to do it for Lanky.

He wondered how many folk were on the pavements. Hundreds of them, nattering away, having a good laugh. Everybody wanted to be outside this summer, basking in the heat. It set his heart off faster, thinking they'd all come to see if him and Jack could defend their title. He could sense the sweat on his forehead now, feel the handbrake slippery in his clammy hand, taste the drought in his mouth. Everyone were out today. Folk he knew. People he'd not seen afore. An old man with springy bands holding up his shirtsleeves. A fat lass sitting on a space hopper. A young mum wearing brown-tinted sunglasses, rocking her baby in a new pram. Flipping heck, that had decent wheels on it. They looked dead fast. Where could they get some like that? No, they couldn't do that to a little baby. There's Elsa, waving at you.

She's got them grotty plastic sandals on again. Be nice if someone bought her some pretty shoes one day. Look at Rodney Hargraves, nowt but two hundred yards away down the hill, standing above the crowd on that top step outside his shop, blood all over his butcher's smock. He looked to be lording it over all and sundry. Akin to a Roman emperor back from battle.

Michael snapped out of it and, staring at the tarmac ahead of him again, tugged at the reins of his bogie chariot. Mr Roe's snotty-nosed son, Terry, boinged across the street on a pogo stick. How the heck could you concentrate? Come on, you've got to win this for Jack. Eh, there's Mum in the crowd, all that love on her face, smiling at you with her head tilted. Hold up, what's she wearing? A white dress. Bit see through, isn't it? She must have been home after work to put it on especially. Dad were there with her last year. Standing behind her, holding her in his strong arms, kissing her long black hair. That's odd, she doesn't look to be standing up properly. Is she leaning back or summat? She is leaning back. And she looks right comfy. Like she's on a giant cushion. But, isn't she...? She's leaning against the person behind her. And he's got his arms round her tummy. And she's letting him. And she's still got a smile on her face. And she's snuggling up to him. Eddie bloody Weir!

"Get set, go!" bellowed Mr Roe.

"Geronimo!" cried Jack.

Michael felt him proper pushing. But why was the bogie hardly shifting? Why weren't the wheels going round? It were like the sun had melted the tarmac and the old girl had got stuck in it.

"What ya doin', Micky!"

Them other bogies were yards down the street already. Michael watched four pairs of trainers kicking fast, getting away, escaping from the Nazis.

"The handbrake!" yelled Jack. "Release the friggin' handbrake!"

Shit, the handbrake! And at last they were off. Steer straight, stay low. Not easy, mind. They were supposed to be going as fast as they could, but everything seemed to be happening too quickly for Michael. The road rushing at his face, the cheering crowd flashing by, the sound of Lanky's sprinting feet pounding like billio. And now them thoughts he got at night, rushing in. The terrible pictures in his brain. Stay low. Do it for...Thud! Jack jumping on the tailboard, panting like a big dog in the hot day.

"Right, Micky, keep her straight! We're catching 'em! Can still win this! Got to win it! Got to win!"

Heck, sounded like he'd kill for victory. They were catching them. Michael got as low as he could. Aerodynamics or summat. He had to have his neck at full stretch, so as to still look down the street. His head were nearly level with the wheels. He listened to them whirring over the ground. His nose was low enough for him to properly smell that mucky tarmac. Hold the steering rope steady. Focus on the street. Focus on the street. The crowd had got to roaring, though. It kept putting him off. Eddie Weir? What's Mum doing with him? The bloke's a knobhead. Has she forgotten about Dad now, then? It's not been a year yet. Come on, concentrate. There's that bastard Rodney Hargraves on his top step, a tall blur. But watch the flipping road. They were gaining on the others fast. He could see the chippings stuck in the nearest bogie's solid rubber tyres. Blurring round and round and round... Round and round and round... Round and round and round...Then he couldn't hear the crowd anymore...Or feel the right warm air on his cheeks... Or smell the sticky tarmac... All he knew were pictures in his head.

Now they were alongside the nearest bogie. Tony Ridley on the back with his Bay City Rollers haircut. Wheel to wheel. James Hunt sticking it to Nikki Lauda. Ridley gawping at them slipping past. Still a bit to go till the corner at the bottom of the street, soon after Bowers' Family Butchers. Next two bogies nowt but inches away. Level with each other. But a gap between wide enough. Nearly as wide as a narrow country lane. Like the lane down the dale that autumn morning. Deer grazing by the woods. Dad with one hand on the butcher's van steering wheel. Making Michael laugh with his daft songs: 'Life is butter, butter, melon, life is but a melancholy flower.' A bend in the country lane not right far off. Caught them two bogies now. Squeezing in between. Stubbsy giving it the big two fingers as they overtook. Lanky must have opened his gob. Corner at the bottom of the High Street coming up fast now. Fair bit shorter if you take it on the inside, that corner. Take that last bogie on the inside. It's just afore the finish line. Dad messing about. Doing squiggles in the lane with his tyres. All because he wanted to put a smile on your face. If only you hadn't been in the passenger seat. All because Dad was after making you happy. They'd take that last bogie on the inside of the corner. Then over the line to victory! The bend in the country lane nowt but a few yards off. 'One last squiggle, Dad.' The corner at the bottom of the High Street coming up. Here we go. Take it a bit tighter. They're on the outside of you. Push them wider. Like James Hunt. 'Dad, watch that bend.' Push them wide. Watch the balance. 'Dad, you're on the wrong side.' Don't tip her over. 'Dad, get over, get over!' Oh shit, she's on two wheels, she's tipping, she's tipping! 'Dad, watch the lorry! Dad! The lorry! Daddyyyyyy!'

CHAPTER FIVE

The weekend after the race was the last of the summer holidays. There might have been a fair breeze blowing this Sunday morning, but it was still roasting hot, so Jack had his cut-off denim shorts on again. Leaning his Chopper bike against the Bowers' house wall on the quiet High Street, he hung his little canvas rucksack off its long saddle and knocked on the front door. He'd caught Michael traipsing round the village once or twice since the bogie crash, with his hands shoved in his pockets and his head bowed. He hadn't got right much out of him, but he had persuaded him to come on Expedition Number Twelve before school started again. To the top of their very own 'mountain', Fowlbeck Beacon. It would be a proper laugh, an adventure, it would do him good. And they'd not conquered The Beacon's tricky North Face as yet. Jack knew he had to bring Michael back out of himself. He should never have pushed their bogie so hard at the top of the High Street. Frigging horrible seeing Micky kakking it when they tipped over, giving that gawping crowd the trapped wild animal treatment. The lad's eyes had been similar to The OB's for a second: 'Get back! Get away from me!' He had been in that van with his dad when he was killed, mind. It shouldn't surprise folk. Poor kid.

When the Bowers' door opened, there was Michael's mum, still in her dressing gown. Her face looked knackered and, even though she sometimes put her hair in a 'beehive', it had the appearance of a bird's nest today. Jack felt a bit stunned, because she was nearly always perfectly turned out. Even tidy enough in her butcher's clobber. And when she had that near as damn it see-through dress on at the bogie race! Fucking hell. He'd been getting a few stirrings in his

Y-fronts lately, looking at lasses, but when his best mate's mum started sparking things off? That really did muck his head up. Maybe it was a good job she did have the look of a scarecrow this morning.

"Jack?"

"What?"

"Are you coming in, then?" said Mrs Bowers. "I've just asked you three times."

"Soz, Mrs Bowers." said Jack, nibbling his bottom lip. "Is Michael in?"

"Yes, come inside," she said, ushering him in, closing the door. "I'm glad you're here. Sit down, sit down."

He sat bolt upright on the worn leather settee, his body right stiff as she slipped in beside him. He could smell toothpaste on her breath.

"Jack?"

"Yes, Mrs Bowers?"

"I'm really worried about Michael," she said, keeping her voice down.

"Are ya, Mrs Bowers?"

"Call me Carol. Sounds daft, you saying Mrs Bowers all the time."

"All reet, Mrs Bowers. I mean... Carol," said Jack.

"He's hardly said owt to me since the race. Don't think he likes me much at the moment. I know he's not happy about... All he's said is that he's walking up The Beacon with you today. I think he's depressed about his dad. Try and jolly him up, will you, Jack?"

She was leaning in closer now, looking right into his eyes. He could see she'd been crying.

"Do my best, Carol."

"Ta very much, eh?" said Carol, her warm hand touching his bare knee. "You're a good boy."

"We'll have a laugh," said Jack, his mouth all dry.

"He loves you, you know."

"No he doesn't."

"Oh, you're blushing. Don't be embarrassed. I mean, he looks up to you."

"Well, yeah, but... Where is he?"

"In his room. I'll go get him for you."

Jack watched Carol's fit arse wiggle as she walked off in her dressing gown. Jesus Christ. Then he could hear her on the stairs, calling up to Michael in a right soft voice, like she didn't fancy upsetting him. Bit late for that, now she's got to shagging Eddie Weir. Funny what she'd said about Michael loving you. Does he love you, then? Jack had never thought about it. Doubtless they did love each other. Not in a sissy way, but...Well, they needed one another. Nowt wrong with that. Don't know what you'd do without Micky. It didn't matter what The OB said that night when he punched your face in. You're not Michael's bum chum. What did the old man know about friendship, anyway? When did he ever give a toss for anyone but himself? No, give over thinking about it. Don't give the bastard the satisfaction. Fight it! Fight it! But he'd said it was a 'good do' Bernard Bowers being six foot under, because this was their chance to bury his 'stick in the mud' shop alongside him. And if they couldn't kill Bowers' Butchers off now, with a geriatric and a woman running the show, they'd never manage it. All they needed was a brand new cabinet... A brand new...Cruuunnch!...That bony fist cracking you one in the gob...Blood dripping on your white pillow...But fight it...Fight it...You can always fight it... Better think about summat else.

He had a gander at the Bowers' front room, looking at all the dead boring traditional stuff. The old sooty-smelling open fire, the stone hearth, the brasses, the copper kettle.

The Yorkshire sideboard, the blue and white china on the oak dresser. Things that loads of folk had round here. Why did people want to be like everybody else? Bollocks to that. Jack had tried fitting in and look where it had got him. He didn't belong in this village. He'd got to get out one day. He wanted to be different.

There were a fair lot of Bowers' family photos about on the flower-pattern walls. He'd not taken much notice before, but summat made him stand up and walk round today, stopping at the pictures for a closer look. There's Micky buried up to his chin in a beach, a grin on his chops, an upturned bucket on his head. Another one at the seaside, where his dad's made him a sand helter-skelter so he can send a tennis ball down. He'd been a lucky sod, having all that with his old man. No wonder the lad got in a state sometimes.

Hanging in fancy frames on the chimney breast were photos of the generations of Bowers' butchers from down the years. Each one standing fine and dandy outside their shop. Jack followed the trail back in time. One of Michael's mum, dad and grandad. Then his grandad when he was younger. Then what must have been his great grandad. Right back to the oldest picture of all, with a shiny brass plaque on the frame that smelt like it had just been polished: *'Bowers' Family Butchers, Founded by Albert Bowers in 1877.'* There's Albert under his **'A. BOWERS' BUTCHERS'** sign. Fists on hips. Chest puffed out. Right serious face. Now that little lot amounted to a fair old weight on Micky's shoulders.

"Here he is, Jack!" said Carol, suddenly behind him. "My one and only butcher boy."

He must have been so lost in the photos that he'd not heard them come downstairs.

"We thought he was hiding up there, didn't we, Jack?"

"No yer din't," said Michael, keeping his head down,

clomping straight past his mum in hiking boots, brown shorts, green T-shirt. He reached the front door and opened it, staring outside at the High Street pavement. "We gettin' out of here or what, Lanky?"

Jack noticed Carol's chin get a wobble on as she tried holding back the tears.

"Have a nice time, then, boys," she said. "Ooh, Michael, your 'pack up!'"

She dashed into the kitchen and came back with a small beige rucksack.

"I'll tek it for him," said Jack, reaching for it.

"There's potted meat sandwiches, love, your very favourite Bowers' pork pies, some pop..."

"Are we off, Lanky?" said Michael.

"Be careful on The Beacon, you two."

"Aye, we will," said Jack.

"Are we off?"

"Should I tell your grandad you'll be round for dinner next Sunday, love?" said Carol.

"You'll do what yer want, won't yer?" said Michael, glaring at her.

Jack could tell that one had struck Carol dumb. Her sexy mouth was catching flies.

"Come on, Micky, let's go," he said, handing Michael his rucksack and guiding him outside into the sunshine. "Where's your Chopper?"

"Down t' back alley."

"Bye, Carol," said Jack, shutting the door.

"Carol?" said Michael.

"I mean... Mrs Bowers."

When Michael had fetched his bike from the back alley, the boys strapped on their rucksacks and set off. Jack was up front. He'd quietly packed his rucksack in his bedroom the night before and was carrying the most important gear for the expedition. An old toffee tin, with cotton wool inside to protect any precious objects they found on their way to the summit. The logbook, with its records of earlier adventures, its wildlife notes, its secret maps. He'd been to the 'spice' shop too, to buy Michael's favourite sweets. Tangy sherbet lemons and liquorice sticks as tough as chewing baccy. He had them tucked away with his sandwiches, ready for when the lad needed a jolly up. He thought it might be time as they rode along a dry track beside the sawmill, on the outskirts of the village, because Micky had said nowt since they'd set off and he was still silent as a mouse. Jack squeezed on his squeaky brakes and stopped, skidding his fat back wheel in an arc through the dirt. Michael pulled up alongside.

"What we stopped for?" he said.

"Fancy a liquorice stick?" said Jack. "It's that hard stuff ya like."

"Aye, go on."

Jack took off his rucksack, delved inside, brought out two liquorice sticks, handed one to Michael.

"How ya doin', mate?"

"I'm reet," said Michael.

"Are you glum?"

"I'm grand."

"Micky, you're not grand."

"Fair to middlin', then."

Jack reckoned he'd better let him alone for now. He put his rucksack back on. Michael knew he could talk to him if he wanted, no bother. That's what mattered. They stood astride their bikes, chewing on the strong-tasting liquorice, looking at the sawmill yard with its log piles and sawn wood stacks. Jack could smell the sharp pine and rich oak on the warm breeze. Frigging hell, what a dusty old place. Molly the Mop would have a field day. Sawdust blowing about like desert sand, now that wind was getting up a bit. He could have been in one of Clint Eastwood's Westerns. A bounty hunter. Cool as owt while the sun beat down. Imagine facing death like that and still being as calm as can be. How would that feel? Was it possible? He wished he'd stayed cool that night when The Old Bastard came into his room. Then he could have stuck his penknife right between those mad goggly eyes.

"Sitha who's laikin' o'er there," said Michael, pointing toward the yard.

Jack spotted three scruffy lads from their year at school, sitting on a half-hidden wood pile, chucking pebbles at a stone watering trough.

"Oh, yeah. Look at the rogues. Could be villains in a Clint film."

"Aye. He'd pick 'em off easy enough."

"No bother," said Jack, at least glad his best mate was talking more.

"Who'd he take out first, then?" said Michael, tearing liquorice with his teeth.

"The nervous one. Allus t' nervous one first."

"Pete the Squeak?"

"Yep," said Jack.

"His voice gets reet jittery, dun't it?"

"Aye, at summat and nowt an all."

"Like climbin' fences," said Michael.

"Or spellin' tests."

Did Micky nearly smile then? A kind of smirk, anyway. They watched the rogues ping a couple more pebbles off the watering trough.

"Who'd Clint kill second, then?" said Jack.

"The ugly one," said Michael.

"Nosey?"

"Aye."

Jack saw Nosey miss the trough, the pebble skidding past it in the dirt like a skimmer on the river.

"Yep, he sure is ugly," he said. "Serves him right for pokin' his nose into fights and havin' it busted for t' trouble."

"One o' them idiots who reckon they're loads harder than they are," said Michael.

"Too right. Well, he's payin' for it now wi' his banana nose."

Micky definitely smiled at that.

"Oy, banana nose!" shouted Jack. "You're a shite shot!"

"Shhhh, Lanky!" said Michael, as the three villains jumped off the wood pile. "Stop it, will yer? Look, they're comin' over."

"We're on bikes, aren't we? Give o'er kakkin' it."

The villains were striding slowly across the yard toward them now.

"We know which one Clint would save till last, don't we, Michael?" said Jack, narrowing his eyes like all the best gunslingers did.

"Come on, let's go!"

"Nasty lookin' Tommy in t' middle. Hairy git."

"Supposed to be on Expedition Twelve, aren't we?" said Michael. "If we don't frame our sens, we'll not conquer that North Face. We're stoppin' at The Waterfall Den an all, aren't we?"

"Ya know summat?"

"What?"

"That fucker's so hairy he could run away wi' t' circus and never be out o' work."

The villains were getting closer, but Michael had chuckled a bit then.

"He's already got a five o'clock shadow," said Jack. "Ya know they never bother cooking owt at their house?"

"Nowt?"

"Not a sausage. Waste o' time, he sez. Reckons it tastes just as good straight out o' t' tin! Spoon-feeding themselves cold spaghetti and meat balls from t' can. Dirty gets! Appen it's what he feeds on that meks him so hairy."

"Appen."

"Spaghetti Yeti, I call him."

"I know," said Michael. "Listen, think on, they're gettin' close."

"Seen his family? Talk about rough. All hairy bastards. Even his mum's got a tache."

Michael couldn't help himself anymore. Jack could see him nearly choke on his liquorice when that one came out.

"And have ya seen him in t' showers at school? I can never stop glancing o'er to see how my pubes are comin' on compared to t' black forest he's got growin' down there!"

Now he knew he had him. The lad was properly pissing his pants. Time to go.

"We off, then, Michael?" said Jack.

"Let's away, let's away, let's away!" said Michael, liquorice slobber sliding down his chin from all his laughing.

Minutes later, they were crossing the old swing bridge that stretched over the river. Jack listened to his tyres whirring on the wooden slats and kept gawping through the gaps at the shallow, brownish water. Doubtless that deep part he'd jumped into a bit further upstream to escape Rocker Billy wouldn't be deep enough anymore, now there'd been six more weeks of no rain. He wondered if there were many trout or grayling this drought season. He'd right missed fishing when he'd been locked up. Proper good for thinking. For dreaming about what was beyond these hills hemming him in.

"Reckon there's many fish in t' river this summer, Micky?"

"Might be if there were any water in it."

Jack stopped at the end of the bridge and planted his feet on the slats. Then Michael was beside him, standing on bike pedals, leaning on him, arm round his shoulder. They looked at the parched, straw-coloured fields sloping up toward The Beacon, with its brown ground, purple heather, jagged limestone rocks they were after climbing in an hour or two.

"The North Face, eh?" said Michael.

"We'll stroll it," said Jack, his long black fringe fluttering round his eyes in the breeze.

CHAPTER SIX

Michael followed Jack as they rode their Chopper bikes across the parched, rock hard fields toward The Beacon, thinking it would have been sweltering if it weren't so gusty. He watched that fancy hanky, which Jack had round his neck, flapping in the wind. What had he called it when he put it on just after the bridge? A bandana or summat. What cowboys wore. It looked like a hanky to Michael, anyhow. Jack was funny, the long streak of piss. He loved stuff like that, no mistake. Blooming heck, it were brilliant being out on an adventure with him again, getting away from all that rubbish going on back home. Good old Lanky. He'd rescued him for a bit. But there were reminders about. Even the sun, which made Michael think of a big butterball on a giant blue plate, because Mum always melted a dollop on her peas at Grandad's. Eddie Weir? He still couldn't believe what she'd done.

When the fields got too steep, the boys hid their bikes in some woods and continued on foot, following the dried-up streambed which led to The Waterfall Den.

"Hope no-one's been messin' wi' our collection," said Michael, trailing a long stick over bone dry pebbles.

"Who knows about t' den except us?" said Jack, straightening his fancy bandana.

"Rats might o' been scrattin' round."

"Ya what? Robbin' fossils for their little ratty museum?"

"Sod off, beanpole. Just watch out for owt precious, can't yer? Eh, did yer remember t' logbook?"

"Micky, will ya give over chelpin'? How could I forget the logbook?"

As they walked, they searched for objects to add to their

hidden collection on the cracked streambed and in the dusty
hedgerows which ran close to its sides. Michael had eagle
eyes. Dead good at spotting stuff like flint glinting in the
dirt. Daft if you thought about it. Collecting ancient stones
or smoothed pieces of coloured glass. Recording them,
storing them away like squirrels in a secret place. Except it
were more akin to what children did, wasn't it? They could
be kids again while they did that. Instead of having to be
grown up all the time, thinking right serious. Exploring,
discovering, being on a mission, that's what they needed.
Besides, Michael loved being out here in nature. He knew
he were going to be a butcher. He had no choice, but it was
what he wanted, anyhow. To make a success of it, to uphold
the family name. But being in these fields, in the beautiful
Yorkshire Dales, happened to be his favourite thing. In
another life he'd have been a gamekeeper. He'd be out here
in nature all hours God sent if he were a gamekeeper.

While Michael looked for things worth collecting, picking
a near perfect speckled eggshell from a holly bush, finding
a nineteen-thirties coin on the streambed, passing them to
Jack for safekeeping in that toffee tin he always brought
for the purpose, he tried taking everything in. Just like Dad
had taught him. Perhaps Dad teaching him how to look at
nature properly was what had given him eagle eyes. And
he'd shown him how to breathe it all in, to smell it, to listen
to it. Something strange about the wind today which made
you prick your ears up. It could have been Dad speaking
in his whispering voice. He'd liked using his whispering
voice when he'd talked to Michael about nature: 'Look on
yon leaf, Son. Can yer see t' tiny white spots? You've got
good eyes, lad. Most folk'd miss them. Know what they
are? Caterpillar eggs. Inside are little caterpillars growin'.
Same as you in your mum's tum. They'll hatch soon. And

they'll grow and grow. And their skin'll grow bigger and harder, until they turn into chrysalises. And what fly out two weeks later? That's reet, Michael. Beautiful butterflies! And every one started as a tiny white spot on a leaf. So remember, whenever a butterfly flutters by, that's nature showin' thee a miracle.'

Michael snapped out of it and looked at Jack, near as damn it six foot tall, black hair blowing in the wind, marching up ahead. Always had to be in front, didn't he? Getting a fair old shift on today.

"Go steady, Lanky! We might miss stuff for t' collection."

"I've got 'em peeled."

"Me dad said you had to take yer time wi' nature."

"Did he?"

As they marched on, Michael listened to the blackbirds chattering away in the hedgerows. Fond of a natter, blackbirds. Similar to Fowlbeck neighbours having a right good gossip. Whenever he saw summat in with the tangled brambles or hawthorn that might be worth collecting, he dropped on his haunches. When you got down that low, you could really see how dry the earth had turned this summer. All powdery. The wind must be have been lifting it a bit, because it kept tickling your nose. You might think all the smells would be dry down here in a drought, but they weren't. Moss still grew on the rocks in the shadows and that smelt damp. Damp, but soft to touch. Like comfy carpet. Even moss were a miracle in nature.

The closer they got to The Waterfall Den the deeper their route cut into the earth. By the time they were near the den, and the collection tin held a few dusty objects, the banks on either side of them had got steep and tall. The sun and wind had been blocked out too now and they were properly in shade. Michael could feel how much cooler it were. He shivered when he looked at the little trees jutting out from the banks, curving upwards, trying to reach the light. It looked like ferns, ivy, sharp-smelling nettles had taken over the world down here. How had they done it with nowt to drink?

The boys followed a final twist in the streambed before the deep, narrow space widened into a big horseshoe shape, carved from layered limestone rock: The Waterfall Den. Except the waterfall was gone. Michael stood and stared at where the old girl used to be. He knew she'd have disappeared in a summer like this, but it still made him proper sad. She were usually so alive, with that white spray falling. She'd give you a decent shower most of the time, if you fancied. He looked up through the horseshoe at the clear sky, imagining clouds and a downpour.

"Checklist and dustin', then?" said Jack.

"Aye," said Michael.

They moved to the edge of the horseshoe, where nooks and crannies had been eroded deep into the limestone over a million years. Pushed inside these deep bits was the collection, hidden away from any folk who might find themselves out here, stumbling across this place. Michael knew that, for the next few minutes, they'd only be speaking to check off each collection object against the list in the logbook. He didn't know why, but they took this part dead serious. Like they were working in their own museum, as if they were taking care of important stuff for the future. They'd never talked about why it happened that way. But if their mates back in Fowlbeck could see them they'd rip the piss summat rotten. Anyhow, it were Michael and Jack's secret. And they'd sworn, as blood brothers, that they'd never tell another soul.

Carefully picking the objects from the rock, they set them

out on a fat slab of moss-covered limestone which lay on the ground in the middle of the horseshoe. Then they took off their rucksacks and sat cross-legged on the right dry earth either side of the stone. Michael watched Jack undo the drawstring on his rucksack, take out a pen and two yellow dusters, then silently remove the logbook, slowly lifting it up and setting it down beside the objects on the soft moss. They looked at it for a bit, as if it was an ancient document you were only allowed to touch with white gloves on. It were just a butcher's order book which Rodney Hargraves had never got round to using, but it had a hardback black cover with a red spine and it looked pretty smart. It were what it had inside that mattered, mind. Jack opened it, angled it so Michael could see it better, took his time turning the pages.

Michael thought about all the brilliant adventures they'd already been on when he saw the wildlife they'd recorded in lists and colourful felt tip pictures again. Kingfishers, hares, water voles, red grouse, otters, deer. Amazing what you could see just mucking about in the countryside. They were lucky lads, having all that. Then there were the maps they'd drawn of their climbs up The Beacon. Different routes dotted out in black, danger zones inked in red with bold biro words written across: **'Boggy', 'Slippery', 'Tangled', 'Jagged.'** On the last page of the map section, Jack had drawn an outline of The Beacon and left it blank. At the top of the page he'd written: ***THE NORTH FACE!*** That made Michael think on what was sometimes put at the end of Starsky and Hutch episodes: **'To be continued...'** Suddenly, the air in The Waterfall Den wasn't just cool, it felt right chilly.

"Lanky?" said Michael, rubbing goosebumps off his forearms. "Get to t' checklist pages, will yer?"

Picking up the yellow dusters, they started cleaning their precious things, sometimes holding them up to the horseshoe filled with blue sky to make sure they were bright as a bobbin. Only after an object had been properly dusted, cleaned, polished, was it placed back gently on the mossy stone. To finish this part of the job, they took the things they'd found that day from the toffee tin, Jack adding them to the checklist, and cleaned them, making the collection even more precious. The last important job, before they put the collection back in the horseshoe's nooks and crannies, was the one Michael reckoned Jack loved best. Always had to be in charge of the checklist, didn't he? Fancied himself a bit, ticking them boxes. Michael nearly got off laughing once or twice when he listened to him calling out like that Sergeant Major in It Ain't Half Hot Mum on telly. Dead funny. Especially seeing as Lanky were always moaning that his old man blithered on too much about having been a soldier in the war.

"Quartz!" said Jack, pen poised over the logbook.

"Check," said Michael, holding up the shiny crystal.

"Mudstone!"

"Check."

"Swan feather!"

"Check."

"Purple glass!"

"Check."

"Belt buckle!"

"Check."

"Horse's bit!"

"Check."

"Slate arrowhead!"

"Check."

"Bird bones!"

"Check."

"Iron key!"

"Check."

"1939 coin!"

"Check."

"Speckled eggshell!"

"Check."

"Mystery seashell!"

"Check."

"Gi' us a listen."

Michael passed Jack the shell and watched him put it to his ear. The lad had his eyes scrunched up, as if he were trying like mad to think.

"Do yer see land yet, Captain?" said Michael.

"Very far away," said Jack.

When they'd finished the checking and hidden the cleaned collection back in the limestone horseshoe, they sat on the ground again and used the moss-covered slab as a table for Sunday dinner 'pack up.'

"Thanks," said Michael, digging his teeth into a potted meat sandwich.

"What for?" said Jack, looking out from under his long fringe.

"Comin' for us today. Bringin' me out here. Getting me away."

"It's nowt. You'd do t' same."

"I'm reet lucky yer me best mate, Lanky."

"I'm lucky havin' you an all, but... Stop bein' soft, will ya?"

"Be a hard bastard like you, eh?" said Michael.

"You've allus got to fight, lad."

Michael looked at Jack chomping on his sausage roll. He was a fighter. He'd crack you one in the gob if you'd got it coming. Oh yes, he were a mad allik all right. A fighter in his head too. You could see it when he gritted his teeth. Michael

Chris Gill

wished he were a bit more like him sometimes.

"Things not good in your house at t' moment, then?" said Jack, wiping pastry crumbs off his lips.

"They're shit."

"Ya mum courtin' Eddie Weir now, is she?"

"Don't wanna talk about it," said Michael, swallowing the last of his potted meat sandwich, grabbing another.

"Don't worry, it won't last. She's too good for him."

"Don't wanna talk about it."

Michael knew they could speak about owt, but he didn't want to think of home and Fowlbeck for now. Best escaping out here a while. Jack was getting chatty, mind.

"You and Elsa courtin', Micky?" he said, opening some Salt and Shake crisps, sprinkling the salt, shaking the bag.

"Yer what?" said Michael.

"She your girrrrlllfriend?"

"No-o."

"Bit poor, her family, aren't they?" said Jack, crunching on a crisp.

"What's that got to do wi' t' price of eggs?"

"I mean, ya can tell by the state o' t' clothes she wears."

"Sod off!" said Michael.

"Oooooooo! Raw nerve?"

Best mate in the world, Jack. But he still loved taking the piss, no mistake. Why couldn't Michael think of a good reply? It were usually like this when Lanky made fun of him. Put panic in his head. He knew he wasn't thick. All he'd got left now, though, was trying not to look riled.

"Don't sulk," said Jack, sticking out that bottom lip with its little bulge.

"I'm not."

"Soz, mate. Listen, ya know me, daft as a fuckin' brush."

They ate in silence a while. Then Jack took a quarter of

74

sherbet lemons from his rucksack, offered Michael one, near as damn it made him smile.

"Reckon you'll be runnin' Bowers' Family Butchers in a few years, then, Micky?"

"Oh aye," said Michael, sucking the tangy sweet.

"For t' rest of ya days?"

"That's hundred years tradition we're talkin' about."

"Yeah, I know," said Jack. "Ever think ya might fancy doin' summat else, though?"

"Like what?"

"You're tellin' me there's nowt else you've ever thought o' doing?"

"Gamekeeper. Sometimes reckon I wouldn't mind bein' a gamekeeper."

"Gamekeeper? Friggin' hell, Micky, there's a whole world out there!"

Michael went quiet again. Then Jack pulled an apple from his rucksack. And a bowie knife with a blade so long and wide it could have been a butcher's cleaver. That slackened Michael's jaw.

"Bloody Nora, Lanky! Where'd yer get that?"

"Never you mind, young man."

"What else yer got in there? Leg o' lamb for carvin'?"

Jack laughed at that, like he'd got to really enjoying himself.

"Bit much for slicin' an apple, in't it?" said Michael.

"Oh, I've not brought it for that," said Jack, looking up at the shiny steel blade against the clear blue sky.

"Eh?"

"Thought it was time we did the blood brothers' ceremony again."

"You're joshing," said Michael. "Wi' that thing?"

"Aye. Let's do t' job right this time."

"Yer can stuff it!"

"Come on, soft lad," said Jack, smirking. "Let's have some nice cuts. Then, when we press 'em together, my blood will really mix wi' yours and your blood will really mix wi' mine. Then we'll be true blood brothers. Till we die."

"But we've already done it wi' penknives."

"Penknives are for girls. Look, we'll never be proper blood brothers till we use a proper knife. You know that, Michael. Ever seen a Red Indian use a penknife in a blood brother ceremony?"

"No, but..."

"See. Be ridiculous, wouldn't it?"

"That's in films, though," said Michael, crunching down the last of his sherbet lemon.

"Tell ya what, you give o'er worryin', mate. It's reet. I'll do my cut first. Then, if ya don't want to be real blood brothers... Well, that's up to you."

"Course I want to be real blood brothers, but..."

Michael wondered what the hell Jack was playing at. Oh yeah, he loved cowboy and Indian films, but it were like he reckoned he belonged in one sometimes. Well, if it makes him happy. Don't want him sad, do you? Especially after everything the lad's been through this summer. Suppose it won't hurt that much. Not as much as seeing Mum snuggling up to Eddie Weir, anyhow.

"Go on, then. Yer mad bastard."

"That's more like my Michael," said Jack. "Me first."

Michael watched him clear the slab of rock and lay the back of his left hand on the moss. He felt his heart pump faster when Jack cut himself, touching his palm with the sharp edge of the steel bowie knife, drawing the blade back slowly across his skin, slicing open his flesh. Cut a bit deep, hadn't he? Michael looked at Jack's face and a little shiver went over it. And his eyes were closed. And he was giving it one long breath out through his nose. And what were that? A smile? The blood was coming out of Jack's hand, oozing thick. Thicker than animal blood on a butcher's block.

"Shit, Lanky!" said Michael, his mouth drying up. "Gi' me t' flippin' knife!"

He took it. Laid his palm next to Jack's. Braced himself. Sliced. Strange how the blood didn't come straight away. How the cut stayed dry for a second. But here it was. Red and dark. They looked into each other's eyes. Raised their wounded hands. Pressed their bleeding cuts together. Then they clasped their fingers round each other's hands. And squeezed. And squeezed. And squeezed.

CHAPTER SEVEN

After the blood ceremony, Jack used his water bottle to wet the dusters and the boys tied them proper tight across their cuts. Then they packed everything up in their little rucksacks and set off in the heat again toward Fowlbeck Beacon. On the way, when the coast was clear, they stopped by a farmyard tap for a water fight. It was a right laugh, and the soaking cooled them off, but they still had that climb to do. They filled their bottles and strode out, reaching The North Face in the early afternoon.

Jack gazed up at The Beacon, with its purple heather and tufts of long sunburnt grass. The summit didn't seem that far away on the north side, but that was because the climb was loads steeper than south, east and west. No messing with The North Face, just straight to the top. They'd have to watch all those jagged limestone rocks which made up most of the climb's terrain, mind. And that narrow ledge right below the summit which it looked like you had to edge along. Jack knew it was more dangerous than the other routes they'd done, which nearly had him kakking it, but that's why he'd been excited about having a crack at it for so long too. Clint was like that in his films. Loved danger, did Clint. Life wouldn't be owt without danger. Jack turned to Michael, who was standing next to him looking nervous, puffing out his chubby red cheeks.

"Ya ready for this, Micky?"

"Suppose it's safer than tryin' to jump o'er The Surge," said Michael.

"Course it is," said Jack. "Just think about all those old Surge stories. Ready, mate?"

"Long as we take it slow. Don't be leggin' it up like a

monkey in a tree."

"We allus stick together, remember?"

Jack watched Michael pointing up at the climb with his bandaged hand, sighting along his finger, doubtless trying to trace out the safest route, as the ends of his yellow duster ruffled in the wind. Just keep an eye on him, make sure he stays close. Pull him up if you have to. Got to take care of Micky. He needed taking care of these days. They needed each other, though. Odd how Jack had felt back there in the blood ceremony. Like he'd been taken over by summat. He wanted to be close to Michael, he was grateful to him for always being there, he loved him like a brother, but there'd been something in his head at The Waterfall Den. He didn't understand it, but it made him want that closeness so much that he just had to get Michael to cut himself open, so they could squeeze their hands together and mix their blood. Or was it that? Maybe he'd just been after an excuse to cut himself with his big bowie knife, because he knew the pain would feel so good. Like when he'd had his first wank and it hurt a bit, but it was fucking ace too. Or had he only wanted the ceremony so he could see Micky in pain? Because he knew he felt jealous of Michael, of what he'd had with his dad. Jealous, even though Mr Bowers was dead now and the poor lad's heart had been broken. There was all sorts of weird shite going on in Jack's head these days. He didn't know what was happening to him, but he felt like flying off the handle sometimes.

"Shall we give o'er stallin', then?" said Michael, stopping sighting along his finger.

Jack shook himself out of it and set off in front, taking it steady, glancing back now and again to make sure Michael was keeping up. The climb was steep from the start, even before it got right rocky, and you could easily slip on the dusty dirt as dry as desert sand, so you had to scramble on all fours in some places to get enough grip. This was a danger zone to put in the logbook straight off. And they'd hardly got going yet. Frigging hell, what a climb, The North Face! They'd just been mucking about on The Beacon till now. Jack was suddenly so excited that he wasn't scared of the danger at all anymore. Loved it, he did. He could have been Clint Eastwood.

After they'd climbed a few hundred feet, Jack reckoned Michael could do with a breather. He hopped up onto a big flat-topped rock, sat there with his long legs dangling over the edge and watched him clambering up just beneath.

"Come on, Micky, lad, you're doin' ace."

"Be jiggered by t' summit," said Michael, puffing hard as he pulled himself up onto the rock and sat with his legs dangling as well.

"Real adventurin', this, eh?" said Jack.

"Aye, but let's be careful."

"We've not fallen yet, have we?"

Jack wished Michael would give over worrying so much. It proper got on his nerves sometimes. The boys wiped their sweaty faces with the tied dusters and took long swigs of water to slake their thirst. Jack kept having to push his fringe out of his eyes because of the wind. It was getting blowy all right, the higher they got.

"Off-cum-dens," said Michael, pointing.

"Ya what?" said Jack.

"One man and his dog."

Jack spotted an old fogie, with a massive mane of silver hair and an Alsatian, walking past down below.

"Oh yeah, Silver Fox and his mangy mutt. I've seen 'em about."

"That bloke's just bought a holiday home off the High

Street," said Michael. "Me grandad reckons there'll be more off-cum-dens buyin' up places o'er t' next few years."

"Good for weekend trade."

"Aye, but what about rest o' t' week? Bread and butter trade, as me grandad says. What if lots of houses in Fowlbeck end up belongin' to outsiders who just come to t' village at weekends? And only sunny ones at that."

"Ya know summat?" said Jack, putting on a fogie's voice. "Thee's soundin' more like thee grandad wi' each passin' day, young un."

"But what about our butchers' shops?"

"What about 'em?"

"It'll cut turnover and profit."

"Oh, I'll be out of here long before that's owt to bother about."

"Will yer?" said Michael, looking at Jack with his gob wide open.

Jack didn't want him upset. He'd have to take his mind off it.

"Eh, listen at this a minute," he said. "See what t' dog does."

Jack stood up, put his neck at full stretch and did a coyote impression, howling at the blue sky like one gone barmy.

"Oww oww owwhhoooo-oooo!"

"Stop messin', will yer?" said Michael.

"Look, Silver Fox has spotted us. And t' mutt's lugs have pricked up."

"I'm not bothered. Listen, did yer mean that? About not stayin' round here?"

Poor lad. Sounded like a nipper at first school. Jack would have to make it better.

"Well how do I know, really?" he said. "Who knows what's gonna happen? We're only twelve, aren't we?

Decisions like that are a million miles in t' future."

Michael gazed at his boots for a bit. Then he looked up at Jack with eyes like a lamb's before the cleaver.

"Suppose," he said.

Jack reckoned it best to get on with the climb. He stared at the jagged limestone rocks above. All dead craggy from now on. Similar to his father's old face. Nowt like Mount Rushmore with its massive, smooth carvings of American Presidents which he'd seen in a textbook once at school. The OB would fucking love that, having his carved baldy head looking out toward Fowlbeck. Better than a picture in The Gazette any day. He'd likely think he deserved it too. Jack felt like laughing at that one. But then his imagination had him thinking himself a deadly spider, about to crawl all over The Old Bastard's ugly mug. Putting the fear of God into it. Conquering it. He couldn't wait any longer. He'd just have to take proper charge. Who was leader of this expedition, anyway? Obvious, wasn't it?

"Let's move on out, partner!"

Jack stepped up onto the next grey rock and they were off again, climbing toward the summit. There were wide gaps between the rocks which they'd have to stride across. And it was like a giant puzzle you had to work out because, if you stood in the wrong place, you'd have to double back to get higher. Frigging hell, tricky standing on these jaggy bits. Not enough surface to put your whole foot down, so you had to use the balls of your feet and be right strong with your ankles. Jack's black trainers were good for grip, but rubbish round the ankles. His bare legs got off dithering a time or two. He'd just have to keep going, mind. Stretching his arms to grab a higher rock and steady himself, then working out where to step next. That wind didn't help much with balance either. You might call it a stiff breeze. Excepting, every few minutes there'd be a noisy gust blowing in from the dry open spaces, taking him unawares. There wasn't any warning, so he had to hold on dead tight to the rough rocks all the time. If he'd had a sensible head on, he'd have wanted it still and calm. But it was... He found it... What was the word? A biddy in a headscarf had come into the shop one windy day and said it. Bracing? Not bracing. Exhilarating! That was it. He found it exhilarating. He liked that word. He wished there were more things in his life to make him exhilarated. Fat chance of that ever happening in Fowlbeck village.

When Jack's 'spider legs' had crept up the craggy face a fair way, he reached a part out of the wind, and where the surface was flatter. This bit looked as if it had been dug deeper into the face somehow. A stinking pipe tobacco mouth? He crawled inside and sat there, waiting for Michael. Being hidden from the wind reminded him of how warm it was today. He reached over his shoulder to grab his water bottle from his rucksack and took another cooling sip. They must have climbed most of The North Face now, no bother. You could see for miles. The parched hills stretching out like huge waves to the horizon. The darker woods dotted about like ships sailing to another continent. The long limestone walls that could have been sea routes on a sailor's map. He'd read a few adventure stories in books he'd taken out of the school library, but there was nowt as good as imagining your own. From this sheltered spot, the world seemed right quiet. As quiet as one of those silent black and white films they showed on Saturday morning television, except without the daft music. And everything looked so far away, as if it would take you a hundred years to get to wherever you wanted to be. Jack looked down at Michael, who was keeping up right enough. But he'd stopped just below now, moving his head about like he'd got to following summat with his eyes.

"What ya gawpin' at?" said Jack.

"A little miracle," said Michael.

"Eh?"

"A butterfly flutterin' by."

Jack could see it now, floating up and away on the breeze with its pretty black and orange wings. Then he realised that his mate had clambered into The OB's tobacco mouth and was sitting beside him.

"Do yer reckon we're about halfway up now, Lanky?" said Michael.

"More like three quarters."

"Bloomin' heck, I'm not even whacked anymore! It's a butterfly miracle!"

"Don't be soppy," said Jack, nibbling at the bulge in his bottom lip.

"I'm serious. I could climb Everest. Me dad said..."

"Look, do ya wanna conquer this craggy old face or what?"

"Aye, but..."

"Let's crack on, then."

Fucking hell, Micky really would be happy just running Bowers' Family Butchers and going for local walks of a Sunday to think about his long gone father. Anyway, Jack hadn't time to mull that one over right now. He'd got to conquer this face once and for all. Not going to let The Old Bastard beat you, are you? Fight it. Fight it. You can always fight it.

After Michael had had a drink, Jack led the way as they climbed out into the gusty breeze again. The rocky slope got even steeper from here, so you definitely had to be like a spider to crawl up now. At least the rock-face had plenty of cracks and holes in it, like The OB's wrinkles and pock-marks, which you could sink your fingers in to get a right good grip.

Jack needed them, because he had a fair job finding places to step here without getting a wobble on. He had to get a decent hold with his hands just to steady himself against the rocks and wind. He knew this part would be one of the first into the logbook as a North Face danger zone, coloured in with red felt tip. Especially when he looked down through his long ruffling fringe and saw how high up they were getting. Not much bother to him, mind. He loved it, didn't he? Like Clint would. Or Spiderman. It was exhilarating. Micky didn't seem right flustered now either. Perhaps he really did believe in butterfly miracles, or whatever it was. He wasn't lagging behind or owt, anyway. He'd be right enough now. Better keep looking up and climbing. You could see the summit getting nearer with every step.

Jack carried on climbing a while up the grey, craggy old face. Reach out an arm, sink your fingers in a wrinkle, find a place for your feet, step up. Reach out an arm, sink your fingers in a wrinkle, find a place for your feet, step up. Climb, climb, climb. Like Spiderman on a skyscraper. You had to be a superhero to beat the baddie. Crawl all over his old face like a deadly spider. Scare the living shite out of him. Reach the top. Reach the top. Don't let him beat you. Reach the top and you've won. But suddenly a big gust of wind whipped round the rocks and into him. It felt as if his body was bending like a sail on an explorer's ship. The sharp blast of air put tears in his eyes, goosebumps on his bare arms and legs. This was fucking ace! Good job he'd been keeping a tight hold. This was proper life. Not chopping up meat on a butcher's block. Another noisy gust blew, making a real racket in his ears, bellowing at him. Similar to The OB in a rage: 'Get out of it! Get out of my face! Look at t' state of you. As if batter wouldn't melt. When are you going to start takin' responsibility as son and heir in this family, Jack?

You'll be running t' shop before you know it. Into your room and stay there! Until I come up them stairs and teach you a lesson you'll not forget!'

Back to his room? Back to prison? Back to being beaten up? Not frigging likely! He was Clint Eastwood. Spiderman. A superhero. And heroes always conquered villains in the end. He reached out his arm again, creeping his skinny fingers over the face, sinking them into another old wrinkle. Find a place for your feet, step up.

He could see that ledge just beneath the summit clearly now. Nowt but a few yards away. Looked right narrow. He'd definitely have to edge along it to get to the top. Piece of cake for a superhero, mind. Feel the danger. Life was nothing without it. And he was like a superhero at school, wasn't he? The best at PE. The hardest kid in his year. Don't mess with Jack 'Spiderman' Hargraves, if you know what's good for you. Another sudden gust whacked into him like a clout round the ear. 'I'll knock some sense into thee, lad!' Climb. Climb. Fight. Fight.

Where was another wrinkle, then? Or maybe that sort of bowl shape scooped out of the top of the next rock would do. The one which the wind and rain had doubtless been sculpting since dinosaurs were about. A giant eye socket with the big bulging eye gouged out. He pulled on its rim and hoisted himself up, trying not to think about what a human eye would feel like in the palm of his hand. Hard as a marble? Dead squelchy? As he stood in the 'socket', he shuddered in the wind. Don't think on it. Just climb. You're a hero, remember. A gunslinger. The toughest kid in town. No fucker beats Jack Hargraves. Step up. Step up.

He'd got under the narrow ledge now, which was just above where he was standing in the eye socket. Should have no bother pulling yourself onto it. Shifting along it, as it sloped up to the summit, might be dicier, mind. One slip and you'll be tumbling all the way down this craggy old face. You'll be like a lump of strawberry jam when they come to scrape you up at the bottom. Better not look down, then. Look up. All you've got to do is edge along the ledge and you're there. At the summit. The conqueror. The hero beating the villain. Standing on top of his baldy head.

Jack pulled himself up and stood with his nose nearly touching the rock-face. Had to be that close to make sure his feet were properly on the ledge. The North Face smelt dry and old and grey. Now he'd got near the summit, the wind was blowing his hair all over the shop. He kept having to push the long black strands from his eyes. And it had started whistling non-stop in his ears, like it was after reminding him of the danger. As if he needed reminding. That's one of the reasons he was doing this. The danger! The exhilaration! He bet that was why Spiderman did it as well. And to defeat evil. Defeating evil bastards was what mattered most.

He started edging along the narrow upward slope of rock. A window ledge one hundred storeys high. Nowt but a few yards to the summit now. Two long spider legs crawling over a craggy face. Two spidery arms reaching for wrinkles and pock-marks to cling to. Edging along, edging along. Once he'd got his technique and balance going, it wasn't as hard as he'd thought. Reach for a wrinkle. Get a good grip. Step with your right foot. Meet it with your left. Breathe. Reach for a wrinkle...And, after three or four paces, the wind seemed to have quietened down fairish. Blowing through his hair more gently. Like it was playing, cooling his skin, keeping him calm under pressure. Reach for a wrinkle. Get a good grip. Step with your right foot. Meet it with your left. Breathe. Fine and dandy, this. Piece of cake. Why wouldn't it be? For a superhero? For Jack Hargraves? The toughest kid in town. The best at PE. The best at climbing trees. And he wasn't scared of danger. Other folk might be, but not Jack Hargraves. He loved it. He found it exhilarating. No wonder he was about to defeat evil, to conquer the big bald villain. Only two steps to go now, then you can haul yourself onto the summit. Nearly there. Reach for a wrinkle. That was a decent grip. Step with your right foot. Meet it with your left...Thwack! Fuck! What was that? Gale force ten coming in from nowhere, smacking him in the guts! Frigging hell, it wasn't stopping this time either! Keep hold! Keep hold! He was a sail bending in a terrible storm! The wind howling at him like The OB in a full on rage: 'I'll knock you into t' middle o' next week, lad!' Fight it! Fight him! Fight him! Shite! It still wasn't stopping! If you let go of that wrinkle you'll be a goner! Tumbling down the rock-face! A lump of strawberry jam! But the wind was buffeting him too much, as if it was trying to wrench his fingers from the rock! Was he losing his grip? Maybe he could get a better hold in that next wrinkle a bit further on, the one dead below the summit. Stretch... Stretch... Stretch... Almost got it... Fuck... Almost... Nearly... Got it! Now step with your right foot. Meet it with your left. And cling on! Cling on! Cling on...But...Was the wind easing off a bit now? It was easing off. Quick! Pull yourself up onto the summit while you've chance!

Then he was on the summit. Standing on top of that baldy head. He'd done it! The conqueror! The hero! He'd defeated the villain. He was Clint Eastwood riding to a new horizon. Stick that in your pipe and smoke it, you evil old bastard!

Jack walked slowly away from The North Face a few paces, toward the millions of acres beyond The Beacon, as the breeze ruffled his hair like a kind father would. Perhaps one day he'd find what he wanted out there. He stood still a while, thinking about it. And now he had a smile on. Course he'd find what he wanted. He was the best, wasn't he? He was Jack Hargraves.

"Lanky!"

Micky? Shite! Micky! Jack spun around. And there, just his head showing above the summit, was Michael, gasping for breath, fear in his eyes, a bloody gash cut into his brow.

EASTER 1983

CHAPTER EIGHT

Michael hadn't planned owt on the freezing, cloudless Saturday night afore Good Friday. But one minute they're walking up the High Street from The Dog and Gun after last orders, Elsa getting him to look at the stars, the next they're outside his house and he's asking her in for coffee. They were just friends, mind. No question of 'funny business'.

"Only if you've got some sugar for me," said Elsa, fluttering her eyelids at him from behind her glasses.

"Oh aye, we've got sugar," said Michael, fiddling with his front door key. "Eh, what do yer mean?"

"Askin' a lass in for coffee, Michael Bowers?"

"Oh no... I din't... I'm not... I just like talkin' to yer."

"Your mum away for t' weekend wi' Eddie an all," she said, winking at him.

"Now hold up..."

But then he knew she were only teasing, because she started giggling in that way which got other folk off laughing. He watched the cold breath coming from her mouth.

"I'll come in for a warm," she said.

Before he turned the door key, Michael had a glance up and down the High Street to check for gossipers. Having nowt to hide didn't matter, that never stopped tongues wagging in Fowlbeck. He heard it six days a week in the shop. You couldn't account for curtain twitchers, but, aside from a mullet-haired poser driving past in a Ford Escort with bolted on headlights, the coast looked clear enough.

Michael unlocked the door and they stepped inside the dark front room, warm from the fire he'd banked up with coal before he'd gone to meet Elsa at the pub. He turned on the tall lamp, with the tasselled shade, beside the drawn curtains. They took off their shoes, hung their big coats on the coat stand by the traditional Yorkshire sideboard, walked through to the kitchen. He flicked on the strip light, put water in the kettle with the spout that whistled, clicked on the gas, set the kettle on the ring. Leaning back against the oak units, woolly socks keeping his feet cosy on the stone flag floor, he looked at Elsa. She was sitting opposite him on the stairs, elbows on knees, face in her hands.

"I like them whistly old kettles," she said.

"Thought yer were a modern girl," he said.

"I am."

"Sheena Easton?"

"Boy George, more like."

Michael could see a bit of the Boy George look going on. Baggy white trousers, long dark hair with raggedy ribbons tied in. What with the amount of clothes and stuff she bought, you could cotton why she needed her Saturday job all the way over in Cropden. She wouldn't stand out so much in that town, but Fowlbeck village were a different story. Folk could say what they wanted, though. She was her own person, Elsa. No mistake.

"What you starin' at, dozy beggar?" she said, tilting her head to one side.

"Nowt," he said. "Nothing...Erm, one sugar, in't it?"

"Yes, Michael."

He opened a cupboard door, brought out a bag of sugar and a jar of coffee, loosened the brown lid, spun it like a flywheel. It was a flywheel when it flew off and bounced across the stone floor toward Elsa. She caught it. Michael strolled over.

"How many ales have you had?" she said, smiling, passing him the lid.

"Only two."

"Two's too many o' that muck."

"Just because you don't drink," he said.

"So, you're sober, but still a butterfingers?"

"Oh aye."

"You dope."

"Thee sez reet, lass."

And they had a good laugh, as he went to the fridge for a bottle of silver top milk, and the drawer where Mum kept teaspoons.

"How's college, Elsa?" he said, back by the kettle, taking mugs off the mug tree.

"Love it, don't I? Even if it is a trek on t' bus to Cropden every day. It's art, in't it?"

"You've allus loved art, haven't you? Dead good at it an all."

"Ta very much," she said.

"Remember when yer painted mine and Jack's bogie like Starsky and Hutch's car?"

"Oh, yeah. Wi' that 'go faster' stripe down t' middle?"

"A real bobby dazzler."

Elsa was twiddling the ribbons in her hair now, as she gazed at the stone floor. Whenever she started twiddling, Michael knew she were off into her own world for a while. He liked leaving her there. Then he could just watch her. Nothing lecherous about it. Anyhow, they were only friends. And did it really mean owt because it sometimes made his heart beat a bit faster?

The gas ring hissed away quietly beneath the kettle. Michael went back to the job in hand, smelling the coffee as he spooned granules into the mugs, poured in milk, made Elsa's sweeter with the sugar. It was 1976, that Starsky and Hutch bogie race. Seven years since. Bloody hell, now they were nearly out of their teens. Back then, Elsa had to wear them milk-bottle specs. The thinner, fancier shaped ones she had on nowadays were much more the job. They showed off the shape of her face, somehow. And Mum had always said she had a pretty face.

"I'll never forget that day," she said.

"What day?" he said, turning to her, leaning his back against the kitchen units again.

"Bogie race, when you crashed."

"Mad dog Jack's fault for pushin' so hard."

Michael laughed. Elsa didn't. She'd stopped twiddling now. She were looking across the kitchen, straight into his eyes.

"Made you poorly, din't it?" she said.

"Only grazed me sen."

"I mean, in your head. No, your heart really."

"Aye."

"Still miss your dad, don't you?"

"Course I do," he said, a lump in his throat.

Michael turned to the mugs again, stirred the milky mixture in the bottom of Elsa's, as if the sugar needed more blending in. Then she were right behind him with her arms round his waist and her head on his shoulder. And his heart had already been going like billio, thinking about Dad! What did they call it? Mixed emotions? He didn't want to feel sad, but he liked the comfort he was getting. He could feel her breasts pushed against his back. Perhaps he'd just stand here a while.

"That were t' day when I knew you'd always mean the world to me," she said.

The water had got to rumbling fairish on the hob now. Michael looked into the kettle's chrome metal. It had bent their faces out of shape, as if they were having fun at the seaside in a hall of mirrors.

"I couldn't have a better friend than you, Elsa."

"How about Jack?"

"His cuddles aren't as nice."

She had a laugh at that one. He was embarrassed, though. He wondered if he'd crossed a line. But then the kettle saved him, blowing its whistle as if to say 'time's up.'

"There she blows!" he said, quickly turning off the gas.

"Shall we sit in t' front room?" she said, moving away from him, letting him pour.

"Aye, if yer like."

When Michael had stirred the coffees and passed Elsa hers, he followed her into the dimmer light of the front room. She sat on the old leather settee, tucking her legs up on it, holding her steaming coffee to her chest. He took off his brown jumper, laid it across the back of an armchair, went to the sooty-smelling fireplace. Shifting the fireguard, he knelt by the hearth, put his coffee on it, took the poker from the set of fireside furniture, started using it to break up the black crust of coal. The fire began to spark and glow and turn his face hot.

"You've got the look of a foundry worker, Michael," said Elsa.

"Workin' a furnace?"

"Yeah. We've done industrial art at college. Had a bash at some paintings me self."

"Wouldn't mind seeing them," said Michael, jabbing at a stubborn bit of crust.

"You can."

"Bet they're smart."

"Do t' job right and they warm you up just lookin' at 'em. Reckon you'd brush up well as a foundry worker. I could do your muscles all shiny in t' furnace heat. You'd make a good subject. Powerful arms, strong jaw line..."

"Short arse."

"Don't talk daft," she said. "You're taller than me. It's a cute arse, anyhow."

"Yer what?" he said, stirring the now loosened coals, releasing more heat.

"Soz, did I embarrass you?"

"No-o. You come down here and see if t' fire makes your face redder."

"All right, then."

There was summat in the way she'd said that. Like she fancied taking charge, as if she were challenging him, rather than the other way round. Michael couldn't put his finger on it, but it set his heart off faster again, he knew that. He watched her take a moorland picture placemat from the stack on the nest of tables by the settee and put her coffee on it. Somehow, she even made mundane stuff look graceful nowadays. How grand would it be having her calmness and confidence, instead of feeling awkward all the time? Some folk might have thought her abrupt, a bit rough because she lived on a council estate, but he could see beneath that. It made him proud of her that she didn't care what people thought. He wanted to know her secret.

She had one of those right short tops on that pop stars wore. As she came toward Michael, he could see her bellybutton and a slice of her tummy in the firelight. It wasn't a flat stomach. It were curvier than that. More womanly, he thought. If they hadn't just been friends, he might have wanted to touch it. She was standing above him now, looking at the Bowers' family photos hanging on the chimney breast, her naked tummy so close to his face that he could smell its soapy cleanness. Oh no, he wasn't getting a hard-on, was he? What would she think if she saw his trousers bulge? Run a mile and that would be the friendship over for good! He didn't want to lose her friendship. She were too important to him. Had been since they were nippers. Shit. Think about summat else. Say something. Take your mind off it.

"I see Thatcher's gettin' into bed wi' Reagan again."

"You what?" said Elsa, giggling as she knelt down beside him.

"O'er this Cold War nuclear business."

"Gettin' into bed wi' him?"

"It's a phrase," said Michael. "Jack uses it. Yer know how he's into politics at t' moment? A deep thinker nowadays, our Jack. Not doin' him any favours, if you ask me."

"Thatcher in bed with Reagan? Oh my God! Can't imagine owt worse."

"Aye, horrible thought, in't it?"

"All that wrinkly old skin rubbin' up against... Oh no!"

"Yeah, hideous."

"Disgustin'."

"Makes yer wanna puke."

Flipping heck, that were better! Like the air being released from an inner tube. Elsa asked him for the poker, then dipped it in the heat, rousing the hot coals with its tip. Michael gazed at it moving about in the fire, while he tried keeping his mind occupied with interesting thoughts. The fire reminded him of one. How stuff could be both beautiful and dangerous. Same as in nature. Yes, when he went walking in the hills and dales, the most beautiful things were often the most dangerous. Like rapids and whirlpools, steep escarpments, The North Face of Fowlbeck Beacon. All interesting enough to focus on. He couldn't resist another look at Elsa, mind. Her face so calm and peaceful and warm. And lovely, actually. Glowing like a sunset in the firelight. But then she caught him off guard, looking right back at him when he must have been gawping at her like the village idiot. He could tell she wasn't annoyed, though, because she gave him a beautiful smile.

"Thinkin' about owt special, Michael?" she said, still stirring the coals.

"What?"

"Looks like there's summat on your mind."

"Oh aye, there is," he said, taking a sip of his coffee. "It's about you."

"Me?"

"Yeah. How come you got so confident in yer sen?"

"I dunno, do I?" she said.

"I mean, yer could allus stand up for yourself, but you were dead shy too."

"Suppose I reckoned bein' meek as a lamb in life wasn't gonna be up to much."

"Not bothered what other folk think either, are you?" he said.

"Don't give a fuck."

"Don't yer?"

"Well, depends who's askin'."

Her joke made him smile. He took a log from the brass bucket on the hearth and put it on the bed of coals. The dry bark crackled and the smoky wood smell reminded him of campfires up the dale with his dad.

"How do yer manage it, though, Elsa? Not worryin' about what other people think?"

"Suppose we've never had much," she said. "So there's allus been a fair number o' folk lookin' down their noses. After a while, you just say 'sod 'em, it's my life.' Easy for me, somehow. Not like that for everyone, mind, is it?"

"No," he said.

"What's it like for you?"

"How long has Bowers' Butchers been in my family?"

"Founded by Albert Bowers in 1877," she said, pointing the poker at the framed photo of Albert standing proudly outside the shop, looking down at them from the chimney breast.

"Aye, Fowlbeck has been brought up on our little shop for o'er a century," he said. "And what's that success been built on?"

"Tell me, Michael."

"Reputation and what folk think."

"True enough," she said, hanging the poker with the other fireside furniture.

"That's reet," he said, sipping more coffee. "And now me grandad's no longer with us, God rest his soul, and Mum seems as interested in dance classes wi' Eddie as butchery, who's virtually running t' show?"

"You."

"Me. I'm even in charge on Friday."

"Good Friday? Good job you're so special, then."

"Eh?"

Why had she started holding his hand?

"Still got them records I lent you?" she said.

"What?" he said, being careful not to spill his coffee as he put it back on the hearth. "Oh, they're in t' stereo cabinet. Sorry, not had time to listen to 'em yet."

"It's okay. We'll listen to them now. Why don't you dance with me, Michael?"

Holding your hand? Asking you for a dance? Is she getting a bit fresh with you? Don't be gormless... Unless... Unless her heart sometimes beats faster when you're together an all. You barmpot. As if. She's over by the stereo cabinet now, opening the dark wood doors, bringing out them singles she loaned you.

"What do you fancy first?" she said, flicking through the vinyl.

"Elsa, I'd just as well have hooves as feet, the way I dance."

"We'll have a slow one, so I can lead."

"Aww, come off it." he said.

"Don't be soppy. I'll be gentle with you."

"Elsa..."

"I've got three slow ones here," she said.

"Which three?"

"Tears for Fears: 'Mad World,' Roxy Music: 'More than This,' Marvin Gaye: 'Sexual Healing.'"

"Bloody hell, not the last one!" he said.

"Roxy Music: 'More than This?'" she said, giggling to herself as she waited a few seconds for his answer.

"Oh, all reet, then."

As Elsa slid the record from its sleeve, set it spinning on the turntable, started cleaning it with the little dust brush, Michael stayed kneeling on the floor by the fire, doing his best to keep calm. Why was he putting himself through this? He didn't have to. He could still change his mind, tell her it were daft and that he didn't much want to. Except he did want to, didn't he? It'd be right enough, wouldn't it? As long as he could control his penis. They'd be dancing close, though. And, because he was a bit taller than her, his cock would be at the same height as that lovely, naked curve of her stomach. Flipping heck!

"Come on, handsome," she said, stretching her hand out toward him.

Right, this is it. Concentrate. If you start getting a stonk on, just think about stuff that worries you. Like nuclear war. You're always flapping about Armageddon. All them big weapons with exploding heads. Mind you, that last thought might be a bad idea. He stood up. She lowered the stylus onto the vinyl. As they met in the middle of the room, static crackled over the speakers.

"Hold me, then," she said. "Put your hands on me waist."

"What, on the... On the naked part?" he said.

"Yes, on the naked part. Come on, lad, frame your sen."

That were beautiful skin to touch. And dangerous. Nuclear war. Nuclear war. Nuclear deterrent! The music had started now. She'd linked her hands behind his neck. And she was looking right into his eyes. Sort of kindly, but serious too.

"Relax," she said. "You're all stiff."

Nuclear war! Nuclear war!

"Just sway wi' t' music. Can you feel the rhythm?"

"Think so," he said.

"Move closer to me. Pull me onto you, Michael."

Armageddon! Armageddon!

"That's better," she said, with a smile as warm as the fire.

They swayed to the music, his feet lifting slightly in time with hers. He was grateful for the simple steps. And to be this close to her. Her hair smelt like spring flowers. 'More than this... More than this...,' came the lyrics through the speakers. She kept singing them three words too. And she had her eyes fixed on his all the time, as if she were singing for him.

"More than this... More than this..."

Between the choruses, she spoke quietly to him.

"Don't worry, everything's going to be all right. Know what I've allus loved about you? You let me be who I am."

And the things she said soothed him, so that he forgot about where his heart might be pumping too much blood.

Then she stopped singing and talking, as they danced slowly together to Roxy Music. But the way she looked into his face made him feel like she were still speaking to him, so that he knew he had to keep holding her close and giving her his attention. It was right strong, that look, but sexy too. And it put a butterfly in his stomach. 'Whenever a butterfly flutters by, that's nature showing thee a miracle.' The final chorus came from the stereo. 'More than this...More than this...' Then the music was over and the room silent, aside from the crackling of the fire and the stylus on the finished record. Summat told him not to let her go yet, though. She moved her fingers gently over the back of his neck and up through his hair. She touched his face and stroked his jaw. Then she came in closer and kissed him on the mouth. Softly at first. Then a bit harder, so it felt like she were breathing a thousand butterflies into his stomach. When she did pull her lips away, he tried kissing her again, but she put her hand on his cheek and he could tell she was asking him to wait.

"You know I'm in love with you, don't you, Michael?"

"Yer what?"

"Been tryin' to tell you for yonks."

"But I'm in love with you too," he said. "It's just, I didn't know it afore."

"Kiss me."

And this time it was much more intense. And it sent his heart, butterflies, blood off giddy. But he didn't have to worry about getting hard and her running a mile anymore, because he knew she wanted him now. And she loved him. And she were rubbing the heel of her hand up and down where he wanted her to. She was still doing it the next time she stopped the kiss and looked dead straight in his eyes again.

"That's funny," she said. "Thought I'd left the poker by t' fire."

CHAPTER NINE

The following Wednesday dinnertime, Jack stood in the cold on the top step outside Hargraves' Butchers, wearing his black leather jacket, leaning his shoulder against the shop window frame and thinking about John Lennon in that dark alley doorway in Hamburg. Perhaps the best photo he'd ever clapped eyes on in the village library, that. Big time. Harrison, McCartney, Sutcliffe walking past right blurry. Lennon, in focus, watching over them. What was that look? Moody? Ice cool? You couldn't take your eyes off the bloke, anyway. John Lennon, Hamburg. Jack Hargraves, hamburgers. At least it was half-day closing and he was out of his butcher's clobber for now. And he'd be meeting Micky for some nosh and a catch up soon. After he'd been back inside for his Good Friday pep talk.

"Jack!"

Frigging hell, he could still crap him up sometimes. There he was in his butcher's whites, pink head in the shop window.

"What?" said Jack.

"Time," said The OB, one of his long, scraggy fingers tapping his watch.

"I'm havin' a cig first."

"Well don't be long," came Father's muffled voice from inside, before he wiped his old breath off the window with a cloth.

Jack gave him the 'peace' sign because he knew it wound him up. Hated 'do gooders', did The Old Bastard. He could have the two fingers the other way round if he fancied. No bother. Why was he still timekeeping after closing, anyway? Only had his military models to go back home to. He loved gluing plastic tanks and planes together, mind. Worked on them every Wednesday afternoon while Mum did her cross-stitch. You could tell he'd been in the army from all the attention he paid to making his little war toys. Perfect hobby for him really.

"All we are saying is give peace a chance," muttered Jack, turning back to the High Street.

He took a packet of Regal King Size from his jacket pocket, pulled out a cigarette, hung it from his lips, lit it with his paraffin-smelling Zippo. A deep drag and the harsh smoke filled his lungs, sending his brain light-headed. He loved the hit. Danger and pleasure rolled into one. Fowlbeck High Street, eh? You had to admit it looked near idyllic after that snow shower. Just enough to cover the truth. Weren't some Dickens novels like that? He didn't know because he'd not read one as yet. Maybe he should take one out of the library next time he was in. Word had it there might be a lot more snow in a couple of days. But Fowlbeck probably wouldn't be cut off before then.

There were a few folk taking tiny steps down the sloping flagstone pavement so they didn't slip. He caught sight of two headscarf biddies doing it as they lugged some shopping. He wanted them to turn their swollen feet sideways and skid down. Weeeeeeeee! But in Fowlbeck you were supposed to keep plodding along. Little steps and not much change. Perhaps when he got old that would suit him too. But he was only nineteen and stuck.

Jack blew a thin stream of smoke out into the freezing air, watched it curl and spread. Should have made those A-Level grades and got off to uni. If only The OB hadn't bullied you into butchering so much when you could have been swotting. All those crucial hours wasted. Then, when you did have chance to study, you got depressed and couldn't do owt half the time. Let alone revise how many men had been slaughtered in The Battle of the Somme. And why did you get on a downer? Who caused that, then? Again, that selfish bastard of a father, who wanted nowt else for you than to stay in Fowlbeck and take over his poxy butcher's shop. Frigging Nora, they were doing underground nuclear tests in the Soviet Union, Reagan thought he was Luke Skywalker with his 'Star Wars' project, and all The OB could think about was how much Easter lamb they were going to shift! Well, this kid was still a fighter, whatever anyone said. He knew it in his gut. And he'd show them all yet. The OB and the blithering Fowlbeck masses. Maybe it was time for his own little Easter Rising. Time for a fight back. All he needed was the bottle to go through with it.

Looking over the snow-covered roofs, opposite, he could see the tops of the white moors beyond. They loomed close, standing out in their wintry coats. He shivered to think how closed in Fowlbeck felt sometimes, and his cigarette shook a moment between his quivering fingers. This High Street put claustrophobia in his head as well. Limestone buildings on either side, grey and cold looking, like prison walls. And pretty narrow, this street. Some folk round here could be narrow as well. Narrow-minded. He knew you found people like that in every town and city too, but in a village in the back of beyond you had a job on escaping it. Especially when you'd read a bit and thought about stuff like Jack had. The Old Bastard could be narrow-minded. Ignorant at times. Racist. Always saying 'nigger' and 'paki.' It made Jack ashamed. Good job he had the best mate in the world to talk to. He drew one last drag from his cigarette. Better get this pep talk over with. He wanted to speak to Michael as soon as he could today.

There was nobody in the shop when he went back inside.

He could hear his parents rattling about in the prep room, mind, beyond the swishy strips of the Union Jack opening. Likely storing the last of the unsold meat for tomorrow. He waited opposite the now emptied, cleaned main glass cabinet, on the posh ironwork garden seat that the old man had lately bought for fogies to use when there was a queue. Slouching, straightening his long legs, he could stretch them halfway across the chessboard floor these days, he sat there thinking about his next move. They should have made these black and white squares carry on out the door, up the street, over the moors and away. Look what he was lumbered with. It felt as if things had been set out in this shop just to get on his fucking wick. Photos of the Royal Family, the Falklands War, Thatcher dotted about. And these walls, which used to be nowt but red, now had white and blue shapes painted in here and there. It wasn't only the swishy opening that was a Union Jack now. Working here felt like being wrapped in a giant one. He knew there was a fine line between patriotism and jingoism, but you didn't have to be the sharpest butcher's knife to work out which camp The OB stood in. Maybe it had influenced what he'd christened his son.

Jack looked at the swishy opening the moment he heard someone come through it.

"All reet, Mum?" he said.

"As I'll ever be," said Mum, in that nervous, half-laughing voice which made him sad for her.

"Where's the ogre?"

"Shhhhh!" she said, looking over her shoulder. "Bloomin' hummer, you'll send him that way out if he hears you. What wi' Easter coming up. You know how he gets."

"Yep."

Mum walked past the end of the cabinet and moved toward Jack in her greasy butcher's whites. She was fifty now, but he thought she looked a decade older. Skinny with worry, grey hair tight-twisted in a bun, right puffy semicircles under her eyes, slightly hunched as if she'd been bent in the wind. Truth be told, she was frigging knackered. No wonder, being expected to work like a dog all hours God sent. She sat next to Jack on the garden seat and gave him a weak smile. It used to be stronger, more reassuring, when he was a nipper, that smile. The thought brought on his earliest memory. Sitting on a blanket in a sunny garden with her when she was still young. Him supping juice from a beaker, sun slanting in under her hat. The two of them playing 'One Potato Two Potato' and laughing themselves daft. Swish! Watch out, The Grand Entrance! Mum sat up straighter now, because The Old Bastard had just strode in from the prep room with his clipboard.

"Reet, then, Team Hargraves," he said, marching back and forth on the chessboard floor in front of the cabinet, looking through half-moon glasses at his notes. "Good Friday in two days. One of our busiest days o' t' year. And we simply must take advantage. Stick it to the opposition! What do you say, team?"

"Yes, sweetheart," said Mum, looking as stiff as the clipboard.

"They don't like it up 'em, Dad," said Jack, still slouching.

The OB stopped marching and peered at him over his specs with those bulgy eyes.

"I do hope you're taking this seriously, Jack."

"Fuckin' hell, how long's this gonna drag on?"

"Now now, we'll have no cursing with your mother present."

"He's only teasin'," said Mum, half-laughing, but with shock on her face. "Aren't you, Jack?"

"It's right, Mum."

"Well, don't be swearin', please," said The OB.

"I can say 'nigger' and 'paki', though, eh?"

"What have niggers and pakis got to do wi' it?"

Fucking hell, he didn't have the foggiest, did he?

"Crack on, then," said Jack.

"Okey dokey," said The OB, looking at his clipboard again. "Jobs for Good Friday morning before we open. I've phoned through the meat order and t' slaughterhouse delivery's arriving early. 5.30 sharp. I've drafted Molly in to butcher some lamb. Any excuse to come out o' retirement. But we'll all have to be ready and shipshape. No muckin' about, Jack."

"I'm thinking of turning vegetarian."

The OB glared at him.

"You'll wash your mouth out, using that sort of language in this shop, lad!"

What chance did Jack have with that line? It was like when he got belly laughs watching Vivian go mental in The Young Ones on telly. Set him off roaring so much he had to hold onto the garden seat. Father must have missed the irony.

"What's so funny, what's so funny?" he said, standing over Jack, ugly mug like a giant radish.

"Oh, sweetheart," said Mum. "He doesn't..."

"Belt up, Judy! What's so hilarious, boy?"

But Jack had suddenly stopped seeing the humorous side, what with the way Mum had just been spoken to.

"Not a boy anymore, Dad," he said, rising to face him.

Any closer and they could have been boxers before a grudge match.

"Eh, have ya shrunk, Dad? Am I taller than you now?"

Frigging hell, he was getting some serious eyeballing here.

"I'll crack you one in a minute, lad," said The OB. "Now

sit down!"

Jack didn't want to sit down, though. He might have been kakking himself, but he didn't fancy backing down. He always had to. But he was getting braver. The old man would get a rude awakening one of these days. Like maybe when he woke up this Friday morning. What are you going to do? Carry on letting him walk all over you, same as he does to Mum? She's not the person she's supposed to be anymore. It put a knot in his stomach, thinking on it. But then Mum had a surprise up her butcher's smock sleeve. She stood, got between them and planted her skinny hands on their chests. Jack looked down at her grey head. She could have been one of those little refs you always saw in heavyweight bouts, knackered from trying to push the big boys apart. Why did they never have heavyweight referees for heavyweight fights? Weren't there any? Mum was proper glaring up at them now.

"Have you two any idea what this does to me?" she said. "Watching my husband and son at each other all t' time?"

Jack didn't know what to say. Looked like The OB had been struck dumb too.

"Churns me up, that's what it does."

"Judy..." said The OB.

"Belt up, Rodney!"

"Mum..."

"You too, Jack! You're as bad as each other! You'll be the death of..."

Then she sat back down on the iron seat, looking exhausted, as if the effort she'd just put in had taken the last bit of fight left in her. Jack and The OB backed away from one another. Jack sat next to Mum. The OB took a while staring through his half-moon specs at the clipboard. He kept peeking over them for a glance at his wife, mind. Felt like a full minute before the bloke settled on his task again.

"So, for lamb, our best Easter seller," he said eventually, marching up and down like a sergeant. "We're bringin' in reinforcements. Molly can cover t' lamb prep. God knows she's been in the game long enough. *On* the game long enough! Ha ha."

It was nowt but a ham-fisted shot at lessening the tension and only the old man laughed. Mum ignored him. Jack wondered if he had time to leap up and jab a quick left into his nose while she wasn't looking. Funny to think he might actually have a chance of flattening The OB now. In top shape at nineteen, he was. And still hard as nails. He knew it. Oh yeah, there'd been a couple of idiots down the years who'd had a pop, and they'd got their comeuppance, but nobody messed with him anymore. As well as being tall and tough, he'd filled out now. Women loved it. Even if he did say it himself, he was built like a brick shitehouse. And Father had turned sixty last year. He couldn't be as strong or fast as he used to be. Left, right, left, right, uppercut! Out for the count. What a champion thought.

"Jack?" said The OB.

"What?"

"Clean your lugs out, Son."

"Oh, did ya say summat?"

"I said, you take care o' t' rump, sirloin and topside. We'll gain most profit on lamb, but there's a lot of folk wi' a preference for beef at Easter. I'll prep the sausages, pork and birds... Judy?... Judy, love?"

"Pies and pasties, I know," said Mum.

"Thank you, love. She's a grand woman, your mother, Jack. Don't know how we'd cope without her."

A John Deere tractor turned their heads as it clattered past, bouncing down the High Street. When it was quieter again,

Jack noticed the droning buzz of the cabinet's fluorescent lights. Strange how you hardly heard such a constant noise after working here full-time a year or two. Pity the same couldn't be said for The OB's droning on.

"Now then, Easter hampers," he said, waving his clipboard at the hamper deal advertised on one of the wall-mounted blackboards offering knock-down prices. "As you know, we're havin' a big push on hampers this year. Money to be made on these. I can smell it. See if we can't steal a march on our rivals from the dark ages down t' road. Right, team?"

"They're not from the dark ages," said Jack. "They're traditional, that's all."

The OB stood silently for a moment, as if weighing summat up.

"Okey dokey, Jack," he said, after a few seconds. "I tek on board what you say. Appen I'm being harsh. Bowers' shop is very traditional, and they make a decent fist of it. But they're stuck in t' past. Will you at least concede that point?"

"I'm conceding nowt."

"Listen, your mother's right. We need to work together more. I'm only tryin' to teach you, Son. I mean, I'm not going to last forever, am I?"

"No."

"So, you'll be takin' over one o' these days."

"What makes ya so sure I'll be tekin' over?" said Jack.

"Well, it's not for your little sister, is it, mate? She likes ponies and cross-stitch."

"And grouse beatin'," said Mum, not looking up. "Doesn't just like girls' things, our Tracy."

Jack stared at the red, white and blue walls, listened to the fluorescent lights' never-ending buzz, smelt the cleaning products clinging to the surfaces. Hard breathing in here sometimes. Like everything was suffocating him. The OB knew he dreamt of being part of summat bigger, more exciting, more important, God knows he'd dropped enough hints, but Father chose to ignore it. Jack hated it when he pretended to be nice to him too. Patronising twat. Nowt but another ploy to get him to do what he wanted. Better if they just had a punch up. Have done with it. Winner takes all. Frigging hell, the git's speaking again.

"It's only because I care, Jack. No crime in a father looking out for his son's future, is there? I don't wish to be mean about your chum's family, but they run that business like Queen Victoria's still on t' throne. And, mark my words, it'll be their downfall. We're not the same as them, see? We're innovators. We try new ideas. We use our nous. We keep ahead of the times."

"What you on about, their downfall?" said Jack. "Bowers' shop's survived o'er hundred years."

"Aye, a past's no guarantee of a future, though, is it?"

"You're puddled, you."

"Look at the facts, lad," said The OB, tapping on the clipboard as if he had them written down. "Granted, good old Maggie's showin' signs of pulling the country out of recession. But there's already a bit less business in t' village because outsiders are buying properties just to use as weekend holiday homes. And, the big one..."

"Watch out, Mum, the big one's coming."

"Supermarkets."

"Supermarkets?" said Jack. "Out here in bumpkin country? Don't talk stupid."

"Not here. Fifteen or twenty mile away in towns, though. Not everyone in Fowlbeck does all their shopping on t' High Street these days, you know. Some of 'em are tootlin' off in their cars to do a weekly shop at supermarkets. Well, you can buy owt there. Including most cuts of meat. These places are even employin' top class butchers now, from the independent shops that have recently folded."

"Will you get to t' point? I'm meetin' Michael in t' cafe five minutes since."

"Someday, there'll likely only be business enough in Fowlbeck for one butcher's shop."

It shocked Jack when The OB said that. He didn't know why. As if he gave a shite about Hargraves' Butchers. Perhaps he was concerned for Michael.

"You're off ya rocker," he said.

"Think about it," said The OB.

Jack thought about it for a second. Mum shifted slightly on the iron garden seat.

"You know what this means, don't you, Jack?"

"No. Tell me, Dad."

"Now we've established this isn't just about rivalry anymore?"

"What does it mean, Dad?"

"Now we know it's likely a fight for survival?"

"What does it mean?"

"I'm sorry, Son, but you've got to stop being friends with Michael Bowers."

CHAPTER TEN

Michael sat supping tea at the only table that had been available in jam-packed Fowlbeck Cafe, listening to the Radio One music playing behind the tatty counter, glancing at the gun-toting film posters stuck to the greasy walls. The table were in a right good spot by the big window, but most punters avoided it on account of one of its legs being an inch or so shorter than the other three. Michael thought about how him and Jack always seemed to end up here. Well, butchers couldn't shut up shop and leave dead on noon like other shopkeepers, could they? Took half an hour just to clean up all the blood. It was a laugh at this table, mind. You could have bets on which condiment would slide off the Formica top first. Funny how they still made up games together, like when they were nippers. You were allowed to tilt and kick the table, but any spilt tea meant disqualification. The odds were loads shorter on Pepper because, being lighter, it won twice as much as Salt. Michael were happy putting his brass on Pepper. Jack backed Salt every flipping time. He'd likely back Shergar to escape his kidnappers and win The Derby again this year, though, just because the odds were so long.

Where was Lanky, anyhow? Michael put down his tea and pulled back his tweed jacket cuff to look at the dull gold watch he'd inherited off Grandad. Ten minutes late and no sign of him. His dad were likely reading him the riot act again. Not Jack's fault, but Michael didn't like him being late. Especially today. Today he had summat to tell him. He leant back on the chair, knotted his hands behind his head and stared at the window, which was all misty with steam rising from plates of hot food and breath coming from punters' chatty mouths. This is love, then, is it? Bloody Nora... Beautiful Elsa.

He knew it were a bit early to be thinking about, things might go wrong yet, but he kept imagining spending the rest of his life with Elsa. Been dreaming of it day and night since Saturday. Maybe she had too. The wedding. A house. Children. They'd be nicely set up, what with Bowers' Family Butchers behind them. He'd support her being an artist, if that's what she wanted. Knowing Elsa, she'd probably not need it, mind. You wouldn't put it past her to be earning brass from her paintings afore long. She was talented and determined. And she loved him. Flipping heck, she loved *him!* He could hardly wait to see Jack.

"All set for the Easter rush, Michael?" said Patricia, the estate agent, sitting with her colleague at the next table, wearing them daft Dynasty shoulder pads and picking apart her lamb chop dinner.

"Near enough, Pat. Slaughtered all t' lambs last week, so we're about ready for Good Friday."

"Oh," said Patricia, stopping mid-chew. "Of course, you have your own slaughterhouse."

"Been in t' family as long as the shop."

Patricia's knife hovered over her food.

"What's it like, Michael? Killing lambs?"

"It's pretty quick," said Michael. "One slit of the throat and t' job's done."

"Yes, well," said Patricia, wincing. "I should imagine you're very... Efficient at it."

"I am a butcher, Pat. How's yer chop?"

"Nice... Yes... Nice."

What had happened to him? Teasing folk like that. Mum had seen a change. This morning, she said he'd been acting like a giddy kipper for days: 'You've even lost the worry lines off your forehead, love.' He shouldn't be making fun of people, though. Even if they did reckon lamb chops grew in rows alongside parsnips and cauliflower. Patricia might be prim and proper, but she was right enough. And she were a good customer. He didn't want to be losing customers.

Michael heard the tinkle of the bell above the cafe door, as someone came in off the High Street, bringing with them a short snap of cold air. It was Jack. Michael watched him stamp on the mat to get snow off his shoes. Judging by his face, mind, he might have been stamping in anger. Looked like cartoon steam were about to blast from them ears. What had riled him? He's coming over now. Slow progress. Stopping to ask folk to breathe in so he can squeeze between chairs. Flipping heck, he's a big lad nowadays. As tall and broad as an oak. And he's got the looks. Could have been a film star in one of them posters on the walls. He'd like that idea. Pulled the girls like a matinee idol, anyhow. Lucky sod. He'd distracted the twins who worked in the pet shop, Laura and Lorna, from the game they were playing on the Space Invaders machine in the corner already. Nudging each other, they were, peeking out at him from behind their Kajagoogoo hairdos. What did Michael have to be jealous of, though? He might be on the short side, a bit flabby-faced, have eyes that were nowt to write home about, but he had Elsa now, didn't he? Who needed film star looks? Just wait till you tell Jack. But he could be in need of jollying up first. He was fuming about summat.

"You'll not believe this one, Micky," he said, reaching the table at last, putting his leather jacket on the back of the chair opposite, plonking himself down.

"Not yer dad, is it?"

"How did ya guess?"

"What's he done now?"

"Reckons I can't be mates wi' you anymore."

"Say again?" said Michael, leaning forward, resting his elbows on the wobbly table, sloshing some of his tea. "Shit."

"Don't worry, he can swing for it."

Not friends anymore? Losing your best mate? Like you lost Dad? Nobody could ever replace Jack. Be like another bereavement. Thinking about it made Michael shiver, as if freezing fog had crept under the cafe door and swallowed the steam.

"Nearly leathered him when he came out wi' it," said Jack. "Can you imagine not bein' mates?"

"No."

"Been pals since God was a lad, haven't we? Don't fret, there's not a cat in hell's of it happening. Ya reckon I could do that to you? You've allus been there. Like after *he* knocked ten bags o' shite out of me, remember? When he eventually let me out again."

"You've allus been there for me an all," said Michael. "Remember when me dad died?"

"Course I do, Micky," said Jack, reaching across, touching Michael's shoulder.

"I'd never find another mate like you, Lanky."

Jack leant back in his chair, then suddenly hammered his fist on the table, turning a few heads, sending more of Michael's tea slopping onto the Formica top.

"Fuck him," he said.

"Listen," said Michael. "Shall we get some grub? And I could do wi' another brew."

They weaved their way through nattering diners and clinking cutlery to the counter. Michael grabbed a handful of serviettes and went to mop up his spilt tea. When he got back to the counter, he stood behind Jack in the short queue.

The queue's front half was made up of Mr and Mrs

Dubois, a couple in their eighties who walked everywhere together in matching anoraks, holding hands all the time. They were as 'ee bah gum' Yorkshire as you could get, so it were a mystery in Fowlbeck as to where the French name came from. They never let on. Michael wondered if they liked the mystery, the romance of it. They most definitely enjoyed getting a bit 'amour dans le public', as Jack sometimes said. Always snogging between ends at the bowling green. It was brilliant, them being so much in love at their age. Maybe that would happen to Michael and Elsa as well. He smiled as he watched them cuddle while ordering bread and butter pudding. Then he remembered Jack saying he'd heard they'd been to the doctor last year to get advice on sex. Rumour had it the flummoxed doctor asked when they'd realised they were having problems. And Mr Dubois had told him straight: 'Twice last neet and once this morning.' Michael suddenly laughed and the randy couple turned to look at him.

"Hello, Mr Dubois, Mrs Dubois," he said. "How are we?"

"Grand, thank you, Michael," said Mr Dubois.

"Bit nippy out."

"Ooh, we keep one another warm," said Mrs Dubois, snuggling even closer to her husband. "Don't we, Maurice?"

"I don't know," said Jack, shaking his head. "You two scallywags. You're like young lovers. What's the secret?" Mr Dubois winked and tapped his nose. "Nudge nudge, wink wink, say no more, eh, Maurice?"

And the four of them got off laughing. When they'd settled down again, and les Dubois had squeezed past, grinning at their custard-smelling desserts, Jack asked Michael what had creased him up.

"That line Maurice is supposed to have come out wi' to t' doctor," said Michael.

"Oh aye. Eh, what's that?"

Jack pointed at the window. Michael spun round to look. But all he got was two stinging earlobes. Lanky and his flicking fingers!

"You bugger."

"Stupid sod," said Jack. "Falls for it every time."

"I'm not thick, yer know."

"Only laiking."

"Yeah yeah," said Michael, nodding toward the Space Invaders corner. "The twins have their eye on you, mate."

"Have they now?" said Jack, turning slowly, suave as James Bond.

Laura and Lorna waved at him and smiled.

"Hi, Jack," they said, above the cafe chatter.

"Hi, Laura. Hi, Lornaaaa!" said Jack, suddenly buckling at the knee, which Michael had just collapsed from behind with his own.

"Yer barmpot, Lanky."

"Little git!"

"Bigger they are, harder they fall," said Michael, watching Jack do his best to play it cool again for the two gigglers in the corner.

Always brilliant, larking about like mad alliks, but summat had got to nagging Michael. Why did Rodney Hargraves not want them to be mates anymore? He needed to know. Lanky was too busy posing for the twins now, mind. And they'd still not ordered dinner. Best wait till you sit back down. Then, after you've straightened out what's niggling you, you can tell Jack all about Elsa.

"Frame yer sens, butcher boys," said scruffy Jed, serving behind the counter.

"Soz, Jed," said Michael, scanning the blackboard menus, breathing in the thick gravy smell coming from the kitchen. "I'll have steak pie, mash and peas, ta."

"Medium rump steak and chips, please, Jed," said Jack, eyes still on the twins.

"Must have strong gnashers, you young uns," said Jed. "Two butchers as supplies this place only sell tough meat!"

"Watch it," said Michael, wagging his finger. "One hundred years of Bowers' Family Butchers buildin' a fine reputation, but a few careless words."

Jed beamed, showing his near toothless mouth, dark as a pothole. Michael ordered two mugs of tea and him and Jack took them back to their table.

"Eh, I could have a threesome on t'cards here," said Jack, pulling up his chair.

"Bloomin' heck," said Michael, sitting down.

It looked like Lanky had forgotten about being angry at his dad, now Laura and Lorna were stroking his ego.

"Twins, mate! Twins!"

"Bloody hell. Lanky, can I ask yer summat?"

"Or we could have a double date. Which one do ya fancy?"

"I don't fancy either of 'em. Look, about what yer dad said. Why dun't he want us bein' mates anymore?"

Jack's mood seemed to change again at that. Michael noticed his broad shoulders drooping a bit and his eyes looking sadder. You could still see the vulnerable little lad in him sometimes. What would it be like having a father being a right bastard to you, though? No matter how tough you were, you must wish things were different. At least when Michael thought about his dad he remembered happy stuff. Even if it did turn him glum to think he'd never be making more memories with him.

"Come on, Lanky," said Michael. "Nowt yer can't share wi' me, is there?"

Jack moved the salt and pepper cellars to the middle of

the table, started fiddling with them, turning them in his fingers, stroking their shiny glass.

"He was jibberin' on about how we'll be battling each other for survival one day. Because, sooner or later, there'll only be business enough in Fowlbeck for one butchers."

"Yer what? Why did he say that?"

"He's reckoning on supermarkets tekin' a bigger and bigger cut, mainly," said Jack.

"Don't talk daft. Out here?"

"That's what I said. But he reckons more folk in t' sticks are drivin' to town and buying meat wi' their weekly shop."

"Well aye, we already know that," said Michael, tugging at his shirt collar. "There's still plenty to go round, though."

"But for how long? That's Father's point, anyway. People like convenience, don't they? And what's in the aisle right next to t' baked beans? Chicken and beef. Whatever ya say about my dad, and I'm the first to admit he's a friggin' arsehole, he is a businessman. Suppose he knows what he's on about."

Michael was dumbstruck. Supermarkets were a challenge, but he'd never reckoned on them being an actual threat to the business. Flipping heck, what if you're the one, fifth generation, to make Bowers' Family Butchers fail? How would you cope with the shame? How could you face folk on the High Street? The steamy cafe air felt proper hot now. It were like a blooming sauna in here! He took off his tweed jacket and hung it on the back of his chair.

"What's wi' t' Sunday best jacket, lad?" said Jack.

"Just fancied it," said Michael.

"Looks like you've got a promise on."

"Does it?"

"Shall we?" said Jack, knocking the salt and pepper together.

"Go on," said Michael, mopping his sweaty brow with a serviette.

"Eh, chin up, Micky. I knew you'd be frettin'. That's why I wasn't sure about tellin' you the old man's reasoning. Might never come to that, anyway. Even if it does, it'll not be for years, by which time he'll likely be long dead. And it's not as if I'll ever be tekin' o'er Hargraves' Butchers, is it?"

"What yer gonna do, then?"

"Fuck knows. But I've got to mek him realise that butchering's not for me first."

"And how are yer goin' to do that?"

"I'll tell you after this game. Come on, thought we were laikin'."

Jack slammed the salt and pepper cellars down dramatically in the centre of the table, and it seemed to snap Michael out of feeling glum. As Lanky had said, the supermarket threat weren't likely to happen for years. Decades maybe. Generations even. Bowers' shop had loads of advantages over Hargraves' shop if it came to that, anyhow. Butchering expertise and customer loyalty established over a century, for a kick off. And there'd be no need to worry about beating the competition and putting their friendship in jeopardy because, by the sound of it, Jack would never be in charge. It had been obvious for ages that he wanted to do summat else.

"Micky?" said Jack.

"What?"

"Wake up."

"Oh aye," said Michael.

"Reet, how much brass in t' kitty?"

"A tenner."

"What's the odds?" said Jack.

"Pepper's at evens. Salt's three to one."

"What's ya money on?"

"A quid on Pepper," said Michael, pulling a pound note from his trouser pocket, tucking it under the brown sauce bottle.

"There's a surprise," said Jack, sliding some of his own notes under the ketchup. "I'll have three quid on Salt."

"Three? You'll near as damn it clear us out if Salt wins!"

"You chose Pepper."

"I'm stickin' wi' Pepper," said Michael.

"Not yellow, are ya?"

"I'm sticking with Pepper."

"Yellow belly."

"Piss off."

They played a while, taking turns to give the table a slight tilt or kick, being right careful not to slosh any tea onto the Formica. Salt and Pepper inched their way, neck and neck, toward the edge.

"Giddy up, Salt!" said Jack, when the race was half run, rubbing his hands together. "Got a gallon of ale ridin' on thee. Your turn, Michael."

But Michael couldn't hold it back anymore.

"Lanky?" he said.

"What is it?" said Jack, bent forward, his face down at table level, looking eager to egg on the outsider some more.

"I've got summat to tell you."

"Can't it wait?"

"It's me and Elsa."

"Ya what?"

Michael waited a moment, as Jack slowly sat up straight and stared at him.

"We're in love with each other."

Just look at his surprised face. Brilliant! He does seem a bit shocked, mind. But hold on for the smile. Here it is...

Except... Except... It's like one of them twisted smiles that villains sometimes have in films. After they've been cracked in the mouth with a fist.

CHAPTER ELEVEN

Jack lay dead still under his duvet, ears pricked like a deer listening for night-time predators. For about the hundredth time in the last hour, he clicked on his torch and shone it at his Sekonda watch. Five to two. Shite, only twenty-five minutes before he had to be out of this God-forsaken house. They must all be fast asleep by now. You could make out The OB snoring down the corridor like some flabby-faced walrus. What were Mum's earplugs made of? Tracy was a right good sleeper, typical thirteen, but, with her room opposite, he'd have to be frigging silent when he left his bedroom. Oh, if you keep stalling you'll never do this thing! Better get a shift on.

He folded back the duvet, sat on the edge of the mattress, reached under his bed for the pile of clobber and packed rucksack hidden there. Setting the torch on his pillow, he dressed in the light of its cone-shaped beam, pulling on jeans, shirt, jumper, woolly socks. Then he took his new leathery-smelling wallet from the rucksack and thumbed through the wad of tenners and twenties tucked inside. That'd be enough, wouldn't it? He stood up, slipped the wallet into his jeans pocket and slung the rucksack on his back. All he had to do now was sneak downstairs, grab his coat and hiking boots and put the note he'd written on the kitchen mantelpiece. Happy Easter, Dad. Surely leaving him in the lurch like this, on Good Friday of all days, would finally make him see that he really didn't want owt to do with his little butcher's shop anymore. Off to help bring attention to summat that actually mattered in this world, eh? An anti-nuclear protest. Maybe the biggest one this country had ever known. They were after having a fourteen mile human chain along the

Nuclear Valley today, stretching from Greenham Common, through Aldermaston, all the way to Burghfield. And he'd be a link in that chain. Photographers, journalists, TV crews would all be there. Perhaps today they'd shake up the world! That's what Jack Hargraves should be doing, shaking up the world, not being forever chained to a bacon slicer in the back of beyond. The OB would likely go ballistic when he read his note about three hours from now, especially when he realised where he was off to. You could imagine what he'd say: 'Greenham Common? Bloody CND. Do gooders, tree huggers, hippies. My son's no butcher, he's a bastard communist!' Well, if it made him wake up at last.

Jack sucked in the air and puffed out his chest. Deep breaths. Compose yourself. Time to go. Maybe just one look out the window first, see what the weather's up to. He shone a yellowy circle on the curtains, moved quietly toward them, opened a narrow gap, peered outside. Still snowing. Not too heavy, but steadily falling against the orange streetlights. Was it settling a bit on the road? Likely getting thicker by the river, along the route he'd be taking. It wasn't the snow that bothered him, mind. He'd grown up rolling round in the stuff. And the forecast had said there wouldn't be much further south of here. He knew right enough what was making him nervous. When have you ever even left Yorkshire by yourself in your nineteen years? Not once. And now you're slinking off in the middle of the night to London, then Nuclear Valley, like some sort of spy. He found it exciting all right, he'd always wanted to do summat like this, but he had to be honest too. He was fucking kakking himself. This was it, though. His big shot. Now or never.

Letting go of the curtains, he moved the torch beam across the room and found the brass door handle. Shiny, tempting, like gold: 'Turn me...Turn me.' He walked toward it, turned it, stepped out onto the landing, closed the door right quietly. The torch lit up the name plate marking his little sister's territory a couple of feet away, with its silhouette horse jumping over black curly letters: *'Tracy's Bedroom.'* Sorry, Sis. Don't fret. Be back soon. Hope Father's not too mardy. He'd never take it out on you, anyway. Loves you too much. You are his favourite. Just a bit.

Jack shone the torch down the long landing corridor, shifting the beam around, letting it rest on the fancy burgundy wallpaper with swirly patterns, the big teardrop chandelier, that table the likes of which were all the rage these days, onyx with gilt legs. If houses were folk, this one would be a proper show off. On top of the polished onyx was a proudly displayed model Spitfire, perfectly put together by The OB's scraggy fingers. All about him really, this house. Jack edged along the landing toward the stairs, which were at the end, next to his parents' bedroom.

Treading as lightly as fifteen stone could, he was making decent progress across the carpet when something made him stop about halfway down, just outside the bathroom. Summat had changed since he'd come out of his room. What the fuck was it? He stayed stock still, listening. Silence. The OB's stopped snoring. Shite! Hadn't woken up, had he? How could you explain being dressed in woollies with a rucksack on your back at two in the morning? Come on, start snoring again, you old git. But now you could hear the bed squeak and the scummy hawking of tobacco phlegm. Well, he didn't have a spittoon by his bed, and would he really fancy swallowing it back down? He'd be getting himself up and going to the bathroom, wouldn't he? Look lively, then. Back to your room. But too late! He's opening his bedroom door! Turn off the torch! Now he'd be feeling for the landing light switch! No escape! Quick, into the bathroom! Bollocks!

This is where he's likely coming to, the bathroom! Torch on. Where could you hide in here? In the bath? Under the bathmat? Inside a tube of toothpaste? The airing cupboard. Yes, the airing cupboard. Good job the shelving in there only spans halfway across and the rest is space for the washing basket. He opened the slatted doors, stood in the part-filled basket, pulled the doors shut. Breathe...Breathe...Torch off! The OB might see it shining between the slats. You could hear him traipsing along the landing now. Don't breathe too loud. He'll hear you. Calm it. Frigging hell, he's turned the bathroom light on. Here he is.

Jack could see slivers of The OB through the gaps between the slats, as he stood over the toilet in his pyjamas. Horizontal slices of his back, the hairy nape of his neck, the roots of that sweep over just above his ear. And now he was hawking up more baccy phlegm, lifting the toilet seat, gobbing into the bowl. He couldn't have been more than one or two arm lengths away. If Jack had been a total airhead, he might have leant out of the cupboard and tapped his shoulder. Now you could hear the sound of piss hitting water in one long stream. Belting send off, Father! As long as he doesn't need owt from the cupboard, that's all. Keep your breathing steady. The air in the cupboard, clingy from the smell of toiletries on the shelves, didn't help with that job, mind. Felt like it was sticking to the inside of his throat.

When The OB finished at the bog, Jack watched him wash his hands in the basin. There was a towel by the basin, wasn't there? He didn't need a fresh one from the airing... No, the red one's on the hook. Right, old man, dry your hands...That's it...Well done. Now back to bed. But he wasn't shifting from the basin yet. Jack put his eyes right up to a gap in the slats so he could see all of him. Leaning against the basin toward the mirror, he was, staring at himself. Bulgy eyes bloodshot, half dead with sleep. He'd got to nattering about something. But you had to properly listen to make out the words.

"Don't worry, Harry, lad."

Harry? Who's Harry?

"We'll lick 'em, them Jerries."

Jerries? He's blithering on about his soldiering in World War Two again.

"Here, have some water, lad. I know, Harry. I know."

Who's this Harry, then?

"I know it's not the desert mekin' thee thirsty."

Desert?

"Oh, don't cry, Harry. Don't cry. I've got you."

Had he just been dreaming or summat?

"I've got you, mate. Now tip your head back."

So, he'd fought in the desert?

"That's it. That's it. Drink. Drink."

He'd never mentioned that before.

"Better? Don't worry, we'll blast yon Rommel fella to kingdom come for you."

Rommel? The old man in The North African Campaign, then, was he?

"Don't upset your sen, Harry, lad... Rest a while now, eh?... Lay your head on me lap... That's the way... Have a little sleep now, eh, Harry?... You have a little kip... You go to sleep now... Goodbye, my friend."

The OB's bloodshot eyes had gone right watery. Two tears swelled and started slipping down his face. Jack gazed at them moving slowly lower on those craggy cheeks. Reminded him of one of the first games he'd played with Michael when they were six or seven: 'Raindrops on Windows'. The old fella must have watched his friend die, then. Comforted him in his last moments. What age would he have been? Early twenties? Late teens? Your age? How come he'd never said owt about Harry? Too painful? Maybe he'd wanted to protect his kids. Poor bloke. Splashing his face now. Dabbing it dry. And now he's walked out of the bathroom and switched off the light.

Jack stayed in the stuffy airing cupboard a while, surrounded by darkness and guilt, waiting for his dad to get off snoring again. Perhaps he should go back to bed too. Call the whole thing off. Did Dad deserve this? But he knew, if he stayed, that he'd be a complete bastard to him in the shop again in a few hours. Same as always. Maybe what had happened to him in the war had turned him nasty and there was nowt he could do to stop himself. Jack couldn't buy that excuse, though. Not after the way his old man had treated him. And as for friendship? The final straw, when he'd told him to give over being mates with Michael? In light of what he'd just heard, The OB should have known better.

About five minutes later, Jack could hear walrus snoring from his parents' bedroom again. He flicked on his torch, stepped out of the airing cupboard, carefully followed the beam of light out of the bathroom, along the landing and down the stairs. Right quietly, from under the stairs, he took his coat and boots. Pulling the note from his coat pocket, he walked through to the kitchen and put it on the stone mantelpiece above the gleaming Aga. As he stretched into his coat and boots, he kept having a gawp at the three words on the envelope: *'Dad, Mum, Tracy.'* He was about to leave, but then he saw the pen clipped to the kitchen noticeboard. And so, before slipping out of the back door and away down the dark alley toward the river, he wrote one more word beneath the other three: *'Sorry.'*

The riverside path was under a couple of inches of snow as he moved along it, his fast pace helping keep him warm while he marched through the torch-lit, white-flecked air, listening to the scrunch of his boots making footprints. Striding on, he checked his watch. Should be right enough for time, to meet the taxi up on the road, if you keep a fair speed. Taxi at three, train at half four, London by half seven, Greenham Common by ten. March, march, march. For a minute or two, he kept having a look over his shoulder at silhouetted Fowlbeck getting smaller. Leaving the place behind put mixed feelings in him. Excitement. Guilt. Freedom. Fear.

After half a mile or so, Jack pulled a cigarette from his top coat pocket and stopped to spark it. Then he shone his torch across the river. Too dark and snowy to see the outline of Fowlbeck Beacon in the distance. He could sense its presence, mind. You and Michael used to have some belting adventures messing about up there, didn't you? What about that day when you conquered The North Face? Back then, imagining being a hero helped you fight the demons in your head. One minute you were Clint Eastwood...The next Spiderman...Crawling up a craggy...A craggy...Who needed that sort of silly shite now, though? Big enough and tough enough to be yourself, aren't you? You're a man for God's sake. What did Clint get up to these days, anyway? Owt good? Should go back to making spaghetti Westerns. Best gunslinger ever. Now look what the world was lumbered with. Rambo in 'First Blood.' Fucking Rambo. Dickhead. Give over stalling, will you? You don't want to miss that taxi.

He pushed on, dragging at his cig till he'd finished it. As the dark river slid quietly by, sound seemed deadened under a massive white cover. The torch lit up the riverbank trees, their skeleton branches collecting little piles of snow that glistened like sugar. Only a few hours and he'd be there, at Greenham Common, telling the Yanks exactly where they could shove their cruise missiles. What would it be like, being part of summat so important? A matter of life and death for millions of folk everywhere. You couldn't get your head round the scale of it. And there was nowt like being a freedom fighter to make you feel free. He might take it up as a career. Jack Hargraves, Freedom Fighter. Nice ring to it. Seeing Michael's face when he'd told him his plan in the cafe on Wednesday had been a classic. Hadn't he looked gormless, gawping at him over the salt and pepper game? Well, Jack had just had a shock himself at the time, what with the Elsa revelation. He'd been going to tell him about Greenham, anyway. He needed to share it. Strange how he'd felt a greater need as soon as Micky said he was courting, though. As if he'd wanted to score an equaliser. Not that he'd been jealous. He was chuffed for him. Why wouldn't he be? She was right enough, Elsa. Nothing to write home about, but maybe her and Michael were meant to be together. They'd always been good friends. Oh yeah, he was going to tell him about Greenham, anyway. That was the thing about Micky, you could trust him to keep his gob shut. You could trust him with owt.

When Jack saw a sharp curve up ahead in the river, he knew he wasn't far from the spot near The Surge where he had to cut up through a field to meet his taxi on the road. It was still dead calm and quiet, save for his scrunching boots. He wondered if the sky hadn't settled a white blanket over the nocturnal animals and they were having a night off in the land of nod. But then, just after he'd leapfrogged a stile, there stood a big daddy fox on the path, staring him out in the torchlight with eyes of ice.

"Friggin' Nora!" said Jack, staggering back against the stile. "What ya doin', Mr Fox?"

Mr Fox thought himself Lord Muck, by the look of it. A

tilt of his slick, snow-soaked head seemed like an answer. As if he was saying, in a right posh voice: 'Don't 'friggin' Nora' me, sonny. I may jolly well ask you the same question. What the frig are you doing in my neck of the woods at this time of night?'

Jack smiled at the thought of such a foxy speech. And Mr Fox, likely way above finding owt amusing, trotted off down the path, all 'la de da', leaving a neat little trail of paw prints in the snow. Talk about crapping yourself! Not done right much for Jack's nerves, that. He set off again on his peace march. He wished he could get a proper grip of himself. And he had to stop blubbing over what he'd left behind in Fowlbeck. Even if he was a bit sorry for The OB now. That had never happened before. Why can't you forget about it? You had to look forward in this life. Peace and freedom. Freedom and peace, man.

He was soon at the place where he only had to leave the path and walk uphill a bit to get to the lay-by for his three o'clock taxi. Even without legging it, he'd be there in five minutes from here, no bother. He pointed the torch at his watch. Twelve minutes to three. Cracked on better than he'd thought. He could hear The Surge a few yards away, pulling in the river, dragging it under, spewing it out. Felt like it was drawing *him* in too. The Surge could do that to you. But somehow he didn't want to fight it. He'd enough time, hadn't he? He'd not be long.

Quick march and he was there, a single stride from the violent stretch of water where the river had to breathe right in and squeeze through a narrow channel, perhaps one tenth its usual width. Snow was still settling on the riverbanks, but here the flakes seemed to melt in mid-air, above the slimy rocks which lined the rolling, spitting torrent. The spray flying at Jack's face might have been freezing cold, but it somehow felt like The Surge was giving off heat too. It had the energy right enough. And it looked like a cauldron, when you watched it swirl and bubble and froth.

He moved the torch beam around, like a wizard with a big stirring stick, among its rapids and whirlpools. Made a hellish racket, didn't it? Such a powerful force in the middle of the surrounding calm! Magic was a load of bollocks, but you might just start believing in it if you stared into The Surge for too long. There were stories, myths, whatever you wanted to call them. That one from centuries back, about the lad who'd had a crack at jumping it with his dog. Stupid mutt holding back at the edge while still on its leash, just as the lad took off. Drowned, poor kid. Because it sucked you under, did The Surge. And it didn't let you back up. They'd find you in the end, after you'd been spat out. Except you'd be downstream a mile or two. Washed up on the bank. Blue and bloated. Dead. Jack could doubtless jump across it, what with being proper athletic. Funny how he'd not tried it, then. Conquered The North Face years since. But he'd never had a crack at this. There weren't many who'd risk it, mind. These rocks were always right wet and slippery, for a kick off. And those old stories had a power all their own.

Jack gazed a while at the water, forcing its way through the gap. Seconds ago, drifting and sleepy, but now fresh and alive, tumbling over the rapids, spinning in the whirlpools. Nowt but a stride away! Micky always said how danger could be proper beautiful. Like a temptress. The mere sight of The Surge made you catch your breath. But there was its noise as well, its spray on your face, its taste in the air. Exhilarating, that's what it was. And maybe it did have a sort of magic. Because Jack gradually seemed to be losing his guilt and fear. Until, after a minute or two, those feelings had disappeared. Abracadabra! What an inspiration, this place.

And now he was buzzing. He felt so free. Jack Hargraves, Freedom Fighter. Hold on, what time was it? Four minutes to. Fucking hell, his taxi!

Getting a shift on, he turned and followed the torch beam, making it back to the right place on the path, then striding up the field to the road. Belted up there no bother, hadn't he? Like he'd been floating on a snow cloud. He was on cloud nine for sure. And now he could hear a car coming. Then he saw the snow falling in the headlights. Thank God it hadn't settled much on the road. The taxi pulled into the lay-by. This is it, then. Here we go. Destination: Greenham Common.

CHAPTER TWELVE

Reckoning his full-timers, Len and Mark, were nicely on top of the butchering in the prep room, Michael had just swapped his bloodied white apron for a clean one washed and ironed by Mum. Now he was standing in the middle of the shop, looking at the mahogany clock above the prep room doorway, watching its pendulum swing. Be opening up in half an hour. He'd been in charge on a few days now, but this were the first time he'd taken the reins for one of the busiest days of the year. Flipping heck, Good Friday! He hoped it went okay. The history of the place was everywhere, weighing on him. Made him right proud too, mind.

He ran his hand over the big butcher's block which, along with the meat cabinet beside it, acted as the serving counter. Look how scarred and bowed the old girl was from years of chopping and scrubbing down. She'd need replacing again soon, no mistake. He'd have to get another exact copy made, though. That was the tradition. Getting a different block would be akin to replacing the altar in Fowlbeck church with a wooden bench. A great chunk of wood like this had been in Bowers' Family Butchers since day one, over a century ago, when Great Great Grandad Albert started trading. Michael loved it being part of the serving counter too. There were still plenty of folk who liked seeing a proper butcher at work, cutting up meat right under their noses. You could sense them smelling its juices as the knife sliced it open. He traced a finger along a couple of cut marks at the edge of the block, where scrubbing down hadn't worn away the wood so much, and thought about Albert making similar marks a hundred years since.

Looking about, there were so much tradition in this shop. That was one of the things which had made the business successful down the years. Which still made it successful, despite the recession and competition from Hargraves' shop. You needed expertise and a top quality product as well of course. Essential, they were. But Dad had always talked about the importance of tradition. There was value in it. Punters liked it. They trusted it. Made them feel special, somehow, like they were part of something which had stood the test of time. Part of summat deeper than just swapping brass for slabs of meat. Well, they had tradition coming out of their ears at Bowers' Family Butchers. Oh yeah, a few years since, Mum decided the sawdust floor had to go. Maybe they'd held onto that for too long, especially with all this health and safety coming in nowadays. But they still had the ancient cash register with buttons like old typewriter keys, the meat scales with little towers of weights, the glossy green wall tiles. And they had the family tradition of hanging photos of each butcher generation standing outside under the shop sign. Michael would have his own picture up soon. He turned from the butcher's block and looked at the white wall, opposite. There was Dad with his arm round Mum, the pair of them beaming at the camera. They'd been so happy, hadn't they? He gazed at Dad a minute. He'd never let him down. He'd rather die.

The sound of a chopping cleaver coming from the prep room snapped Michael out of it. That proper clean striking which could only be Len's work. The bloke were as much an artist with a set of knives as Elsa was with her paintbrushes. They were lucky still having him there after donkey's years. He might have been the most miserable old sod the world had ever known, but you couldn't argue with his butchery skills. And whenever Michael went to auction to buy new livestock he'd never go without Len. You'd have to be a total barmpot not to want to learn from a man with such an expert eye. He could spot the finest beasts a mile off. And nowt mattered more than getting the best quality meat in the first place, did it? You could kill it, hang it so it aged just right, butcher it perfectly, but if your original stock was crap you'd just as well sell it for dog food.

Michael moved slowly along the front of the cabinet, toward the point where it met the meat display in the shop window, checking that everything looked in prime condition. He had to admit it were hard finding fault. The chickens were plump, them sausages nice and fat, there was a lovely shiny glaze on the pork pie crusts, the red meat seemed to glow with succulence. Nobody could deny it, their shop sold only the very finest of products. Locally sourced, well reared, carefully stored, skilfully butchered. All Michael had to do was keep up the age-old traditions and everything would stay just grand, wouldn't it?

He went to the serving side of the cabinet, where lamb and beef hung from hooks in the ceiling, ageing among the dangling knives and cleavers. You could tell the beef was firming up right enough because of how dark it looked. But he slapped some of it, like Dad and Grandad used to, just to check. Pretty solid. Smelt drier than younger stock too. Another week and it would be beautifully tender inside. Ripe for a carve up. He loved it that they still hung meat in the shop as well as the prep room. Wouldn't feel like a proper butchers otherwise.

A minute or so later, Michael walked to the shop door and stepped out into the daylight and the cold High Street air, being careful not to slip on the snow-covered pavement in his polished market boots. Best chuck a bit of salt down. At least it hadn't settled right much on the street. And the sky was clear. Perhaps they'd seen the last of it. Hopefully, it wouldn't put a dent in today's trade. The shop front seemed in good order, anyhow, with its string of fresh game birds hanging like a feathery necklace under that olde worlde lettering:

'Bowers' Family Butchers ~ Finest Quality Meats Since 1877.'

There were a few folk pottering about on the High Street, wrapped in woollies, stopping for a natter, popping into the newsagents for tabloids and baccy. An Austin Metro chugged past up the hill, its exhaust spluttering foggy fumes, its driver straining at the wheel like a jockey urging on a doddery nag. Hold up, Rodney Hargraves had appeared outside his shop up the street. Opening out his 'Specials' board on the pavement. What brilliant offer did he have in store today, then? Michael could just make out the big bold words:

'EASTER HAMPERS - £4.99. LOWEST PRICE. HIGHEST QUALITY.'

Highest quality, my arse. They don't even select their own meat. Get it shipped in from Cropden Slaughterhouse. What's the nasty bugger doing now? Standing there dead still with his arms folded, looking in this direction. You could near as damn it feel them bulgy eyes glaring. Michael cottoned on to his meaning right enough: 'You knew what Jack had planned, didn't you, lad? You two's thick as thieves!' You could sense his anger from here, as if the top of his bald head might blow off any minute. Lanky must have gone through with it, then. Rodney were off back up Hargraves' shop steps and inside again now.

Michael dipped into his shop to fetch a bag of road salt outside. As he spread it across the white pavement, like a yesteryear farmer scattering seed, he got to worrying about Jack. He'd have already got to London, likely heading for

Greenham Common by now. You had to admire the lad, didn't you? Even if you disagreed with his politics. Wasn't having American nuclear weapons on British soil the best deterrent a country could have? Michael knew Jack were mainly doing it to get his message into his dad's thick skull, but he believed in the cause too. Everyone was entitled to their opinion, mind. You had to hope he looked after himself, that's all. Bloody hell, his dad will go nuts at him when he gets back tomorrow! Well, if he tries clouting him like he used to, Lanky might be inclined to retaliate this time. He'd been properly wound up with his old man on Wednesday, when he first came into the cafe. And when he'd talked about his Greenham plan a bit later. There could be one hell of a showdown come Saturday.

By mid-morning, Michael had stopped fretting over having a good day on takings, because the shop had been busy since opening, and there was still a stream of customers keeping everyone on their toes. The staff were pulling together as well. Len and Mark were making sure the cabinet and window displays stayed well stocked. And part-timer Mum had turned up on the dot, after a late one out dancing with Eddie, to help her son serve folk. He felt like he were in his element. They were doing a belting trade with him as boss, he still had that buzz from last Saturday night, Elsa loved him too. He might have been a bit concerned about Jack, but the lad was usually decent at taking care of himself. Things were champion, really. Mum seemed on good form as well. Always the same after a Thursday night jive with Twinkle Toes. Good for her, anyhow. As Michael served one of the new computer generation a dozen sausages, no wonder the kid was so spotty with the amount of bangers he got through, he kept looking across at her. She were at the butcher's block, trimming a lamb shank for Susan from Susan's Antiques. Funny old woman, Susan. Forever carrying little knick-knacks round in her cardigan pockets so she could work on them all the time. And her nose was more like a beak. Its tip moved when she spoke. About right for her, that hooter. She were as beaky as hell. Always pecking at folk for gossip.

"I am partial to a lamb pot roast at Easter, Carol," she said, dirt-ingrained fingers polishing an antique spoon with a rag.

"Well, this little smasher won't disappoint," said Mum, holding the trimmed shank under Susan's nose. "I'll put a Bowers' guarantee on it."

"By gum," said Susan, beaky tip aquiver. "I can smell it roasting now."

"All right for you, love?"

"Just the job."

Mum turned to the long wooden table along the back wall, where the two sets of traditional scales sat. As she weighed the meat, worked out its price on a notepad, wrapped it in greaseproof paper, Susan kept nattering. Michael had a laugh to himself. You could tell when the antique lady was fishing.

"Out dancing last neet, Carol?"

"That's right, Susan," said Mum. "Every Thursday."

"You and Eddie?"

"Me and Eddie."

After Michael had given the computer whizz kid his change, he spotted Susan giving more attention to her silver spoon, as if she had nowt on her mind other than getting it highly polished.

"You'll be wearin' yon spoon away, Susan," he said.

But she'd not heard him. That nose had got to twitching again.

"Surprised you and Eddie haven't tied t' knot yet, Carol."

"Are you?" said Mum.

"Well, you have been courting a long while."

"Nearly seven years."

"Seven year," said Susan. "And he's not even popped t' question?"

"We're happy as we are," said Mum. "Thanks for asking."

"Appen he needs a size nine up his backside," said Susan.

Mum laughed as she turned to her and passed her the greaseproof-wrapped lamb.

"You're a rum one, Susan. One pound twenty-five, please."

Susan stuffed the spoon and rag into a cardigan pocket, delved into the other pocket to pull out two crumpled pound notes, handed them over.

"Thank you," said Mum, moving to the ancient cash till.

Michael picked up a steel sharpening rod and his favourite butcher's knife from the long table, started swiping the blade, waited for what Beaky was going to spout next. Knife and rod clashed like a sword fight. Mum handed Susan her change.

"Seventy-five pence," she said, reaching over the butcher's block.

"Ta," said Susan. "Seven year. By gum! Not thinking o' moving Eddie into your place yet, then?"

Mum put fists on hips at that one, like Albert outside the shop in Victorian times. It weren't a look of pride, mind. She had a proper scowl on.

"Any further questions?" she said.

"Only teasing, lass," said Susan.

"You'd do well keeping your nose out."

"Mu-um," said Michael, stopping sharpening. "It's reet."

"Honestly!" said Mum.

She tugged her apron straight and started wiping down

the butcher's block. Michael noticed a strand of long black hair escaping her white pork pie hat to hang over her flustered face. He clashed away with the knife again, like it were a warning to Susan to bugger off. She'd not shifted yet, though. Not hanging about for more gossip, was she? But one thing Susan liked as much as cottoning on to gossip was dishing it out.

"Summat's biting Rodney Hargraves this morning, you know," she said.

"What makes you say that?" said Michael, trying to sound casual between swipes of the knife.

"Well, my shop's opposite his, isn't it? And he looks in a bit of a flap to me."

"That's Rodney Hargraves for yer, Susan."

"No, Michael. I mean like really...What's t' word? Agitated."

"It'll be something and nothing," said Mum, tucking the strand of hair under her hat.

"Wonder if summat's gone on. Is he keeping a secret?" said Susan, her beaky nose sniffing at the meaty air like she was onto it. "I've not seen young Jack about, you know."

"Haven't yer?" said Michael, stopping the knife mid-swipe.

Mum and Susan must have sensed something because they stared straight at him.

"Michael, where's Jack?" said Susan, eyes narrowing.

"How should I know? Appen he's sick."

"Right, Susan," said Mum. "Enjoy your lamb. We'll be seeing you."

Susan hung on a few more seconds. But then she must have realised there'd be no more change out of Bowers' Family Butchers, because she was away through the door and up the High Street.

"That woman!" said Mum. "No prizes for guessing where she's off to now."

"Hargraves' for mint sauce?"

"She's got plenty o' sauce already, love. Now, what's going on?"

Michael looked down at his shiny boots. Jack had sworn him to secrecy. And he'd kept his gob shut so far, course he had. But it would be through Fowlbeck like wildfire pretty soon, anyhow, what with Beaky Nose sniffing around. It would be right just letting on to Mum, wouldn't it? No-one else in earshot. Len and Mark clattering about in the prep room, the shop empty of customers for a minute. Flipping heck, first time that had happened this morning. The place had been jam-packed afore now. Weren't flagging already, were they? On Good Friday? They needed to keep that till ringing.

"Mum, what's happened to all t' punters?"

"Give over fretting, Michael. There'll be another rush soon. Take a breather. Now where's Jack?"

"He's gone to Greenham Common."

"Greenham Common?" said Mum. "What for?"

"They're havin' that nuclear protest, aren't they?"

"Well, who's he gone with?"

"Nobody," said Michael.

"Nobody?"

"He's by him sen. Sneaked out last night while everyone slept."

"Blooming heck!" said Mum. "Hope he's all right."

"I'm more bothered about what happens when he gets back tomorrow. I reckon his old man's seething."

"Blimey."

"You mustn't say owt, Mum. There's only me supposed to know."

Michael could tell Mum were worried about Jack. In the next half hour, she kept asking him questions: 'Where's he staying tonight?' 'Has he enough money?' 'Will he have wrapped up warm in this cold weather?' He loved it that she had a soft spot for Lanky. No wonder, mind. She knew better than anyone how he'd been like a brother to her only child.

Mum had been right about the shop getting a mad rush on afore long too. By the time the pendulum clock said quarter to twelve, it were as busy as hell again. A chattering queue let the cold in, as it stretched out of the open door and a yard or two along the pavement. As if a place like Bowers' ever stayed quiet for long, anyhow. Why had Michael even fretted about it? He was pushing and pulling a ham through the white enamel slicer on the long table now. The circular blade whispered as it cut thin slices off the cooked joint, sending that sweet-savoury smell floating into the chilly air. When he reckoned he'd done enough, he slid his palms under the greaseproof and lifted the little meat stack he'd made. Then he turned to the right posh family waiting on the other side of the cabinet in their best hiking gear. They were staying in the village for Easter, in a holiday cottage they'd lately bought. The young lad had a Darth Vader mask on and was looking up at Michael, who tried doing a frightened face as he held the ham for them to see above the lit cabinet.

"Is that all right for you?"

"Perfect," said the father. "Splendid for our sarnies. I must say, you have a marvellous place here."

"Thank you," said Michael. "We've been working at it long enough."

"Super to see the old country ways being maintained," said the mother, who had the look of Princess Di.

They might have been a bit snobby, but Michael would take compliments about Bowers' Family Butchers from all and sundry.

"I'm the fifth generation butcher in my family to run this shop," he said, wrapping the greaseproof paper round the ham.

"And so young!" said the father, taking a crisp five pound note from his wallet, passing it over the top of the cabinet. "Michael, isn't it?"

"Aye. Erm... Yes, that's right."

"I'm Rupert. This is Jane. And Clarissa. And, The Lord of Death here, that's Teddy."

When Michael had finished serving them, he told them to take care hiking in the snow-covered dale and that he looked forward to seeing them again soon. A kindly word here and there made all the difference to customer loyalty, no mistake. Dad had taught him that. Mum were brilliant with punters as well. Unless they riled her. A flipping decent butcher too, she was. As Michael put the ham joint back on the top shelf in the cabinet, above all the uncooked meats, he listened to her cracking a cleaver through a shoulder of pig on the butcher's block. One strike per chop, that's all she ever needed. She still mollycoddled him in the shop at times, but he knew he'd be at a loss without her. Could be galling, mind, being mothered in front of folk. Perhaps he should stamp his authority more, now he was running the show. What did people think when they saw him treated like a kid? Hold up, there were one or two beef cuts running low in this cabinet.

"Len! Mark!" he shouted toward the prep room.

Mum stopped her chopping at that. And the queue gave over chattering. A line of heads in caps and hats stared at him. Must have fairly bawled them names. He felt his face go proper red. Could take some getting used to, this being in charge business.

"Boss?" said Mark, appearing at the prep room door, heavy metal hair in a ponytail.

"Could we have more fillet steak and silverside out here, please?"

"Yes, boss. Reet away, boss."

Was he taking the piss?

"Ahhhhhh! Let go, Len! Let go!" yelled Mark, tugging his ponytail and vanishing backwards through the doorway, as if Len had just yanked him off stage.

The daft joker got a good laugh from customers for that.

"Don't be encouraging him, everyone," said Michael, smiling anyhow.

"Needs no encouragement, that one," said Mum.

Michael went to wash his hands in the sink by the long table, as Mum drove her cleaver through the pork shoulder a couple more times for Donald, a dry stone waller in his sixties. Strong as a bull, Don, and camper than Christmas. He'd been 'living over t' brush' with Irish Brian for years. It tickled Michael pink that Bowers' Family Butchers always had a good variety of punters coming through its door. Put him in mind of how important the shop was to the whole community. Interesting little batch in now. Clive, the wine merchant, who only drank stout. Mr Hodgson, Michael's old Maths teacher, who was still young. Mrs Jones, the noisy librarian. Mrs Taylor, the hill farmer. Oh, Elsa had just walked in. Edging through the crowd in her parka coat. Mum had got to grinning at her son now. No flipping surprise there.

"Michael, your girlfriend's here!" she said, sounding so happy she was all but singing.

"Mu-um," said Michael, feeling nowt but twelve again.

"Hello, Elsa, love."

"Hiya, Carol."

"Oh no, you've got to call me Mum now."

Mum got off laughing with a couple of customers at that. It pleased Michael, seeing her chuffed for him. She'd nearly picked him up and spun him when he'd told her about Elsa a couple of days since, but did she have to make a song and dance of it? Elsa wasn't a lass to hold back nowadays either, though. In private or public. Afore he knew it, she'd got down the side of the butcher's block and was with him at the sink, flinging her arms round his neck and planting a long, juicy smacker on his lips. The shop went quiet for a second. Then there was a titter, a bit of gossip, a teasing cheer, Mrs Jones the librarian shouting for an encore. Michael's head were a beetroot. But at that moment he was more like Elsa too, because he really didn't give a toss what folk thought, he had that much love in him.

Elsa turned to the punters when she'd kissed him, leaning back into his chest, snuggling up. It felt right, cuddling her, even if they did have an audience. Dad used to cuddle Mum whenever he fancied.

"That's your lot for today, folks," said Elsa, giggling.

"Oh, it's so sweeeeet!" said Donald, clapping his strong hands light and quick.

"Someone chuck a bucket o' water o'er 'em," said Mrs Taylor.

Could a lad be happier than Michael was right now? Standing there in his family's busy, century old butcher's shop with the girl who'd sent him smitten? His heart were full to bursting! By the sound of it, so was Mum's.

"Awww, look at my little boy and the lovely Elsa, everyone."

Then Michael noticed that Beaky Susan had appeared again, pushing her way in at the shop door. Flipping heck, she must have smelt there was summat new going on. Make a cracking bloodhound, she would.

"Oh, Susan, you're back," said Mum. "Thought you might be missing something, did you? Have you not heard that Michael and Elsa are courting now?"

She definitely seemed shocked by the news, anyhow.

"What's the matter, Susan?" continued Mum. "Cat got your tongue?"

"It's Rodney Hargraves. He's dead."

CHAPTER THIRTEEN

Wrapped in his coat, Jack was sitting out of the rain at last, on a bench in Cropden bus station, eating salty fish and chips off newspaper with a little wooden fork. Fairly lashing it down against this tinny shelter roof. What a racket! One of these 'chippy' paper headlines could have been: *'Snow Washed Away In Biblical Monsoon.'* Not that a bit of weather was enough to put the crowds off a Saturday night on the town. He could see folk along the road at the other side of the oily station turning circle, darting between lit up restaurants and pubs. Lasses wobbly in white stilettos. Lads, shoulders against the downpour, having a crack at looking tough. You had to wonder whether any of them had given a thought to the nuclear issue this Easter. Or in a long while for that matter. Doubtless most had put it down as a bad job ages since. When your number's up and all that bollocks. They likely reckoned they'd just as well be partying if the 'commies' got twitchy about the prospect of cruise missiles in Europe and flicked the big red switch. At least 'good old Maggie' got our precious Falklands back, eh?

The peace protest had put Jack in mind of more important stuff than hanging about alehouses of a weekend. But he had to admit there was still a certain part of him that fancied joining the fun. He'd have no bother finding a pretty lady to keep him warm till morning. Got enough brass left from Greenham for some drinks and a cheap hotel room. No, he'd got to get back to Fowlbeck tonight. Promised it in that note he'd left on the kitchen mantelpiece. Mum and Tracy would likely be worried sick, especially seeing as he'd not contacted them these past two days while he'd been away.

Not let on to anyone where he was staying last night either. Somehow, he'd needed to be properly independent and free on this trip.

A red single-decker pulled a wide arc in the turning circle, fairly blinding Jack with its headlights for a second. As it lumbered noisily out of the station, it coughed black smoke into the rain. The smell of diesel hung in the air, putting him off the last of his fish supper. He screwed up what was left in its right greasy newsprint and chucked it in the bin by the bench. Then he pulled back his coat sleeve and looked at his watch. Quarter past eight. His bus should be here before long. Be home soon after nine. Frigging hell, what sort of reception was he in for from the old man? Oh well, it had been worth it, anyway.

When the Fowlbeck bus arrived a few minutes later, and the incoming passengers had got off, he picked up his rucksack and ducked through the double doors. He clocked how fat and squashed against the steering wheel the driver's belly was when he paid him, shirt buttons set to pop. The bloke could have counted out change on that gut. How did he manage round corners?

"How do," said Jack, just stopping himself from adding 'you manage round corners?'

"How do," said the driver.

Jack went to the smoking area at the back of the empty bus, where the musty-smelling seats were proper threadbare and torn, mucky yellow foam spilling out of them. Sitting down, he pushed open the squeaky narrow sliding bit at the top of the window. Spits of cold rain fell on his hand. Taking a packet of cigs from his pocket, he lit a fresh one and squinted through the smoke at a couple of passengers who'd just got on. The bloke in best bib and tucker tuxedo looked fucking arseholed, didn't he? Had he lost his coat? Soaked to the skin, he was. He tottered along, like a regretful groom drowning his sorrows, and made it about halfway down the aisle before plonking himself on a seat. The scruffy lass in a duffel coat had one of those boomboxes. Did she have any decent tunes? None of that New Romantic shite. She sat near the front and, with only three on board, the driver sparked up the juddering engine. They were off. Fowlbeck bound.

When they passed the old cinema on the road out of town, Jack gazed through the raindrop window at the brightly lit sign advertising *'Gandhi'*. Better look sharp and go see that film. It had been out a fair while now and, from what he'd heard, you didn't want to be missing it. Belter of a movie, by all accounts. He already knew about Gandhi taking on the British Empire with non-cooperation and non-violence. Peace as a weapon of war. Summat else, that, wasn't it? Genius. It had worked as well. India got her independence, didn't she? Mahatma might not have used guns and fists, but he was a freedom fighter up with the best of them. And courageous as hell. That was heroism for you, right there, inside the skinny little guy with round specs.

Now the bus left Cropden and started along the dark country road. Jack crushed out his cigarette butt on the metal stubber stuck to the back of the seat in front, then slid the narrow window panel shut. The women he'd seen yesterday, from the Greenham Common Peace Camp, were heroic the same as Gandhi, weren't they? Wasn't like they'd not had provocation. They'd been evicted many a time, taken shite off the coppers, been made to stand trial, sent to prison, faced vigilante attacks. But they'd not bitten, had they? 'No violence, no violence, no violence.' That's what one of them, pierced nose, rainbow coloured jumper, had said to thousands of protestors over her megaphone, just before everyone stretched out and linked arms in that massive human chain. It wouldn't surprise Jack one bit if Gandhi was the Greenham Women's inspiration.

The bus carried on rumbling through the darkness. The only streetlights were in the hamlets now, where they shone on the wet road and rusty signposts, counting down the miles to Fowlbeck. **15... 12... 9...** Jack thought more about the peace protest. Summat altered in him yesterday, didn't it? Standing in solidarity, shoulder to shoulder, all the way along Nuclear Valley. How many did today's Guardian say had turned up? Seventy thousand? What a mind boggler that was. If nowt else, they'd shown Thatcher and her American buddies that they weren't about to take their nuclear policy, their propaganda, lying down. As one of the CND leaders said at the rally afterwards, the protest had been 'a great victory.' It would be a long road to make a proper difference, mind. Much longer than the fourteen mile chain they'd managed yesterday. Gandhi had known how much it took. But he'd kept going, kept believing. Big time. You had to carry on fighting. That's what the Greenham Women needed to do. And CND, and the seventy thousand, and millions more. And Jack. Then, one day, if you never gave up, if you kept fighting, maybe you'd change things too.

Just before the next hamlet, the bus hit a pothole and arseholed tuxedo bloke sat bolt upright.

"We in Leeds yet, fella?" he bawled at the driver. "Leeds yet, pal?"

"We're off to Fowlbeck, mate. Told you that when yer paid," said the driver, raising his voice, his bloated face glaring down the bus through that angled rear view mirror like some oversized goldfish.

"Fowlbeck?" slurred The Tuxedo. "Where the fuck's that?"

"End o' t' line. And watch yer mouth."

"I'm heading for the end of the line all right! Oh God. Oh God. Stop the train! Stop the train!"

"We're off back to Cropden after Fowlbeck," said the driver. "If you behave yer sen, I'll let you stay on till then. You can get yer train to Leeds from there."

Jack watched The Tuxedo bury its bedraggled head in its hands and start to blubber. What a state! No wonder scruffy lass with boombox seemed relieved when the bus stopped to let her off near the next signpost. **Fowlbeck 7 miles.** Quarter of an hour and Jack would be back there.

As they set off again on the bumpy road, he stared at his reflection shaking like a mirage in the black windowpane. He'd been trying not to think right much about home. But now he was nowt but fifteen minutes from seeing The OB, and you'd have to be a total dimwit to reckon he'd taken kindly to being left in the lurch. Had he fuck. That's really what you want, though, isn't it? To shock him into realising he's wasting his time trying to tie you to Hargraves' Butcher's shop.

Another mile or so and the rain looked to be easing, yet it still fell steadily against the window, showing up like teardrops on Jack's reflected face. He pushed his hand through his still wet hair once or twice, trying to style it like in that early John Lennon photo again. He knew he was good looking, in decent fettle, had no bother handling himself, but you really didn't need all that to be heroic, did you? You didn't need that to change things. And wasn't it time to give over fighting fire with fire? Perhaps you've been reacting too aggressively to The OB of late. You could fight peacefully, couldn't you? And still be strong and stand your ground. You might have more luck with him that way. Jack would never forget the Greenham Women scaling that perimeter fence yesterday in teddy bear clobber. The fence that they'd decorated with toys and photos of their little children. Teddy bears, toys, kiddie pictures. Symbols of life, they'd called them. Talk about total opposites to nuclear weapons. It was funny, because the authorities didn't know how to respond to all that peace. Coppers had looked proper awkward. You couldn't help thinking they'd much prefer a good old scrap.

The Tuxedo had fallen asleep now, snoring like a pig above the noise of the diesel engine. He'd give champion snorer Rodney Hargraves a run for his brass. His head and shoulders were starting to loll across the aisle, so Jack went to help him sit up. As he lifted him upright, The Tuxedo grunted and he got a stale, beery stench in his nose. Then the silly pisshead slowly slid the other way, until he was laid out on the seat, doing piggy impressions again and dribbling from the corner of his gob. At least he'd got to lying on his side, so he wouldn't choke if he puked. And it didn't look like he was going to fall anymore.

Jack went back to his seat. You had to do what you could to help others in life, didn't you? That's one thing he'd learnt on this trip. Seventy thousand uniting for the well-being of millions. Jack and Michael were always there to help each other. But sometimes you had to do that for folk even when they weren't deserving of it. Sometimes you had to do the right thing, show people the light. Like Gandhi had the British, like the Greenham Women were trying to do with the nuclear brigade. Maybe your dad needs your help to look at things differently.

Soon the bus rattled through the last cluster of limestone houses before Fowlbeck. **3 miles**. It surprised Jack how calm he felt, what with being right close to home. He smiled at himself in the dark window. He knew exactly what to do when he got back now. No arsing about. No shying away from owt. Face Father eye to eye. You've done it before.

Only this time you'll be serene inside. There'll be no biting or getting riled. You'll not be angry, like The Surge, but as tranquil as the river when it's gliding by. Strange how everything seemed to be fitting into place. And now he even knew what to do when he left Fowlbeck and Hargraves' Butchers behind. Get a new job, any job, as long as it gives you time to swot. Find work in Cropden, Leeds, Bradford. Wherever. Cheap digs. A-levels at night-school. Shape yourself and you'll get those grades this time, no bother. Uni next year. Study a worthwhile subject. A decent degree and there'll be no stopping you making summat of yourself. Making a difference. You're still young.

A few minutes later, the bus swung round a corner and there were the lights of Fowlbeck, a mile away at the bottom of the dale, glowing like candles on a birthday cake. Jack thought how chuffed he was going to be to walk into that house and be met by his family relieved at his return. But he knew he'd be getting a frosty reception that would linger about the place a while. Maybe three or four days? A week? After that, things would likely thaw. And eventually his dad might accept his decision. If not, he'd be packing his bags, anyway. To have the old man's blessing, mind. How ace would that be? Well, weirder stuff had happened. You just need to be peaceful when he's riled, give over getting wound up. It could work, because there were times when he showed a human side, weren't there? Mostly with Tracy, but what about Harry in Africa? Nobody could have watched him crying into that mirror two nights since, listened to those gentle words for a dying friend, and not seen a drop of humanity in him. There were even moments when he'd had a crack at being kinder to his son. Once he'd said it pleased him that he was a good grafter, sometimes he called him 'mate'. It wasn't much, and he could be a manipulative bastard, but, if you looked hard enough, there was definitely summat softer under that craggy old skin.

Jack was glad of the stop near his house, because it meant he could get off there and dodge being gawped at through the bus windows on the High Street. He knew it would be all round the village about him upping sticks, and he couldn't be doing with gossipmongers staring or nattering at him tonight. He just wanted to get inside and face the music.

"Cheers, mate," he said, standing next to the driver as he stopped the bus.

"Cheers," said the driver, putting his podgy thumb on a button to open the doors.

"Stopped rainin' at last."

"Aye."

"Keep an eye on tuxedo bloke, eh?" said Jack. "He'll be reet, but he's laid out for now. Hope ya can shift the great lummox back in Cropden."

"I'll shift the bugger," said the driver. "Swift kick up the backside usually suffices."

"Happy Easter."

"Aye, happy bloody Easter."

Stepping onto the damp flagstone pavement, Jack swung his rucksack across his shoulder, waited for the bus to set off again and crossed the road. Not fancying bumping into anyone, he decided to go the back way. Up Sugar Hill Lane, along the snicket, down the alley to the house. Sugar Hill Lane was barely lit, but he could make out someone coming toward him. With bow-legs like that, it had to be Geoff, the joiner. Doubtless off to The Dog and Gun for a Saturday night ale. Better give him the time of day.

"Evenin', Geoff."

Acting odd, wasn't he? Sort of half-waving, head down. And now he'd crossed to the other side of the lane. Jack stopped and watched him walk past. What the frig is up with him? Anyway, better crack on. Up the lane, along the snicket, down the alley.

He noticed the quiet just before he put his key in the lock. Not a sound coming from the kitchen on the other side of this back door. Was it the only room in the house with a light on? Were they out? No, that was a chair scraping on the floorboards. Right, you're calm, aren't you? Calm and peaceful, remember? Breathe. Breathe. Key in. Turn it.

"Hello, Mum. Hi, Tracy," he said, closing the door behind him.

Fucking hell, this kitchen's boiling. What going on? They look zonked out. In a proper daze. Neither of them has so much as looked at you yet. What's Tracy doing at the kitchen table? Colouring in one of those horsey books she used to read when she was about eight? Not even a colouring in book, is it? Scribbling felt tip over photos? And why is Mum sitting right close to the Aga with its door open, staring into those roasting flames? She sort of had her back to him, but, from what he could see of her face, it was so red hot it looked like it might blister. He dropped his rucksack on the floor. For some reason, his mouth had gone dry. He walked past Tracy.

"That's nice colourin', Sis."

Jack reached his Mum and stood behind her. She had her grey hair down. How straggly did it look tonight?

"What is it, Mum?" he said.

He put his hand on her shoulder, felt it go rigid.

"Mum? Where's Dad?"

She turned slowly to him.

"You've killed him," she said.

CHAPTER FOURTEEN

Michael wondered if Jack were hankering after the past when he wanted them to stop and skim stones across the river. They'd not been skimming for years. Jack had said nowt since he'd sent that first one over the surface, and they must have been throwing from this pebbly bank, in black coats and suits, trousers tucked in wellies, a full five minutes now. Michael scuffed at the little stones, making them click as they knocked against each other, and uncovered what looked like another right good flier, thin and flat. He dropped on his haunches and picked it up. Some weight to it, but not too heavy. Sat right enough between finger and thumb.

"Try this one, mate," he said. "It's a good 'un."

Jack didn't say owt, but turned to him with his arm outstretched, that blank look he'd had all day still on his face. Michael tossed him the stone, watched him twist his broad shoulders and fling it low above the brownish water. It skipped away silently, leaving an arc of widening circles before sinking near the opposite bank, where a heron stood in tall grass. Michael could see that ringed, dotted eye on the side of its sleek head. Fixed on them, it were, like the bird was trying to freak them into moving from there. Odd creatures, herons. Looked to be lording it over all and sundry afore they started taking off, when they were more akin to gangly barmpot inventors wearing cardboard wings, until they somehow turned graceful in flight.

Perhaps Michael should ask Jack if he fancied walking on further. Because he'd just begun opening up when they were on the move coming down here, after he'd said he needed to escape from all the accusing stares he reckoned he was getting from folk at the after-funeral buffet. Giving the impression he wanted to stay put for now, mind. And you had to respect that, didn't you? You had to use a bit of gumption in a situation like this. How had it been when Michael's dad died? Sometimes you needed to talk, but sometimes you wanted to say nothing and have everyone else keep their gobs shut as well. One thing you couldn't bide was someone blithering on or preaching. Michael best button his trap. Felt like a day for silence, anyhow, didn't it? Because of the funeral, yes, but it were really quiet out here this afternoon too. The air as still as could be, not so much as a whispering breeze under the cold, clear sky. And was there less birdsong than usual? Everything strangely peaceful.

Jack kept skimming. Michael noticed how he gazed at the water each time one of them stones sank, as if waiting for it to jump back out and start hopping along again. He were still in shock of course. How could he not be? These last few days, he'd been more like a zombie than owt else. But that's how it was when you lost your dad out of the blue. It knocked you for six, you went right numb. It was a smack in the guts, you felt sick, you couldn't believe it, you were empty, you didn't know where the hell you were. No doubt it could be the same even when your old man had been a flipping sod to you. If you blamed yourself for his death, anyhow. And Lanky did blame himself. He'd said that much at least.

Michael watched the heron flap its wings, drag itself into the air and fly off downstream, disappearing among the leafless sycamores and oaks. Oh yeah, it was never going to be easy for Jack, but knowing his dad had a massive heart attack on the very day he'd disappeared to Greenham Common? And knowing that on Good Friday morning the bloke had been proper fuming about him going off in the middle of the night? From what he'd said, his mum had made that clear to him, no mistake. How could the lad not cotton on to the affect he'd had, then? Anyhow, the whole village was talking now about the state of Rodney Hargraves that morning. Afore little sister Tracy found him round the back of their shop, laid out on the snowy ground. Just popped out for a smoke, by all accounts. And now he were turned to ash. Maybe it would have been possible to persuade Jack not to go to that nuclear protest. It had been obvious how set he was on the idea, but Michael was the only one who'd known about it, the only one who'd had any chance of stopping him.

"Ya know my dad fought in t' war, Micky?" said Jack, stopping skimming at last.

"Aye," said Michael.

"He was in The North African Campaign. Heard of it?"

"Sorry, no, I haven't."

Jack picked up another handful of stones and started throwing them, one by one, high into the sunny sky. Michael shielded his eyes and watched them climb and fall, then splash like mini bombs in the water.

"Heard him talkin' to him sen about it," said Jack, dropping the stones he had left on the pebbly bank. "The night I sneaked off... He could've easily collared me... Easy... If he'd copped me then, he'd likely still...I hid in the airing cupboard... He came into t' bathroom... Staring in t' mirror, he was... Cryin'..."

He went quiet again. Michael didn't know what to say, so he was glad of it when Jack suggested summat half a minute later.

"Let's walk up to t' waterfall."

"The old den?" said Michael.

"Aye."

"We've not been there for donkey's years."

"You're right," said Jack. "Stupid idea."

"No, it's not. Let's go."

"A fair trek an all."

"Not that far," said Michael. "Come on."

"Can't think straight..."

"Come on, Lanky."

"Suppose we can."

The recent snow, and the rain which had washed it away, had left the narrow riverside path muddy, making their welly boots squelch in the dark earth as they walked. Michael had set off in front, but it didn't seem right, somehow. Perhaps because, when they were nippers, Jack had always been leader on their adventures to secret places like The Waterfall Den. 'Bagsy me first!' he used to say, 'Bagsy me first!' Until, eventually, they'd accepted that's how it would be. Even though Michael's life was pretty champion nowadays, he did miss them times dossing about with his best mate.

They were soon approaching the big sycamore that had been their favourite for ambushing. Wouldn't be much use for that job at the moment. Bare branches like crooked fingers in the bright light. Michael could see one or two buds about to sprout when they got closer, mind. Another month and the old girl would be leafy enough for camouflage. He wondered if there were still nippers about using her to fire water from at passers-by, making them mardy. Had some good laughs, him and Jack. He stopped under the tree and waited for him. Looked to be struggling. Sort of dragging his feet, hands deep in the pockets of his coat, as if he fancied losing himself in it. Michael knew what he were going through. He felt right sorry for him. But all you could do was be there, wasn't it? Especially when you loved someone like he loved Lanky.

When Jack reached the tree, he sparked a cigarette.

Michael could smell the chemicals in the wispy grey smoke as it mixed with his own frosty breath.

"Yer know which tree this is, don't you?" he said.

"Wonder what happened to Rocker Billy," said Jack.

"Rocker Billy Rebel, eh?"

"Just upped sticks and left."

"Flippin' heck, still can't believe you jumped into t' river from way up yonder!" said Michael, looking up at the sycamore's highest branches.

"Not seen or heard of since."

"Up in smoke." ,

Bloody hell, why did you say that? You've only been back from the crematorium a couple of hours. You need to think on a bit! Thank God it didn't seem to have registered with Jack, who were brushing the hair out of his blank eyes. The cool, gelled up 'John Lennon in Hamburg look', as he called it, had disappeared now. Got rid soon after he'd found out about his dad. Gone back to how he used to have it a long while since. He really did have a hankering for the past.

"You all reet, Lanky?"

"Eh?" said Jack, staring at Michael like he'd forgotten he was there.

"Why don't you lead t' way?"

"Suppose I can."

"Yer did when we were kids, remember?"

"Don't mind."

"Dun't feel right, me up front."

"Don't mind."

Jack led the way along the rest of the path and over the swing bridge, but, as they strode up the boggy fields' more open spaces, between ancient walls of limestone, through herds of Friesian cows and flocks of sheep, Michael got to walking alongside him. The farmers had been muck-spreading nearby and the air were ripe with it. Yet there were crocus clusters here and there and bluebells would soon be emerging in the copses. Spring was peeping through. Wouldn't be long afore she were in full bloom. Michael couldn't wait to be here with Elsa, when all the flowers were out and the trees in leaf. She could bring her watercolours. He'd make them a Bowers' Butcher's picnic.

"It was Tracy who found him," said Jack, as they crossed the third field.

"Aye, I heard," said Michael.

"Poor lass. If they'd not broken up from school the day before..."

"There's nowt you could have done about that."

"Nowt I could have done?" said Jack, stopping and looking straight at Michael, eyes flickering in the cold sunshine. "You off ya rocker or summat?"

"I mean about Tracy breaking up from..."

"Nowt I could have done? Fuckin' hell."

They moved on a while, across the cattle-trodden acres, over rickety stiles, through wooden gates with iron fasteners. Michael picked up a stick and found himself swishing at thistles, like when he were a kid, until Jack told him to pack it in. He'd sounded pretty pissed off. But you'd got to leave him be. Let him do what he needed to.

At least he seemed to have calmed down by the time they were nearing the stream which led to the waterfall, when he mentioned his little sister again.

"Tracy doted on Dad, mate."

"I know she did."

"No wonder, seeing as he treated her like a princess. They doted on each other, to tell t' truth. Not that he didn't want the best for me an all, Micky. Don't be thinkin' that."

"Course not," said Michael, wanting to whack summat

with his stick.

"Just because he could be a bastard to me doesn't mean he didn't care, ya know."

"Course."

"I've allus known that about him, actually."

"Good, mate."

"Oh aye, no bother on that score," said Jack, swinging open the gate to the last field before the stream.

Michael glanced at him once or twice as they walked side by side. Had he put more purpose in his stride, now he'd got a bee in his bonnet about how much his dad supposedly used to care for him? There looked to be some determination on his face, anyhow. You could glimpse a bit of the fighter in him again. He'd need a fair lot of fight to get over this, wouldn't he? And to get his sister and mum through it. Not to mention all the other things he'd have to help get sorted. Like going through his old man's stuff for a kick off. Deciding what to keep or get rid of were trauma in itself. Michael would never forget how it was eight years since. Sitting on the stairs, listening to his mum go through some of his dad's belongings in what had been their bedroom. Doing her best not to cry because she knew her boy would hear, but not being able to stop herself.

Thinking of what had belonged to *Jack's* dad, Michael knew the shop had been the jewel in his crown, and what were the family going to do about Hargraves' Butchers now? His mum seemed knackered, so she'd likely not have the heart to run it. They'd have to get a manager in. Or else sell up. What would that be like? A new rival butcher in the village? If a buyer wanted to keep the place as a butcher's shop. Could end up as summat else. If they thought like Rodney Hargraves had, that sooner or later there'd only be room enough in Fowlbeck for one butchers. They might think it, especially when they saw how respected and established Bowers' shop was. How grand would that be? No competition. No need to worry...Flipping heck, what the hell are you playing at? Thinking like that on today of all days. Bloody shameful!

When they reached the lively stream, they stood beside it a moment and watched the fresh water washing over its mossy stones. Michael listened to its gentle murmur.

"She dotes on me now," said Jack.

"Yer what?"

"Tracy. I said, she dotes on me."

"She's allus looked up to you," said Michael.

"Aye, but these past few days it's like I'm her surrogate father or summat."

"Oh."

Michael wished he could find the right words. Jack plunged his hands into his coat's pockets again and sort of drew his head back into its collar, like a preyed on animal hiding in its shell.

"She follows me round all t' time," he said. "Same as a lapdog. Dead clingy. Be easier if she put some blame on me, like Mum does. I'm tellin' ya, I can't stand it. Nearly told her to fuck off once or twice. How shite is that, Micky? I mean, what sort of a person am I? Only thing that stops me is knowing her childhood's in ruins."

After another silence, Michael offered Jack the stick, saying he might find good use for it hacking away undergrowth on the stretch upstream to the waterfall.

"Well, thee's best at bein' up front, remember?"

Jack took the stick and set off in front. They edged slowly toward the hidden spot which used to be their secret den, walking in the stream where it was shallow, and through the undergrowth on its banks in places where the water would have sloshed over their welly tops. The narrow route grew darker as it cut deeper into the rocky earth, but it weren't long afore Michael cottoned on to the sound of the waterfall. And, a minute or so later, as they rounded the final bend in the stream, it set his heart off faster to hear the full force of it. Then the space widened into a horseshoe shape and there they stood, under the bright, cloudless sky again, looking up at that lovely cascade of white water glinting in the sunshine.

"A reet beauty, in't she?" said Michael.

"You forget, don't ya?" said Jack. "Seems smaller than it used to."

They moved about separately in The Waterfall Den a while, as if they were in need of rediscovering it alone at first. Michael was after taking it all in. His eyes traced the tangles of ivy creeping over the walls of layered limestone rock. When he got down on his haunches to search for what grew, he could smell the damp decay of fallen leaves left over from autumn. He touched the smooth bark of an ash tree stretching up toward the light. But it was the waterfall he really wanted to get near. Remembered being drawn to it when he were a nipper. Likely Dad's influence. Teaching him the wonder of nature, the power of it. And this was a force of nature, right enough. He skirted the deep pool at the bottom of it to get up close. Flipping heck, the rush of noise in his ears, the shock of freezing spray on his face! If you were in need of a liven up, this was the place.

Michael looked through the spray at Jack, a few yards away. Them fine, sun-sparkled droplets gave him a sort of golden glow, despite his black clothes. He were by where they used to hide their collection of objects, his coat and suit sleeves pushed up, his hands feeling around in the rock's nooks and crannies. A few years since, he'd been in his element in charge of the collection... Hold up, he's found summat now...Two things...Grasping one in each hand. And now he's moved to stand next to that big slab of moss-covered stone on the ground by the stream, the one you used for your blood brother ceremony that time when he scared you a bit. He's gesturing for you to go over.

Michael jumped over the stream, to stand opposite Jack on the other side of the mossy stone, and saw that he'd found the belt buckle and mystery seashell. He seemed more interested in the buckle than the shell. Proper rusted up, it were. Not polished and shiny, like how they used to keep it. Jack held it up to the blue sky and stared at it.

"What about our mystery seashell?" said Michael. "Still full o' t' sound of far off places?"

"Dad used to have a buckle similar to this," said Jack. "On one of his belts."

The way he'd said that, Michael wondered what job, other than holding up trousers, that belt had been used for.

"Suppose there'll be lots of similar belt buckles kickin' about, Lanky. You still got our logbook at home? Wouldn't mind having a gander at that again. For old times' sake."

Jack put the seashell in his coat pocket, held the belt buckle at waist height, rubbed away at the rust with his thumbs. Michael could hear him muttering something to himself. He wasn't right sure how much of it he'd caught, though, what with the noise of the waterfall: 'Have a... Kip now... Goodbye... Friend...'? But then Jack, eyes still on the buckle, thumbs still rubbing the rust, started talking directly to him and speaking up.

"Fought in The North African Campaign, Dad, Micky. Helped defeat Rommel in t' desert. All heroes, those men. Courageous men. Dad included. Don't get me wrong, they'd have taken peace any day o' t' week. But what choice did they have, eh? Wi' them murdering Nazi cunts after killing

owt in their way? What must it have been like, knowin'
you might get blasted to fuck any minute? What must that
have been like, eh? Can you tell me? No, what do we know
about it? Nowt. Send you fuckin' bonkers, it would. Shells
exploding round your head. Wonderin' how long it'd be
before one ripped your face off. Aye, what do we know about
what that does to a bloke? Fucks him up for t' rest of his born
days, I'd say. What do you think, Micky, lad? How old do
you reckon he was back then? I've worked it out. Our age.
I'm not muckin' about. Nineteen, twenty at most. Can you
put ya sen in his army boots at nineteen?"

"No, I can't..."

"Naa, what do we know?"

Jack was scratching hard at the rusty buckle with his
thumbnails now, as if desperate to find some shiny silver
underneath. Michael wanted to take it off him. It were
worrying, seeing him that way. He had started opening up,
mind. Good and proper.

"You know t' worst of it, Michael? He saw his friend
die in that desolate place. That's reet. Harry...Harry was his
name. Died in Dad's arms, he did. Dad comforted him in his
final moments. 'Goodbye, my friend.' Helped him as best he
could. Because he had that in him, mate. I know he did. Can
you imagine going through summat like that? What do we
know, eh? I mean, how would you not be scarred by it? Spent
t' rest of his days knowing how tough life could be...And...
And...And now I can see it. That's why he was a bastard to
me sometimes. Toughenin' me up, that's all. Trying to help
me. In his own fucked up way, he was actually doin' his best
to protect me."

Michael had his own ideas on that score, but he kept his
gob shut. Then Jack stopped scratching the buckle and, tears
swelling in his eyes, looked straight at him over the blood

brother stone, like he were pleading with him.

"I should have been more peaceful to him, Micky. Should have been more peaceful."

"You can't keep blamin' yer sen," said Michael.

"Easy for you to say," said Jack, a tear slipping down his face.

"Sorry, I don't get you?"

"Well, you've never had to feel guilt o'er your dad, have ya?"

"We'd probably best head back, eh?"

"Your perfect dad."

"I were in t' car wi' him, Jack," said Michael. "He started drivin' daft because o' me. To set me off laughing. If it hadn't been for me, he'd still be alive. And what did I come out wi'? Not a scratch."

Michael suddenly had a struggle on fighting his anger. He knew Jack was messed up, that he wasn't in control of what he were saying, but he'd hit a flipping nerve there all right. He looked into his teary eyes and saw the blank stare below that long black fringe. Just remember what he's going through.

"You've got to help me, Micky," said Jack.

"Course I will."

"Remember this stone we're standing o'er?"

"Aye, I do," said Michael.

"We're blood brothers."

"Always."

"Don't forget it," said Jack. "My blood's in yours. Your blood's in mine."

"That's reet."

"You've got to be there for me."

"Always, Lanky."

Michael listened to the waterfall a moment. Then Jack

said something else.

"I came round to yours last night."

"Mum said. Sorry, I..."

"You were out."

"Aye, I was," said Michael.

"You and Elsa."

"Me and Elsa."

"But it's me who needs you," said Jack.

"I din't..."

"You've got to help folk in life."

Michael felt himself getting more riled, as if that blood of Jack's he had in him were firing up his own. Jack had got to gawping at the belt buckle on his palms, though. Like he'd discovered a rare butterfly or summat. And, because his palms were facing the sky and his sleeves were still rolled up, you could see the inner sides of his forearms and wrists. Scarred with crisscross cuts, they were. Right red and raw. Michael's anger turned to shock.

"What yer done to your arms?" he said, pointing.

"Eh?" said Jack, looking up.

"Not been hurtin' yer sen, have you?"

"That? It's nowt."

"Oh, mate."

"Needed to do it, that's all."

"Bloody hell."

"Used to do it years since. Never let on to you, mind. Well, you are a worrier."

Michael could feel a tear running down his cheek now. Then Jack was looking at him with a load of concern on his face and reaching across to wipe the tear away with a rust-smudged thumb.

"Don't worry, Michael," he said. "Everything's going to be all right. I'm here for ya. It's gonna be fine and dandy.

Promise. You've got to help folk in life. Do the right thing. Don't worry, Micky, lad. I'll be here for you. I mean, not goin' anywhere now, am I? Got to stay put and take on Dad's shop. Can't leave him in t' lurch anymore, can I?"

AUTUMN 1989

CHAPTER FIFTEEN

J ack had loved being high up since climbing trees as a lad, so the modern, top floor flat he'd not long been renting was just the job. Tucked away in the roof of a converted Victorian house set on the hillside, he could see far and wide from his dormer window with its three glazed sides. He was standing in the dormer now, on this cloudy Sunday morning in early October. From here, directly above the top of the High Street, you could look out over Fowlbeck, see a fair way up and down the dale, look across at the heathery Beacon, turned from summer purple to autumn brown. The narrow village streets were pretty deserted as yet. He'd just been for a stroll to get the paper and there was barely one man and his dog about. Well, what did folk have to get up early for on a Sunday round here? Excepting a Yorkshire breakfast. On his way back from the newsagents, he'd smelt one frying somewhere and got to wondering whether it was Hargraves' or Bowers' bacon sizzling in the pan. Michael would likely tell you. Had a nose for it. No wonder. In his blood and marrow, wasn't it?

Apart from the odd early riser, Fowlbeck was still asleep and it made Jack fancy some sleepy jazz. He ambled over to the stereo, pressed the power button and slipped the album he'd lately bought from a record shop in Leeds out of its sleeve. You could get a lot on compact disk these days, but the proper best stuff was still only on vinyl. This one was a classic, Miles Davis's 'Kind of Blue'. He set it spinning on the turntable and, with the small lever at the side, lowered the stylus onto it. Static crackled through the speakers. Shite, turn that volume down before Miles drifts in. Clare's still asleep. Better not wake her.

As the quietened music started, he wandered across the room to the bedroom door he'd left open, leaned against the doorframe, watched Clare sleeping a moment. She was only partly under the duvet and those naked curves were a tempter all right. He'd been seeing her just a few weeks, but he'd found out three or four times already that she wasn't averse to sex before breakfast. She'll likely want to run her hands through your thick black hair before long, rip this denim shirt off your back, unbutton your 501 jeans. He was definitely getting in with her again soon. She was fucking lovely. And she fucked lovely as well. But he had other things on his mind too.

Jack went back to the dormer window, pulled up what had been his dad's armchair, a hollow made by the old man's backside still there years later in the creased leather seat, and settled in to read The Observer. A decent spot, this dormer. When he was nowt but a kid, he'd have likely imagined it a cockpit with him at the controls, flying above a little world. Dad, given the choice, would have doubtless had it down as a Spitfire.

As he began turning the broadsheet pages, getting whiffs of dirty newsprint, glimpsing inky smudges on his thumbs, he couldn't help but notice how much was in the paper again this week about the anti-communist protests in Eastern Europe. He'd been following events in the Baltic States, Poland, the German Democratic Republic for months now, half wanting to be out there on the frontline, mucking in with the rest of the freedom fighters. That peaceful Baltic Chain of Freedom in August, two million people linking arms between the three capitals, had fairly sparked memories of Greenham Common back in '83, hadn't it? As if he'd ever have time to get involved in owt like that these days, though. With Hargraves' Butchers to run? Fat lot of good it had done him last time, anyway. But perhaps he should join in with one of those marches Clare went on. Sometimes he didn't have a frigging clue, did he?

Well, at least he cared about folk fighting for their freedom. More than you could say for some people in Fowlbeck. And the times had been a-changin' all over the shop this year. Bob Dylan could do a remix with Jive Bunny, no bother, there'd been that much going on. How about these so called celebrations in Berlin yesterday, to mark forty years of communist rule? He scanned the double page spread with photos of Honecker laying it on thick for guest of honour, Gorbachev. Look at that, thousands lining the streets. Not celebrating their government, but protesting against it. **'GORBI! GORBI! HILF UNS!'** one banner said. Reading a couple of paragraphs, it looked like Gorbachev was up for helping too. Was he a freedom fighter, then? Go on, Mikhail, lad, stick it to 'em! Jack had always known protestors could make a difference. Pity you couldn't do it from an armchair, eh?

When he'd finished reading about yesterday in Berlin, he noticed that Miles Davis's trumpet had ditched its sleepy tone and was now doing high-pitched somersaults at breakneck speed. Was there owt the guy couldn't do? You had to wonder if those frantic notes had woken Clare, despite the speakers being turned down low. Jack gripped the paper in one hand, then turned round to kneel on the chair and look over its back. No, you could see her still sleeping through the bedroom doorway, her body moving gently with her breathing. Couldn't blame the lass, being in a right comfy bed like that. Same as most stuff in this mainly open-plan, clean-smelling, cutting edge place, with its sharp lines and gleaming black and white surfaces, it was top quality. Looking about, everything was fine and dandy. The yuppie landlord had not scrimped on expense, had he? He'd said everything was the latest in design and technology when he'd done his guided tour. The spotlighting in the kitchen area, the new television, the video recorder, the shagpile rugs and plumped up three-piece suite. He'd even seemed proper chuffed with his bookshelves, which he reckoned were from Sweden. By all accounts, the trendiest place for bookshelf design these days. 'I kid you not,' he'd said. Silly twat. More important what you had on them than where they were designed, wasn't it? The 'Tiananmen Square Tank Man' picture, which Jack had bought and hung above the shelves, seemed to say as much. You'd never forget that image, would you? Four monster tanks lining up. And this ordinary bloke, holding a carrier bag or summat, like he's just popped into Happy Shopper, standing slap bang in their path. Jack turned back round and sat down. What was it that gave some people such courage?

It might have been a minute later, maybe five, when a bright red pram being steered down the High Street in the grey day made Jack realise he was gawping out of the dormer again. Michael and Elsa and their newborn baby boy. He folded his newspaper, placed it on the arm of the chair, stood up to get closer to the windowpane. Where were they off to, then? Maybe a wander by the river. Doubtless Micky would be skimming stones with his nipper before he knew what was happening to him. Once they'd got it out of nappies. Folk did say time flew when you had sprogs. Jack had already lost count of how many of his punters had uttered summat like: 'They'll not know where t' years have gone, they grow up that fast.' Mr and Mrs Michael Bowers seem happy enough, mind. Well, suppose it's what they want. Each to their own and all that. And the baby is cute. Jack had held him once and he had to admit it. But it was a relief when the little sausage started blubbering and he was forced to give him back. He wasn't much cop at the coo-cooing lark. And he'd kept wanting to crack up when he looked at the poor kid, because of what they'd called him. A great honour, being named after his grandad. But 'Bernard'? For a baby? Frigging hell. With a name like that, you'd be wanting the years to fly by just so you could reach an age where it didn't sound so daft. Could be worth a bet on Bernard looking older quicker than most babies, though. Knowing his daddy, he'd have him in a flat cap at six months.

They'd stopped at the bottom of the High Street now. Elsa fiddling with the pram, by the looks of it. Micky shaking a toy for Bernard. He seemed to have taken to fatherhood, no bother. Jack had to hand it to him, because he was totally knackered, what with the family shop *and* a shiny new arrival. Suppose he was a bit tougher these days. Whatever you think of Elsa, she has been good for him. Not that he's given over being too sensitive. He didn't take kindly to that sign you put up outside your shop a few weeks back, did he?

'TRADITION'S TRADITION. BUT TRY SOMETHING *DIFFERENT.'*

When the Bowers had set off again and Jack had watched them disappear round the corner, the music stopped and he heard the stylus crackle as it lifted automatically off the record. Felt like the static had clung to the air and prickled his skin with electricity. He'd not meant owt by that sign, had he? Shame it had caused more tension between him and Michael. But all he wanted was a fair slice of the action. Just after doing right by his family, wasn't he? Whether he liked it or not, he still had an obligation to his mother and sister. For the time being, anyway. Things could always change, like in Europe, but sometimes you'd got to do right in life. Even if it wasn't what you'd dreamt of. Sometimes, you'd got to make the best of a bad job and carry on fighting. And, for as long as he had to stay in Fowlbeck, the least he deserved was a fair slice.

"Jack!"

Clare? He went to the bedroom door. She'd thrown back the duvet and was sitting up dead straight in the middle of the bed. Her naked body looked right warm against the dull light. He could almost smell her from the doorway. Smell how beautiful she was. Fuck, he wanted her. But she'd got such a stern face on.

"What's the matter, Clare?" he said.

"Shut up. Take all your clothes off and get in this bed. Now."

So that's how it's going to be this morning.

In the late afternoon, before Jack gave Clare a lift back home to Leeds, they set off to his mum's for tea and biscuits. Mother had been edging her nose in for a week or two now, nattering him to bring his latest girlfriend round to meet her and Tracy: 'Folk who've seen her in t' village say she's near enough as tall as you, Son. And very elegant. It'd be grand meeting her. Tracy's plannin' on making shortbread and brandy snaps.' Jack had suggested driving the half mile or so and going straight on to Leeds afterwards. But, because they'd been inside most of the day, reading the newspaper, jumping into bed, Clare fancied fresh air. And so, with the sky clear now, they walked to the Hargraves' family home.

He held her hand up Sugar Hill Lane and along the snicket, where ash leaves were yellowing and brambles, their fruit scarce and shrunken in the new season, snaked among the hedgerows.

"Used to pick blackberries down here wi' Mum every summer," he said.

"Did you make jam?"

"Oh aye."

"Oh aye," she said, her silver teardrop earrings shimmery in the low sunlight.

"You tekin' the piss?" he said.

"Oh aye."

He stopped and kissed her.

"I like how you speak," she said, stroking his stubbly Sunday face. "And how you kiss."

They stood there a few moments, looking into each other's eyes. Jack reckoned Clare's could have been cut from sapphire. And those cheekbones were like sculpture. That short blonde hair you always wanted to touch. Those lips. What Mum had heard about her being elegant was right enough too. No point denying it. There was nowt quite as good as being seen out and about with a woman like Clare. Other blokes got jealous. You could tell when they tried too hard to act natural around her. Jack enjoyed watching them work their bollocks off attempting to be cool. Drinkers offering her cigarettes at the bar in The Dog and Gun. Mucky farmers, caked in mud at that country show last month, getting a bit too friendly with their chatter at the stall where Clare had helped promote Hargraves' new bakery range.

"Come on, then," she eventually said, smiling at him. "I want to meet your mum and sister."

As a blackbird sang, they started walking along the snicket again, their fingers interlocked, the edge of her woollen poncho tickling the back of his hand. It wasn't just her beauty, her elegance, the way she sent men gormless that Jack liked about her. She was an interesting person. And she'd travelled fairish, seen a bit of the world. Where had he been? Ibiza once, on an '18-30' holiday with the lads. The Isle of Man twice, with Micky for the motorbike TT Races. Clare had been to university as well, like Jack had wanted to. And now she was helping others. Disadvantaged folk. Giving them some freedom in life. Doing summat worthwhile. Hard to believe she was only twenty-two. Three years younger than him and look what she'd done already.

When they reached the last bit of the snicket, they turned into the alley, the smell of yesterday's rain still on its mottled limestone, and began walking down the back of the row of big semi-detached houses where Mum and Tracy lived at the far end.

"What are you thinking about?" said Clare.

"Nothing."

"You must be thinking about something. Besides, I can tell by your face."

"You've copped me," said Jack. "Liberty, then."

"Liberty?"

"Aye, freedom. Imagine living in East Berlin right now."

"With freedom perhaps so close?" she said.

"Tantalising," he said, almost tasting the word as it shaped on his tongue.

"Must have been dreadful, having your liberty snatched away like that."

"Do you think The Wall's gettin' bulldozed before long, then?"

"If the will of the people has anything to do with it," she said. "But that's not always enough, is it?"

"Not when it's got dictatorship to contend with."

"Oh, I don't think Gorbachev is a dictator."

"Oh no," he said. "But he's still got to work within the Soviet system, hasn't he? The *apparatus* of dictatorship."

"That is an excellent point."

He was glad it was an excellent point.

"I think he's already started dismantling the system, though," she said. "Honecker's looking more like a lame duck too."

"Especially after yesterday."

Jack loved talking to Clare about this stuff, but soon he was knocking on the back door of the last semi in the row. Then he could hear Mum's little tapping footsteps approaching like toy clogs on the wooden kitchen floor, catch the smell of Tracy's baking coming from the Aga.

Mum, looking fine and dandy in her brightly coloured Sunday best dress, asked Clare whether she'd like to go through to the lounge for afternoon tea. Clare thanked her, but said it felt cosy in the kitchen with the Aga on. Jack was sitting at the head of the kitchen table now. Mum and Clare were just in front of him, sitting opposite one another, chatting across Mum's swirly pink and gold china, waiting for the tea to mash. Looking down the table between them, Jack could see Tracy a few feet away. She was standing by the Aga, her apron doing nowt to cover up the size she'd got to these days, sliding a spatula under pieces of buttery-smelling shortbread, being right careful as she lifted them from the baking tray to a cooling rack.

"That shortbread smells the business, Sis," said Jack.

"I can't wait to try a piece," said Clare.

"And don't forget my little girl's brandy snaps, Clare," said Mum. "Has Jack not told you about those, then?"

"No. The first I knew of them was just now, when Tracy put them in to bake."

"What were you playin' at, Son?"

"No better surprise than one o' my sister's brandy snaps. Is there, lass?"

"Ja-ack," said Tracy, in a near whisper, looking embarrassed.

"Stop ribbin' her," said Mum. "You know how fragile she is. Aren't you, Tracy?"

"Give over, Mother," said Jack. "I'm tellin' her how good she is. And you're not fragile, are ya, Sis?"

Mum glared at him over those puffy semicircles under her eyes, before getting back to chewing the fat with Clare. Forever protective of her daughter, wasn't she? More so these past six years. Especially in new company, when Tracy tended to get shier than usual. About time Mother eased off. Suppose you could understand it, mind. Frigging hell, it was probably down to Jack that Tracy was like that, anyway. Not that Mum ever let him forget it. She had her sly ways of dropping a hint now and again, just to remind him of his obligations and keep him on his toes. It made him right fidgety sometimes. Even now, after one disapproving look, he caught himself tugging at his shirtsleeves, fiddling with the ring on his finger.

"What do you do, then, Clare?" said Mum, leaning forward slightly, as if she had an inkling the answer might be tasty like Tracy's baking. "Jack mentioned beggars in Leeds."

"I didn't say beggars. I said homeless people."

"Sorry, Clare. Homeless people, not beggars."

Clare showed no sign of getting riled at Mum saying 'beggars' as if it was a manky word. She'd likely be a bit narked inside, but Jack had never met anyone with such poise.

"I work for a homeless charity, Mrs Hargraves," she said, calm as the river on a breezeless day. "And many of the homeless people we're working with have been forced into begging to survive."

"Well, that's smashin', sweetheart," said Mum. "That's really nice."

"What, for the poor buggers begging?" said Jack.

"I mean, the work that Clare does."

Jack knew what she meant. He watched her lift the lid off the teapot to check on the brew, then dip a clinking teaspoon inside to give it a stir. Was that what you were supposed to do when you invited folk round for tea and biscuits? Clare didn't bat an eyelid. But Clare wouldn't.

"Tea still needs a minute or two," said Mum. "How much longer for those brandy snaps, Tracy?"

"Comin' out soon," said Tracy, red-faced, oven gloves on, quietly putting the now empty baking tray in the sink.

"Must be rewarding, that kind of work," said Mum, turning to Clare again.

"It can be. Yet frustrating at times. There's a lot involved. As well as the practical day to day stuff, like providing food and shelter for people, there's the fundraising, the lobbying of local government. But do you know what I think our greatest challenge is?"

"What is it, sweetheart?"

"The mental health issues we're facing out there on the streets," said Clare. "The terribly low sense of self-esteem felt by those we're trying to help."

"I see."

"People feel trapped in a situation which they often regard as their own fault."

"Yes, I can understand that," said Mum.

So can I, thought Jack.

"But homelessness can happen to anyone, " said Clare, upturning her hands as if to show what it was like to have to beg.

Jack could see her getting passionate about the issue. It made him fancy joining in.

"Thatcher's Britain, eh?" he said, wishing he'd mustered summat more interesting.

Mum shot him another glare. Loved Thatcher, didn't

she? Same as the old man had.

"There are two former millionaires that I know of living on the streets of Leeds at the moment," said Clare.

"Millionaires?"

"Yes, Mrs Hargraves. As I say, homelessness can happen to anyone."

"Are you listenin' to this, Son? Best keep your father's shop up and running."

And she was off jabbering away to Clare again, only this time about Hargraves' Butchers. Jack noticed how Clare kept a smile on her face and had her head tilted to one side a bit, like she was fascinated by what Mum was offering up. But those sapphire eyes were definitely blinking fairish, as if to remind her not to show that she was actually bored out of her skull. Made him think of when he'd first met her in that Leeds wine bar a few Saturday nights since, and how he'd sensed her hiding her surprise when he said he ran a butcher's shop out in the sticks.

Mother's little mouth was going ten to the dozen now. It put Jack in mind of the Samuel Beckett monologue he'd seen on BBC2 recently. He couldn't remember what the play was called. It was just a woman's mouth, though. Talking. Everything else blacked out. The whole stage, the woman, most of her face. Excepting her mouth, gabbing away. Strangest thing he'd ever seen. So strange he'd found it hard to listen to what the woman was saying. Mum's gob got through some work these days too, didn't it? Fucking hell, she'd become a right chatterbox. It was like, after Dad died, all he'd suppressed in her had come flooding out in words that wouldn't stop flowing. She'd never utter a word against her dead husband, mind. He'd been a bastard to her, you couldn't deny it, but she'd stayed loyal to him as yet. Till death do us part and then some. Jack doubted she'd ever hitch up with anyone else.

Perhaps it was some of the old man's things that had stayed put in the kitchen which made him think that way too. His model battleship, tank, Lancaster Bomber, on that shelf, looked like they'd been lined up to ward off any back door chancer for a kick off. Then there was his fishing rod still hanging on the wall above the PVC window, loaded with blood-red fly hook, as if he'd left it primed to catch sly widowers and fling them back over the threshold like knackered old trout. And you couldn't ignore his pipe on its stand in the middle of the stone mantelpiece, which seemed to need nowt but its sturdy permanence to keep any local Lotharios at bay.

Mum's mouth was still blithering on about the shop... About what a smashing job Dad had done building it up... About how important it was that Jack kept... But, like with the Beckett monologue, you could block out the words if you buckled down and stared at those lips moving. Forming 'O' shapes... Thin straight lines... A grimace... A grin... She did wind Jack up at times, especially when she badgered him about the business, but he was chuffed for her in a way. Her voice might have been in danger of wearing out, but at least it wasn't squeaky and downtrodden anymore. And, credit to her, she was a stronger person than before. More confident. Walked more upright. Wore brighter clobber. She'd ditched the grey hair, dyed it brunette. She looked younger than she had six years since. And the energy in her! Frigging hell, you'd never have guessed it. Look at how many Fowlbeck societies and committees she was involved in now. Could just do with losing that shell suit she'd started wearing while organising jumble sales and whist drives. That and the bigotry she sometimes let slip from her lips. Mothers, eh? Anyway, she was in a better state these days. Like she'd ever admit it, but a better state than when the old man had been around.

Now Mum must have stopped to take breath or summat, because there was a moment quiet enough for Jack to hear a sigh from Tracy near the Aga. She looked flustered and sweaty, as she set out the shortbread on that posh three-plate tower arrangement with the thin gilt pillar running up its middle. Better go check she's all right.

He went to her, saw she was fretting over getting the shortbread pieces perfectly spaced on the bottom plate, put an arm round her, turned her slightly so they had their backs to Mum and Clare.

"Stop stressin'," he said softly. "Clare won't be bothered."

"She's like a princess, though," whispered Tracy, as she carried on trying to space the shortbread.

"Aye, she is. But she's no fusspot."

"I just want it doin' right, Jack."

"You're mekin' a great job. It's lovely what you're doing."

"Oh, why do these plates slope toward t' middle? Shortbread keeps slidin'."

"Chill out, eh?"

But Tracy wasn't one for chilling out. Excepting maybe when she worked at the stables. Sometimes, on his way back from delivering meat down the dale, Jack would pick her up to take her home and he could see how the horses settled her. Once or twice, he'd switched off the engine so she'd not hear the butcher's van, freewheeled down the dirt track, put the handbrake on behind the barn at the top of the field where the stables were. Then got out and stood at a barn corner, watching her too engrossed to look up, while she groomed the piebald or soothed her favourite, the headstrong grey, with that right quiet voice of hers. He loved seeing her peaceful. Jack wished she was that way more often. Didn't like herself, though, did she? Ate too much comfort food, wore massive cardigans to cover the consequence. Did that nervous thing with her fingertips, touching her face loads, as if trying to massage it lean again. And she couldn't look folk in the eye, could she? Life shouldn't be that way for a lass of nineteen. She should be out enjoying herself on the razzle-dazzle of an evening. Not stuck inside doing cross-stitch with Mum. Or shut in her room listening to Jason Donovan. There were fuck all answers in that. He couldn't stand how things had turned out for her. Sometimes when he thought of it he got this image in his head. A girl, barely a teenager, kneeling beside her daddy laid out on the snow. His last breath in the frosty air, thinning to nothing. Why had Tracy never cast blame on her big brother? It was more like she blamed herself.

"Can't do it," she muttered, still bent over the pieces of shortbread. "They won't stop still."

"What about puttin' a paper doily on t' plate?" said Jack.

"Doilies. How come I forgot them? You're brill, Jack. Why am I so useless?"

"You're not..."

But before he could finish she'd set off to fetch a packet of doilies from a kitchen cupboard. Seconds later, she was returning the shortbread from the bottom plate to the cooling rack, then reaching for scissors from a top drawer, cutting a doily to its centre, fitting it dead carefully round the little gilt pillar. And now, starting to place the shortbread on the plate again, she let out another sigh. Only, this time, Jack could hear relief in it. He felt relieved too. That doily's doing the trick: **'Paper Doily Averts Afternoon Tea Disaster'**. Maybe it would make The Observer next Sunday.

As Jack watched Tracy have a crack at the world

millimetre biscuit spacing title, he could hear Mum still carrying on to Clare about the shop.

"Eh, Sis," he said. "Mum's jaw's gonna drop off any minute."

Tracy glanced over her shoulder and had a quick laugh at that jaw going like billio. Then she smiled up at her brother, warm like the Aga, and got back to shortbread spacing.

What exactly was Mum blithering over now? Oh yes, today's CBI report predicting another recession. Jack had spotted it in the paper's business pages this morning, skimmed over it sharpish. And she was on about supermarkets flexing their muscles again. Say summat he didn't think about near as damn it every day. She could mention high interest rates and an albatross business loan, thanks to the old man's bouts of spending on the shop, too if she fancied. How about the fact he'd not taken out any life insurance either? That was a belter. You could do half an hour's 'stand up' on the whole frigging scenario.

"No, you've landed a smashin' lad really, Clare," said Mum. "I'll admit it, Tracy and I do rely on him to keep Hargraves' Butchers in rude health, as his father was fond of saying. Yes, there's Tracy's part-time job at the stables. But it's got to feed three, that shop, yer know. I'm sure he'd prefer to be gallivantin' off to Leeds to see you every day, sweetheart, but he's aware of his responsibilities here. You understand what I'm saying, don't you? No, he's doing a champion job, he really is."

"You tryin' to warn her off me, Mother?" said Jack, suddenly riled. "That brew mashed yet?"

"Bloomin' hummer, the tea," said Mum, her hand shooting to her mouth before lifting the lid off the china teapot again. "Do you prefer it strong, Clare?"

"I do, actually," said Clare.

"What a smasher you are. Isn't she, Jack? What a... What... What's that smell?"

As soon as Mum had asked the question, Jack could smell it too. Similar to burnt treacle.

"The brandy snaps!" screeched Tracy, grabbing the oven gloves.

She opened the Aga door, pulled out a smoking baking tray, stared at the two neat rows of rolled up brandy biscuits, part blackened, like they'd been welded to the metal. Then she looked up, the tray hanging pathetically in those oven-gloved hands. Jack just wanted to take his little sister away from there.

"Mum, the brandy snaps."

"Oh, Tracy," said Mum.

CHAPTER SIXTEEN

It put Michael in mind of midsummer, winding up the narrow lane toward Fowlbeck Beacon, sitting in the back of Eddie's new BMW convertible as it purred along, soft top down. You could see a light mist above them distant hills, Elsa had called it a milky sky a minute ago, but over The Beacon and nearby fields and copses it were pure blue. Must have been a long while since it had got this warm in mid-October too. More often than not nowadays, they'd have Sunday dinner at Mum and Eddie's, but it was such a grand day that all four of them had been inclined to a trip out. How could you beat a stroll up The Beacon's gentle eastern slopes and a Bowers' Butcher's picnic at the top? Besides, a certain bundle of joy would always be able to say he'd conquered the big hill at nowt but five months old. Good lad, Bernie! Michael gazed at his son strapped snugly in the baby seat between him and Elsa, that toothless mouth beaming up at Mummy acting the berk.

"Yes he is," said Elsa, slowly, eyes wide as saucers behind her thin-rimmed glasses. "Oh, yes he is. What is he? What... Is...He?" And then, zooming in, rubbing her nose against that tiny button one, speaking fast. "He's a bonnie bobby dazzler! A bonnie bobby dazzler!"

Michael couldn't weigh up what swelled his heart most. The anticipation on Bernie's little face afore the nose rub, or his squeal of delight when it happened. How come you got so lucky in life? At times these past few months the question had all but flummoxed him. But then, whenever he looked at Elsa, he saw the answer. She'd changed everything since... When did they get together? Six years ago? Six and a half?

"Just look at them chubby chops," said Elsa, giving

Bernie's cheeks a squeeze. "All rosy like Daddy's. Yes they are. Oh... Yes... They... Are."

"Hold up," said Michael. "Are mine rosy, then?"

"No, yours are more ruddy, love," said Mum, turning to him and smiling from the front passenger seat, her sunglasses and long dark hair giving her the look of a film star. "You've got ruddy cheeks."

"No need to be rude, Carol," said Eddie, at the wheel.

"And you've cheek enough for the lot of us, haven't you, Mr Weir?"

Mum reached over to give Eddie's black beard a teasing tug. He did his pirate impression.

"Why thank yee, Mrs Weir! Thank yee!"

A proper double act sometimes, weren't they, Mum and Stepfather? Eddie never needed much egging on, mind. Any excuse for some showing off or posing. Forever playing silly buggers, acting twenty instead of fifty. Nowt wrong with being young at heart, though, eh? Michael still reckoned Eddie was a bit of a knob, but he were right enough. At least you couldn't deny he made Mum happy. Not that it wasn't shit hearing her referred to by her second married name. She'd always be Mrs Bowers to Michael. But Mr Weir treated her with respect, he was thoughtful toward her, and he obviously loved her. Anyhow, Dad would have wanted Mum happy. That's the sort of man he was. Dad, the love of her life, would be chuffed for her. So, all told, how could you not think Eddie were right enough really? Even if he did look like a nasty sea captain nowadays, that bushy beard having overgrown them mutton-chop sideburns he used to have, that hooped gold earring swinging from his left ear.

"You sure yer not an actual pirate, Eddie?" said Michael.

"What's that you be callin' me, landlubber?"

"I be callin' thee an auld sea dog."

"Where be me cutlass?" said Eddie. "Where be me cutlass?"

"It be away wi' t' fairies," said Elsa. "Same as you."

Bernie must have cottoned on to the silly voices, because he suddenly let out a shriek of pleasure which got them all off laughing.

They soon reached the small gravel car park at the foot of Fowlbeck Beacon, the open-top's tyres scrunching to a stop next to a Land Rover, which looked in need of a right good wash alongside Eddie's sparkly metallic paintwork. Minutes later, hiking boots on, they were walking up The Beacon's thin muddy trail in single file, acres of flowerless heather stretching away from them on either side. Michael was at the back. He watched Elsa, just in front, that little wiggle of her hips catching his eye as usual. Then Mum, with her straight-backed walk which made her appear an inch or so taller than her five foot four. Then Eddie, leading the way with that swagger that made him look cocky, except it were starting to seem a bit daft, now he'd clocked up half a century in years. The three of them had rucksacks on their backs, carrying essentials. It reminded Michael of how, years since, Jack had to be in charge of the important stuff on Beacon expeditions. That were Jack Hargraves for you. Always after being top dog. Still the same nowadays. No mistake. But best give over dwelling on that. Michael had what was most precious of all on his back today. Baby Bernie in a framed canvas seat, making contented gurgling noises and playing with Daddy's ears.

The good thing about being last in single file was that you could stop for a gander at the view whenever you fancied without getting in anyone's way. And it were so beautiful this morning that, for the first part of the climb, Michael found himself stopping about every hundred yards. Bernie wasn't bothered, because he loved it each time his dad pretended to be an aeroplane, or did a run like a demented chicken to catch up again. Fairly giggled away to himself riding 'the chicken'. But, after a while, when the five of them got to a place where some limestone boulders along the edge of the trail looked like a row of decent seats to rest on, the grown-ups decided to sit down for a scan of the view.

"God's blessing us this morning, folks," said Mum, on her stone seat, pushing her sunglasses up into her hair.

"Aye, today's a belter in God's County," said Eddie.

"Fowlbeck looks a picture from up here."

"It does that, Grandma."

Michael noticed Mum's silence for a second or two, before she turned slowly to Eddie and spoke again.

"Would you have me down as a grandma?"

"Appen if grandmas were twenty one and gorgeous."

"Nice one, Eddie," said Elsa, taking a sketchpad and tin of artist's pencils from her rucksack. "Should be on Blind Date wi' a line like that, mate."

"Good answer, Contestant Number One," said Mum, reaching across to pat one of Eddie's strong builder's hands. "Might keep him a while yet, Elsa."

"Do yer not like bein' called Grandma, then, Mum?" said Michael.

"Course I do. Nothing makes me prouder. Just don't fancy looking like one."

"No need to fret on that score," said Elsa.

"Oh, love, you are sweet."

Michael watched Mum stand and kiss the top of her daughter-in-law's head, as Elsa sketched away, glancing back and forth between paper and autumn landscape. They were like sisters sometimes, weren't they? He'd hit the flipping jackpot there too.

Mum was standing beside Michael now, stretching her arms out toward Bernie, a smile across her face as broad as the one on Elsa's sunny-faced rave T-shirt. Bloody hell, T-shirts in October! They'd already edged past a couple of hikers coming down the trail with jumpers tied round their waists and a sweat on.

"Think it might be time for another cuddle with Grandma," said Mum.

"You goin' to Grandma for a bit, Bernie?" said Michael, pulling the lad's thumb from his earhole.

"Course he is. Aren't you, little man? Shall we go see Eddie? Eh? Shall we?"

Mum lifted Bernie from his canvas seat, cuddled him as she went to sit back down, started bouncing him on her knees.

"Who's a little bruiser, then?" she said. "Just like your daddy... Just like Daddy."

As Mum and Eddie fussed over Bernie and Elsa lost herself in drawing, Michael took in the dale below. Been here all his twenty-five years, hadn't he? He'd live the rest of his days here as well, no mistake. Why settle for elsewhere? No wonder they called Yorkshire God's County. You could reckon on the Big Bloke having used the rest of the world as practise, so he finished up in The Dales with perfect technique. Michael had always loved this countryside. Just like Dad. And he remembered Grandad Bowers being the same. Some of his earliest memories were of holding his hand through the fields, spotting farm animals and tractors and fish in the streams. Grandad had told him how he'd done similar with his grandad too. Except there wouldn't have been tractors round here in them days. Grandad's grandad, eh? Albert, founder of Bowers' Family Butchers.

Michael were glad Elsa felt the same about the countryside surrounding Fowlbeck as his family had since decades back. Meant they could love it together. And with Bernie too now. Elsa's inspiration, wasn't it? Mind you, you'd have to be blind, or else stupid, not to appreciate such a landscape as this. Especially on a day when the sun had the sky to itself. Them rolling hills seemed so green in this light they almost shone. And the early autumn leaves looked like yellow and russet flames in the sunshine. Vibrant as flowers in bloom. Funny how nowadays Michael sometimes saw things the way Elsa did. Like a painting. She were only a couple of feet from him and so he leaned over to see how her pencil drawing was coming on.

"Did yer not bring colours today, darlin'?" he said, looking at the shades of grey.

"Grey's a colour too, me darlin'," she said, sketching in a dark little cube for one of the farm buildings dotted about.

"Aye, it is."

"When there's so much colour, folk often as not miss what's most interesting."

"Don't get yer?"

"The shadows, me laddo, the shadows."

And she were away in her own world again. In art, same as life, she didn't let much pass her by, did she? Michael used to tell himself he had a sharp eye for nature until he'd been out with Elsa once or twice, watching her at the easel. Not surprising she'd sold one or two paintings. Brilliant, she was. Flipping heck, he loved her.

A few minutes later, as Michael listened to the calls of grouse nestling in the nearby dry-smelling heather, he heard Bernie giggling like a mad allik. He looked to his left, past Elsa, and there was his son on Eddie's knees now, mesmerised by that pirate beard and pulling on it with his tiny hands. Eddie acting daft, shaking his head as if trying to wrestle free. Bernie going nuts for it. Mum and Elsa laughing too now. Suppose it were a laugh. Bernie adored Eddie, didn't he? You'd just as well admit it. Whenever he saw him, his little face lit up. No use denying it. Likely a good thing, anyhow. He'd learn of his proper grandad when he got old enough to understand. Understand what a wonderful man he was, what he'd done for his family and Bowers' Butchers. Then he'd see why he'd been named after Grandad Bernard. Perhaps he'd be inspired by him, like Elsa was by the Yorkshire landscape. Maybe inspired enough to run the shop one day. Bloody hell, you couldn't be mapping out the lad's future already. It were the worrier in Michael that had him thinking that way. Been dealing better with his worrying of late, though, hadn't he? Likely just the old habit. What had he to fret over anymore? Life was perfect, wasn't it?

"Shall we crack on, then?" he said, edging past Elsa and turning his back to Eddie so he could slot Bernie into the canvas seat again. "Best see if we can reach t' top afore me boy wants feeding."

When Bernie was safely in place, they continued in the same order as before up the gradual slope. As they climbed higher, it stayed warm for autumn, but the air started to feel a bit cooler on Michael's ruddy cheeks, crisper in his throat. After a while, he saw a red kite gliding above the dale and tried pointing it out to Bernie. The lad was too content blowing raspberries to bother about owt as graceful as a bird of prey, though. But he would in time, wouldn't he? Course he would. It were daft stressing about that.

More people were walking down The Beacon toward them now. Mostly Fowlbeck folk, so they had to keep stopping for a natter. Michael liked it that a lot of the older generation, even when they were skiving off church for a hike in the hills, still dressed in clothes akin to traditional Sunday best. He might have been in brown cords and checked shirt for the walk today, but many a time of a Sunday he'd be out in smarter trousers and one of his tweed jackets. Not that he didn't take to the modern clobber his own generation had a preference for, he wasn't averse to wearing the brighter stuff, it were just that traditional clothes had summat comforting about them.

After they'd bumped into retired dry stone waller, Donald, out with his partner Brian and their labradors, Eddie asking if he missed the old trade but mostly going on about his own fancy stonework, Michael noticed another twosome coming down the trail from near the summit. They'd lately bought a weekend retreat in Fowlbeck. Despite them being half a mile off as yet, there was no mistaking who they were. Set against The Beacon's dark earth and fading heather, the bulky 'his and hers' white jackets and trousers stood out like new bedsheets. Eddie, up front as they kept climbing, had the couple spotted too.

"Watch out, lads and lasses," he said. "Look who's comin'. Hide yer cocaine, everyone, it's Miami Vice!"

"They look like a washing powder advert," said Mum.

"Doin' a turn for sunbeds an all," said Elsa. "You seen their faces this weekend?"

"Saw 'em peerin' in at t' shop window yesterday," said Michael. "Very... Orange."

"Didn't they pop in?"

"No, Mum. They've never been in."

"Well, there's time, love. Remember they only bought that place this summer."

Michael reckoned on the married couple not being many years older than him and Elsa. Must have had a bob or two, mind, snapping up a little terraced on the High Street as a second home to one they owned in Leeds. Seemed to be a lot more Fowlbeck properties going that way lately. Mr Miami Vice were apparently making a killing in stocks and shares. According to tales he'd been telling in The Dog and Gun of a Saturday night, anyhow. Grandad would have called the couple 'off-cum-dens', but Michael had grown to dislike that word. What it really meant was 'ones from outside who weren't properly welcome'. The village wasn't like that. They were welcome. Provided they showed consideration for the community, supported local businesses, shopped at Bowers' Butchers once in a while. Now that Mum had given half ownership of the family business to Michael, it were only right that he should expect that. Especially if Mr and Mrs Vice were set on leaving their holiday home, which had previously been occupied by a regular customer all year round, empty most of the time. At least there was someone who looked like he might get brass out of them.

"Eddie?" said Michael.

"Aye?"

"Did yer give 'em a price for puttin' a swimming pool in their cellar?"

"Not as yet, Michael," said Eddie. "Not done one afore."

"Oh yeah," said Elsa. "Is it legit, then, this swimming pool?"

"Don't even know as it's possible in a house that size."

"How big's their cellar?"

Elsa had got to twiddling her hair in the sunlight as she walked. Michael were glad she'd never lost the habit. Sexy as hell.

"Not big enough for a swimmin' pool," said Eddie.

"But they'll allus be able to say they've got one."

"That's likely the size of it, Elsa," said Mum, glancing

over her shoulder. "Clever cookie, your mummy, Bernie."

"Too clever by half," said Michael, waiting for the friendly punch to the chest his wife usually planted on him for smartarse comments.

"Cheeky bugger," said Elsa, turning, landing her fist, but looking at him like she did whenever she wanted him.

There'd be time enough when they got back home and Bernie had his afternoon kip.

As they continued up the eastern slope toward the dazzling white couple on their way down, Michael made out gunshots coming from Tattersall's country estate, a short distance away to the south. Noises so harmless sounding they were akin to popping wine corks. Them weekend grouse shooters must have bagged a sackful of birds by now. No doubt they'd be packing in for a meal up the dale at The Yorkshire Arms soon. At least that were the tradition. One or two might order the best partridge or pheasant around, game supplied by Bowers' Family Butchers since the days Queen Victoria ruled half the world. Thinking on that fairly warmed your blood with pride, didn't it? Puffed out your chest so much that, if there were plumage on it, you'd likely set about having a preen.

Michael carried on preening himself until Mr and Mrs Vice had got to within about fifty yards and you couldn't help but be distracted by the sight. As out of place in the world of hiking as a pair of pork chops on a vegetarian's plate. They were a matching pair, no mistake. As well as the 'his and hers' clothes, you could see the trouser turn-ups all mucky from the trail now, they'd got yellowy blond highlights in their hair. Hairdos which they'd clamped down with them personal stereo headphone contraptions. Whatever happened to listening to nature when you were out in it? People would be walking round staring at hand held televisions next. One day, folk might just give over talking to one another altogether.

When they were only a few feet away, the couple took off their musical headbands and wore them like necklaces. Now Michael could hear faint tunes coming from the sponge earphones. Gloria Estefan? Erasure? Flipping heck, how orange were them tans in the sunshine? Sunbeds or from a jar? Bet they could afford gold-tinted tans if they fancied. How posh were that big bag the woman had hanging off her shoulder?

"Hello, Eddie," said the bloke, shaking his hand enthusiastically.

"Morning, Gary. Morning, Vanessa."

"Afternoon, Eddie," said Vanessa, tapping her flash watch.

"Is it? Already?"

"Five past twelve."

"Just had some dinner at the top," said Gary.

"Aye, Bernie might be ready for his. Think he's gettin' cranky," said Michael.

He didn't reckon much to the thought of a long natter with Gary and Vanessa. They put him on edge, somehow. Made him right uneasy. Maybe because they were so flash. Stopping to chat to them had bunched everyone together on the trail, which made the group spread a bit, like a loosening knot, onto the springy heather. Now they were high up, Michael could feel a soft breeze and, unless Mum's mention of an advert had sparked his imagination, it were lifting hints of washing detergent off Gary and Vanessa's clothes.

After some quick introductions, it was only Eddie who'd really spoken to them before, and them talking about the breathtaking views, and about how lucky they were to have been able to buy a second home in 'pretty little Fowlbeck', and about how funny it was that they could afford two houses but hadn't bought any hiking gear yet, Gary got on to the subject of the swimming pool.

"So, Eddie," he said, turning his chunky gold wedding ring on his tanned finger. "Now you've had some time, two questions. How long will it take? How much will it cost?"

"You're forgetting t' third question, Gary," said Eddie, stroking his beard as if he'd been doing a lot of thinking on the third question.

"And what's that?"

"Is it possible?"

"That's not a 'no can do', is it, Eddie?" said Vanessa, inspecting her perfect nails.

"It's an 'I'm not sure yet.' As I've already told yer, there are contractors about these days who'll sink a swimmin' pool into a basement. I'd have to subcontract a job like that. Very specialised. Pricey an all. But the main issue you've got is space."

"Space?" said Gary.

"Pretty small, that cellar."

"Small?" said Vanessa.

"For a swimmin' pool, aye," said Eddie. "Chances are, yer pool's edges would be reet close to yer exterior and adjoining walls. There'd have to be fairish o' reinforcement going in, diggin' down that close. Don't want the whole house sinkin' into t' ground, do you? And you'll need consent from yer neighbours on either side o' course."

"Consent?" said Gary.

"Adjoining walls? Wi' it being a terraced? Unless you downsize your plans."

"Downsize?" said Vanessa.

"Have summat like a dipping pool instead."

"Dipping pool?" said Gary.

They seemed shocked by Eddie's reality check, mouths gormlessly open. Elsa must have cottoned on to the reaction as well. Michael recognised that cough she'd just had as cover for what would have been a blurted laugh. He couldn't look at her, otherwise they'd both be in fits. Best make excuses.

"Listen," he said, "Vanessa, Gary, apologies, but I can feel the boy gettin' restless. Needs feeding. So we should get to t' top for dinner really. Sorry about that."

"No probs," said Vanessa, coming over to give Bernie a tickle under the chin.

"Yeah, no probs," said Gary, starting to move off downhill again. "I'll be in touch, Eddie. If we have to reinforce and get consent, then that's what we'll do."

It was the moment before Vanessa said goodbye and set off following Gary, as she gave Bernie a last bit of attention, when her big posh bag were open right under Michael's nose, that he spotted the oblong wicker basket inside with the plastic plaque on the lid which said **'Hargraves' Hamper'**.

When the five of them reached the top of The Beacon, they had the flatter, grassier summit to themselves. Mum joked that Gary and Vanessa had likely scared everyone off. Bernie was getting cranky now so, as Mum and Eddie laid out a tartan blanket and started unpacking picnic stuff from the rucksacks, Elsa sat down to breastfeed him at the foot of the tall limestone cairn which marked The Beacon's peak. Michael said he wanted a minute to himself and stood watching the others from a little way off at the north edge of the summit, the top of The North Face. He was lucky, wasn't he? Didn't he know it? He only wanted a few moments to himself, that was all. Nowt but a minute.

Turning toward the sunny, shadowy dale, he noticed that the milky sky had almost burned away now above them far hills. He realised he'd got a proper sweat on, despite it being more exposed and cooler at the summit, and dragged his palms across his face and neck. Then he gazed down on his lovely Fowlbeck, with the river running by it like a dark brown ribbon. Except for the odd bird call, it were near enough silent up here. Funny how Vanessa had carried that meaty-smelling hamper in her posh bag. Perhaps Mr and Mrs Vice were more sensitive than appearance suggested. Decided on hiding it when they saw Michael coming, out of respect for him being the other village butcher. He weren't even arsed about the Hargraves' hampers, anyhow. He'd seen a few of them knocking about this past year. Dressing up meat in a fancy basket? More like a cover up. No need for it if you only sold the finest quality products, like Bowers' Family Butchers did.

Something had niggled Michael, mind. Maybe it were just Mr and Mrs Vice sticking out so much. A brash white and orange reminder of more houses being flogged off as less occupied second homes, and the impact that had on trade. Or the thought they'd tried hiding the hamper, because they reckoned Michael needed protecting or summat. Bloody hell, that idea did rile him. Or maybe it *was* the hamper that rankled, a jab in his side telling him that Jack's innovations were attracting decent custom from second homers and tourists. Perhaps all them things bothered him. Oh, he didn't flipping know!

He wiped his clammy hands on the seat of his corduroy trousers and tried putting stuff in perspective. The way Elsa had shown him once, using one of her paintings of the High Street by way of demonstration. Get a grip, lad. Yes, the shop had seen a dent in takings this last year or two. But it wasn't owt to fret about, was it? And the business did well enough with folk coming in from outside. Plenty of them preferred the more traditional. Bowers' shop were the most traditional in Fowlbeck. The most established. The one with the longest standing reputation. There might have been other factors to consider, supermarkets in towns attracting more rural custom, the economy getting in a right state again, but Bowers' Family Butchers stood as safe as houses really. At least ones without swimming pools in their cellars, undermining the foundations.

Perspective, that's all Michael needed. A fair old perspective from atop The North Face. He leaned over the edge and peered at them rocks sloping away, which him and Lanky had climb up that time in 1976. Seemed steeper back then. Definitely more dangerous. They'd been mere whippersnappers, though. It had blown a hell of a gale that day. He could have been a goner. It put shudders through his bones now, thinking on it. This ledge just beneath your feet, isn't it the one you edged along to reach the summit? Aren't you standing beside the spot where you made it to the top and saw Jack with his back to you?

Anyhow, Michael still felt sorry for Lanky sometimes. The lad wasn't exactly doing what he wanted with his life. He still worried about him, even if they were supposed to be business rivals nowadays. Friendship cut deeper than rivalry, didn't it? Jack felt trapped. Oh yes, he were fonder of a jibe about Bowers' Butchers than he used to be. And that sign he'd put up last month, suggesting punters shun tradition for something new, had been a flipping dirty trick. But being dissatisfied did queer things to folk.

At times, Michael thought it was lucky that him and Jack had a joint project. Restoring the nineteen-fifties motorbike they'd bought helped keep their friendship going somehow. You might compare it to way back, when they'd built and raced their bogie together. They'd have their Norton motorbike properly firing and looking brilliant soon. And, you never knew, once they started racing the old girl next year, it might feel just like them good old days again.

"Michael?" called Mum. "Food's ready, love."

He looked toward the others. Mum and Eddie sitting on the tartan blanket, dishing Bowers' Butcher's cooked meats and Mum's homemade coleslaw onto picnic plates. Her digging her elbow into his ribs, no doubt in return for him playing silly buggers again. She were happy being with him. Elsa with the sun in her hair, still feeding Bernie, but watching Michael with her head tilted in that silent way she had of asking him if everything was all right. She always knew when he got to bothering over summat.

"How about Elsa, Mum?" he said.

"Don't worry, love. I'm making a plate up for her."

"And I'll have it whenever his lordship stops guzzlin'," said Elsa. "You okay, darling?"

"Oh aye," said Michael. "Luckiest bloke in t' world, me."

Not right easy telling, but Michael reckoned Jack must have been standing somewhere between where him and the others were now, that time in the summer of '76. That time when Michael had stuck his nut above The North Face, breathless, a big cut across his forehead from when he'd lost his bloody footing and cracked it against the limestone. That time when Jack had his back to him. When he'd forgotten about him. When he'd left him alone on the jagged rocks.

Michael ran his fingers over where the cut had been, feeling for the ridge which had stayed there along the healing. Strange how sometimes it were like it still hurt.

CHAPTER SEVENTEEN

On the last Saturday night of October, Jack was standing at the bar in The Dog and Gun, fidgeting with a ten quid note, waiting for George the landlord to come up through the floor from the cellar where he'd gone to change him a barrel of ale. The cellar entrance was a wide rectangular opening in the middle of the lino-covered space behind the bar that smelt of spilt beer. Now that its right heavy looking hatch was up, held on a chain to prevent it crashing into the ground level drinks cabinets, the other bar staff, collecting punters' orders, were edging round it so as not to fall down the hole and join George among the crates and empties. Heavy Metal Mark, butcher at Bowers' Family Butchers, moonlighting in a Megadeth sweatshirt and serving Joan from the ladies' dominoes team, pushed up a tall glass under the gin optic. Jack watched air bubbles rise in the upturned bottle.

"What's ya preference, Mark?" he said. "Bar work or butcherin'?"

"Butcher boy to t' core, me, lad," said lank-haired Mark, reaching down to take a tonic from one of the cabinets.

"Same as ya Bowers' Butchers boss, eh?"

"And thee."

"Not me."

Mark picked up a bottle opener, prised the top off the tonic, the sound similar to someone saying 'psst', and poured it into the glass. Jack heard it fizz like aspirin. Gave him recollection of hangovers. Not that he'd be making out fizzy little noises in an hour or so, mind, when the pub had filled up a bit and alcohol set about loosening some rowdy tongues. Pretty quiet with chatter and drinkers as yet.

Doubtless there'd be more folk traipsing in soon. Same as they'd done every Saturday night since history began. Look at this old fucking alehouse. Talk about stuck in the past. In this main part of the pub, the saloon bar, if it wasn't for the fruit machine by the toilets and the jukebox in the far corner playing Fine Young Cannibals, you'd be forgiven for thinking you'd landed in eighteenth century England or summat. Dick Turpin might trot in on horseback any minute, stand and deliver a round of drinks. The place seemed forever dimly lit, as if electricity had never properly reached here. It was like the scant light bulbs, fixed to the oak beams and wooden wall panels, were nowt but a string of candles. George likely controlled them with a secret dimmer switch in the cellar. Tight bastard. Taking a while down there, wasn't he? Must have a struggle on. You could hear him clanking metal barrels around on the cellar floor and cursing in that Lancastrian accent which had never left him since his defection from Clitheroe twenty years since.

Looking about, Jack knew it wasn't only the dull lights that had you thinking the pub better suited to the dark ages. The darkness of all the wood in here did that too, somehow. That of the chunky tables, chairs and barstools, the panels cladding the walls, this polished bar that smelt of beeswax, the low oak ceiling beams which, when you happened to be six foot three, made you duck in places to avoid bumping your head. There was something...What word had Clare used that first time she'd been in? Oppressive. Something oppressive about this pub. Oh yes, you could put it down to darkness, the room's dimensions, the air turned smoky by burning cigarettes and a stoked open fire, but you'd just as well lay it at history's door. Stifling everything, holding everything back.

Jack tugged at his pinstripe shirtsleeves, fiddled with the

ten quid note, caught himself glancing at ancient objects dotted along the room's edges. A rusty scythe, an old single furrow plough, a massive coopered barrel, the likes of which would send George loopy if ever he had to shift it. Then there was the sound of market boots clacking on the stone flag floor, just as they must have three hundred years since. Little Richard, who wasn't little, but near as damn it Jack's height and broad as a bull in the shoulder, walking in off the High Street. Farmer's son, mid-twenties, big gap in his front teeth. Stonewashed jeans and John Deere baseball cap. Dressing up, was he? He clacked to the bar, sat on the barstool he always sat on, nodded at Jack.

"Hargraves."

"Little Dick."

"Fuck off."

They'd never much liked one another since Little Richard smacked Jack for six in that 'friendly' cricket match at Fowlbeck Country Show and Jack followed up with a quick one right in his bollocks. Wasn't his fault the thick twat had neglected to wear a box.

"Language gentlemen, please," said Mark, putting on a daft pompous voice, popping Joan's change into her bony, blue-veined hand. "There's a lady present."

"Sorry," said Little Richard.

"Apologies, Joan."

"You two great lumps aren't too big for o'er my knee," said Joan, a glint in her eye.

She picked up her gin and tonic and tottered back to the table where, decked out in floral frocks, the other three members of the ladies' dominoes team were waiting to play another practise game.

"Usual, Ricardo?" said Mark.

"I'm reet for t' minute, ta," said Little Richard, tugging

the peak of his cap.

"Has thee not got a thirst needs slakin'?"

"Aye, but Wendy's servin' me."

Jack reckoned Little Richard close to drooling as he gawped across at Wendy. She'd just served someone on the taproom side of the bar and, with George still out of the way, was lolling beside the pickled eggs, flicking through a celebrity magazine with Cilla Black on its cover.

"Sez who?" she said, head buried in gossip.

Opted for one hell of a tight miniskirt tonight, hadn't she? Fairly caked on that make-up as well. Brickie's trowel job, by the looks of it. Bit rough, our Wendy. Not too bright either. Elsa's mate.

"Wendy?" said Jack. "Anything in that magazine regarding the plight of eastern Europeans struggling for liberation from Soviet totalitarianism?"

"Naa. Couple o' tips on how to pull a fit bloke like you, mind."

She looked up from the glossy pages, winked at him awkwardly because her eyelashes were sticky.

"What *is* your opinion on the current political situation in Berlin, Wendy?"

Now she ditched the magazine and glared at him.

"Piss off!"

"Let her alone, Hargraves," said Little Richard.

As Wendy got round to pulling a pint of lager for Little Richard, her 'sulk on' giving his advances nowt by way of encouragement, and Mark went to clear glasses from the saloon's central table, occupied by three middle-aged bikers and foggy with cigar smoke, Jack heard George climbing the cellar steps. Then up through the floor came that hairless head, bald as one of the pickled eggs, the sheep's fleece jumper and the breathless panting of a grumpy Lancastrian landlord. Better not ask the mardy frigger what took him so long. After he'd closed the hatch, hand-pulled some froth off the new barrel into a bucket, got his breath back, George turned his hangdog face to Jack.

"What is it yer wantin' agen?" he said.

"Two pints o' bitter, a small red wine and...And..."

"Better if yer told me today, would it not?"

"One sec, George," said Jack, looking over his shoulder toward Clare, Michael and Elsa, at the table by the lit open fire. "Elsa, what was yours?"

"Fresh orange juice, ice and a slice."

"Fresh orange juice, ice and a slice, please."

"At long last. Yer doin' me shed in here, lad."

"Sorry, George."

An hour or so later, the saloon bar was busy with drinkers, the smoky air filled with laughs and chunter, clinking glasses and gossip, the smell of clingy perfume and sweat, Black Sabbath from the jukebox. Jack had a decent view of the room from where he was sitting, next to Clare at the table near the warm open fire. They were on an ancient pew-like seat which backed against the panelled wall running parallel to the bar, Michael and Elsa sitting at the other side of the table, Elsa opposite Clare, Michael facing Jack.

Jack wondered what went on in Michael's head sometimes. The ladies' dominoes team had just gone home, leaving the 'doms' behind the bar, and Micky, for some daft frigging reason reckoning Clare might appreciate a game, had fetched the little oblong box to the table with his round of drinks. A silly fogies' pastime? It was embarrassing. Not that Clare said owt when Michael suggested she have the honour of upturning the box, mixing the bone dominoes face down on the tabletop and choosing her seven first. She'd only met Mr and Mrs Bowers in passing before tonight and you could tell she was after being respectful. She had too much class to get in a flap over a stupid pub game, anyway.

"Now then," said Michael. "Who's got double six?"

"Oh, that's me," said Clare, placing it in the middle of the table.

"Your turn, Lanky."

"Tell me we're not actually laikin' dominoes on a Saturday night out," said Jack.

"Laiking?" said Clare.

"Playing," said Elsa.

Jack put a domino down, offered Clare a cigarette by way of solace, lit one for himself when she declined.

"How is your baby boy, Elsa?" said Clare, as the game continued.

"Bernie?" said Elsa, twiddling her hair. "On good form, the little ratbag. Thanks for askin'."

"Bernie. I like that name."

"Do ya?" said Jack, immediately regretting it.

"Why, don't you, Jack?" said Elsa, giving him dagger eyes through her glasses.

"Aye, course I do."

"We named him after me father," said Michael, placing his second domino.

"Yes," said Clare. "Jack told me."

"Did he now?" said Elsa.

"He also told me what a wonderful man your father was, Michael."

"Did yer, Lanky, lad?"

"Well, he was," said Jack.

"Used to take us campin' up t' dale, din't he?" said Michael.

"Remember that time he got kiddin' on about that wild boar?"

"Oh aye."

The two of them had a proper chuckle at that. It put Jack in mind of all the laughs they'd had as kids. He somehow needed reminding of how close they used to be. They were still good mates, but it put sadness in him to think how different they were from one another now. Maybe they'd always been chalk and cheese. It was just that these days, Micky, tied to his new young family, repeating the histories of his old family, was lashed tighter than ever to Fowlbeck and its ways. Never appeared to question it, mind. Kept stumbling blindly on from one day to the next. Not that Jack wasn't lumbered here too. For now, anyway. He knew it. But *at least* he knew it.

"So, where is Bernie staying tonight?" said Clare, taking a sip of wine.

"At me mum and stepfather's," said Michael. "They've got a barn conversion just out o' t' village. Me stepfather converted it not long since. He's a builder."

"Nice place?"

"Very glam," said Elsa, weighing up her next domino option. "Bernie's got his own room. They did it out especially. He's still a bit young to be in a room by him sen, though, so he's in wi' them for now."

"Aww, how lovely, Elsa," said Clare. "And your place is on the High Street?"

"Nowt but a few doors up from here."

"We're in the old family home," said Michael. "Been in me family since way back. About to buy it off me mum. We'll have a mortgage sorted afore long. Yer know, security for Bernie's future."

"Albatross," said Jack, tearing the corner off a beer mat to prevent him tearing his hair out.

Michael was staring across the table at him now, dark

brown eyes gleaming like marbles in the firelight.

"No, Jack," he said. "Security. If you ever have children you'll understand."

"Friggin' hell, Micky, you heard ya sen? It's like listenin' to my mother blether on."

"Well, yer will understand."

"I'm not having fuckin' kids."

Jack saw the other three stiffen at his words. Why did he have to say it like that? Had George not been keeping this ale right or summat? Course he didn't ever want sprogs. Why hang more millstones round your neck? Wouldn't hurt to tone his gob down sometimes, though. Michael and Elsa had to make their own choices. It just wound him up to think they probably never wondered what life might be like outside this dale. And did they even consider the importance of events happening on their planet at the moment? Millions of folk in Europe and China fighting for their freedom. Well, it didn't affect the Bowers, did it? Ignorance is bliss, eh? Clare was a world away from being like them. Since she'd come into Jack's life, she'd been a reminder of how different he was from them too. He suddenly felt depressed, surrounded by the same old Saturday night noise, while sitting at a table silently tense.

As they carried on playing the game, Michael looked riled, his face even redder than usual. It almost surprised Jack that he still had it in him to get angry, like at times when they were nippers, because these days he seemed to have convinced himself he was so happy with his lot. What with having a son and heir now, as well as a wife forever by his side. Elsa didn't look right chuffed with the nasty kids comment either. The lass had always been touchy, mind. Fairly slammed that domino down on her last turn a few seconds ago. Now Michael had got to rapping his two remaining dominoes on the table to show he couldn't go. That steam kept coming from his ears, didn't it? Poor lad. Perhaps he still needed his friend's reassurance. He didn't have to rely on his wife all the time, did he? Jack better try calming him a bit.

"Listen, Micky, I meant nowt bad about Bernie. Come out wi' idiot stuff sometimes, that's all. You know me, if anyone does. We go back a long way, don't we, mate? Been through a lot together. Michael?"

"That supposed to be an apology?" said Elsa.

"It's right, Elsa," said Michael.

"No, it's not."

"It's reet, I said."

"Hey, everyone, I think I've won!" said Clare, placing her final domino.

During the next few games, perhaps because Jack had decided he'd do better keeping his trap shut, it felt like some of the awkward atmosphere might be lifting from the table. At any rate, by the time Clare was at the bar getting in the third round of the night, to Jack's relief returning the dominoes to grumpy George in the process, Michael's cheeks had gone back to their natural shade of red and Elsa had given over snarling. Now the two of them were chatting about summat or other, doubtless Bowers' precious shop, or baby Bernie's future, or mortgage rates, but Jack couldn't be arsed trying to catch snippets of their conversation above the increasing din of punters. Besides, he was too busy looking over their heads, watching Clare order drinks.

Not exactly short of attention from the blokes knocking about, was she? No surprise there. How gorgeous did she look in that silky, sleeveless turquoise top? The perfect skin of her lovely arms glowing like toffee in the dullness of the room. That slender neck which he liked to kiss and make her catch her breath. You want to be careful. You'll be falling in love with her next. No, that's just thinking daft. What he did love, mind, was sitting here keeping an eye out for any men pretending they'd not seen her, but sneaking sly glances when they reckoned no-one would notice. Jack might not always feel right great about himself these days, but this was one little game he'd lately discovered which put a satisfying smile on his face.

How many blokes could he catch having a shifty peek at Clare while she waited for George to pour the drinks? There were those three bikers at that central table for a kick off. Knocking on a bit, but they still knew proper beauty when it smacked them round the chops. The one with Kawasaki badges on his leathers had definitely got to turning his grizzly head in Clare's direction every other moment. The best of it was clocking his pals follow suit. They were like bony old dominoes in a row, falling for her one after another.

Who else can you spot? Fine and dandy Colin from Fowlbeck Dramatic Society. Reckoned himself a ladies' man, chinless wonder, wearing his Saturday night cravat to try hide the fact. Oh yes, he was treating himself to a gawp all right. Over the shoulder of Beaky Susan, who'd collared him by the toilets for a chinwag. Good luck with that, Susan, love. And how about the blokes nearer to Clare at the bar? Little Dick peering at her from beneath his John Deere cap. She's out of your league, sonny Jim. Doctor Clegg with his handlebar moustache, sipping white wine, faking backache so he can stretch either side of his fat wife for a quick eyeball. But maybe that one's your imagination. Hang on a minute. Where had that fella in hiking clobber just turned up from? Must be on a Dales walking weekend. Perhaps he'd booked into The Dog and Gun for bed and breakfast. Come round from the taproom, had he? Seen Clare through the serving hatch and fancied a closer look? Handsome bastard. Dead skinny, mind. Long streak of piss. Appearance of a Swedish high jumper. He was leaning on the bar and in toward her now. You could see them in profile. She didn't seem right averse to his move either. Laughing at summat he'd said. Locking him in with that piercing sapphire gaze. Michael and Elsa stopped talking when Jack stood up.

"Off to give Clare a hand wi' t' drinks," he said.

As he moved the short distance across the stone floor toward the bar, bending his head under a low beam, getting a dry whiff of ash as he passed Wendy tipping cig-ends from an ashtray into a tin bucket, he tried to steady his heart, keep an air of cool, not give the impression he felt the need to rush. He approached and placed himself squarely by Clare's side, facing Swedish high jumper guy. The bloke looked snotty at Jack's presence, giving him the slightest nod, which somehow seemed to be telling him to sling his hook. You could still hear a trace of laughter in Clare's voice when, seconds later, she asked 'Swedish' something.

"What do you do?" she said.

Had she not noticed Jack standing beside her, then?

"I'm studying journalism," said Swedish, precisely pronouncing each syllable. "Final year. Then out into the big bad world. I'd like to be a foreign correspondent."

"Oh wow!" said Clare. "Where are you studying?"

"School of journalism in Leeds."

"Really? That's my neck of the woods."

"Really?" said Swedish, ears pricking up, all perky.

Jack put his arm round Clare, pulled her in tight, felt her body go rigid.

"Aren't you going to introduce me?" he said.

"This is Jack," she said, after a pause.

"Boyfriend," said Jack.

But the cocky twat was ignoring him now.

"A foreign correspondent, you say?" said Clare.

"Yes, I have a passion for foreign affairs."

I bet you have, you streaky fucker.

"Certainly enough happening on the world stage this year," said Clare.

"Indeed," said Swedish.

"Indeed," said Jack. "Looks like George has nearly got your round ready, darling."

"Why have you come over here, Jack?" said Clare, slipping from his grasp, looking him dead in the eye.

"To help you carry t' drinks."

"Do you think me incapable?"

"No, but..."

"To help me carry the drinks? Is that the reason?"

"What other reason would I have?"

"I wonder."

Her face looked proper serious now. But Swedish had a smirk on which wanted wiping off. The three of them were quiet for a moment. You could hear retired copper, Alcoholic Trevor, slurring his way through his new song, 'I'm a Yorkshireman and I'm All Right', in the taproom.

"Listen, Jack," said Clare, her lovely face softening again. "Everything's fine. Okay?"

"Aye, okay."

"And I'm getting a tray for the drinks."

"Sorry," said Jack.

"I'll join you at the table in a minute."

"Fair enough."

Better be polite to matey-boy first, though. Before leaving them to talk 'foreign affairs'.

"Didn't catch your name," said Jack, offering a handshake.

"Giles," said Swedish, obliging.

"Pleasure."

Pleasure watching him wince in the grip of a good old bone-crusher, anyway.

Back at the table, Jack hated himself for having shown Clare how weak he could be. Not that she looked to be giving him owt by way of a single thought, as she carried on chatting to future Observer correspondent at the bar.

"You all reet, Lanky?" said Michael.

Mr and Mrs Bowers appeared content again. All loved up. Her holding his big butcher's hand in both of hers, slowly turning his wedding ring with those thin, artistic fingers. Maybe they were the luckiest folk about, wanting for nowt in their Fowlbeck world. Perhaps they were. Jack's heart jumped, as the smoky-smelling fire beside him suddenly cracked and spat. He found himself nipping his bottom lip between his teeth and licking at it. Odd how he'd kept the tendency. You could still feel a slight bulge in it all these years on. Likely never leave him, would it?

"What's up, Jack?" said Michael.

"Eh?"

"Don't seem yer sen tonight."

Look at the lad. Same old Micky. Excepting one traditional piece of clobber.

"What's wi' t' green tweed waistcoat, anyway?" said Jack.

"Elsa bought it me," said Michael, running his free hand over the cloth. "Yer like?"

"Thought you had a preference for beige."

"He's tryin' summat different," said Elsa, her glasses reflecting the fire's flames.

"It's all a bit beige round here," said Jack, ripping up another beer mat. "Don't ya reckon, Michael?"

"Don't get yer?"

"No, didn't think ya would. But nowt much changes in Fowlbeck, does it, lad? Unlike, say, in Europe of late. Shaping up to be quite a year for t' freedom fighter, isn't it? What do you say, mate? What's your opinion? I'm of the view it's pretty frigging exciting. No? Something so important having that air of inevitable change about it? There's fairish occurred this year already, of course. As I'm sure you know full well, Michael. Seen some news, haven't ya? Even if you're not reading broadsheets, doubtless you're tuning in to the old goggle box occasionally. Just consider t' goings on these past few months. 'Solidarity' wins Polish elections, Estonia flies national flag for first time in forty odd years, Soviet Communist Party severely weakened, Hungary votes for multi-party democracy. It's all happening. If you're in any way interested in justice and freedom. You are interested in justice and freedom, aren't you, Michael? Those two million protestors in t' Baltic states certainly were a couple o' months since. 'Baltic Chain of Freedom?' Any bells, lad? Oh aye, never underestimate people power. That's what's driving change in Eastern Europe. And just because we're a thousand mile away doesn't mean we can't have an impact. You should know. Into dominoes, aren't ya? Well, it's the domino effect. Take Greenham Common six years back. We inspired folk worldwide that day with our fourteen mile human chain. Showed everyone the power of protest. Started a chain reaction, we did. And, believe me, we're seeing it's culmination on the continent in 1989. Human chains now stretching from Tallin to Riga to Vilnius. NATO and the Soviet Union holding talks about reducing their number of nuclear weapons. Who would have thought these things possible six years since? Eh, boy? What's your opinion?"

"We didn't realise you'd saved the world, Jack," said

Elsa, jutting her chin at him. "You don't half spout bollocks. Quite finished?"

"No, let him carry on," said Michael. "I'm enjoyin' me sen."

But Jack could tell Michael wasn't enjoying himself. If there was a safety valve in the top of his skull, it would be whistling the same as a pressure cooker. His face had the look of raw rump steak. Poor Micky. It's just that sometimes he had his head buried so deep in Fowlbeck muck it put him in need of a wake-up call.

"Summat else happened the day I was at Greenham, though, didn't it? My old man died. Bless his cotton socks. That meant I had to stay in this village. I tek my obligations seriously an all, ya know. And I'm stuck here. For t' time being, anyway. Not forever, but for now. I accept it. Yet there's a difference between you and me, Michael. Maybe there always has been. I can see I'm stuck. I'm allus looking out, whereas you're forever looking in. We're both in a rut, but you're the one who's *truly* trapped. By all that family tradition, generation after generation. By Bowers' Butchers, generation after generation. By a way of life, generation after generation. You're a man trapped in history, lad. And the trouble is you can't even see it."

CHAPTER EIGHTEEN

Michael couldn't sleep, and he knew it wasn't down to the clocks having been put back an hour at the weekend and throwing his body out of kilter. Anyhow, since Saturday night at The Dog and Gun, it had been his *mind* playing up and he was aware of why right enough. He rolled away from Elsa as she slept and looked at the alarm clock on the small table at his side of the Victorian four poster. The red digital numbers, glowing like miniature heat elements in the dark room, said 02:46. Always paid to get an early start of a Monday morning, but weren't it crackers contemplating a crawl out of bed at this time? He'd never properly sleep, though. Jack had buggered with his head too much for that. Wouldn't he be better off at the butcher's block than lying here staring into darkness, working himself into an even worse state?

He rolled back toward Elsa. The faint light from the digital alarm and the glow lamp clipped to Bernie's cot at the foot of the bed meant he could make out her head on the pillow. He listened to her gentle breathing, smelt her clean hair, which she'd washed while having a bath with Bernie afore his bedtime. Couldn't beat perching on the bath's edge, could you? Watching them have a good old-fashioned laugh splashing about with the toy boats and rubber ducks. Made you give over fretting for a bit. A brilliant mummy, Elsa, no mistake. She'd been as pissed off as Michael about Lanky's Saturday night lecture, and she'd told him exactly where he could stick it afterwards, but she'd not let it spoil Sunday's family trip to York, had she?

Yesterday was Bernie's day, feeding geese on the Ouse, chomping cake by the Minster, giggling at entertainers juggling fire on cobbled streets, and Jack Hargraves wasn't putting a dampener on that. Not when Elsa Bowers had owt to do with it. Michael moved his hand toward her head and, soft enough so as not to wake her, stroked her cheek. Took no prisoners, did she? But he'd glimpsed some hurt in her eyes once or twice yesterday and he suspected Jack had been the cause of it. Michael's pain were Elsa's pain, the same as Elsa's pain were Michael's. It riled him to think their way of life had been attacked like that. Couldn't take that lying down, could you? And now, for some reason he wasn't quite sure of, more than just being tempted by an early start at the shop, he felt the need to be there. He rolled over to face the digital clock again, flicked off the alarm switch to avoid Elsa and Bernie being disturbed in a couple of hours and quietly got out of bed. Then, doing his best not to tread too heavily, he took his stack of work clothes off the top of the chest of drawers and walked out of the room.

After he'd had a shower, got dressed, been down to the kitchen to sup a cup of tea, Michael went back upstairs to the bedroom and carefully made his way toward the dim glow of the lamp clipped to Bernie's cot. Just look at the little lad cuddling his Care Bear. What a bobby dazzler! Kicked off his covers as usual. Best tuck him in again. There you go, boy. Don't worry, Daddy will take care of you. Off to work at our shop now. See you in a bit. He bent over and kissed his son's forehead. Then he could hear the drowsiness in Elsa's voice as she quietly spoke.

"Bernie all right, Michael?"

"Oh aye," he whispered, moving to her. "Snug as a bug again now."

"Kicked them covers off for a change?"

"What do yer reckon?"

"Bless his cottons," she said, through a yawn.

"Sorry for wakin' yer."

"Darlin', you're about as light on your feet as a prize bull. Are you dressed?"

"Couldn't sleep," he said. "I'm off to work."

"What time is it?"

"Quarter past three."

"Quarter past bloody three?" she said, seeming more awake now.

"Sorry," he said, watching her prop herself up on her elbows.

"Come here, you. Your wife wants a kiss."

He sat on the edge of the bed and kissed her.

"You all reet?" she said.

"Just think I'd be better off at work."

"Whatever's best for you, darlin'."

Michael stood, walked to the bedroom door, turned to Elsa again.

"Will you and little man come see me in t' shop later?" he said.

"You mean like we allus do?"

"Aye."

"Well course we will, dafty," she said.

"Good."

"Michael?"

"Yeah?"

"Love you."

"Love you too," he said.

"And Michael?"

"Yes?"

"Promise me summat,"

"What?"

"Don't let him win."

"Who?"

"You know who."

A few minutes later, after taking his thick brown coat off a hook behind some of Elsa's art gear under the stairs, and finding his market boots hidden beneath a pile of Bernie's toys next to the Yorkshire sideboard in the front room, Michael was on the High Street pavement locking his front door. Flipping heck, there were a fair old frost about. It was already biting his face. He put his hood up to take the sting off, slipped his keys into his coat pocket and started walking downhill.

His boots sounded hard and crisp on the stone flags. Best go slow in case of ice. Might be one or two patches underfoot, judging by how frosted over the car windscreens were. White and brittle looking, akin to icing that you'd have no trouble poking your finger through. Sent you frozen-bowlegged, this weather. Made the High Street bonnie, mind. Everything coated in sparkle under the streetlights and star-filled sky. What did it matter that nowt much changed in Fowlbeck? Why would you want it to? A place like this, pretty as a picture, in the middle of such a beautiful part of the world? With folk salt of the earth too. Mucking in for one another, because it had always been a way of life out here. In the blood. What the hell had Lanky been jabbering about on Saturday night? Yes, nothing much changed in Fowlbeck, but that were a compliment in Michael's opinion. Jack had meant it as an insult. He'd said similar stuff about the village afore, but there'd been an edge to his words on Saturday, a real nastiness which he'd thrown in with the rest of his lecture. Not as if he were arseholed after just a couple of ales either. Come to think of it, there had been a change round here lately. It had been in Jack. What was Michael nowadays, then? A piece of shit, to be talked to like that?

As he continued steadily down the hill, he sensed the

anger that had been in him most of Sunday rising in his chest again, setting his heart off faster, quickening his breath as it came out into the cold like little clouds of freezing fog. He tried distracting himself, as if he were still an excited kid, by counting the witch-faced pumpkins set out on the doorsteps ready for tomorrow night's Halloween street party. That didn't do a right good job, though, because it only reminded him he was about to pass opposite Hargraves' Butchers with its fancy display of Halloween pumpkins. Don't even bother looking across at it. You've seen the thing a dozen times already. Just another 'stack 'em high, sell 'em cheap' promotion designed to shift more meat at knock-down prices. But Michael seemed to have an instinct at the moment for keeping an eye on what were happening at Hargraves' shop, so he couldn't help having a quick glance.

A split second later, his feet were in mid-air and he landed flat on his back. Stupid lummox! What had he been telling himself about icy patches? Lucky not to bang his head, but he'd had enough wind knocked out of him to make it feel like someone had caught him unawares and punched him in the stomach. He stayed lying on the pavement, stargazing, while gasping to get his breath. Nobody had seen him, had they? He could do without embarrassment on top of pain. He'd not spotted anyone else barmpot enough to be out in the dead of night, but he listened a minute for approaching footsteps just in case. Silence. Except the distant bleat of a sheep out in the fields somewhere, and the low buzz of the streetlight outside Hargraves' Butchers, opposite.

Was his breathing improving a bit now? Look at all them stars. Thousands of them. Nowt other than a typical clear Dales night. No pollution worries in Fowlbeck. Why settle for living elsewhere? Michael knew stuff about the goings on in the world nowadays, he wasn't thick, he wasn't *forever looking in*, as Jack had accused him of, but you could keep your smoggy cities and Valdez oil disasters.

When Michael's breathing had near as damn it returned to normal, he sat up slowly. He'd likely be sore for a day or two, but at least it didn't feel as if he'd broken any bones. Best sit here a minute, chilly as it made his backside, till he were sure he'd got proper composure. He didn't fancy another crash landing. Similar to being shot with the grouse, that fall, coming like a bullet out the blue. Looking down the High Street from this low level brought on memories of them childhood bogie races. Head down, clinging to the steering rope, mad allik Lanky pushing like a nutjob and jumping on: 'Hold her steady, Micky, lad! Hold her steady!' They'd been top dogs, hadn't they? What a team! Won every year they'd raced. Apart from in '76, when it tipped and sent you doolally. That was the day Jack was let free by his old man too. After being locked away all summer holidays while he recovered from the beating he'd got. Recovered physically, anyhow. And, despite what he'd suffered, a day or so after the race he'd been thinking of you when he got you to go on that North Face expedition. Done it as a means of lifting you out of the doldrums. But then there'd been that abandoning near the summit. Most likely just got carried away with himself. Flipping heck, why start mulling that one over again? Happened a few times of late, thinking on that. It were years since and you were only nippers. Now's what matters. And now it looks like you've trouble enough in your friendship.

That were most definitely an eye-catcher across the street, if nowt else: **'HARGRAVES' HALLOWEEN DISCOUNTS'.** An outdoor display as orange as Mr and Mrs Vice's tans, with its orange pumpkins set on orange painted orange boxes under an orange streetlight. That was the thing about Jack, you could tell he reckoned himself too good for butchery, a lad only in the trade because he'd been obliged to shoulder it. Yet he were as competitive as hell. Michael hated thinking of them as being in competition, but how could it be otherwise? Two butchers' shops on the same street, in the same village, vying for the same punters? What if someday there was only room in Fowlbeck for one butcher to have a livelihood? Bowers' Butcher's sales were down a bit on what they were a couple of years since. The thought that his lifelong friend might be the biggest threat to everything that mattered to him mucked his brain up sometimes. But it did you no favours, did it? Sitting on your frozen arse, bothering about what might or might not happen. Besides, you're stronger nowadays, remember? Not so much the worrier, remember? And you've got a family that needs feeding now. So you have to give over nattering about the competition and keep your own shop shipshape. He picked himself up and carefully walked the last couple of hundred yards to Bower's Family Butchers, his eyes peeled for ice, his mind on butchering them two sides of beef which had been hanging for just long enough.

After Michael had opened up the shop, switched on the ceiling strip lights and Calor Gas heater, swapped his coat for an overall and apron, washed his hands, he strode into the walk-in prep room fridge with his butcher's saw and went to the two sides of Longhorn beef hanging with the other carcasses. Within a couple of minutes, he'd sawn half off one of the sides and was carrying it out of the fridge. When you held it across your chest and shoulder like this, seventy kilos were nowt. Akin to burping Bernie really. Dad and Grandad lugged heavier in the old days.

He took the meat to the prep room's long table and laid it down. More often than not, he worked on one of these big pieces here, but this time he hankered after butchering in the shop itself. Among the history of the place. Near the cash till with buttons like old typewriter keys. And the weighing scales with little towers of weights. He weren't ashamed of any of it. Following the natural seams of the meat with his ten inch knife, he removed the forty kilo 'top of beef', then took it into the shop and put it on the bowed butcher's block. When he'd been in and out of the prep room again to fetch his knife, passing under the mahogany clock's pendulum clicking out time above the doorway, he swiped the edge of its blade along the sharpening rod a few times to keep it razor-like. Then he set to butchering, taking the shin off at the joint, setting it aside to cut the meat from later for top quality mince and stewing steak, tracing the blade's tip round the pelvic bone to release the hip-bone, exposing the seam to the femur so he could start splitting the piece into its three primals.

Changing to a smaller knife for the more precise work, he removed the flank primal with the confident, clean cutting expected of a fifth generation butcher and turned it on the block a couple of times to properly cast his eye over it. Longhorn cattle made for champion beef, didn't it? The Dales' finest, no mistake. You could feel how well it firmed up under ageing, see that rich flavour in its deep redness and marbling, tell by the slight yellowness to its outer layer of fat that it had been reared in the right way and allowed a free-range life. Not that suchlike ever came as surprising when you sourced your Longhorn from the herd out at Akers' farm. Alan and his lads knew how to keep livestock, nowt more certain than that. Popping across there earlier in the month, to give this beast the once over afore buying it, having it transported to his slaughterhouse, killing it, the health of the cattle had been as evident as ever to Michael. Clear eyes, glossy coats, good muscle structures, even gaits. As he put the flank to one side on the butcher's block, used his strong hands to loosen the seam between the two remaining primals, started releasing connective tissue with his small knife so as to free the beautiful topside, he got to thinking more on Alan Akers and his beef farm.

He must have only been eight or nine when, over boiled eggs for breakfast, Dad asked if he fancied jumping alongside in the butcher's van and heading out to see the herd afore school. Riding shotgun, eh? How flipping grown up was he that morning?

Just gone dawn when they arrived. Rising sun painting the sky pink. Smells of slurry and silage. Longhorn feeding on hay in the meadow, all bunched up and quiet, steam coming off them. Dad and Alan chewing over the state of the Common Market or summat, as Dad took a gander at what he'd be paying for.

Standing with them beside the livestock for the first time put a young boy in mind of being a real butcher himself. Daft as it sounded, it were one of the most exciting experiences of his life. If he'd been bored out of his brains, he'd most definitely have still paid attention to Mr Akers, though. When you'd never met the man before you couldn't help it. Back then, as now in his seventies, he was squat and barrel-shaped, as if a massive hand had come down through the clouds and squashed him a bit. There must have been some jolly dust on that hand as well, because Alan was a right barrel of laughs. Always cracking funny ones, with Dad all them years since, nowadays too, and shaking at the joy of it. Hard to remember a time when that tough, weather-beaten face hadn't seemed happy. Tough and happy, was he? Dad had given a different perspective on the drive back from the farm that morning.

Michael had all three primals off the bone now and so set to work on the flank, skimming off excess sinew and tissue to expose the good stuff, taking his ten inch knife to the middle seam to divide the meat in half, cutting each half into silverside and rump joints. As he began tying up the joints, his mind drifted back to that journey home from Akers' farm with Dad. The van's diesel engine making a proper racket on the country lanes, windscreen sun visors down, dog-eared butcher's order book slung on the dashboard.

"Unwind thee window, Son," said Dad. "I've just farted."

"Awww, Daddy."

"Must be them boiled eggs."

"You've got t' smelliest bum in t' Dales," said Michael.

"I'll not deny it."

"Kawww, Daddy, it stinks! Them's rotten eggs, not boiled!"

They'd had a laugh for half a mile with the windows open, as fresher-smelling pine woods blurred along the roadside and rabbits dodged being Bernard Bowers' latest roadkill. But Michael had wanted to ask about Alan Akers, and so, when they'd given over chuckling, he'd put the passenger window up again to make things quieter and turned toward the driver's side. Dad's brown eyes still had mischief in them under his bushy eyebrows and he were having another crack at getting his boy off laughing. A silly-arse gear change this time, his thick, freckled forearm swerving snake-like through the air, a single meaty finger hooking round the lever and pulling it.

"Daddy, is Mr Akers allus happy as Larry?"

"Who's this Larry fella?" said Dad.

"Come on, Daddy. Is he, though?"

"Allus comes across that way, any road."

"What d' yer mean?" said Michael.

"Well, some folks put on a front, don't they?"

"A front?"

"They pretend," said Dad.

"But why?"

"Lots o' reasons, lad. Mr Akers is a very proud man."

"And that's why he puts on his front?"

"I'm not sayin' he puts on a front all t' time. Appen sometimes."

"So he's not allus happy?" said Michael.

"Nobody's allus happy."

"But you are, Daddy."

"Oh, Michael."

"When's Mr Akers sad, then?"

Dad had done some thinking when that question came out. Michael remembered watching his shiny, clean-shaven face looking right serious, as he wound his window up and shifted about in his seat afore speaking again. When he did speak, eyes fixed on the road, his hard Yorkshire voice seemed softer than usual and there were moments when it sounded like a lump had taken to lodging in his throat.

"You've heard o' foot and mouth disease, haven't yer, Son? Sends the whole community into shock when it strikes, no mistake. I'm not tryin' to put frighteners on yer, but we're each links in a chain out here. Farmers supply butchers, butchers supply customers, and when summat like that happens it affects all of us. Just remember it's farmers as feel it most when foot and mouth takes hold, though. One o' their livestock gets it and the lot's got to go. Might have taken ten year to build a top class herd, then one bright mornin', appen the same as this, every animal destroyed. Buried in a big pit to prevent t' disease spreading."

"Is that what happened to Mr Akers, Daddy?"

"Aye, sorry to say it did."

"The Longhorns?" said Michael.

"Twice," said Dad. "I were stood beside him t' second time. Cryin', he was."

"Mr Akers?"

"He were sad. But next time I saw him he came across happy. Like today."

"He were puttin' on his front," said Michael.

"I knew thee weren't thick, Son," said Dad, smiling warmly at him. "Growin' up fast, aren't yer? Listen, all as I'm sayin' is that folk jolly along nicely in and about Fowlbeck. We pull together so as to preserve our way of life, businesses, families, traditions, and we mostly do it wi' a smile. But I don't want yer thinkin' that means it's allus easy. Oftentimes, it's a tough life and you have to work hard to look after it, that's all."

"I won't let yer down, Daddy."

"I know yer won't, Son."

Nowadays, sixteen, seventeen years after that morning, fourteen years since Dad were killed, Michael still thought about never letting him down. How could a son not think on it? It would stay with him forever, course it would. He had a lump in *his* throat now.

Tying up the last of the silverside and rump joints, he laid them out pride of place in the cold, previously empty meat cabinet. Then he took to butchering the topside primal at the block. Once you'd removed the odd sinew here and there, trimmed off a fair lot of fat but left on plenty, you had a lovely piece of beef to divide into three cuts for jointing. Just straight down twice with the big knife. The blade sank so easily through that solid muscle which retained its blood so well.

As he split the topside into joints and cut lengths of string for more tying, Michael kept having a look at the framed black and white photographs on the white wall, opposite. It had seemed best steering clear of colour for the picture of Elsa and him taken outside the shop front a short while after they were wed. What had been the way for a previous four generations was flipping well right enough for them too. Made him hellish proud to be up there with the full set of Bowers butchers, but the photo his eye returned to settling on most were that one of Dad with his arm round Mum. Dad had been right that morning when he'd likened everyone to a link in a chain in this community. Looking out for each other, helping one another along so as to protect what mattered. Especially when things got hard. How brilliant was it that he'd made a point of being beside Alan when the poor bloke had to watch his herd get destroyed again? He'd not done that because he were trapped in owt to do with history, or generations, or tradition, had he? He'd done it out of good old-fashioned decency.

Jack had spouted some bullshit on Saturday night, no mistake. What had he really meant by saying Michael was the one *truly trapped* in Fowlbeck? And that he couldn't even see it? Trapped *because* he couldn't see it? Was that it? He likely reckoned he were too stupid to work it out or summat. Left it in the air like that to make himself feel superior. Michael wasn't thick, though. Trapped because he couldn't see it. That had been Jack's meaning. But his meaning was wrong. He had an opinion, but it were bloody well wrong.

CHAPTER NINETEEN

Jack hadn't taken a Saturday off from Hargraves' Butchers for ages. He might not have been exactly in love with the job, but Saturday was the busiest day of the week and he felt the need to make sure the brass kept coming in. When he'd spoken to Clare on the phone yesterday, though, and she'd invited him over to Leeds for this march from the university to City Square, he'd not hesitated drafting Mum and Tracy in as cover to lend his two full-timers a hand. Mother hadn't understood why it was so important to him to be here with Clare, and you had to bear in mind she'd likely never completely get over what happened the day he went to Greenham, but this was a global event they were celebrating. A moment in history, as Chancellor Kohl had described it last evening on the news. There'd been no way Jack was staying away from this. Besides, he'd not seen Clare since the weekend they'd gone out with Michael and Elsa, a fortnight previous, and he'd got to wondering time and again whether she'd missed him as much as he'd missed her. He was walking alongside her now, in the thick of it, where he'd always wanted to be. How about this for a buzz? Doubtless nowt like being in Berlin itself, where, since midnight on Thursday, they'd been joyfully swinging sledgehammers into those graffiti-covered concrete slabs. This Leeds gathering was one hell of a second best, mind.

As the colourful, noisy crowd of marchers moved away from the university under a blue and crisp morning sky, past Leeds General Infirmary on the right, into Calverley Street packed with weekend traffic, Jack soaked it up. He belonged in the middle of this, didn't he? It was like his destiny being played out in these celebrations of The Wall starting to come down at last. And today, among a couple of hundred students snaking through the fumy city streets, holding aloft their freedom banners, beating their drums, blowing their whistles, singing their freedom songs, he felt free. It was giving him a right high too, being part of this. He didn't reckon you could put it down to the dude a bit nearer the front, in a rainbow kaftan, making a crap job of pretending that was normal baccy in his oversized roll-up. Oh yes, it smelt like some strong shite when you copped a whiff, and maybe they'd all be floating into City Square by the time they got there, but for now Jack was on a natural high. Frigging hell, there was so much life in this crowd! What have you been these past few years, half-dead? Well, not this morning. Not here, surrounded by everything a half-dead person needs to be properly alive again. The energy coming off these folk was enough to put breath in a corpse. Breathe it in.

When they'd been walking for about ten minutes and everyone started chanting 'Gorbi! Gorbi!', and then, this also being a march for battles not yet won, 'Free Nelson Mandela!', 'Thatcher Out!', it made it near impossible for Jack to hear Clare's Cuban heels clicking on Calverley Street's wide pavement. He'd missed even that, the sound of how she walked, the rhythm of it. Anyway, he'd got hold of her hand right enough now. After a bit of bother with her deciding whether she could just as well grip that **'BERLIN - ONE LOVE'** placard with the hand further from him. He'd caught a glimpse of the two of them nowt but a hundred yards back, in the dark as treacle glass of one of the modern office blocks squeezed between the older greyish stone buildings at the edge of the pavement. He had to admit the two of them looked good together. Well, to have it right, she looked a damn sight better than him. In her tatty Levi's and Amnesty International top with pinned on CND badge. Dress her in rags and she'd not be out of place beside Claudia Schiffer. As for himself, he didn't think the bomber jacket, white T-shirt, Samba trainers combo gave him an air of Tom Cruise in 'Top Gun'. But, bright as it was today, he'd done well deciding against the sunglasses. Perhaps he had made a bollocks of it by trying to impress Clare with this clobber, though. Oh, give over being soft, can't you? This is a great day for freedom and justice! Soak it up, lad.

The crowd grew as it marched toward the crossroads with the city's main shopping street, The Headrow. Jack clocked a fair mix of people being drawn to it now. A lass in luminous leggings along for the ride on roller skates, a square-jawed BMX rider bouncing on and off the kerb, a couple wearing Pringle jumpers with a snotty toddler in a pushchair similar to the one Mr and Mrs Bowers traipsed baby Bernard round in. Then there were three folk with a student look about them tagging along. Stray, bedraggled, still arseholed from an 'all-nighter', if that beery smell was owt to go by. Then a Goth lass with legs like twigs slotted into clumpy Doc Martens. And now a strumming busker bloke belting out 'Heroes' and getting marchers near him to help with the first chorus. There was talk Bowie's song had been a catalyst for change in Berlin. He'd performed it at the Reichstag a couple of years since, hadn't he? Stage in darkness. Excepting a spotlight on him. And grainy black and white film behind. Of families split when The Wall went up. Tearful. Distraught. Candles in Bowie's audience. Ballerina from the East. Circling him. At the edge of his light. A lover he'd never have.

"Ow!" said Clare, turning sharply to Jack, her face a scowl.

"What's the matter?"

"Why are you squeezing my hand so tightly?"

She yanked it away and shook it.

"Oh fuck," said Jack. "Sorry… I… Didn't… Didn't know I was doing it."

She looked straight ahead.

"Sorry, Clare. You all right? I didn't mean… "

But then she transferred the **'BERLIN - ONE LOVE'** placard, as if it was a shutting door, back to the hand he'd been holding. Well, better not badger her, eh? Just keep marching. She'd be right enough with him again soon. She must know he didn't mean it. Why would he do summat like that on purpose? Keep marching. Anyway, she'd been ratty with him a fortnight since, when they'd left The Dog and Gun after last orders, and it had been worth it for the making up at his place. The first time he'd really understood what they meant by 'making love'. And 'falling in love'. Because they'd been falling… Falling… Falling. And then caught each other in the final moments. And then he'd drifted back up and realised what he'd perhaps been suspecting. He was in love with her.

When they turned left into The Headrow, the busker yelled 'big finish!' and Jack heard what sounded like the whole crowd giving it some stick for the final 'Heroes' chorus. Instead of dwelling on the hand incident, he had let being in love put him on another high, and listening to everyone singing lifted him higher. You could feel like a real hero on this march, couldn't you? Even if it ended up being just for one day. Marking events in Berlin with a public celebration showed its importance, highlighted what mattered in the world. And this being a protest as well, against what still needed putting right in places like China, South Africa, Northern Ireland, Thatcher's Britain, made it a proper freedom march. Turn up today, same as if you'd been at Greenham Common six years since, and you were a freedom fighter. Jack wanted more of it.

The pavement here was as broad as Calverley Street's, but, busy with Burtons, Top Man, C&A shoppers lugging bulging bags of new clobber, it wasn't right easy for the marchers to move along. By way of compensating, the crowd of celebration and protest, like a metamorphic animal, gradually got longer and narrower, four or five abreast thinning to two. Jack made sure he stayed beside Clare, despite her placard 'door' staying firmly shut. He smiled to himself. What a woman she was! Strong, determined, principled, took no shite. Stubborn when she fancied it. Even if they didn't properly make up all day, they'd do it tonight at her place. And it would be fucking mind-blowing. He kept patient and got back to enjoying himself. He wasn't going to miss out on feeling as alive as this. He'd missed out on too much life these past few years. No, he was after taking everything in today. Shouldn't be any bother, seeing as just being here seemed to have sharpened his senses.

All the way down The Headrow, and it must have taken them fifteen minutes to reach Vicar Lane, Jack looked at, listened to, smelt the world around him. Noticed a fair lot more when you had freedom in your heart, didn't you? After their 'big finish', aside from the odd chant, burst of laughter, rattle of a tambourine, the marchers went quieter for a while, so it was easy picking out bits of conversation the nearby ones were having in their pairs.

As they were alongside a cafe with swirly lettering and real coffee aroma:

"See their faces when they opened them checkpoints, man?"

"Must be overwhelming."

"Big time."

Whilst they passed a grimy newspaper stand looked after

by an old watery-eyed fella:

"If they could just solve Palestine and Israel."

"Different ball game, Mandy."

When a dirty bus rumbled by, a fading poster of 'Dead Poets' Society' on its side:

"Check this guy coming out of Next."

"Which?"

"Michael Jackson lookalike."

"He's bad!"

Near a manky looking building with a smell of blocked drains about it:

"So I said to him, I'll only do it with you if you buy me a curry."

That little belter came from the lass immediately in front, university rugby top, long loping strides, and it nearly cracked Jack up. He managed to catch Clare's eye and she smiled at him from under her placard.

By the time the march turned right and started moving along wide and straight Vicar Lane, staying 'two by two' on account of a load of pedestrians still knocking about, Jack had got to hold Clare's hand again. Everything was fine, just like he knew it would be. And so, in among the excitement, conversation, debate of others, as someone toward the back played Simple Minds' 'Belfast Child' on what sounded like a ghetto blaster, he raised his voice and spoke to her.

"Do ya reckon Germany will unite, then, Clare?"

"Yes," she said, loud and clear. "The dam's burst now. I think it's inevitable."

"I agree with you. Kohl says he wants to bring unity to the German nation."

"Yes, I listened to the translation of his speech on Radio Four. It's going to be a transition fraught with difficulty, though, Jack."

"Oh, absolutely," he said.

"You can't assimilate eighteen million people overnight. Think of all the economic implications for a start."

"Absolutely."

"They'll have to invest billions," she said. "In infrastructure, industry, education, health, welfare. Especially in the most deprived areas of the east. Then there are the political challenges of merging states which have held opposing ideologies for the past few decades. Not to mention the democratic freedoms that need putting in place."

"Didn't Chancellor Kohl mention those in his...?"

"Freedom of speech, freedom of the press, freedom to form political parties, freedom to have equal elections. These are basic human rights we're talking about. All you have to do is watch the pictures coming out of Berlin to see how important these rights are to those denied them for so long. Change will take time, but what's happening in Berlin at the moment is a huge victory for freedom. It's so symbolic too."

"Symbolic?" he said.

"Of course! Can you think of a more powerful symbol of oppression than the Berlin Wall?"

"Well..."

"Exactly. These actions, by the people for the people, offer hope to those oppressed across the globe."

He looked into her sapphire eyes.

"You're amazin', ya know that?"

"Don't," she said.

For a second, Jack wondered whether Clare was after sticking her barrier between them again. But you could tell by the calmness on her lovely face that she wasn't really annoyed at him. Maybe he'd interrupted her train of thought with his soppiness, that's all. How frigging intelligent was she? He wished he could reach her level sometimes. Another chant, accompanied by drum and whistle, started and he watched her calmness turn to passion as she joined in with the other freedom fighters:

"No more Tory cuts! No more Tory cuts!"

At least he thought they were shouting 'cuts'. Too good an opportunity, anyway. So he joined in as well and quietly slipped an 'n' between the 'u' and 't' a time or two.

As the chant died away, the march continued carrying its bright banners in the sunshine, passing tall red-brick buildings with fancy sandstone mullions and lintels, then the old oily-smelling bus station. Jack kept soaking stuff up. The students' high spirits, the amused glances of passers-by, the welcoming of more folk, a pensioner and a Rasta man, into the long line. His mind was mostly on the woman at his side now, though. A Sierra Cosworth, with its lights on full blast in the daylight, went tear-arsing by, a dog was yapping summat rotten across the street, he could feel the breath of the six foot hippie chick close behind him on his neck, but he wasn't about to be distracted from Clare. Besides, he always loved it when they talked politics. He turned to her as they marched.

"Did ya catch Thatcher on television at that press conference yesterday? Outside Number Ten?"

"Yes," she said.

"Is it me, or is she gettin' to look more like her Spitting Image puppet?"

He was glad to see her have a laugh at that.

"For sure. Of real concern, however, is that she's also *acting* more like it."

Jack had been wanting to impress her with an opinion on how Thatcher was acting.

"She's such a hypocrite, Clare," he said. "That correspondent asks for her reaction to events in Berlin and she makes out she watched with the same joy as everyone else. Did she hell. It's only a couple of months since she was in Moscow grovelling to Gorbachev not to let The Wall come down, because she's bothered Germany might get too strong. And yesterday she says you can't stifle people's desire for liberty. What I mean is..."

"I know what you mean."

They marched on until they were alongside the bustling indoor Kirkgate Market, with its rows of glinting windows and biscuit-coloured stonework, where they turned right, up narrower Kirkgate. Jack listened to Clare, eloquent as ever, speaking of what was really galling about Thatcher. How the woman had always believed in a small state, where government took care of defence and fiscal policy, and then, as much as possible, got the hell out of the way to leave people to fend for themselves. How this might be all well and good if everyone in society had equal opportunities. How continuing public sector cuts and an erosion of the welfare state had created a Britain ever more polarised between the 'haves' and 'have-nots'. How there was little wonder charities like the one Clare worked for had become a necessary lifeline for the homeless. A cruel irony, she said, that those forced to live outside walls had also been robbed of their freedom. How fucking awesome was his girlfriend? All the way down the rest of Kirkgate, along Commercial Street, Bond Street, Park Row, Jack thought about what an inspiration she'd been to him. And, by the time they reached City Square, he was all for doing his sums on Hargraves' Butchers again. Sell up and get your arse out of Fowlbeck. Hang the consequences. Mum and Tracy will just have to cope. Why not move over here to be with Clare? Why not get involved in the kind of things she's involved in? Why not do summat with your life that matters? All you need is for her to say she loves you.

With the sun high, the marchers stopped in the middle of City Square, in the large open space between the Old Post Office building and the huge bronze statue of the heroic Black Prince on horseback, and spread out a bit. Some clustered in groups, some stuck in their pairs, some wandered off a few paces, alone. Jack spotted a bloke close by who looked proper homeless. Sitting on the ground, he was, his back against one of the smaller statues of local historic figures dotted round the edge of the open space. Long manky coat, big scabs on his hands like islands on a globe. Had a right gawp on him too. Seemed out of it, poor sod. Clare said she knew the guy and, still carrying her placard, went to check he was okay. Jack watched her walk over, listened to the fading click of her Cuban heels, thought about how it would be making love with her again tonight, got a little kick and shiver from it as he felt for his cigs and Zippo in his bomber jacket pockets.

As he waited for her to come back to him, he sparked up a cigarette and had a scan of the scene. The lead-domed clock tower on top of the Post Office building, sharply outlined against the blue sky, showed quarter to twelve, as a couple of hairy student lads set up a soapbox, amp and microphone by The Black Prince. Clare had said the speeches were due to kick off at midday and Jack was looking forward to it. A genuine political rally, eh? Perhaps one day it would be him on a soapbox. Speaking out about injustice and human rights. What a frigging buzz that would be, in front of a gathering like this. All these folk listening to what he had to say. Maybe he could inspire them in the way Clare inspired him.

On a day the same as today, that hum of chatter would fall silent as he stepped up to speak. Folk would turn down those freedom songs on their tape recorders so they could hear his voice. Even those two coppers watching over proceedings might stop plodding in their shiny boots just to listen to him. Jack Hargraves, political speaker. Fucking dreamer. But you never knew, did you? At twenty-five, he still had time, didn't he? Trouble being, you couldn't really do it stuck behind a butcher's counter. Well, you could, but you'd likely get pelted with pork pies in Fowlbeck. He had a laugh to himself at that and took another deep, satisfying drag on his cigarette. Something about being here today, wasn't there? Somehow made you feel that life might turn out just fine and dandy.

While Jack sucked up the second half of his smoke, almost giddy like a kid on it, he got to imagining in the way he had as a nipper. Still one big kid sometimes, but this cig was a cheroot and he was Clint Eastwood. Ice cool eyes narrowed against the sun. Hero for a day. Maybe more. Saw, heard, smelt everything, did Clint. Like in that desert cemetery gunfight in 'The Good, the Bad and the Ugly'. Senses cocked for the twitch of a finger hovering over a holster, the sound of a vulture's beating wing, the smell of fear coming off Lee Van Cleef, sweating under his dusty bounty hunter's hat fifty paces away. Excepting, here in City Square, Clint would have noticed that lass dancing to 'Redemption Song' having a crescent of six studs in her left ear, that **'FREIHEIT'** banner having a wonky pink **'H'** on it, that smell of the fish and chips this passing builder was shovelling into his gob. How good did they smell? Wonder if Clare fancies some nosh after the speeches.

Crushing the tab end of his 'cheroot' under his Samba trainer, Jack turned to watch her about thirty yards off. Good that the crowd was sparse in this part of the open space, so he had a right decent view of her. Down on her haunches, she was, talking to the homeless bloke, her **'BERLIN - ONE**

LOVE' placard resting against the small statue. How much love did she have in her? Helping others was in her heart. The same as a shed load of folk, she wanted to make a difference, but she'd actually got round to doing summat about it. Look at the way she's reassuring the poor fella with big scabs on his hands, the way she's gently holding his shoulder, the way her beautiful face is so full of understanding and sympathy for him. Jack made up his mind. You can't keep it inside any longer. You've got to tell her you love her. You've got to tell her today.

When Clare got off her haunches, Jack could see the homeless bloke gawping up at her, the same as if she'd been a goddess. Well, she was one. Looked like she was saying a final word to him. Doubtless something inspiring. And now, having left her placard with him, perhaps she reckoned it would bring him more brass, she slowly started coming back to Jack across the open space. Her face had gone glum. Must be a tough job, hers. You couldn't do owt but admire her. Now, though, maybe twenty yards away, she'd suddenly got to smiling as bright as the sun. Happy to be returning to her man, of course. She's not looking at you, mind. And she's stopped in her tracks. Spotted someone else, has she? That long streak of piss journo student she'd bumped into at The Dog and Gun a couple of weeks since! What the fuck's he doing here? Wait on, didn't he say he was studying in Leeds? Not been on the march, though, had he? This just coincidence, then, 'Swedish' rocking up in City Square? Likely story. He must have arranged to meet her here. Were they seeing each other? Bastard! Look at him, closing in on her in his brogues and chinos. Not that she's averse to it, gazing into his cocky mug like he's the hero in this scene. How close were they to each other now? Near as damn it touching one another. Get any closer to her and I'm over there, lad. I'm over there and I'm launching your scraggy head off your scrawny shoulders. What's he doing now, going in to kiss her? I'll kill the streaky cunt! No. No, he's not. Calm down. He's just whispering something in her ear. Calm down. Breathe. What's he whispering? She's laughing at it. She's laughing. Oh, he's off now. He's going. Breathe. What had he whispered, though? What had he whispered?

Seconds later, Clare was with Jack again, facing him, looking straight into his eyes. But it didn't seem to be a look of affection or love. It had a kind of challenge in it, a resistance, and it riled him.

"What did he want?" he said, trying to control the crackling emotion in his voice.

"You mean Giles?" she said, her face set against him like chiselled stone.

"Aye, I mean Giles."

"He didn't want anything. He was just saying hello."

"Ya reckon I'm stupid?" he said.

"No, I don't... "

"What did he whisper to ya?"

He got a sigh off her for that, and a roll of her eyes before they fixed back on him.

"With the greatest respect, Jack, it's not your business," she said.

"Not my business?"

"No, it's not."

Anger was pulsing through him now. He could feel it in his temples, neck, chest. You'd better settle down or you'll be doing summat silly. He fumbled in his jacket pockets for his lighter and cigarettes, sparked up another, took a breath of smoke, breathed it out, watched it drift toward the sound of those students 'testing testing' their microphone. When he looked at Clare again, she'd not shifted an inch. He took a second drag on the cig, fiddled with the ring on his finger, tugged at his bomber jacket sleeves.

"What's so funny about me?" he said.

"What do you mean?" she said.

"Funny. You and him were havin' a reet laugh at me o'er there."

"We weren't laughing at you, Jack."

"Likely story."

"Why would you think that?"

Her face had softened slightly. She tried reaching out to touch his shoulder, like she'd done with the homeless guy. Jack backed off a bit. He could do without her sympathy.

"How come fella-me-lad left so soon?" he said. "Not counted on findin' me here, eh?" He didn't fancy asking the next question, but he had to. "Clare, are you seeing him?"

"No."

And, because she'd sounded so sure, because she'd not hesitated before answering, because he knew she would never lie about owt anyway, he believed her. The relief was so strong inside him he went in for the hug. She patted his back.

"Jack?" she said.

"Yeah?"

"I'm really sorry, but this isn't working for me."

"No bother," he said, coming out of the hug for her. "Thought you loved my hugs."

"It's not that..."

"Listen, sorry I was so... You know... About Giles."

"This has nothing to do with Giles. I hardly know him. This is about us."

"Don't get ya?"

It was the way she stroked her forehead at that moment, knitted her eyebrows, pinched her chin, that made him think summat might be up.

"I'm sorry, Jack," she said, looking composed and strong again, locking him in with those eyes. "I don't want us to be together anymore."

Eh? She didn't mean it. Did she? She couldn't have meant what she'd just said. But she didn't lie. She never lied. And her eyes hadn't shifted from his, telling him she meant every word of it. But he loved her. Perhaps he could persuade her she was making a mistake. Those beautiful sapphire eyes were still locking him in, though. Making him see that she'd made up her mind and it was useless trying. Reality hit. He couldn't speak. A kind of cold shudder went through him. It felt like an iron curtain had set to crushing his heart. He nipped the little bulge in his lip with his teeth, took a final drag on his cheroot, as if he was some freedom fighting hero.

CHAPTER TWENTY

Michael hoped it weren't going to piss down, now that he'd wheeled the 1957 Norton motorbike out of the back yard shed, put it on its stand in the corner where the ancient flagstones were slimy green and always smelt damp, and removed its front section. He'd been working on this section for the last few minutes, unbolting the handlebars, headlight, wheel, mudguard from the front forks. And he'd got to wondering whether the thick clouds, above this little yard of the house he'd lived in all his life and was soon to buy off Mum, had got darker, lower even. Perhaps because it were mild for autumn, the air felt 'close', as if there might be thunderstorms about. Anyhow, it wouldn't take long to put everything in the shed again if it slung it down. The main thing was that Elsa had picked up Bernie's plastic pushchair cover afore they'd set off to her mum and dad's for Sunday dinner. They could be in need of it on the way back. A twenty-minute trek, that. Stop your fretting. If it gets wild, there's nothing to prevent you fetching them in the van. Michael had felt bad not going with them to Elsa's parents, they didn't see them often enough, but he'd agreed with Jack about a month since that they'd have a crack at getting the motorbike finished today. Near as damn it only this front bit to restore to its former glory now. Then they'd be ready to ride the old girl in races. It'd be like their bogie racing days. Except it wouldn't really, would it?

Leaving most of the front section components on the ground near the main, restored part of the bike, Michael carried the two greasy telescopic forks, with heavy gauge tubes and alloy sliders, to his Black and Decker Workmate bench in the middle of the yard. Placing one fork alongside his toolbox, on the dustsheet which he'd laid down to protect the flagstones, he then carefully clamped the other fork vertically between the two moveable pieces of wood that made up the bench's work surface. Getting down on his haunches to look under the surface gave him a right good view of the screw near the bottom of the alloy slider, which the Haynes Norton manual said you needed to take out to release the old fork oil. Likely been in there thirty odd years, that oil, if the state the rest of the bike had been in when they'd picked it up for next to nowt was anything to go by.

Michael reached for a screwdriver from the metallic-smelling toolbox. Hold up, had he forgotten summat? Flipping heck, something to catch the oil in. He'd stopped thinking straight lately. Too much dwelling on what Jack said to him in The Dog and Gun a fortnight back. Not exactly improved matters, stewing on it for two weeks. It had wound him up further, if owt. Trapped by history and tradition? What a load of codswallop! Was there an ounce of truth in what Lanky had spouted? Maybe he regrets his words, now he's had time to think on them. Perhaps he's realised he were speaking rubbish. Doubtful. Not while he's got a bee in his bonnet. Always been the same. He definitely didn't sound regretful when he phoned you on Friday to say he might be late this morning, because he was off to Leeds on Saturday to meet Clare and 'celebrate Berlin', then stopping at hers overnight. Got to leave time for a long Sunday morning shag, he'd said. As if he could ever regret his words of a fortnight ago. Too wrapped up in himself, that one.

Instead of taking a screwdriver out of the toolbox, Michael grabbed a rag from it, got off his haunches, wiped the grease from his fingers. Rolling up his checked shirtsleeves, he glanced at the dull gold wristwatch with bent hands that he'd inherited off Grandad. Half eleven. Jack wasn't turning up, was he? So obsessed with Clare, he'd likely not be back in Fowlbeck for hours yet. Should be annoying, but it's more a relief. Best get a shift on, anyhow. What's good to pour the oil into?

He scanned the edges of the yard where, down the years, things had been left next to the limestone walls, which seemed greyer than usual in this grey light beneath the low, grey sky. One of them terracotta plant pots, stacked on the millstones Dad had intended making something out of, would do the job. No, they were that sort with holes in the bottom, remember? Owt else suitable in among the coalbunker, stone trough, corroded wheelbarrow, hanging baskets waiting for Elsa to replant with colourful perennials and hang back on the house wall? They'd make this house more their own, wouldn't they? Just because you wanted to keep original features, stuff that had been part of the place for generations, didn't mean you weren't after making it your own too. Respecting tradition and family history didn't mean you were trapped in it, did it?

Michael must have got to drifting off with these thoughts, because then it were like he'd been startled into waking, by someone's angry shout in the High Street near the front of the house. Silence again. Apart from the whirring washing machine, which you could hear through the open back door to the kitchen. Another load of Bernie's baby clothes spinning round and round, round and round. Come on, shape yourself. Must be summat in the shed to catch the oil in. He moved toward the tired old shed, but then saw Jack peering at him over the yard's solid wooden gate.

"Bloody hell, yer scared the shit out o' me!"

What the heck was he playing at, landing from nowhere? The shock of it had set Michael's heart off like the high compression pistons they'd put in the Norton's engine to get her up to race speed. Not just the shock that had done it, mind. Since a fortnight previous, he'd only seen Jack at a distance on the High Street once or twice. And suddenly having him up close, a mere seven or eight feet away, seemed to have triggered something akin to proper dislike in Michael. He'd never felt that way afore, at least not about Jack, but it were like an instinct he couldn't stop. Best speak to him, though. They couldn't stay staring at one another over the gate till the cows came home.

"All reet, lad? What kept yer? Nothing to do wi' a certain young lady, was it?"

No response. Nowt but that continuing stare through red and puffy eyes. He's in a state. Hair all over the shop, unshaven face mucky looking, somehow. What's up with him? Too much ale last night? Well, if he's after sympathy, he's come to the wrong place.

"Let us in, Micky, will ya?" said Jack, his voice rough and dry sounding, like he'd swallowed gravel.

None too keen, Michael moved toward him, copped for the whiff of stale beer and cigarettes on his breath, unbolted the gate to let him into the yard. Jack walked past him in what might have been new jeans, T-shirt, bomber jacket, except it looked like he'd slept in them a week. Michael managed to calm down a bit and watched him stop in the corner between the millstones and the Norton, paying the bike no attention, as if he'd not so much as noticed the strong petrol smell coming off its still to be cleaned fuel tank. Were his hands shaking as he dragged the stack of plant pots, terracotta scraping, to the edge of the top millstone? Jack sat on the heavy stone, almost slumping, and let out a fair old sigh.

"What's up?" said Michael.

Jack's puffy eyes looked at him.

"Clare's finished wi' me," he said.

"She's not, has she?"

"You think I'm lyin'?"

Now Jack had got to glaring at Michael, like it were his fault he'd been chucked.

"I love her. Ya know that?"

"Love her?" said Michael.

"You reckon every woman's just a fuck to me?"

"Well..."

"Well not Clare!" said Jack, nearly shouting.

"Eh, what's wi' t' pop at me about it?"

Michael's heart were racing again. Never properly got used to standing up to Jack, had he? But things had taken a turn of late. And when you were being personally attacked like this you'd got to stand your ground. By the sounds of it, his so-called best mate was carrying on where he'd left off in the pub. If you were inclined to it, you might stride over and clout him so as to shut his trap.

"I'm sorry, right?" said Jack, head bowed, elbows on knees, big hands pressing his temples. "Wasn't havin' a dig at you. I'm gutted, that's all. Not felt so shite since...I need someone to talk to, Micky."

What sounded like a Land Rover pulling an empty horsebox rattled past the front of the house, somebody slammed a back door a few doors down, the washing machine went into a fast spin, whining as if it fancied a rest. Michael could tell Jack were suffering fairish, but he had a struggle on being sorry for him. Oh yes, he comes round for support when it suits. Anyhow, he'll be over Clare in a week or two. Had he really fallen in love with her? More like put her on a pedestal. Because the way she looked and spoke suited his ego or summat. Or because her life was more akin to what he wanted for himself. But love? The same as you and Elsa have? Did he really know what that was? He'll be shagging another lass by Christmas and Clare will be nowt but water under a bridge.

"Listen," said Michael. "No use sitting there being glum. How about we carry on wi' t' bike a while? Help take yer mind off things."

"Ya what?" said Jack, sitting up straighter, lighting a cigarette.

"The Norton, Lanky. That's what we're here for, isn't it?"

"Oh, the friggin' Norton."

"Frame yer sen, eh, lad? I'm gonna drain the old oil out o' t' forks and put some fresh in. Why don't you clean the bike a bit for now? Petrol tank's in need of a polish, all t' chrome wants a buff up. Look, I've got some Autosol here."

Michael went to the opened toolbox by the workbench, got down on his haunches, rooted out the tube of Autosol polish and a rag from in among the hard-edged spanners and screwdrivers, took them to Jack.

"Here."

"All heart, aren't ya?" said Jack, gripping his cig with his front teeth as he held out his hands for the rag and polish, the smoke rising into his red-rimmed eyes, making him squint.

Michael wondered whether to give him a little show of support, smile at him, put his arm round him even, but then somehow couldn't bring himself to do it.

"Just off into t' shed for something," he said, turning on his heels.

Inside the musty shed, as he rummaged around among stacks of dinted paint tins, bottles of weed killer and vapour-smelling turpentine, trays of rusting screws on a woodworm-bitten shelf for summat to catch the fork oil in, Michael kept thinking about Jack. The lad would put this Clare business behind him soon enough, wouldn't he? Being besotted weren't proper love. He'd be better off without her, anyhow.

She'd most definitely had one hell of an influence on him these past couple of months. Not that it was her fault if he'd started acting the dickhead. He had to take responsibility for that. But, perhaps with her not about anymore, he'd settle down again afore long. In the meantime, though, you've got to give as good as you get. No matter that it gives you jitters. What did Elsa say? Don't let him win. And what did you promise Dad on the way back from Alan Akers' farm that morning? That you'd never let him down. You don't just have to stand up for yourself, do you? There's your whole family to think on. Oh, that old margarine tub with flower bulbs in it will do for the oil. He upturned it, the bulbs tumbling onto the white Formica worktop which had been there donkey's years, took the Haynes manual from the shelf, steeled himself before stepping out of the shed again. Just carry on as normal. Don't take any shit off him, that's all.

Striding to the middle of the yard, Michael put the grimy motorbike manual on the workbench and got down on his haunches to place the margarine tub under the clamped front fork. Then he picked a screwdriver from the toolbox, removed the screw near the bottom of the alloy slider, watched the oil slowly stretch, like mucky honey, from the hole into the plastic container. Likely take a minute or two for the lot to drain. He stood up, slipped the screw into one of his corduroy trouser pockets, looked at Jack a few feet away. He'd not shifted. Rag and polish beside him on the millstone, cig gripped and seemingly forgotten between nicotine-stained fingers, an inch of ash set to fall from it. Sort of lolling forward, he were, stringy black hair covering his forehead. Flipping heck, you couldn't cotton his words, but he'd got to muttering to himself. Best speak over it like it's not happening.

"Reckon we've done a reet job on this bike," said Michael, opening the manual at the page with its top corner folded. "First crack at owt like this an all. Remember Smithy and Stubbsy taking the piss when we laiked 'em at darts last year? Din't give us a cat in hell's, did they? Well, they can wait till they hear her all fired up. Cos she's got a fair auld grunt on her, han't she? And how about t' dirty great fumes comin' off her when she's got a growl on? A real racer. They can chew on them fumes while they watch her fly. Reckoned on us not so much as gettin' our licences, din't they? We showed 'em. Eh, lad?"

"Aye, we showed 'em."

The inch of ash dropped onto Jack's jeans near the knee. Michael watched him trying to dash it off, but he made a right mess of it and the ash became a grey patch, like a little rain cloud, on the dark blue denim. He rubbed at it, gave it up as a bad job, crushed out the rest of his cig on the millstone. Michael had a scan of the front fork section in the manual, then took his adjustable spanner from the toolbox.

"I'd best go steady loosenin' this nut, Lanky," he said, sizing up the big one at the top of the fork. "There's a spring underneath that's liable to fire it from t' tube. Don't fancy eatin' shrapnel!"

"Have ya seen this?" said Jack, pushing back his fringe, holding it flat and tight to the top of his head. "You've got to see this."

"Don't get yer?"

"Well, some twat must have burnt 'Muggins' into my forehead wi' a brandin' iron."

"Stop bein' daft," said Michael.

"I'm not being fuckin' daft! She's teken me for a right mug!"

"Listen, mate, carry on gettin' riled at me and yer can

piss off!'"

That gobsmacked the lad, didn't it? He weren't expecting that. Michael had surprised himself as well. He'd felt his cheeks redden, his heart kick into a faster gear, but he'd stood up to him, no mistake.

"Should I... Erm...Start on the exhaust?" said Jack, after a moment's silence, holding up the rag and polish.

"Aye, go on. I'll get you a dustsheet so yer can sit on t' ground. Slimy, them flags."

Michael fetched a thick, disused curtain from the shed and laid it on the ground alongside the Norton. Then he went back to the workbench to undo the nut, pushing down on its greasy top with his free thumb so as to prevent the spring launching it when it came loose. He could see Jack out of the corner of his eye, hauling his massive frame off the millstones, sitting on the curtain dustsheet. He looked proper miserable. Blooming heck, if he has to talk about Clare then you'll listen to him. You've always listened to him when there's been need. No sign of an apology for what he said the other week, mind, was there? That might be a good starting point.

For the next ten minutes or so, they hardly spoke. Jack seemed elsewhere, suddenly lost in polishing the chrome exhaust pipe. Michael wondered if he'd taken to searching for a shiny new Clare in it. He let him alone and cracked on with his job, removing the nut and spring, putting the screw back in the slider when the old oil had drained, pouring fresh oil into the hole left by the nut at the top of the fork, fastening the spring and nut tight again. When he got to unclamping the first front fork and replacing it with the second, he noticed that the light had darkened under the low clouds and that the air were starting to feel colder on his bare forearms. The washing machine had stopped now. He could make out thunder in a faraway dale, rumbling like a distant stampede. How long till they'd have to shove everything back in the shed? Hold up, Jack's speaking now.

"I asked her why," he said, gazing into the mirror-like chrome while he buffed it. "She said I'd become *too controlling*. I told her I didn't know what she was on about. She said, if I didn't know, that showed it was just normal behaviour for me and I should seek professional help. What the frig does that mean? I'd be better off in t' nuthouse?"

"As if," said Michael, checking the tub had room left for the second lot of old oil.

"Appen she's right. Might be t' best place for me."

"Now you are talkin' silly buggers. Smell o' that polish has gone to yer head."

"Wasn't she gorgeous, Micky?" said Jack, stopping polishing, biting his bottom lip, turning to look at Michael with them bloodshot eyes.

"Suppose so, aye."

"Suppose so? You've got to be kiddin' me. She was unbelievable, man! Seen a woman more beautiful than her, then, have ya?"

"Elsa's the most beautiful woman in t' world to me."

"Aye, well..."

"What does that mean?" said Michael.

"Calm down, mate. Fuckin' hell, you're defensive today."

"Defensive?"

"See?"

It could have been a weapon, but Michael picked up the screwdriver with the intention of releasing the oil from the second fork. Jack, by the looks of it not giving a toss about owt he'd said to cause offence, started polishing the exhaust again. That pop at Elsa were typical of him, weren't it? Something awry in his life and he couldn't help but take it out on someone else. Well, he wasn't taking it out on Michael's family anymore. Be it Elsa, Bernie, all the generations that had come afore and served this community with pride. Michael had anger pumping through his veins now. That new instinct for disliking Jack was kicking in again. What did the bloke have against Elsa, anyhow? He'd never been right fond of her. Even when they were all nippers, climbing trees together, laiking about in the river. Forever trying to put her down. Most likely that was because he'd always reckoned himself above her, but nowadays it was as if she made him jealous or summat. Why the hell would she make him jealous?

They carried on working a while. Every minute or so, the thunder rumbled. It were definitely getting close. A strong breeze started, now and then rattling the back yard gate. A flurry of dead autumn leaves blew over the limestone walls and scattered across the flagstones. As Michael put the screw back in the alloy slider, after the oil had drained, he knew they'd be forced to pack up soon. Maybe he should have it out with Jack first, though. All this disrespect he'd been slinging at the Bowers' family of late. How long could you bide it? Come on, you're stronger nowadays, aren't you? Stand up to him. Remember what Elsa said. *Don't let him win.*

Getting off his haunches, screwdriver in hand, Michael stood up straight and looked down at Jack sitting on the ground five or six feet away. Despite the chain being on the opposite side of the bike to the exhaust, he'd somehow managed to get a smear of that thick, sticky chain oil on his neck, just above his bomber jacket collar. He weren't right in the head today, but there were things that needed saying.

"Lanky?" said Michael, hearing the quiver in his voice, feeling it in his throat.

"Ya might reckon me incapable of loving a woman, Micky," said Jack, out of nowhere. "But Clare wasn't just an ordinary woman."

"Oh aye? And I suppose..."

"Let me finish, will ya? I've told you I need to talk about this."

Jack was peering up at Michael now, them sore eyes like dim red lights in the growing darkness.

"Love's a bitch," he said. "You know that? Clare's sliced through my heart like it's nowt but a pig's on t' block. Doubtless I'll stop blubberin' over her one fine day, but I'm telling ya she's knocked the stuffing out o' me. Oh aye, she was stunnin' looking, classy, elegant, fit as fuck, I'll not deny I got a kick from bein' seen wi' her, but she had much more going on than that, Micky, lad. She carried a placard for what's right, wanted to fight injustice in the world, got off her arse and did something about it. I didn't just love her. I admired her. She was an inspiration to me. For a moment there, she even had me thinkin' I might do summat worthwhile with my own life. Stupid twat that I am. Oh aye, one hell of a freedom fighter, me!"

The blustery wind constantly rattled the back yard gate now.

"I reckon you're better off without her," said Michael.

"Ya what?"

"She did yer no good, lad."

"Fuck off."

"Look at the state of you. Elsa would never do that to me."

Michael watched Jack's teeth clench, his unshaven jaw tighten. Then the lad was up on his feet, dropping the polish and rag, taking a stride which left him nowt but inches from Michael and towering over him. Michael's instinct had him levelling the screwdriver at Jack's chest.

"Back off!" he said.

"All right, big man. All reet," said Jack, smirking, not shifting, slowly raising his grubby hands like he were taking the piss. "You're not gonna use that thing, are ya?"

Michael's heart was racing, the screwdriver shook in his hand, his cheeks felt hot with blood.

"I'll have that apology now," he said.

"Apology, lad?"

"Aye, to me and my family."

"What you on today, you?" said Jack.

The thunder had got loud and close. It suddenly cracked above their heads like a bullwhip, sending shudders through Michael's bones. Then a flash of lightning lit up Jack's face against the dark grey clouds. He looked flipping demented.

"We're owed an apology," said Michael. "For what yer said to me in t' pub a fortnight since."

"So that's what's botherin' ya."

"You insulted me. And Elsa. And Bernie. And all t' Bowers' generations afore us."

"Ah yes," said Jack. "The Bowers' generations. Lest we forget the Bowers' generations."

"I'll not forget them."

"How could you?"

"I don't want to."

"You won't. Mind if I have a final cigarette?"

"Stop takin' the piss," said Michael, keeping the screwdriver levelled at Jack's chest, gripping it tighter. "Sod the cigarette. Apologise."

They stayed dead still, locked in a stare. Another thunderclap had some kids on the High Street screaming. Michael felt a raindrop splash on his taut forearm.

"Can't bring yer sen to say sorry?" he said. "That ego o'

yours gettin' in t' way again?"

"My ego's fucked," said Jack, biting his bottom lip.

"You were wrong sayin' I'm trapped in Fowlbeck, yer know. Same goes for me family since Victorian times an all. Suppose it's hard for you to understand, what wi' your family not havin' been here right long in comparison, but I know you're wrong about us Bowers. I mean, how can we be trapped if all we've ever wanted is to be here? Trapped means being stuck where yer don't want to be, dun't it? Or am I just thick?"

"How can ya know you're not trapped when you can't see a place for what it is?"

"Here we go!" said Michael, breathing hard. "Trapped and the trouble is we can't even see it, eh? That's us, blind as well as thick!"

Another lightning flash. Then steady rain. Droplets like glass on screwdriver metal and shiny bomber jacket leather.

"Any chance I can put my arms down yet?" said Jack, grinning.

"Never told yer to put 'em up."

Michael watched Jack lower his arms to his sides, then he locked into them puffy red eyes again. He thought about dropping the screwdriver, but it were as if his instinct had got too powerful to let him. He could feel adrenalin driving out the fear he'd had of standing up to Jack now.

"Trapped because we can't see our lives for what they are," he said, the words pouring out. "That's what you meant t' other Saturday night, I know. I've not come across such bullshit in a long while. We can see our lives crystal clear, ta very much. As if it's owt to do wi' you, anyhow. Not just us Bowers, but most Fowlbeck folk can see that our way of life, our community, our families, our livelihoods, these beautiful Yorkshire Dales we're blessed to live in, are actually worth lookin' after. For ourselves and future generations. And, you'll not make me ashamed to say, out of respect for them who came afore us and built everything that's so precious to us nowadays."

"Nice speech," said Jack. "Need a soapbox?"

"Allus havin' a dig, aren't yer?"

"Eh, watch where you're jabbin' that screwdriver, will ya?"

"Listen to me, then!" said Michael, raising his voice above the noise of the quickening rain. "We've been blessed wi' what we've got out here. Don't tell me yer can't see that. But, as me dad once told me, we need to work hard so as to preserve it. We have to help one another preserve it. We're all links in a chain out here. You don't attach much importance to it, but I'm proud to be one o' them links. I'm proud that our shop is one of them links an all. And has been for o'er hundred year. Take Bowers' Family Butchers by way of example if yer like..."

"No thanks."

"Well, you'll not get reet far wi' *your* shop."

Michael wondered if that dig at Hargraves' Butchers might rile Jack good and proper, push him too far, have him grabbing for the screwdriver, or taking his chances with a right hook. That were thinking daft, though. As if he cared about his shop as much as Michael cared about his.

It was as dark as dusk now, and the rain had got to belting down. It made a racket on the flagstones, somehow lifted their dank smell into the air, felt like needles on Michael's forearms, stuck his checked shirt to his skin. He looked at Jack's black fringe plastered to his forehead. It covered his eyebrows, stopping just short of his eyes, which seemed to be glazing over, as if the lad were elsewhere again. He'd get over Clare soon enough. Most likely in shock more than owt. Flipping heck, how brilliant was it standing up to him for once? Face to face. Eye to eye.

"You know what irony is, don't you?" said Jack, suddenly looking alert, almost shouting against the rain's din.

"Course I know what irony is!" said Michael, the downpour just about making him yell too now.

"You'll see the irony in likening Fowlbeck folk to links in a chain as if it's a good thing, then, yeah? What about being chained *down?* I mean, you Bowers should be able to see that if anyone can. Can you see it, Micky, lad? All that history and tradition chaining you to this village out in t' middle o' nowhere? No choice but to follow in ancient footsteps? Obliged to it. Chained to it. Like being fettered to your own Berlin Wall. History holding you back. To have been lumbered with such a predictable life, to know what's expected and to have to follow it every step of the way like a bunch of blind old sheep. What a fuckin' bag o' shite fate that is! If ya could but see it. Whatever happened to individuality? To fulfilling your own potential? Eh, Michael?"

Michael's instinct pressed the screwdriver hard against Jack's chest now, its tip digging into the triangle of T-shirt left showing by the partly zipped bomber jacket, sopping white cloth transparent to the skin. What with years at the block, this forearm's as strong as Dad's were, isn't it? How easy would it be plunging metal between bone? Through muscle and tissue? You've done it thousands of times afore. Jack Hargraves seems to reckon you capable, anyhow. Judging by the rapid rise and fall of his chest against the end of this screwdriver. Not much fear on his raindrop-spattered chops, mind. More like defiance. Or even a challenge to you to have a crack at stabbing him.

"What can you get out of life for yer sen, eh, Jack?" said Michael. "Appen that's how you see things, but guess what? We're not all the same as you. The way you've behaved lately has got me thinkin' maybe I never realised how selfish you've always been. Our expedition to t' North Face of The Beacon in '76 is a bloody decent example. Remember that? I've thought about that a lot recently. Why were you after another blood brother ceremony by the dried up waterfall? Why did you cut so deep? That about control, was it? Controlling me? I reckon Clare had that right about you. And why abandon me on The North Face? So blustery I could have been dead on t' rocks. Too selfish to give me a single thought, I know."

As they stood in the gushing rain, drops dripping off Jack's fringe into his blinking eyes, next door's leaking gutter making its own noisy waterfall, Michael thought he'd never expressed himself like this. His anger had given him power to speak as he'd not spoken afore. Jack Hargraves needed telling and, at last, Michael was finding the words to do it. He were near as damn it enjoying himself now.

"And while we're on home truths," he said. "If Fowlbeck in't good enough for yer, why not sod off elsewhere? If you're so superior, go and save the flippin' world. As you said yourself, though, not much of a freedom fighter, are yer? What have you ever done out in t' wider world? A human chain at Greenham Common a few years since. One march in Leeds yesterday. Summat and nowt, I'd say. Oh, and another thing. You can give over havin' a pop at Elsa all t' time. What's she ever done to you? It's like you're jealous of her. Appen you're jealous of what Elsa and me have. Is that it? After all, it's true love. And look at you. The one woman yer reckon to have fallen for and you've made a right pig's ear of it!"

Michael watched Jack's red eyes still blinking out rain. Hold up, though. The lad had just kept them shut tight for a second or two. And again. He's screwing them up like they've been stung. Was he crying? Michael slowly lowered the screwdriver to his side.

"Lanky?"

CHAPTER TWENTY-ONE

Jack never had much enthusiasm for Monday mornings, but with Clare rejecting him on Saturday, and Michael Bowers fucking him over yesterday, he'd been inclined to stop in bed today. His heart like mincemeat, he didn't know where he'd found the strength to get up, shaved and showered, let alone walk down to Hargraves' shop in the darkness to take delivery from Cropden Slaughterhouse and do some prep before opening time. Perhaps it had been Bowers mentioning that North Face expedition in '76, a reminder of how Jack had fought to conquer what he'd imagined to be his old man's craggy face. Had some fight in him back then, didn't he? Maybe he'd got a bit left.

Standing by the main cabinet, he looked at the digital clock above the shop door. Nearly time to open for another long week. Better put the cabinet lights on, then. He flicked the switch. The fluorescent tubes began their droning buzz, shining on the herby sausages, pre-packed mince, pork pies with different toppings of tangy pickle, apple sauce, blue cheese. Stank summat rotten, that cheese. Mother had laughed at him when he'd trialled it in the pie range, but it sold well enough.

Speaking of Mother, Jack could hear her blithering on at Tracy in the prep room as they experimented with new products for the bakery range. Did she have to be so patronising to the poor lass? How could treating her like a baby give her confidence? What the hell were they doing here, anyway? Like it wasn't frigging obvious. Mother's meddling. Rocking up on a quiet Monday, when they usually only helped out once in a while on right busy days. Mum telling full-timer Dennis on Saturday that he could have today off. Cheeky cow. Jack knew she was here to keep her beady eyes on him, after he'd jumped ship for the Berlin Wall celebrations. She'd had a grumble about it when he'd told her he was going, but doubtless the idea that Clare might end up luring him away from the shop for good had her kakking it. Of course she'd not forgotten Greenham Common's consequences. How could she? It wound him up that she felt the need to drag Tracy along to play on his guilt, mind. He hated it when his sister got used like that.

Only three minutes until opening time now. The two dots flashing between the numbers on the digital clock. Time slipping away like a dream when you wake. Was this it for Jack Hargraves, then? Hargraves' Butchers till he died? Was this the sum of his worth? He walked slowly along the front of the cabinet a couple of times, running his hand over the cold glass, the replacement for the original pane he'd smashed when he was nowt but twelve. Today he felt like shattering his father's pride and joy again. Maybe he could plough his fist through it and hang the bloodshed. Look at the white trays of pale pork loin, lamb chops, brisket, edged with false green sprigs of plastic. What did any of it mean to him? These past few years, he'd just about coped with being responsible for this place, grudgingly accepting his family obligations. But Clare had reawakened summat in him that stretched way beyond Fowlbeck. Then he'd gone and fallen for her too. To have to come back here and carry on with a broken heart. The mere thought of her set off pain like a deadweight in his guts. He turned his back on the cabinet, leant against it for support. Mother might well have fretted over whether Clare could tempt you into upping sticks forever. Because, if she'd had a mind to, she could have. You'd have packed all this in for her, no bother. That's the kind of selfish bastard you are. You'd have left your own mother and sister up shite creak. A shop just about breaking even and no-one to run it. That's what you'd have done for Clare.

Jack tugged at his dark blue apron with white pinstripes, twisted the ring on his finger, nipped the slight bulge in his bottom lip between his teeth. As he tried steadying his breathing, aware of Lisa Stansfield's new single, 'All Around the World', coming to an end on the quiet radio in the prep room, he wondered how he'd managed to do his best with this shop until now. You might say that was heroic. Being tough enough to put your own stamp on something you had fuck all passion for. Doing it out of duty to others. Or you might reckon you'd somehow used duty as an excuse. Perhaps the truth was that Jack Hargraves had never really pursued what he wanted because he didn't have the bollocks for it. Maybe he'd used the shop as an escape from the big, bad, scary world. Convincing himself he was carrying on after the old man on account of it being the right thing to do, when really he was just being a coward. Replacing the iron garden seat, which aforesaid Father had bought for fogies to rest on, with that tall silver fridge displaying dairy products and fruit juice. Fixing more blackboards to the walls for chalk advertising of special deals and bargains. Lately putting that metal shelving unit on the chessboard floor alongside the tall fridge to house the new bakery lines. All excuse and escape in a place like a silver and white mirage. He laughed a bit at that. Remember painting these walls white to cover the Union Jack jingo walls the old man favoured post the Falklands War? And ripping down the red, white and blue strips from the opening to the prep room. But why laugh at yourself? Performing great political acts, weren't you?

"Bloomin' hummer, Son, have you forgotten the time?"

Mother emerging from the prep room. Jack turned to see

her standing behind him. Her expression looked like it had witnessed murder under that pork pie hat. She rattled on.

"Yer can't afford to open up late wi' a recession round the corner. There's talk of it every day on the news now. I don't know, Son. It's not Clare who's taken your eye off the ball, is it?"

"She's finished it."

"What?"

"I said she's dumped me. Happy now?"

You could tell Mother was happy, mind. That noisy little mouth a dead giveaway, trying like hell not to smile.

About twenty minutes later, Jack was serving behind the cabinet, putting a foil tray of breakfast meat together for Gary and Vanessa, the couple who'd bought a second home a few doors up from the shop in the summer. Gary had just remembered he needed to call his stockbroker and had asked to use the shop phone by the prep room opening. All fine and dandy in his crisp business suit, he was, spare hand on hip like Tom Cruise in 'Rain Man'.

"You're bugging me big time now, Phil," he said. "If it doesn't make a quid a share, it's a no can do, right? Right."

"What's your best tasting sausage, Jack?" said Vanessa, pouting her glossy lips at him over the cabinet.

Gary was preoccupied, but Jack could tell Mother had sensed the suggestion in Vanessa's voice. She gawped at her from the bakery unit, opposite, where she was working on a display of home-cooked breads, pastries and biscuits with Tracy.

"Well," said Jack, not much in the mood for mucky innuendo. "We have herby ones, leek ones, spicy ones..."

"Do you have a nice juicy pork one?"

That got Mother's eyes bulging like her husband's used to, fit to burst.

"You all right, Mum?"

Frigging hell, someone had rendered her speechless at last. She quickly got back to helping Tracy.

"Yes, Vanessa," said Jack. "We do plain pork ones too."

"Make it butcher's choice, Jack," said Gary, off the phone now and moving to the punters' side of the cabinet. "You know best what Fowlbeck folk eat for breakfast."

"Fowlbeck folk?"

"Didn't Vanessa say? We're donating this tray for the meat raffle they're having in The Dog and Gun tonight, after the dominoes match. Told George we'd drop it in this morning, before we go back to Leeds. Like giving to good causes when poss. Don't we, honey-pie?"

Jack watched Gary put his arm around Vanessa, that tanned hand with chunky gold wedding ring keeping a tight grip on her waist. Did she wince a bit then? She'd given over smutty flirting, anyway. Gone aloof again, like she often did when you saw her with her husband.

"Ya can have a mixture," said Jack.

He reached for some scissors from a drawer in the long table stretching along the wall behind him. Then he started snipping a couple of sausages off each different string of them laid out in the white plastic trays, putting them in the foil tray beside the bacon and black pudding. Bit of a twat, Gary, but was he controlling Vanessa too? Did he always keep a right tight grip on her? Is that how Jack had been with Clare? He'd not thought about it before she'd suggested it on Saturday, but maybe he was a controlling person. The same as his old man had been to him. The same as Mother, with her baby talk, sometimes was to Tracy. Must be in his blood. Bowers had likely been right when he'd said that blood brother ceremony was about control. Jack Hargraves, bastard all his life, except he'd never been able to see it.

More like Gary than you'd care to admit, eh? In another life, you might have ended up posing round in a Toyota MR2, same as the one Gary's left on the High Street outside the shop with its engine running. Hint of petrol coming in under the shop door, mixing with the bloke's cloying aftershave. Controllers could even control the air you breathed. High Street's quiet this morning. Not many folk about. Excepting Beaky Susan, standing outside Susan's Antiques, opposite. Polishing some ancient piece of bric-a-brac, glancing across at the MR2 once or twice, looking out for any 'goings on'. Yesterday's storm long gone now. Just the limestone buildings left damp. A kind of dull shine on them in the weak sun.

"Hello, Jack. Is there anybody home?"

"Eh?" said Jack, realising Gary was waving at him from across the cabinet like a superfast windscreen wiper.

"I said, we're having a swimming pool put in the cellar of our Fowlbeck house."

"How ya gonna fit a swimmin' pool in there?"

"We'll get one in, no probs," said Gary.

"Be a bit small, won't it?"

"Small?"

"You must come round for a dip, Jack," said Vanessa, fixing her eyes on him.

Jack noticed Gary's grip on her waist tighten even more at that. He was suddenly proper irritated with both of them.

"Look," he said. "You want owt else in this breakfast tray?"

"Eggs, if you don't mind, Jack," said Gary. "Who doesn't like eggs for breaky?"

"Folk who are allergic to 'em, probably. Tracy, bring us half a dozen eggs from t' fridge, please."

Tracy moved past Mother, who was still fiddling about

with the bakery display in silence, opened the tall fridge, brought half a dozen eggs over for Jack. Why were Gary and Vanessa properly looking down their noses at his sister? Because she was out of shape and image was the same as religion to them? Thatcher's children. Expensive fashion labels and gleaming super-white teeth made them better than Tracy, did they?

"Thanks, Sis," said Jack, as she went back to her mum. "You're the best, ya know?"

She said summat, but her whispery voice meant he couldn't catch it.

"Yes, we'd like to do our bit for the village when possible," said Gary. "Today a meat raffle, tomorrow a community centre. Who knows? We love Fowlbeck and The Dales, don't we, honey-pie? When I make a killing on Eastern Bloc shares, which I'm bound to do now the Berlin Wall's coming down and all those new markets are about to open up, we might even buy another house here. A third home. I tell you, Jack, now they're tearing that wall down, you should jump on board. I can put you in touch with my stockbroker if you like. You'll make a killing. I kid you not."

Jack wondered if it might be best to just smash his stupid orange face in.

By mid-morning, with Gary and Vanessa long gone back to Leeds, Mother's vocal cords had fairly loosened up again. She was taking a turn serving at the cabinet now, wrapping Old Ken, who'd lived in the village donkey's years, some chicken thighs and plucking coins from his arthritic hand. Jack, rearranging the bakery display with Tracy to make the brandy snaps she'd just baked in the prep room oven more prominent, kept glaring at Mother whenever she hinted at his obligations. Could you ever escape her natter?

"As you know, Ken," she said, at the digital till. "His

father was a keen fisherman, same as you, but Jack's not kept up with it. Not sure why. Of course, he's got fairish responsibility these days. And not only to his self. He knows that. You'd think he'd find time to relax with a pastime the like of fishing, though. Of an evening, just as soon as he's finished what needs seein' to here. Maybe in the spring when it's lighter nights. He deserves it, Ken. You could go to the river with him. I'm sure he'd benefit from your experience."

"Oh, I don't get about so easy nowadays, Judy," said Ken, tucking the chicken thighs into the tartan trolley you saw him trundling up and down the High Street day after day.

"How about takin' up fishin' wi' Ken, Son? It might help you relax."

"He's not getting about too well, dear," said Jack, like she was senile. "Ya goin' deaf?"

Mother opened her gob again, but, before more words could spill out, Jack gestured 'shush' to her across the shop with his finger over his lips. She looked to have got a sulky cob on at that, her fifty-six year old face as stern as weathered stone. She straightened her pinstripe apron and set to tidying the cabinet a bit. Ken had started shuffling across the chessboard floor now, like an ancient rook, toward Jack and Tracy. Squeaky trolley in tow, beige coat grease-stained and zipped up to his chin.

"You young whelps partial to mint humbugs?" he said, in his shaky voice when he reached them, digging into his coat pocket and producing a crumpled bag of sweets.

"Want one, Sis?"

"Thanks," said Tracy, taking one, eyes averted.

"Ta very much, Ken," said Jack, putting a sticky humbug in his mouth.

The old fella stood there a moment, watching them suck

on the sweets, a crooked grin on him as if the pleasure was all his. Faint whiff of piss about him, but a nice fogie, Ken.

"Mek yer hair curl, them," he said, turning and heading for the shop door.

"Got a sweet tooth, Ken?" said Jack.

"Oh aye. Truth be told, it's a mystery how I've kept a full set."

"Fancy a complimentary bag of Tracy's delicious brandy snaps, then?"

Ken stopped to look back at brother and sister.

"Any good?" he said.

"Any good?" said Jack. "You'll not taste better in a month o' Sundays!"

"Ja-ack," said Tracy, blushing, gently jabbing his arm with her elbow.

"Go on, then," said Ken. "Much obliged."

"Best not give too much stuff away, Son," said Mum. "What with talk of..."

"Shut up, Mother."

Jack picked a little paper bag of brandy snaps from the display, took it to Ken, made sure to speak up for Tracy's benefit.

"You do know my sister's very talented, don't ya, Ken? Oh aye. Tek her cross-stitch pictures for a kick off. Ever seen 'em? Belong in a gallery. And she's a miracle-worker with horses. Sixth sense goin' on or summat. Never witnessed the like. But her brandy snaps? All I'd say, Ken, is watch out. So scrumptious they'll blow ya socks off!"

"Ja-ack," said Tracy.

"Thank you, Tracy," said Ken, taking the bag of brandy snaps from Jack and putting it in his coat pocket with the humbugs. "I shall cherish eating these. Tata, folks."

Ken scuffed his way toward the door. Jack overtook him,

opened the door for him, helped him down the three worn stone steps and onto the pavement. Back on the top step, he watched him move off slowly down the street, pulling his right squeaky trolley.

"Look after yourself, Ken."

"You an all, lad. Mek yer hair curl, them humbugs."

Jack wondered if they might. Had a fair kick to them, anyway. A sharp mintiness filling his mouth, freshening his nostrils, moistening his eyes. Too much moisture in his eyes these past couple of days. Ken making steady progress downhill now. Back home in time for a chicken thigh, brandy snap dinner and a fireside afternoon kip. Set your watch by this High Street, couldn't you? Folks' routines. Predictable as time itself. Or a Michael Bowers' tradition. Had that shop of his near the bottom of the hill changed at all these last hundred odd years? That string of game birds hanging across his shop window could just as well have been stuffed in 1877 as killed in 1989. Not right fond of change, was he, Bowers? Frigging hell, how knackered would he be if he ever had to adapt his business to stay afloat? He had changed lately, mind. Laying into you yesterday, instead of supporting you when you needed him most, proved that. Fucking arsehole! That's it, anyway. Friendship over. You're having nowt more to do with him.

Jack went back into the shop, shut the door, ignored his mother as she cleaned surfaces behind the cabinet, walked straight to Tracy.

"How's it lookin', Sis?"

"Not sure," said Tracy, standing back from the bakery display, sucking on her sweet, touching her face with her fingertips.

"Not sure? You've done a crackin' job on that."

"Tracy?" said Mother, coming over.

"Yes, Mum?"

"Your apron strings need fastenin' properly. I don't know, little girl. Come here."

"She can fasten her own strings," said Jack. "She's not a baby, ya know."

"I know she's not."

"So stop treatin' her like one!"

They were all silent a moment. Buzz of dairy fridge, ringing of horseshoes on the tarmac High Street, 'Ride on Time' by Black Box on the turned down radio in the prep room. Then Mother looked up at Jack, those semi-circles under her eyes still dark in the shop's artificial light.

"Tracy's suffered, Son," she said. "You should know that more than anyone."

"Here we go," said Jack. "Guilty as charged."

"I'm not sayin'... "

"Yes, you are. You're sayin' it's my fault Dad died, my fault Tracy found him laid out in t' snow, my fault the way it's affected her these past six years. Well, ya know what? I accepted all that ages since. I don't need you remindin' me every minute, that's all. That's why you're here today, isn't it? To remind me of my obligations. As if I could ever fucking forget!"

Gone right still at that, hadn't she? All stiff, as if she'd been showered in starch. She couldn't stand it when he swore. She'd not brought him up like that. Useful weapon to have when you wanted her to belt up. Looked like she wanted to say summat else now, mind.

"Listen, Jack, I know you're upset about Clare..."

"What's Clare got to do wi' you?"

"I'm sorry, Son," said Mother, reaching up to touch his shoulder. "I know she's hurt you, but you're better off without..."

"FUCK!"

That one seemed to have really stung her. She slowly returned to the cabinet, her narrow shoulders slightly hunched, like they used to be under the weight of the old man's tyranny. And now Jack felt guilty about how he'd got to treating her too. Even a bastard to those he supposedly loved, eh? He hated himself. Clare had rejected him because he was a controlling bastard, hadn't she? She'd said as much. Had that been her only reason, though? Maybe you just weren't in her league either. Perhaps that's what she whispered to Swedish in City Square on Saturday. 'This guy's not in my league. Whereas you, Giles, you...' Maybe she'd had Giles spotted as proper freedom fighter material. Whereas you, Jack Hargraves? You? More like a day tripper. A day at Greenham. A day in Leeds. As Bowers said yesterday, summat and nowt.

"Jack, you okay?"

"What?"

"You okay, Bro?"

Tracy beside him, looking up for once, concern on her plump face.

"Oh aye, Sis," said Jack. "Don't worry. Fine and dandy, me."

"But you're not fine and dandy today, are you? Please don't pretend just to protect me. I wanna be here for you."

"Allus said you were the best. I don't deserve a sister like you."

"Ja-ack," said Tracy, blushing. "You're a brill brother. You've always looked after me. I wanna look after you an all."

"Don't. Please. You'll set me off blubbin'."

"I'm sorry it din't work out wi' Clare, Jack. It meks me sad. She was special."

"Aye, she was. And so are you. Thanks, Sis."

Jack heard the creak of the shop door and there, minus postbag, was postman, Jimmy-Whizz. By the looks of it, another early finish for 'Yorkshire's Quickest Postie'. Late thirties, lean, neatly clipped sideburns and tache. He held the door open with a low bow, as estate agent Patricia ascended the steps.

"Me Lady," he said, like Parker from Thunderbirds.

"My man," said Patricia, walking past him into the shop, her needle-like heels tapping on the chessboard floor, the shape of her out of fashion blouse shoulder pads showing through her long fawn coat.

"All as I'd say, Tricia, is I'm glad I bought me house a few years since," said Jimmy, shutting the door behind her.

"Indeed, Jimmy," said Patricia, the smell of her hairspray already getting up Jack's nose. "It's all the people from outside seeking a Dales bolt-hole who are pushing up prices. Most of them only stay in the village say once a fortnight, but they'll pay top dollar. Take that young couple who bought number thirty seven, just up the street here, in the summer."

"Oh, Gary and Vanessa?"

"Money to burn."

"Carries on t' same way and Fowlbeck will end up a ghost town, Trish."

"It's the nouveau riche, Jimmy."

"The nouveau riche, Treash."

It was almost dinnertime when Beaky Susan could resist temptation no more and popped over the High Street into Hargraves' Butchers. Jack knew she'd have been itching all morning to find out why Mum and Tracy were working of a quiet Monday.

"How come you two are working today?" she said to them from near the cabinet, them in the corner by the dairy fridge, sitting on stools they'd brought in from the prep room, supping brews of tea.

"Christmas will be here before we know it, Susan," said Mum, picking up what used to be the old man's clipboard from her lap and waving it at the antique biddy. "Helpin' with some Yuletide hamper ideas."

"Dennis not capable, then, Judy?"

"Folk deserve a day off sometimes."

"You mean t' same as young Jack here on Saturday?"

"The same as me on Saturday, aye, Susan," said Jack, stopping trimming brisket for her on the long table behind the cabinet, looking at her over his shoulder. "No bother to you, is it?"

"Not at all, not at all," said Susan, that beaky nose twitching, as she rubbed what smelt like beeswax into a little wooden Buddha with a cloth. "You not have any bother at t' weekend, then, lad?"

"It's none o' your business, Susan," said Mum.

"Leave it, Mum," said Jack.

"It's just, he doesn't seem himself today."

"Susan!"

"Mum, it's all right."

If Beaky only knew how much bother Jack had been through at the weekend, she'd be gossiping for Britain. He finished trimming, ripped a flimsy plastic bag off the wall-mounted reel of them, put the meat in it, sealed it with a sticky blue tag, weighed it on the digital scales.

"As they say in the land of onions, Susan, that's shallot," he said, passing her the brisket over the top of the cabinet.

"How much?" said Susan, stuffing the Buddha and cloth into one of her dog blanket cardigan pockets and taking the meat.

"A quid and ten, please."

When she'd dug around in the other cardigan pocket for some change, and put a pile of it on top of the cabinet so Jack could do the counting himself, she had more to say.

"River's nearly burst its banks this morning, after yesterday's storm. By gum, I'll bet The Surge is a sight today! Eh, did you hear about that rave up t' dale on Saturday night? A load o' druggies commandeered a barn, they did. Commandeered a barn! What next, eh? We're being invaded by all and sundry nowadays. Oh, Jack?"

"What is it?" said Jack.

"What's your take on the massive new supermarket they're set to open about three mile this side o' Cropden?"

"Supermarket?"

"Have you not heard?" said Susan. "Land sale's just gone through. It's goin' to be huge, apparently. Nobody will have seen the like. Start building in the spring. No doubt there'll be plenty more Fowlbeck folk shopping there. Why wouldn't you? It'll be nowt but a few mile away, much closer than t' other supermarkets, and you can do a full shop. What's up, lad? Oh, I see. Well, they'll have a big butchery department, it's true. Take a lot of trade off you and your mate. Question is, afore long, will the village have need of two butchers?"

"I don't know, Susan," said Jack. "That nose o' yours extend into t' future, does it?"

She looked riled at that. They stared at each other across the cabinet, like Clint Eastwood and Lee Van Cleef.

"What's this about a new supermarket, Susan?" said Mum, a tremble in her voice.

"It's reet, Mum. She's just leaving."

"Keep the change," said Susan, stomping off. "Might need every penny soon."

At the shop door, nimble for a biddy, she did a kind of quick half-spin and fired a parting shot before she left.

"How's it going wi' that lass you've been courting, Jack? Not seen her in a while. Hasn't moved on to pastures new, has she? Found someone a bit more in her class?"

Beaky Susan had gone now. The shop door rattled for a second with the force of her shutting it. Mum was saying summat from the stools by the dairy fridge. But Jack couldn't make it out right well. The buzz of the cabinet strip lights suddenly seemed dead noisy, as he looked down at the white trays of pale meat. *Bit more in her class*. Summed the job up. Clare was out of your league. Bowers had likely been right about you being jealous of what him and Elsa have as well. Face it. Not good enough to keep the one woman you've ever loved. *Made a right pig's ear of it.* Not good enough to do summat worthwhile in life either. Jack Hargraves, freedom fighter? Fucking joke. You might hate him for it, but Bowers had that right too. Time to face reality good and proper now, lad. This shop is all you'll ever be worth. Just a butcher, that's you. Always will be. Same as Michael Bowers. A bag of shite butcher.

CHRISTMAS 1992

CHAPTER TWENTY-TWO

Michael had not long said goodbye to the last customer of the day and was outside his shop near the bottom of the High Street, unhooking the string of pheasants and partridge from beneath the *'Bowers' Family Butchers – Finest Quality Meats Since 1877'* sign. Another flipping shit day for sales. He'd banked on more, what with nowt but a fortnight till Christmas Eve. The shop had been struggling for a couple of years now. Things were starting to look desperate. He were pinning his hopes on this festive season. A bad Christmas and you might have to... No, give over fretting... It does you no good...How many times does Elsa have to tell you? Yes, but what if? What if?

He held the line of limp-necked game at his side and bowed his head. The long pheasant tail feathers brushed against his brown market boots until the string of birds stopped swinging.

"Cheer up, Michael," said Craig, the local mechanic, striding past in overalls, a battered fish butty in his greasy hand. "Might never happen."

"What might never happen?"

"No idea, lad," said Craig, looking over his shoulder and waving his sandwich about as he moved off down the street. "The Queen might never have another annus horribilis, the IRA might never plant another bomb, Nick fuckin' Berry might never be allowed to sing 'Heartbeat' again! Come on, gi' us a smile, mate. It's nearly Christmas."

As if Michael needed reminding of that. Or of how crucial it could turn out to be. Plenty enough reminders about already. All them multicoloured lights, bright as Blackpool under the darkness of the late afternoon winter sky, for a kick off. Forming reindeer pulling sleighs high above the street, and Santas lugging sacks up lampposts, lighting up Christmas trees in near as damn it every shop window. There were the wreaths of holly and ivy hanging on house doors too. And the blackboard sign outside the off-licence offering mulled wine. And the bunch of school kids and teachers belting out carols by the war memorial. And the sparkly poster on the village noticeboard, opposite, advertising Fowlbeck Dramatic Society's Christmas panto. And the smell of hot mince pies. Or was that his mind playing tricks? More than likely. His mind got up to all sorts nowadays.

As a blue Renault Clio went by on its way uphill, a horse trotted past downhill on the other side of the street, its glossy chestnut coat standing out against the grey limestone buildings.

"Busy day, Michael?" said Mrs Taylor, the hill farmer, on board the chestnut in jodhpurs and luminous jacket, curly hair sprouting from under her riding helmet.

"Oh aye, Mrs Taylor," said Michael, twisting one end of the string the birds were tied to tightly round a couple of his fingers. "Allus busy this time o' year."

"Glad to hear it. I'll be sure to pop in for me turkey next week."

"Only the finest quality turkeys sold in this shop, Mrs Taylor. Why not try a pheasant this year as well? Only the very best..."

But she'd clip-clopped out of earshot. Michael realised he'd got to holding the string of birds aloft, like some poor street vendor living hand to mouth. He lowered his arm again. Busy flipping day? Who were he kidding? He'd resorted to lying now, so as to try preserving Bowers' reputation. What had made him sink so low? Being in the middle of the longest, deepest recession he could remember didn't help. What was it now, six quarters? And Black Wednesday to boot. That supermarket akin to an aircraft carrier, which opened virtually down the road a couple of years since, had stolen a fair chunk of custom as well. More Fowlbeck properties empty most of the time too, due to yet another rise in folk from outside buying second homes in the beautiful Yorkshire Dales. All stuff that had had a big impact on trade these past two or three years. You'd have to be a barmpot to deny it. But that was *what* had made Michael and Bowers' Family Butchers sink so low. There were also the question of *who* had made that happen.

His tired eyes looked up the High Street and fixed on the brightest festive lights of all. Them blazing out through the window of Hargraves' so-called butcher's shop. So bright, they made Michael think of when his dad used to tell him not to look directly at the sun. Make you blind, staring a while at that cheap, nasty promotion of Christmas deals at knock-down prices. Butcher's shop? Nearly half the gear Jack Hargraves shifted nowadays wasn't even meat. Truth be told, he'd just about taken to running a crappy little grocers. And the meat he flogged weren't worthy of being sold in a proper butchers. Never had been, mind. When had he ever been to a farm or auction to source top quality stock? Phone your order through to Cropden Slaughterhouse and they'll do the rest. Job'll be right. Not so much as a need for casting your eye over what you're buying. Be good to ask Hargraves how he slept at night. Except they'd not spoken to one another for three years. But what was even more galling was that, despite recessions, supermarkets, second homes, judging by gossip and how many punters walked up them steps and through that door, the bloke seemed to be making a real success of his business. At whose expense, though? Hold up, he's appeared atop his shop steps now.

Suddenly riled, Michael watched Hargraves close his shop door, spark a cigarette, slip the packet and lighter into the front pocket of his butcher's apron. You couldn't make out his face right well from two hundred yards off, but that body language seemed a giveaway. Leaning against the door, looking heavenward, exhaling smoke slowly. You might think that showed satisfaction, but Michael reckoned it meant the opposite. Hargraves couldn't bide that shop, could he? He'd always hated it. Why were he so *hell bent* on its success nowadays, then? So much so that he wasn't averse to underhand tactics either. Undermining Bowers' shop time and again. He used to say all he wanted were a fair slice of the pie. He used to say he was only running the place out of obligation to his family. Now it looked like he wanted to destroy Bowers' Butchers into the bargain. To think there was likely still enough trade to go round even now. If Hargraves had any decency left. Michael were forever trying to work out what had been driving him these past three years. Surely, you couldn't just put it down to a grudge from when they'd had their fall out. Not as if the bloke hadn't put his *own* two penneth in back then, was it?

A knackered looking wagon made its way down the street, past the smoking Hargraves, the newsagents, the chip shop, Ye Olde Tearooms. Michael smelt its mucky fumes as it clattered by, glimpsed its piled load of dark earth, stared at the two teenage boys in hoodies chasing dead close after it on bikes. Not seen them kids afore. More folk from outside? Off-cum-dens, as Grandad used to call them. Everyone's welcome, though. So long as they spend brass at Bowers' shop. Course they're welcome. But Michael felt like shouting after them all the same: 'There's nobody alive who's ever seen this High Street without Bowers' Family Butchers on it, you know!'

Come on, lad. You're dwelling on stuff too much again. You must have been standing here holding this bloody string of birds nearly five minutes now. Best get back inside and crack on. Got to help Mum clear everything away. Then put them decorations up. A fortnight afore Christmas Eve, that's the shop tradition. He turned to go inside, but couldn't resist one last look up the High Street at Jack Hargraves. The bloke had finished his cigarette. Now, brightly lit on that top step, he were facing down the street. Staring straight at Michael, by the looks of it. Standing dead still, legs wide apart, arms folded across his chest. There were summat permanent in that stance. Something you could never shift.

Back in the shop, Michael asked Mark, the only full-timer he still employed, to hang the string of birds in the walk-in prep room fridge afore he clocked off for the day. When Mark emerged from the prep room again, out of his butcher's gear now and in his denim jacket covered with heavy metal badges, he walked past Mum, who was washing knives and cleavers at the sink, and up to Michael as he scrubbed down the bowed and bloodied butcher's block.

"Sorry I've got to get off a bit early today, boss," he said.

"It's reet," said Michael, stopping scrubbing, standing up straight to face him.

"Christmas dinners are flyin' out at t' Dog and Gun now and..."

"I know, Mark. George needs an extra pair of hands in t' kitchen."

"Ya know how he gets. I need to stay on t' right side of him, that's all. In case..."

"I understand."

"In case..." said Mark, his sharp grey eyes darting about nervously.

Stopped acting so daft lately, hadn't he? Not his self

since it dawned on him that he might not have a job for life anymore.

"See yer bright and early tomorrow," said Michael.

"Boss?" said Mark.

"Aye?"

"Is everythin' gonna be all right?"

Michael sighed and shook his head.

"I don't know, mate."

Mark pulled his ponytail from under his denim jacket and began sloping off, past the black and white photos of the Bowers' generations toward the shop door.

"Remember to remind George we can supply him wi' t' finest game in Yorkshire for his Christmas dinners," said Michael. "It's not everyone as wants second-rate turkey from Hargraves' shop."

"Aye, boss."

"Bye, Mark," said Mum.

"Bye, Carol," said Mark, stepping out onto the High Street pavement, shutting the door.

Michael took to scrubbing the butcher's block again in long, hard strokes. The brush's stiff bristles scoured away at the beech wood, making a kind of whooshing sound, akin to the ebb and flow of a harsh tide. It set him thinking on the Sunday he'd had at the seaside this summer with Elsa and Bernie. Elsa snuggled in his arms, the same as Mum used to with Dad, while they watched barefoot Bernie running away from incoming waves, then chasing them back out again, laughing his little head off.

"What's up, love?" said Mum, hanging a cleaver from a hook above the long wooden table on the back wall.

"Nowt."

"Come on, Michael. You've been quiet all day."

"Yer know what's up, Mum," said Michael, still

scrubbing.

Half an hour later, they'd finished scrubbing down, clearing everything away, storing the last of the unsold meat in the prep room. Now they'd swapped their butcher's whites for everyday clothes and were kneeling opposite each other in the middle of the floorboard shop floor, sorting through the right dusty-smelling box of baubles and tinsel that Michael had fetched from the prep room loft. The Christmas tree he'd had delivered from Tattersall's estate this morning stood bare in the corner closest to the butchers' photos, where Bowers' Christmas trees always stood, planted in a sand-filled, galvanised bucket. 'O Little Town of Bethlehem' was playing quietly on the portable compact disk player Mum had bought for the purpose of treating Bowers' punters to the old classics. 'Let's have a listen to Carol's carols,' she'd said, when she'd put the CD on a couple of minutes since, by the sound of it doing her best to stay light-hearted.

"Saw Hargraves on his top step when I were outside a bit back," said Michael, eventually, trying to untangle fairy lights from a long length of glittery red tinsel.

"Forget him," said Mum, taking baubles from the box, collecting them like an apple-picker in her roll-neck jumper.

"Starin' straight at me, he was. And cocky wi' it."

"Could you tell from that distance?"

"Well, if not cocky, defiant. I cottoned that much. He'll never let up."

"It's not about him, Michael. It's about us getting this place back on track."

"Yer reckon I've dropped me standards, then, Mum?" said Michael, finally separating the lights from the tinsel.

"I didn't say that. It's not your fault, what's happened."

"I know I've kept up t' standard of what we sell. But this shop's gettin' shabby."

"Could do with a lick of paint, maybe," said Mum, her big brown eyes scanning the smudged white walls.

"And them cracked Victorian tiles could do wi' bein' replaced. And that pendulum clock's losing time and wants fixing. And we'll need a new butcher's block afore long."

"Oh, Michael, you must try to keep positive."

Mum had concern on her face now. Even them laughter lines seemed to have lost their jolliness. That worried look was similar to the one Michael remembered from when he'd been a nipper and she'd picked him up whenever he took a tumble. Made him feel like he'd gone back to being a little boy, that look. What a flipping downer! Now Mummy stood up, one arm cradling the baubles in her jumper, walked to the tree, set to decorating it like someone who'd never wanted apples to fall.

The CD choir sang 'Away in a Manger', as Michael took the cable of fairy lights to the tree, put it on the floor next to Mum, went to the prep room for stepladders. Back in the shop, gathering up the long length of red tinsel from the box on the way, he carried the ladders to the corner by the shop door, climbed them, took a drawing pin from the pocket of his brown corduroy trousers, pinned one end of the tinsel to the old lath and plaster ceiling. Then, dragging the ladders with him, he started moving diagonally across the shop, stopping every couple of feet to pin up the length of tinsel, so it made curves in the air akin to toy hammocks. He'd best keep cracking on with what needed doing. Not that he could shift the picture of Hargraves, arms folded on that top step, out of his head.

Disgusting, the way he's been these past three years. No mistake. Is there nowt beyond him? Has he turned into his old man? Getting more like him, anyhow. His nasty little games started with them blackboard signs outside his shop that his dad was so fond of using. Advertising his shitty little produce, but having a swipe at the only proper butchers in Fowlbeck while he were at it: **'TRADITION'S TRADITION. BUT TRY SOMETHING *DIFFERENT*.' 'SICK OF LIVING IN THE PAST? WANT MORE FROM YOUR BUTCHERS? TRY OUR DELICIOUS BAKERY RANGE.'** Them signs and all the rest. Including the most galling of the lot, half of it a downright dirty lie: **'CHEAPER PRICES. SAME QUALITY.'**

Hargraves had used similar tactics in his door-to-door leaflet campaigns too. Never neglecting to put one through Michael, Elsa and Bernie's letterbox of course. Then there were his cheap little digs in his Gazette newspaper interviews, about traditional butchers supposedly not offering folk what they needed in *these challenging economic times*. But it was the bloke starting rumours to mucky Bowers' Butcher's reputation that mostly got Michael's goat. In light of everything else he were up to, it had to be Hargraves spreading gossip. Over his shop cabinet, no doubt. Down The Dog and Gun, on the High Street, whenever the flipping chance presented itself! Michael cottoned on to bits of conversation right enough, read people's faces, picked up on their body language. He wasn't thick. In the last few weeks alone, he'd caught folk saying that his shop was losing money, that his standards were slipping, that corners were being cut. That the meat wasn't as good as it used to be, that the case of food poisoning in the village earlier this year could well have been down to Bowers' Family Butchers. Well, this place might be losing money, it could do with a lick of paint, but the rest were a pack of bloody lies! And Hargraves had to be responsible. Michael didn't want to hate him for it, but he was being humiliated.

"Ow!" he said, up the ladders in the middle of the shop

by the butcher's block now.

"What's the matter, love?" said Mum, looking up from the tree, fairy lights in hand.

"Pricked me thumb, that's all."

"You daft thing. Have you just got those pins loose in your pocket?"

"Aye."

"You silly sausage."

"Yer sound like Elsa talkin' to Bernie."

It seemed like Mum wanted to say summat to that. But then she sort of half-smiled at him and got back to decorating the tree, hanging the unlit cable of fairy lights among the shiny baubles.

Michael, the top of his head almost touching the buzzing ceiling strip light, his ruddy cheeks feeling hot under its heat, took in the shop from above. Could all be gone soon. Might be no need of a new butcher's block. Fridge cabinets ripped out. Original cash till and weighing scales slung in a skip somewhere. Framed generation photographs taken down. Would Bernie even want to keep them after his mummy and daddy were no more? Oh yes, photos would likely end up in a skip one day as well. Crushed and forgotten. Along with owt else ever associated with Bowers' Family Butchers. Perhaps the only thing remembered, the butcher who failed his forefathers, left his son no legacy, broke a link in the chain of the Fowlbeck way of life. And to think that butcher once told his dad he'd never let him down. Left an ache in his heart, that thought, put a knot in his guts, filled his mind with shame.

Making another 'toy hammock' under the strip light, Michael pinned the next part of the tinsel to the ceiling. Just pushing a blooming drawing pin into soft plaster somehow took a big effort this time, mind. Felt like the energy were draining from him. Was he a bit unsteady on his feet too? The ladders wobbled, as he climbed down to move them to the serving side of the butcher's block.

As he was about to go up the ladders again, Mum switched off the strip light and flicked on the fairy lights.

"Ta da!" she said, doing a little curtsey, like she'd just finished a dance with Eddie, then opening her arms wide, as if she fancied giving the glowing tree a hug. "What do you think, love?"

"Looks reet enough," said Michael, stepping onto the bottom rung. "Put t' big light on again, will yer?"

Mum switched on the strip light and went to rummage in the box of decorations. Michael climbed the ladders, reached across for the dangling end of tinsel, took another pin from his pocket. The CD choir had got to singing 'Silent Night' now, the noise of a car horn came from the High Street, the sharp smell of disinfectant rose from cleaned surfaces. How could Hargraves live with himself? Nowt wrong with growing your business, of course. But, while you were at it, doing your damnedest to ruin the shop run by the person it meant everything to? The person who relied on it to feed his family? The person who'd once been your best mate? To think they used to practically love one another. With that kind of betrayal, was it any wonder it hurt so much? How could Hargraves do it? Michael kept getting flashes of anger, at times he even felt like he wanted to kill the selfish git, but it were the depth of hurt which betrayal brought that was crushing him. Why had Hargraves gone to such extremes? Yes, maybe he still felt an obligation to his family. Yes, he'd always been competitive. Yes, he likely still resented being told some home truths three years since. Yes, he probably didn't feel right brilliant about himself. But to become such a bastard as a result? You couldn't flipping well fathom it!

"What shall we have at the top of the tree this year, Michael?" said Mum, standing by the box, putting a big smile on, holding up the options. "The star or the fairy?"

"Listen a minute," said Michael, realising he hadn't got round to making another toy hammock yet, but looking down at Mum from the top of the ladders, anyhow. "Yer say we need to put this place back on track, right? But what more can we do? Tell me that. We've advertised, sponsored events, done country shows, kept spreading t' word that our meat is still the finest, stuck to principles that have served this shop since 1877. So what more can we do? If yer know, can you tell me? Cos I'm strugglin' here, no mistake. Know the truth? Whatever we set about doing to get this shop back on track, we're fighting a losin' battle. Know why? Because that bugger up t' road is doing all he can to muck up our reputation! And I'm not retaliating by stoopin' to his level, I'm tellin' yer. Never! Us Bowers are better than that. Folk know they're buying crap from his crappy shop, anyhow. They don't need me pointin' it out. But they still bloody well buy it! It's beyond me."

"Calm down, love," said Mum. "You might fall."

"How can I calm down? How? Jack Hargraves is sendin' this shop under! He's destroying it! He's destroying Bowers' Family Butchers, Mum!"

CHAPTER TWENTY-THREE

With ten days until Christmas Day, and the digital clock above Hargraves' Butcher's glossy red shop door showing less than an hour until opening time, Jack was setting out pre-packed meat on the white plastic trays in the main cabinet. He could hear Tracy singing along to the radio in the prep room. A fucking *decent* Christmas song, 'Fairytale of New York.' At least nowt like the rest of the festive shite folk had to endure these days.

"Enjoyin' ya sen in there, Sis?" he said, standing up straight too quickly from the cabinet as he raised his voice, feeling a stab of pain in his brain from another hangover.

"Yes ta, Bro. This song's brill!"

Good to have Tracy working here part-time now. Jack was chuffed for her as well. What had happened to that whispery voice? Just about gone. Yes, she still got shy and embarrassed plenty, but she looked folk in the eye more now, stood up for herself a bit, especially with regard to Mother. She'd even lost weight. The lass liked herself more and that was always the most important thing. Done her wonders, having a boyfriend. Young love, eh? Oh yes, remember that?

When Jack had finished putting the batch of packed meat in the now three-quarter full cabinet, he reached for his clipboard and pen from the long metal table behind him. Better get through this checklist and make sure you're on top of the job. Doubtless make another killing on sales today. Knock Bowers' Butchers into the middle of next week again.

If gossip was owt to go by, Michael Bowers' stuck-in-the- mud shop had a right struggle on now. And, judging by the bloke's miserable demeanour whenever you saw him about, the rumours were true. Likely not be long before his shop was six foot under. Well that's life, sonny Jim. Jack gazed at the checklist on his clipboard, remembering how him and Bowers used to keep a checklist for their secret Waterfall Den collection. Oh, give over being soppy and get a shift on, lad.

Nibbling at the little bulge in his bottom lip, he started moving around the shop, intent on ticking off jobs on the list that had already been done. Not right far off a military operation, this. But with full-timers, Frank and Dennis, out and about, busy motoring round the dale making deliveries and boosting profit, you had to be organised like a sergeant in that Bosnian War that kept on raging. Fucking horrific atrocities going on over there! War in Europe again, eh? Only three years after The Wall had come down too. The world never learnt, did it? Enough to make you puke. But come on, shape yourself. Better get some jobs ticked off.

Knackered Christmas light bulbs replaced, check. Back to two hundred or so in good order, strung about the place. Christ, bright as the sun in here! Attracted punters like moths, mind. Today's deals chalked up on the blackboards, check. Folk need value for money these days, Bowers. Not that you'll ever cotton on, history boy. Chessboard floor mopped, check. Poultry, mince, pie range, lamb chops and joints, check. Festive sausage range, brisket, rump, sirloin, check. Dairy fridge restocked, check. Bakery range bread and sandwiches out and ready to fly, check. Good lass, Tracy. Bargain Christmas hampers, check. Cranberry sauce, brandy sauce, chutneys, pickled onions, check. Free cheese and wine tasters on top of the cabinet, check. Be ready for opening, no bother.

Jack was next to the shop door, about to swap his clipboard for the cigs and Zippo in his apron pocket and step outside, when Tracy walked in from the prep room carrying a baking tray in oven-gloved hands.

"Mince pie, Jack?" she said, on her way to the bakery display, that new lightness to her voice.

"They smell sweet," said Jack.

"That'll be me special recipe. Want one, then?"

"Better not. Likely not keep it down."

"Charming!"

"Too much ale last neet, Sis."

"Oh, Ja-ack," said Tracy, turning to him from the bakery display, looking him straight in the eye. "You all right?"

"Bit rough."

"No. I mean, are you *all right*?"

He couldn't help being happy for her. She had some sparkle in her eyes now, held her head up more, didn't do that nervous thing of touching her face with her fingertips so much. There was summat grown up about her these days, as there should be at twenty-two, but she'd been similar to a kid until a few months since.

"Earth to Jack."

"Eh?"

"You okay?"

"Fine and dandy," said Jack, putting his clipboard on top of the cabinet, next to the cheese and wine tasters. "Ta for doin' extra hours in t' Christmas run up, Tracy. I know you're only supposed to be part-time, and you've fairish on at t' stables, but you're a big help."

"No probs," said Tracy, setting out the pies precisely on an angled shelf. "Are you sure you can afford me wages, though?"

"Come off it, Sis. Ya know how busy we've been these past two or three years. All t' shop's debt's paid off now, we're nicely in profit, course I can afford it. You're worth every penny an all."

"Thanks."

"How's it goin' wi' lover-boy?" said Jack, rummaging in his apron for cigs and Zippo.

"Ja-ack," said Tracy, turning properly red.

"I'm happy for you."

"How's *your* love life goin', anyhow?"

"Up and down. In and out."

And they had a good laugh.

A minute later, Jack was out in the cold morning, having a smoke on his top step. Pretty dark as yet. High Street Christmas lights aglow like lanterns in a cave. The surrounding hills, rugged moors, jagged-rock Beacon made this village seem similar to a dark cave sometimes, day or night. That darkness often came from feeling glum too, though. He took a hard drag on his cigarette, tasting its filthy smoke, feeling its harshness in his throat, not giving a fuck. Another day in Fowlbeck. He watched the street getting busier with traffic and passers-by. And shopkeepers taking deliveries or setting out window displays in squares of light. The paper girl had set to swinging her empty bag round her head like a lasso. A right scruffy school kid, slouching his way to the bus stop, buttons dangling off his blazer, was playing on one of those Nintendo Gameboys that were all the rage. Peggy White's ancient dog was yapping at her while she wiped condensation off her biddy's glasses with her beige scarf. Everyday life and not much change. But sometimes you had to give over moaning. Accept what fate had dealt. Make the best of a bad job.

Jack stubbed out his cig on the steps' frosty iron railing, tugged at his apron, fiddled with a silver ring on his finger, as he looked down the High Street, beyond the river, toward Fowlbeck Beacon three miles away. You could just see its outline now. It set him thinking on times when he'd climbed it with Bowers and gazed at far off horizons from its summit. Only horizons he gazed at these days were pictures on telly or in broadsheet newspapers. Enough murderous bastards about in the world again this year, weren't there? Balkan Wars, Middle East, South Africa, fifteen hundred massacred in Bombay only last week! Plenty of heroism about too, mind. U.N. peacekeepers in Somalia, Mandela taking no shite off de Klerk, Yeltsin and Bush stopping pointing their big dick nuclear weapons at one another, three hundred thousand protesting in Berlin against right wingers attacking immigrants. He wondered if Clare had been on that protest. You wouldn't put it past her. He knew he still thought about her too much. But they could have been part of that scene together. Altruistic. Heroic. But she'd rejected him. Oh yes, he'd ended up failing before he'd started with that job. Jack Hargraves, failed freedom fighter. Summat and nowt.

A fair old bite in the air this morning, chilly breeze cutting to the bone. There was talk proper wintry weather might be on the way too. And here were Mr and Mrs Dobson from Doncaster, recent purchasers of a Fowlbeck bolt-hole, dressed as if they were ready for snow. Striding past, all puffed up like giant gaudy maggots in hiking clobber.

"Brass monkeys this mornin', Jack," said Mr Dobson, from somewhere in his hood.

"Ya look prepared for it. Early start?"

"We're planning on conquering The Beacon by lunch," said Mrs Dobson.

"Oh, Jack?" said Mr Dobson, stopping a few yards down the street, a fat mitten shooting to his head. "Our Christmas hamper ready yet?"

"Aye."

"That's a good do. We'll pick it up later. Off back to sunny Donny this aft."

"Reet you are."

"Ta-ta, Jack."

"Ta-ta, Mrs Dobson."

Doctor Clegg drove past in his growling, highly polished Jag, checking his oiled moustache in his rear view mirror, blasting out Beethoven so the world could hear it through his shut windows. Beaky Susan was letting herself into her shop, opposite, sneering at Jack over her shoulder as she stepped inside. Would she ever die?

Jack put his hands deep into his trouser pockets, drew his arms close to his sides, bit the bulge in his bottom lip. Making the best of a bad job, eh? Folk might reckon there was nowt right special in it, and it was nothing like being a freedom fighter, but he knew it to be a kind of heroism too. If a butcher boy was all you'd amounted to, and you frigging despised it, then the more of a success you made it the more heroic you were, weren't you? Especially if you helped others in the process. Especially if those you'd set to helping were Mother and Tracy, the ones you'd hurt so much, damaged so much, in the first place.

Jack stared down the street at Michael Bowers' dimly lit shop. Shame that a consequence of Hargraves' Butcher's success looked like it might be Bowers' Butcher's downfall. Shame that a former mate's pride and joy could be going under, over a century's tradition and all that bollocks, but what did the bloke want? Sympathy? Just the way of the world, lad. He should have kept his gob shut three years since, anyway. What did he expect now then, after that? Sympathy?

Half an hour before opening time, Jack was back in the shop, putting meat under the cabinet's buzzing strip lights again, while Tracy neatly laid out her pastries and chocolate Christmas logs on the bakery display's silvery shelves.

Annie Lennox was singing 'Walking on Broken Glass' in the prep room. It got Jack thinking on the day he'd crashed that bastard lintel through this cabinet when it was brand new. His old man's icy glare bearing down on him from right bulgy eyes. From that moment, he was likely destined to finish up staying here, wasn't he? His fate forever tied to this cabinet.

"Went to t' cinema the other day, Tracy," he said, cramming cellophane-wrapped mince between turkeys and pork.

"What did you see?"

"'Unforgiven.' Clint Eastwood. Best thing he's done in donkey's years."

"Allus liked Clint, haven't you?" said Tracy, stepping back from her display and inspecting it.

"No-one plays a gunslinger like Clint."

A tractor lumbered past on the High Street, Annie Lennox faded, the fluorescent tubes kept on buzzing.

"Anyway," said Jack, half sighing it. "Crackin' on and all that. Got a couple o' Christmas promotion ideas I fancy running by ya when we have a brew before openin', Sis."

"Oh yeah?"

"We'll mek a right killin'. Bowers won't know what's hit him."

"Is that really what you...?"

"I'll tell you as soon as we've stocked t' shelves. When we have a brew."

While Tracy put finishing touches to the bakery display, Jack squeezed the last of the meat into the cabinet. Then he brewed up in the prep room, carried two mugs of steaming tea into the shop, sat with his sister on stools that she'd placed in the middle of the chessboard floor.

"There ya go, lass," he said, passing Tracy her tea.

"Ta. Din't put sugar in, did you?"

"Thought you'd given over tekin it."

"I have."

"Well then."

She smiled at him as she held the hot brew up to her chin in both hands, the steam rising over her leaner face, her brighter eyes.

"Out on t' razzle dazzle with David tonight, Tracy?" said Jack, running his spare hand over the short haircut he'd lately had cropped with clippers.

"Off round to his. He's makin' spag bol."

"Decent cook, is he?"

"Brill," said Tracy.

"He's a good lad, Sis. I like him."

"I'm glad."

"He treats you right and he meks you happy," said Jack. "Both."

"His clobber's a bit knackered, mind."

"Ja-ack!"

"I'm joshin' you. What do they call it? Grunge?"

"All the rage," said Tracy, blowing on her tea.

"He's a good un. Has Mother teken to him yet?"

"She can't see past his clothes."

"Doubtless she'll be here soon," said Jack. "Checking up on the shop. I'll have a word if you like."

"I've already told her to butt out."

"Different person these days, aren't ya?"

Jack slowly started turning full circle on his stool, taking in the brightly lit shop, fit to burst with stock. Still a bag of shite butchers, this place. But at least he'd not just settled for selling meat, like Bowers. Oh yes, Hargraves' Butchers smelt of raw, cold meat, but it smelt of baking and dairies and grocery shops too. Even stuck in a fucking butchers,

Jack Hargraves had managed to broaden his horizons. That was the difference between him and Michael Bowers, right there.

"What you grinnin' at, Cheshire cat?" said Tracy, as he faced her again.

"Summat and nowt."

"Got more Christmas promotion ideas, then?"

"Here's two," said Jack. "Number one. Let's have a stall out on t' pavement. We'll bung a load of products out. Your homemade Chrimbo jams and chutneys, those delicious smellin' mince pies, full cheese selection, mulled wine. All quintessential Yuletide stuff. We can call it 'A Taste of Christmas.' Put a big banner up. And taste's the key. Taste it and they'll likely buy it. Same idea as we've got wi' this cheese and wine on t' cabinet. But right outside the shop, so folk think twice about walking by. Doubtless there'll be a fair few traditionalists round here averse to it, but there'll be lots that won't be. These people with second homes in t' village lap up owt new as well."

"Not a bad plan, Bro."

"Cheers."

They raised their mugs, supped some tea. Slade started belting out 'Merry Christmas Everybody' in the prep room.

"Not this again!" said Tracy.

"They'd just as well sling it on a loop," said Jack.

"It's always on. What's your other idea, then?"

"Leaflet campaign. I know we've done door-to-door leaflets before, but not in t' run up to Christmas. We'll mek them nice and bright, highlight our best deals, put a picture of a festive hamper on there. And your bakery display of course."

"Obviously."

"Goes wi' out sayin'. But the main job will be to print

some reminders on it."

"Reminders?" said Tracy, shifting on her stool, like she had to be sitting comfortably.

"First, a reminder that we offer a much wider product range than fella-me-lad down t' street. Ya know, we're definitely a butchers, but we've got similarities to supermarkets an all. Folk expect choice and variety these days. Second, we do good quality, but we also do it a damn sight cheaper than Michael Bowers. Providing for people in tough economic times. And third, a nudge in t' direction of hygiene. Just to remind folk that it wasn't Hargraves' Butchers that caused food poisoning in the village early this year."

"Nobody proved it were Bowers' Butchers either."

"Come off it," said Jack. "Those two fogies shopped at Bowers' shop the day before they got poorly."

"But they went to about five other shops together that day too. Anyway, one of them said they weren't right sure it was food poisoning. Reckoned they might just have had a dicky tummy."

"You stickin' up for Bowers now, then?"

"No," said Tracy, averting her eyes a moment. "All I'm sayin' is we shouldn't spread rumours that might not be true."

"You are sticking up for him."

Jack was suddenly riled. Tracy must have known it, because now she had cheeks as red as Bowers' ruddy chops. And she'd reverted to touching her face with her fingertips. Frigging hell, he'd better go easy on the lass.

"Listen, Sis. Sorry if I sounded narked then. It's too much of a coincidence for me, that's all."

Tracy held her tea in both hands again, shifted on her stool, looked her brother dead in the eye, right serious.

"I'm pretty happy at t' moment, Jack," she said. "But

know what still makes me sad?"

"No."

"This falling out between you and Michael. Remember how close you used to be? Remember all them good times you had? More than that, even, remember what you helped each other through?"

"Well, course I do," said Jack, after a moment.

"I were so worried about you after Dad died. And Michael was the one who was there for you."

"Well..."

"And can I be honest with you, Jack?" said Tracy. "I don't think it's right that, when we're promoting our shop, we seem set on puttin' his down at t' same time."

"What you on about?" said Jack. "I'm doing this for you and your mum, ya know. I hate this job. But I'm still after mekin' the best success of it I can. Don't I get any credit for that? Eh? Bowers just happens to be the competition. It's the nature o' t' situation, that's all. Anyway, if his business ends up dead and buried, he can always sell the building, can't he? And that slaughterhouse that's been in their family since the dark ages. You know how much property prices have shot up round here recently. He's joint owner of those buildings wi' his mum, ya know. Same as we've been joint owners of this building along with Mother since I sorted it. With that little nest egg he's sittin' on, he could start another business. No bother. Or just get him sen a different job. When we were kids, he said he wouldn't mind being a gamekeeper."

"But Bowers' Butchers means the world to him."

"I said, when we were kids, he mentioned he wouldn't mind being a gamekeeper. Anyway, I've told you how he spoke to me three years back, haven't I? He's had it comin'. Don't be giving him any sympathy, Sis... Look, I know what that business means to him...Course he's set on keeping it

goin' for another hundred years... But... Eh, don't be showin'
him any sympathy...The way he spoke to me... You should
have been there... Besides...Anyway... Don't I get any credit
for how successful I've made..."

"Jack? Are you all right?"

"I've made..."

"Jack?"

CHAPTER TWENTY-FOUR

F ive days before Christmas Day, Michael and Elsa were finishing preparing Sunday dinner in their kitchen, as Bernie made a hellish racket with his train set under the dining room table.

"Choo-woo! Woo-choo-woo!" came his voice again through the opened door between the two rooms.

"Time to put them trains away, Bernie, darlin'," said Elsa, big mittens on, pouring meat juice from the oven tray, which had topside resting in it, into the saucepan of beefy-smelling gravy simmering on the hob.

"I've told him three times," said Michael, draining carrots at the sink by the lattice window, steam putting sweat on his face. "God knows why he din't set his flippin' trains up in t' front room."

"Choo-woo! Woo-choo-woo!"

"Bernie! Do as Mummy says!"

"Awwwww, Daddy's shoutin' again, Mummy."

Elsa put the tray on a chopping board, took off the big oven mitts, looked at Michael through her glasses in that questioning way she'd lately taken to using.

"What?" he said.

"Please give over shouting at him, Michael."

He watched her walk silently to him across the stone floor in her stocking feet and white jeans, twiddling them ringlets she'd recently had put in her hair because she'd taken a shine to how Madonna had hers this year. You'd likely say it looked sexy. Not that he felt much like sex nowadays. And how much had she spent on that haircut, anyhow? She were up close to him now, face to face, her Sunday best perfume swallowing the smell of boiled carrots, her hands linked behind his neck, akin to that night when they'd danced to Roxy Music in the front room. No danger of him getting a hard-on today, mind. It was the rest of him that had gone right stiff.

"Drain the bloody cabbage, then," said Elsa, turning from him and marching into the dining room. "Come on, Bernie, let's clear your trains away till after dinner."

"Mummy?"

"Yes, darlin'?"

"Why was Daddy shoutin' again?"

Michael leant back against the oak units and stared at the whirring washing machine, opposite. Another load of Bernie's clothes spinning like a patchwork whirlpool. Round and round and round. Life carried on, but what were going to happen to the little man now? With Christmas sales turning into a nightmare and the shop seeming close to finished? Perhaps the lad would never have entertained owt to do with Bowers' Butchers, anyhow. But it looked like he'd be the only Bowers in that long, proud line as had no choice.

The wind picked up outside, whistling among the cast iron gutters and drainpipes, rattling the back yard gate. Michael turned and peered through the lattice window at that bit of dusty snow from last night getting blown about between the millstones, slimy green stone trough, rusting Norton by the shed that him and Hargraves had never got round to racing. Best get the old girl slung afore long. Why have you kept the pissing thing? For the memories? Truth be told, looking at it puts sadness in you. But perhaps you'll feel sadder getting rid. His wife and son were chatting in the dining room now.

"Mummy?" said Bernie.

"Yes, darlin'?" said Elsa.

"Which chimney will Santa climb down? This room or t' front room?"

"Depends which hearth we leave Rudolph's mince pie on."

"But does Rudolph like mince pies, though?"

"Oh aye, gobbles 'em up for breakfast!"

Bernie giggled like a mad allik as Elsa 'gobbled him up for breakfast'. Somehow put a tear in Michael's eye, listening to that. He looked at the corroding chrome on the motorbike, remembered the day three years since when he'd set Hargraves to polishing it. The bugger had never let up after that day, had he? As if war had been declared or summat. You couldn't fathom it. Looked like he was after sticking his boot in one last time over Christmas as well. That leaflet shoved through your house door this morning suggested as much. Promoting Hargraves' shop while twisting the knife into Bowers' Butchers too. Same old bullshit. Bullshit! Bullshit! Michael hammered his fist down hard a few times on the oak units, blood raging through him.

"Bullshit! Bullshit! Bullshit!" he said, keeping it under his breath for Elsa and Bernie's sake.

But they must have heard his pounding fist.

"What's up?" said Elsa, in the doorway between the rooms, Bernie alongside, chubby arm around Mummy's thigh.

"What's up?" said Bernie, laughter still in his moist eyes, cheeks as red as Daddy's.

But Michael's words had dried up like a drought in summer. Nowt he could say to put things right. The wind died down outside. The washing machine whirred to a stop. You could hear the steady ticking of the grandfather clock's pendulum in the dining room. He tried steadying his racing heart. Bernie skipped across the kitchen and hugged his leg.

"Daddy, Daddy, Daddy," he said.

Michael ruffled his fine brown hair.

Minutes later, they were sitting at the table in the long, narrow dining room, with its lattice windows at either end letting in dull grey light from the back yard and High Street. Michael, at the head of the table, checked shirtsleeves rolled up to his elbows, was slicing through the Longhorn topside on one of Grandad's hand-me-downs, the blue-patterned carving dish. Elsa and Bernie were sitting opposite one another, just down from Michael, Elsa piling vegetables onto the three plates, Bernie messing about, swinging his legs back and forth under the table, kicking Daddy every other second.

"Hold up, Bernie. Stop kickin' me, will yer?"

"Sorry, Daddy," said Bernie, unbuttoning the cuffs on his shirt that was identical to Michael's, rolling his shirtsleeves up too. "Din't mean to."

"I know yer din't, mate," said Michael. "Fancy some best beef in Yorkshire?"

"But is it topside, though?"

"Longhorn topside."

"Flippin' heck!" said Bernie. "Yes pleeeaaaase!"

Michael trapped two slices of beef between his bone-handle carving knife and fork and lay them on Bernie's plate.

"Oh, thanks."

"That's all reet, Son," said Michael, putting meat on his and Elsa's plates.

"Best daddy in t' world, in't he, Mummy?"

"Course he is," said Elsa, catching Michael's eye.

As Elsa dished up her special cauliflower cheese, suggesting Bernie smell how tasty it was when he got a grumble on about eating it, Michael carved a couple more slices off the topside. You could tell by the way the knife cut through it how tender it were. Finest quality, no mistake. As Dad used to say it should be. Owt less and you'd never see it in Bowers' meat cabinet. He looked at the photograph of Dad in his butcher's gear, hanging on the wall, opposite. Michael wished he'd give over glaring back at him like that. Same went for Grandad, meaty forearms on show, on the wall nearest the kitchen too. And Great Grandad, with his long beard, on the wall behind him. And Great Great Grandad Albert, fists on hips, founder of Bowers' Family Butchers, on the chimney breast above the lit open fire. Generations on all sides, surrounding him, closing in, staring him out. Well, what did he expect? He was letting the lot of them down.

While Elsa put a dollop of horseradish on the side of her plate, poured gravy on her food, tried persuading Bernie to pour his own, Michael were drawn to that photo of Dad again. And this warm room, with its dark furniture, brasses, traditional ornaments, brought on memories of when he'd been nowt but three year old, lapping up Sunday dinner here with his mummy and daddy. And the smell of the tender Longhorn beef reminded him of that first early morning trip to Alan Akers' farm, sun painting the sky pink. And the fire's smoky smell set him thinking on them brilliant father and son camping trips up the dale. Oh yes, you're failing four generations all right, but it's your own father you're letting down most. Driving away from Akers' farm that morning had got in his head now: 'I won't let yer down, Daddy.' 'I know yer won't, Son.'

"Gravy, Michael?" said Elsa, passing him the gravy boat.

They ate in silence a few moments at the gingham-covered table. Logs crackled on the fire, a car revved up the High Street in the wrong gear, the grandfather clock ticked out time. Then Bernie piped up.

"Daddy?" he said, fork in both little hands, mashing up his roast spuds.

"Aye?"

"What's t' best present Santa ever give yer?"

"Dunno," said Michael.

"Aww come on, Daddy. The very bestest one?"

"Likely a push bike."

"Push bike?" said Bernie, mixing gravy and cabbage in with his potatoes.

"Left me a Chopper. Popular in them days, Choppers. Reet long seat, fat tyres, handlebars that curved up like cow horns."

"Cow horns? That's funny."

"Used to fairly bomb round on them, we did," said Michael.

"Did someone else get a Chopper bike off Santa an all, then?"

"Jack... I mean..."

"But who's Jack, though?"

"Give o'er messin' wi' that food and just eat it, lad!"

"Michael?" said Elsa, putting down her knife and fork.

"Sorry."

"Please stop."

As they began eating in silence again, Elsa somehow elsewhere, Michael watched Bernie trying hard with his table manners. Sitting up right straight, cutting his food properly, chewing with his mouth shut tight. Bless him. Deserving of more festive cheer in his own home, wasn't he? Not much merriment in this room. If it weren't for them Christmas cards dotted about, and a couple of half-wrapped presents they'd just about managed to afford on the sideboard, destined for Mum and Eddie, you'd be forgiven for not cottoning on to Christmas Day being just days off.

"Sorry for snappin' at yer, Bernie," said Michael, eventually.

"It's all reet, Daddy," said Bernie, before clamping

his tongue between his teeth and concentrating on cutting another corner off a juicy slice of topside.

By the time they'd finished the main course and started on their trifle, Elsa had put some jolliness in proceedings and got a game of 'I Spy' going for Bernie. Michael joined in for his boy's sake, if nowt else. The lad was flipping well loving it.

"I spy with my little eye something beginning with... Erm..."

"Shape your sen, Bernie," said Elsa, beaming at him.

"I am shapin' me sen, Mummy," said Bernie, dropping his spoon in his bowl, making a pointy roof shape above his head with his arms. "Triangle! Do yer get it, Daddy?"

"I get it, Son, I get it. Come on, I spy... "

"With my little eye something beginning with... Erm... M.B.P."

"A word beginnin' wi' MBP?" said Elsa, giggling.

"Three words," said Bernie, looking proper chuffed with himself. "One begins wi' 'M', one begins wi' 'B', one begins wi' 'P'."

"You dafty."

"Let's have t' job right, Bernie," said Michael. "That's not how yer play."

"He can play how he likes," said Elsa. "Can't you, darlin'?"

"Sorry I spoke."

Michael put his hands up. He felt akin to a nipper again, getting caught scrumping apples or summat.

"Man's big paws?" said Elsa, pointing at Michael's hands.

"No," said Bernie, folding his arms, shaking his head.

"Mummy's bowl... Em..." said Michael, lowering his big paws.

"Ooo, ooo, yer got one word right, Daddy!"

"Mummy's?"

"Yeah, yeah," said Bernie. *"Mummy's, Mummy's."*

"Mummy's *beautiful* paws?" said Elsa, wiggling her fingers over her trifle.

"Nope. Do yer give up?"

"Aye, we give up," said Michael.

"Mummy's brilliant pictures!" said Bernie, smiling his little head off, pointing at Elsa's oil paintings of The Dales that were alongside the generation photos on the burgundy walls.

"Aww, thank you, darlin'. Come here, gorgeous boy."

Michael watched his wife and son lean across the table and meet above the double cream for a kiss. If only life were that happy.

"Can you keep tellin' folk they're brilliant, Bernie?" said Elsa, as she sat back down. "Appen they'll sell a bit better then."

"Yer should find out Damien Hirst's secret," said Michael. "What do they reckon that 'Shark' of his is worth?"

"That piece in formaldehyde? Millions, most likely."

"Start painting sharks and we'll pay t' mortgage off on this place. Might even get to sellin' meat for fun, wi' out frettin' over making brass on it."

"Yeah, Mummy, start paintin' sharks, start paintin' sharks!"

Michael watched Elsa chuck her spoon in her half-eaten trifle and push her bowl away. Must have cottoned on to the sharkasm in the mortgage and meat comments. Like she could have missed it. She'd got to staring at the smeary mess of cutlery, crockery and leftovers on the table now, as if it were the state of their lives. The fire hissed and spat behind its meshed guard like caged anger. Bernie started kicking

Michael under the table again.

"Your turn, Daddy."

"Think we've finished, Son."

"Awwww."

"Sell up," said Elsa, eyes still on the messy table, firelight reflected in her glasses.

"Yer what?" said Michael, shock sending his blood cold.

Elsa glared at him, stony-faced.

"We can't carry on like this," she said. "*I'm* not carryin' on like this, Michael. And there's a family to feed. Sell the shop."

"Mummy? Should we leave summat for Santa to eat an all?"

"Quiet a minute, Bernie!" said Michael.

"Don't talk to him like that."

"What you on about, sell the shop?"

Elsa sighed and pushed her hands through her Madonna hair.

"Let's discuss this later, eh?" she said, nodding to indicate Bernie, who had his head over his bowl, scratching around its rim with his spoon. "I shun't have said owt while..."

"No, come on," said Michael, leaning toward her, hands on his thighs. "Yer reckon I should sell up now, then? Afore it's definitely all over?"

"You've been saying the shop's finished for months."

"*Headin'* that way, I've said. *Heading* that way. It's not over till it's over."

"We'll talk about it later," said Elsa.

"I'm telling yer, I'm not doin' it until I've no choice. Any road, me mum would have to agree first. She owns half o' t' business and buildings, dun't she? Thought yer knew that, darlin'."

"Carol would do whatever's right for her family, I know

that."

Michael had not been this riled since that time in the back yard with Hargraves. Now he *did* feel trapped. Trapped into selling up by his own wife. What price loyalty? He leant back in his chair, linked his hands behind his head, tried ignoring Bernie scratching away at that bloody bowl.

"Listen to me, Michael," said Elsa, reaching across to him, touching his face. "I know this is hard for you. But let's not put it off any longer, eh? We can start afresh. You and me. Make summat new. Together. For the three of us. Make our *own* history."

"History?" said Michael, voice trembling. "Don't blether on to me about history. I know all about it."

He stood, walked away from the table, started circling it as he strode round the room pointing at the framed generation photographs, all the while gesticulating in Elsa's direction with his other arm, a kind of madness flickering through him like a thunderstorm.

"Dad... Grandad... Great Grandad... Great Great Grandad... That's history for yer!"

"Bernie, darling, are you all right?" said Elsa.

"Hold up a sec," said Michael, stopping circling a moment, gripping his forehead. "Just... Just... Hold up..."

"This is not the..."

"Shut up, Elsa! Shut up! Can you not see it? I'm letting them down! After all they built up, after all they left me, I'm bloody well letting them down! Bernie, give o'er scrapin' that spoon!"

"Stop it, Michael!" said Elsa, standing up, yelling too now. "Stop it!"

"But once I sell up I've let them down good and proper! Can't you see that? And you once told me not to let Hargraves win! You said never to let him fucking win!"

"MICHAEL!"

They all froze, akin to a game of musical statues. But then Bernie moved first and climbed off his chair. Michael watched the tears slipping down his boy's little face, as the lad pushed the chair back neatly under the table and walked out of the room.

CHAPTER TWENTY-FIVE

Early on the Sunday evening, Jack was sitting at the bar in The Dog and Gun, smoking, supping his first pint of ale. A few strings of red and green Christmas lights hung about the place, Grumpy George's concession to festive cheer, making the dark wood wall panelling, low oak beams, scythe, plough, coopered barrel at the room's edges, a bit easier to see than usual. Still seemed as dark as frigging death in here, mind. Despite the extra light and that from the jukebox in the corner, the fruit machine by the toilets, the glow of the smoky open fire. Stubbing out his cigarette in the ashtray on the polished wooden bar that always smelt of beeswax, Jack chucked the rest of the pint down his neck and put the empty glass on the copper drainer by the beer pumps.

"Same again, bartender."

He noticed Heavy Metal Mark freeze on his haunches a second, before continuing to empty a box of bottled tomato juice into one of the drinks cabinets.

"Sayin' please could help," said Wendy, behind the bar too, but currently a few feet away at the end near the pub's front door, flirting with her latest boyfriend, Little Richard.

"Aye, Hargraves," said Little Richard, on his usual barstool, gap-toothed grin appearing under that knackered old John Deere cap. "Sayin' please could help."

"Reet you are, Little Dick. Please could you just fuck off, then?"

"Ooooo!" said Wendy. "Proper moody nowadays, in't he?"

"Proper moody," said Little Richard, looking smug, doubtless tickled pink that he'd actually managed to pull in his life.

Wendy sneaked in under the peak of his cap, leaving smears of make-up on his ugly mug as she came up for air and they smirked at Jack.

"Right miserable sod, in't he?" said Wendy.

"Right miserable sod," said Little Richard.

"Same again, please, Mark," said Jack, turning his back on them.

He watched Mark as he put the last of the tomato juice in the cabinet, stamped the empty cardboard box flat under his Doc Martens, took a fresh glass from above the bar, started pulling another pint. Early Sunday evening at The Dog and Gun, eh? Not many folk in as yet. Same as always at this time of a Sunday. The few that were in, doing the same shite as last week. Joan and the floral-dress dominoes team, practising for tomorrow night's league match at the table nearest the fire. Donald and Irish Brian in Santa hats, pampering their Labrador by the jukebox. Smithy and Stubbsy, visible through the serving hatch to the taproom, playing darts and talking the same old bollocks. But you're not like that, Jack Hargraves. Because you're never sitting on this same barstool, are you? At this same time near as damn it every day. Drinking the same ale, having the same conversations, thinking the same thoughts. Because you're not set in your ways like every fucker else, are you? Oh no, you're above all that.

"A quid sixty," said Mark, putting the fresh pint on the copper drainer, drying a damp hand on his Guns N' Roses T-shirt.

"Guns N' Roses, mate?" said Jack, digging in his jeans pocket for brass. "Bit tame for thee, aren't they?"

Mark grunted summat, took the money, rang the till, handed Jack his change.

"What's up wi' you today, bartender? Face like a slapped arse."

"Thee's pulled some stunts, but yon leaflet I got through me door this morning? Lowest o' t' low, that were! There's a barrel o'er there ya might wanna scrape!"

Mark grabbed the flattened cardboard box off the floor, strode out from behind the bar, disappeared through the door at the back of the pub. Jack turned to Wendy and Little Richard again.

"What you two smirkin' at?" he said, not waiting for an answer, picking up his drink instead.

That familiar frothy smell under his nose, he pulled smooth ale down his throat. Some of the dominoes team kept knocking their doms hard on the table now because they couldn't go. Donald and Brian had just shoved Whitney Houston's 'I Will Always Love You' on the jukebox. Stubbsy had got to chelping at Smithy in the taproom.

"Eh up, he's on double one! He's in t' madhouse!"

Jack bit the slight bulge in his bottom lip. Putting **'EAT WELL, STAY WELL.'** on those leaflets had been a low blow, hadn't it? You couldn't blame Mark for being narked. As Tracy had said a few days since, you'd have a job on *proving* Bowers' shop had caused that food poisoning. If it actually was food poisoning. He'd been doubting he should go through with it ever since she'd pointed these things out to him. Along with her saying she didn't reckon right much to them slagging off Bowers' Butchers all the time, that it made her sad he was no longer mates with the bloke, that Bowers had been the one who'd been there for him when the old man popped his clogs. All that coming from his little sister, who'd kept her mouth shut so much of her life, had shocked him, done his head in for a day or two, set him thinking on all the shite he'd subjected Michael Bowers to these past three years. But he'd frigging well gone ahead and had those leaflets delivered to the whole village anyway. What was happening to him?

"Evenin', Gary and Vanessa," said Wendy. "The usual?"

"Please, Wendy," said Gary.

Jack felt a chill from the High Street before the pub's heavy front door settled shut again. He watched Gary and Vanessa hang their 'his and hers' coats on the brass hooks above the doormat and stamp their boots to rid them of snow. An inch on the ground now. Village might be cut off by Christmas.

"Mr Hargraves!" said Gary, striding to the bar in a Pringle jumper like he was on the eighteenth fairway, Vanessa following languidly. "Just the man we wanted to see. Thought you'd be in."

"That predictable, eh?" said Jack, shaking Gary's offered hand, copping for a whiff of that doubtless expensive aftershave.

"Could we have a word in your shell-like?"

"What's it about, Gazza?"

"I'll get these drinks. Then we'll find a quiet corner. Can I buy you a beer?"

"Just got one, ta."

"No probs. When you've finished that, then."

"Hello, Jack," said Vanessa, dressed in posh labels, eyes wide.

"Hello, Vanessa."

A minute later, Jack found himself walking across the stone flag floor with them, ducking his short-cropped head under the low oak beams as they made their way to the darkest corner of the pub near the back door. Not that he cared right much for their company, but owt that differed from usual proceedings might be worth a shot. And Gary did seem a bit more human these days. They sat on stools at a little round table, Vanessa's glossy red lips and Gary's super-white teeth defying the dim light.

"Fire away, then," said Jack, supping more ale.

"Here's the thing," said Gary, leaning forward slightly. "Vanessa and I absolutely love Fowlbeck and the Yorkshire Dales. Don't we, honey-pie?"

"Sooo beautiful," said Vanessa, picking up her wine, little finger in the air.

"And we'd like to move here full-time, so to speak."

"Full-time?"

"Sell our house in Leeds," said Vanessa. "And the one here on the High Street."

"Pool our resources," said Gary.

"*Pool* our resources! Do you get it, Jack?" said Vanessa, stroking his bare forearm.

"Afraid not, love," said Jack, lifting her hand off his skin.

"My wife is trying to make a joke because we have a swimming pool in our Fowlbeck cellar. Very funny, Vanessa. Not."

Vanessa seemed to get a sulky cob on at that, a frown crumpling her orange forehead, a huff escaping her high-gloss mouth. The pub's back door opened and Mark appeared, shivering his bollocks off in his T-shirt, lugging a full coal bucket. As he shut the door, planted a glare on Jack, walked past toward the fire, the coal smell lingered about the little round table.

"Listen," said Gary, fixing his piggy eyes on Jack. "Here's the upshot. We're going to sell both houses, buy one big one here and make Fowlbeck our proper home. I've made a lot of money on the markets these last couple of years. A lot of money. So we can afford something special out here."

"Thought you had an office in Leeds," said Jack.

"I'll commute when necessary. Not much more than an hour's drive. I do most business over the phone, anyway. And you've heard of the World Wide Web, haven't you?"

"Oh aye, read newspapers and everythin', me, ya know."

"Well, it's just taking off. Be massive before long," said Gary, stretching his arms as if he'd lately reeled a giant trout from the river. "Massive. Mark my words, Jack."

"I will, Gary, I will."

"Pretty soon, people like me will be doing business worldwide without even..."

"That's all fine and dandy," said Jack. "But can ya get to t' friggin' point? Why are you telling me all this?"

"The upshot is that Vanessa is going to need something to occupy her out here."

"I want to start my own business."

"Selling hiking and camping gear, that sort of thing," said Gary. "There's nothing around here that really caters for the great outdoors. Now there's an untapped market, if ever I saw one. A place of such natural beauty, thousands of hikers and campers passing through."

"But what's all this got to do wi' me?"

"I'm going to need the right premises, Jack," said Vanessa, widening her eyes at him, pouting her lips.

And suddenly the penny dropped.

"You're asking me to sell you the shop?"

"Ideal location, Jack," said Gary, flashing him a super-white smile. "Slap bang in the middle of the High Street."

Jack sat up straighter, stared at that stupid fucking pout and smile, took a swig of ale, sparked a cigarette. Ridiculous proposal. Anyway, the place wasn't just his to sell, was it? Mother and Tracy owned a third each. Oh yes, they were in the best position they'd ever been to flog it. No bother on that score. But... Ridiculous... Stupid.

"Sorry, it's a 'no can do.'"

"I did tell you it was a long shot, honey-pie."

"But, Gary, it would be perfect!" said Vanessa, grabbing his heavily-ringed hand like a spoilt brat. "You said we'd be able to knock through into the prep room and open the whole place up!"

"I still don't understand what set ya thinkin' on Hargraves' Butchers," said Jack.

"Well, there is its location and potential size," said Gary. "Also, there's nothing else available on the High Street at the moment. And we thought you might be willing to sell, that's all."

"But why would I?"

Gary took a long pull on his lager. Then looked right serious.

"Are you happy, Jack?" he said.

"No, I'm miserable as sin, but what the fuck's it got to do wi' you?"

"Thought not. People talk, you know. Gossip's rife in a tight community like this. And we've lost count of how many times we've seen you in this pub on a downer."

"It's true, Jack," said Vanessa.

"We know you're not living your dream," said Gary. "We've heard all about it, mate. We know you're not doing what a man of your potential was put on this earth to do."

"Potential?" said Jack.

"Yes, potential. You still have your life ahead of you. How old are you?"

"Twenty-eight."

"Twenty-eight!" said Gary, as if such a number was a mere blip in a lifetime of achievement. "Bloody hell, you could have seventy years left!"

Jack took a slow, deep drag on his cigarette, exhaled,

gazed at the smoke rising from the table, floating like cobwebs among the ceiling beams. Maybe Gazza was right. You never knew, did you? Some smokers lived to a hundred. Stupid proposal, anyway. Funny how it made him excited, mind. There's a whole world out there. You can read about it every day in the papers. He'd not thought much about leaving Fowlbeck these past couple of years, though. Kept his head down instead. Finally accepted his butcher's fate. Made the best of a bad job. But the shop was debt free now. A few grand profit in the bank. If it wasn't for family duty...

"Still with us, Jack?" said Gary, pulling his jumper sleeves halfway up his forearms.

"Just about."

"I've heard Bowers' Butchers isn't doing as well as it used to."

"Eh?"

"Suppose we could ask Michael Bowers if he's willing to sell."

"Wait on, Gary," said Jack, draining the rest of his pint. "Wait on, lad. Tell me a bit more about this proposal of yours."

"No probs. Do you own the building as well as the business?"

"Aye. Me, my mum and sister own a third each of everything."

"Right," said Gary. "Well, we'd pay full market value for the building. Do you know how much property prices have shot up around here lately, Jack?"

"Course I do."

"We're talking big bucks. Over a hundred K. Think about that. You might never get a better offer. Remember we're still deep in recession and the property bubble has burst in many places. Who's to say it won't burst here too before long?"

"What about the business itself, though?" said Jack. "Not after buyin' that, are ya? You're plannin' on selling hiking clobber, not meat. Who's to say we couldn't sell to another butcher? Get brass for the actual value o' t' business that way too. Doin' pretty well these days, Hargraves' Butchers, ya know, despite the recession. Bet there'd be a few takers."

He could see Vanessa's strained face pleading with her husband now.

"Okey cokey, Jack," said Gary, eventually, puffing out his cheeks. "We'll compensate you for the value of the business as well."

"Yes!" said Vanessa, clapping her hands. "What do you say, Jack? What do you say?"

Jack stubbed out his cigarette, peered through the dark, smoky atmosphere at the pub stuck in history. Last chance saloon?

"I'll need to speak to my mum and sister."

The next minute, Jack was lifting his coat off a hook by the pub's front door, striding up the cold High Street under its bright Christmas lights, making tracks in the glittering snow toward his mum's house. Hopefully Mother and Tracy would be in.

When he'd reached the snicket and the mottled limestone alley that ran down the back of the row of semis, he knew for sure what he was after. Last chance saloon. And what could you do with forty grand in your pocket? Likely be that much, no bother. Tidy sum for all three of them. And Mum would be drawing her pension soon. And Tracy was stronger now, happier, more independent. His thoughts had him buzzing summat rotten by the time he got to knock on the back door of the house. Kitchen light's on. Here come Mother's little feet, tapping away on the wooden floor. But what if she won't go through with it? She's bound to dig her frigging heels in. Tracy might want nowt to do with it either.

"Who's there?" said Mum through the door.

"It's me, Mum."

The door opened and there she was in a saggy purple cardigan, looking questioningly at him over those dark, puffy semi-circles.

"Everythin' okay, Son?"

"I need to talk to ya."

"Well, come in. You'll catch your death out there. Especially wi' your hair that short. What were you thinkin'?"

"Don't start, Mother, please."

Shutting the door behind him, he stepped into the kitchen, with its big table in the middle, its Aga making the room toasty, its never-ending reminders of The OB. Fishing rod mounted on the wall, pipe on the mantelpiece, model weapons of war on that shelf.

"Where's Tracy?" said Jack, as Mum sat at the table and started working on a cross-stitch.

"Round at her boyfriend's again," said Mum, sounding glum.

"Oh. When will she be back?"

"No idea."

"Right. Appen I'll catch her later."

"Bloomin' hummer, Jack. Give over pacing and tell me what you want to talk about."

Still in his coat, he stood opposite her at the table, put his hands on the back of a chair, gripped its hard wood.

"I've had an offer for t' shop."

"I beg your pardon?" said Mum, stopping mid-stitch.

That had thrown her, hadn't it? Nowt to say for once. Sitting there with a gawp on. Putting down her cross-stitch. Come on, Mother, frame yourself. Tell me you're interested.

You know I want out, don't you? You've always known it. I stayed for you and Tracy. Perhaps even for The OB as well. But I've done my time now. Likely my last chance, this.

"It's a right good offer, Mum. You know that loaded couple, Gary and Vanessa? They're after starting a business sellin' hiking gear, and our shop... "

"Have you been drinkin' again, Son?" said Mum, picking up the cross-stitch once more, pulling thread like the last half minute had never happened.

"They'll pay top whack for t' building and compensate us for the business."

"*Compensate* us? Did you just say *compensate* us?"

She flung the cross-stitch across the table, face and neck almost the colour of her purple cardigan. Jack gripped the chair tighter as he looked down at her. And now Mother was off on one, sitting there like in that Beckett monologue, gabbing away ten to the dozen.

"We're reliant on that shop. Where's the brass comin' from if we sell up? Answer me that. How am I paying my bills? Gold at the end of a rainbow? And the place is doin' well now... And another thing..."

But you could sort of turn down the fucking volume if you focused on those lips moving so fast, same as that monologue. Everything blacked out, excepting the gob going like billio. Forming shapes that blurred together, words that blurred together until they almost disappeared. Why listen to shite that was so predictable, anyway? Jack tuned back in when he caught mention of the old man, mind. Not like he hadn't been expecting it, but it still properly wound him up.

"Give over rollin' your eyes, Jack. So you reckon your father would give you his blessing on this, do you? The shop he grafted all hours for? He did it for us. The three of us. But especially you. So you would have summat of value in life.

He wanted to hand the place on to you more than owt. Not that he ever got bloomin' chance to see that day. Never got chance, did he, Son? And now you're repaying him like this? This is how you respect his memory?"

"Whatever happened to Father's belt, Mother?" said Jack, sensing the simmering of his blood, gnawing away at that bulge in his bottom lip like he wanted to bite it out.

"What belt?" said Mum, suddenly sheepish, reaching for her cross-stitch again.

"The one he was fond of keepin' in t' bottom o' my wardrobe."

"I don't know what you're talking about."

She had her head right over the cross-stitch now, puffy eyes up dead close to needle and thread, as if she'd gone half-blind. He walked round the table, stood behind her, slowly bent down until his chin was resting on her shoulder, whispered in her ear.

"The one he used on me whenever the fancy took him, Mother."

Jack kept his chin there, felt her shaking like she'd got to shivering in the winter snow, watched her little hand tremble as it pushed and pulled the shiny needle. He could sense her fragility now, but he wasn't ready to let up.

"Let's remember Dad in his true light, shall we?" he said, voice quiet, but above a whisper now. "Let's at least pay him that respect. Dispense wi' t' rose-tinted specs and tek a proper look at the man. What exactly was he? Tell ya what, let's just cut to t' chase. Rodney Hargraves was an abuser."

"No..."

"Yes, Mother. Your husband was an abuser. Give him his due, not of Tracy. He allus protected Tracy. But of me. Definitely of me. And I'm not blamin' you for standing aside, Mum. Honest, I'm not. Know why?"

"I'm sorry..."

"Because you were bein' abused an all. Don't know if he ever took a belt to you..."

"No... "

"But he was a controlling, psychological bully to you, Mum. I witnessed it every single day. He's not deservin' of any loyalty or respect from us. We owe him nowt!"

"I'm sorry, I'm sorry," said Mum, sobbing, ditching her cross-stitch, starting to curl up, as if the heat from the Aga was shrivelling her.

"No, I'm sorry, Mum. I'm sorry."

Jack kissed the top of her head, moved to the stone mantelpiece above the Aga, picked up The OB's pipe off its stand, walked back to the table to sit opposite Mum who was still crying.

"Sometimes think I'm turnin' into him," he said, clutching the pipe.

"Don't say that, Son," said Mum, looking at him intently. "Don't ever say that."

"I don't want to end up like him, Mum."

"You won't."

"But I can feel it happening... And t' longer I stay here... I've paid my dues now."

Why had he fetched this stinking old pipe from the mantelpiece? Did he really need a reminder of the bastard he didn't want to be? He turned it over and over, ran his finger across its worn, curvy stem, its gnarled wooden bowl which still smelt of tobacco and ash. Ashes to ashes. He was glad The Old Bastard was dead.

"We'll not get a better offer than Gary and Vanessa's, Mum," he said, chucking the pipe on the table. "Property prices could have peaked round here. Look at what's gone on in a lot o' t' country. Appen we've rode our luck a bit wi' t' business too. Doubtless the competition from supermarkets will carry on increasing, recession could get worse yet. And you'll be nicely set up if we sell. You'll come out with summat like forty grand, no bother. And you've fairish put by, haven't ya? And you'll be drawin' your pension next year, won't you? And this house is worth a packet now. Why not sell it and get a smaller, cheaper place? Pocket the difference. Don't fancy rattling round in this big old house forever, do ya?"

"Got it all worked out, haven't you?" said Mum, looking a bit calmer.

"If we don't sell now, I'll likely stay stuck here."

"I know what your father was, but I still..."

"I'll finish up like him, Mum."

"I still feel loyal to him."

"Keep the fuckin' shop, then!" said Jack. "Buy me out instead."

"I can't afford... "

"I need that money to start afresh. Buy me out and get a manager in. Or else buy me out and you and Tracy run it."

"Jack, I can't afford to buy you out."

"We'll *have* to sell, then."

"And what about Tracy?" said Mum. "Does she get a say?"

Jack watched his mother take a handkerchief from under the sleeve of her cardigan and dry her tear-stained face. Why was she keeping a hanky up her sleeve? Not got a cold, had she? Maybe she needed it every time Tracy went to see her boyfriend or summat. About time she cut her daughter some slack, wasn't it?

"Mum, listen to me," said Jack. "Tracy's stronger now. I know she's precious to you, but it's time to let her go."

"What do you mean, let her go?" said Mum, shock in her

voice.

"She's her own person now."

"I know she's her own person. Not keepin' her under lock and key, am I?"

"No, but..."

"Well, then. I let Tracy make her own decisions, you know. And I reckon she'll be averse to sellin' an all. You know how she doted on her daddy. That cross your mind? That would be two versus one."

"Two versus one counts, does it?" said Jack.

"Course it counts. It's democracy."

"So Tracy has the casting vote?"

But now Mum didn't look right sure. After a moment or two, she tucked her hanky back under her sleeve, sighed, looked at Jack over those dark, puffy semi-circles.

"One condition," she said.

"Go on."

"Neither of us tries influencin' her. We just give her the option."

"Aye, of course."

"As you say, Son, Tracy's her own person now."

"Mum?" said Jack, reaching across the table, gently holding her little hands.

"Yes?"

"Thank you."

CHAPTER TWENTY-SIX

wo days before Christmas Day, trade at Bowers' Family Butchers was still way below what it had to be, and by dinnertime it had put Michael on a proper downer. At one o'clock, he asked his mum and Mark whether they could cope without him for a couple of hours, because he were in need of a long walk.

"Job'll be right, boss," said Mark.

"Take as much time as you want, love," said Mum, concern on her face.

An hour or so later, after walking across the swing bridge and the sloping, snow-covered fields that led up to Fowlbeck Beacon, Michael stood in his big coat and hiking boots at the foot of The North Face, its jagged grey rock cutting through the snow like serrated knives, pointing at the heavy grey sky. Brought on memories of that climb with Hargraves back in '76. Blue sky and strong winds that day, mind. Flipping heck, he could have died! Might have been better for all and sundry if he had. Why had he come here today? He couldn't fathom it. But he wanted to reach the summit again. Perhaps he'd finish up as mincemeat if he took a crack at The North Face, though. Best take the gentler eastern slope.

When he'd headed east a few minutes, he reached the gentler slope and began making his way up The Beacon, managing to pick out the stony path beneath the couple of inches of snow, because he could see the acres of flowerless heather poking through on either side of it. As his boots crunched up the path, the air got colder, stinging his fingertips, numbing his face. If he kept climbing, perhaps it would see fit to numb this pain he was carrying inside too. The guilt, the humiliation, the aching sadness. Hadn't he always found comfort in nature? Looking about now, mind, across the miles of whiteness stretching out beneath him, broken by nowt but limestone walls and farm buildings, or clusters of dark, leafless trees, nature appeared desolate. Not a sound up here either. Not so much as a soft breeze that, when he were a nipper, he'd reckoned akin to Dad's whispering voice: 'Whenever a butterfly flutters by, that's nature showin' thee a miracle.'

Michael trudged on, snow sticking to his boots, the low cloud like a mass of lead. Everything seemed to weigh him down nowadays. Close to jiggered, he was. He kept trying to imagine Fowlbeck without Bowers' Family Butchers on its High Street. But each time it were as if his thoughts frosted over and he couldn't picture it, didn't want to picture it, refused to picture it. Bloody hell, what would folk think if he sold up? Everyone knew how much the shop meant to him, so they'd cotton on to him being forced to sell. They'd see him as a failure, no mistake. And they'd remember Dad and Grandad making a success of the place for all them years and compare him to the past generations. Oh yes, tongues would be wagging like nobody's business, nattering away about what a shame it was for Michael Bowers, about how he'd not cut it as a butcher, about there being nowt else for it but to pity the poor lad.

Around halfway up, he stopped for a breather, sat on a boulder at the path's edge, pulled back his big coat's heavy sleeve to see the dull gold watch with bent hands that he'd inherited off Grandad. Half past two. Fairly dingy already under this greyness, you might reckon there was more light coming from the white ground than the sky, but it started getting properly dark by mid-afternoon at this time of year. And he'd not brought a torch. Best not stay right long at the summit, then. Maybe he should get back to the shop for soon after four, anyhow. Could be a late surge of punters. All hands on deck time! Fat flipping chance. You had to admit the business were in a pretty hopeless state now. What hope was there when even Christmas sales were shit? How could you ever turn things round? How was it even possible? And how long could you carry on losing brass? Michael had had a job on not getting despondent lately. Was there really any point fighting anymore?

He should get a shift on again soon, avoid his backside freezing to this rock. But he suddenly felt dead knackered and so sat there a bit longer. It were as if the cold had taken to gnawing at his energy. But these temperatures didn't sap you, did they? Likely depression doing it. The weather kept weakening his senses, though. Not much feeling in his fingers now. Raw nose near as damn it useless. And maybe it wasn't right silent here at all. Perhaps his ears had iced up or summat. He shivered and used his sight. Just a white and grey world. A world without colour. Like one of Elsa's canvases afore she'd mixed her paints. Like his own life nowadays. He stared at the frozen Dales through smarting eyes.

It could have been a minute later, perhaps it was ten, but Michael didn't think to check his watch as he stood and carried on up the path. At least he knew his ears were working now, because he could make out distant gunshots, like popping wine corks, coming from Tattersall's country estate to the south. Festive shooting season in full swing. Maybe one or two shooters would keep their tradition of having a meal up the dale at The Yorkshire Arms today. Order the finest partridge or pheasant, supplied by Bowers' Family Butchers since Victorian times. A bird of prey darted past to his right, high above The North Face, then slowed and turned in a wide arc over the dale. A red kite. He watched it soar and glide and dip, as it flew out toward Fowlbeck. You could see the place right enough from here, in the bottom of the dale, High Street Christmas lights shining through the gloom.

For the rest of the way to the summit, ever more jiggered, the bitter cold eroding his senses, Michael kept glancing down at Fowlbeck. Fretting about the shop, Dad, the generations, what folk thought of him. He was so sodding tired of it all. But what his village made him think on most was Elsa and Bernie. How could you not think of them? They'd likely be wrapping the last of the presents now, or else food shopping for all the trimmings, or making the Christmas pudding. Elsa keeping things fun for little man, having a good old laugh with him, trying to make him believe everything was all right. Strong as ever, Elsa. She were suffering fairish underneath, though. And how about Bernie? Yes, he'd still seemed as excited as owt these past couple of days, asking a hundred questions an hour about Santa, bouncing round the house like a mad allik. But he must be upset as well. He wasn't four years old yet. The lad shouldn't have a care, should he?

When Michael reached Fowlbeck Beacon's summit, he walked the few yards to the limestone cairn in the middle of the flatter land there and scrambled up it. See many a mile in all directions, standing atop this pile of stones on a clear day, couldn't you? Still enough light about today to look a fair way, mind. Gentle white hills rolling out like billowing sheets in a breeze. Was there a bit of a breeze now he'd got this high up, this exposed? He reckoned he could feel summat on his face, despite its numbness, then wondered if he could hear a whisper in the air. Dad had always helped him appreciate the beauty of The Yorkshire Dales, hadn't he? And they were even beautiful today, course they were. Nowt but your state of mind, them thoughts of desolation. Pretty as a Christmas cake. Elsa would see it. Elsa would bring it all out in a painting. Because she loved The Dales too. She knew how lucky they were to live in such surroundings. She appreciated why folk flocked from all over the world to walk here. Why settle for elsewhere? This was no flipping trap, even if some might reckon so. This was heaven on earth. This was God's County. And them as lived in The Dales had the privilege of looking after them, being custodians of them. All links in a centuries-old chain. Mucking in together. Supporting one another. And Bowers' Family Butchers were a link in that chain round here, weren't it? Didn't sourcing livestock from local farms help sustain them and allow farmers to stay on the land and maintain it? And hadn't the shop contributed to the local economy, provided employment, fed the community for the past hundred odd years? Wasn't all that vital for a place to thrive? For people to stay here and take care of this God-given landscape?

For a moment or two, these thoughts got the better of him, and his pride had him imagining the shop and his family still having the same impact in and around Fowlbeck as they'd had for decades. But then the stones beneath his boots shifted a bit, as if the land saw fit to serve up a reminder of how times were changing, and he had all on keeping his balance. As he tried steadying himself, reality gave him a clout and he dragged himself off the cairn and toward The North Face, his shivery body sapped by a new wave of tiredness.

Standing at the edge of the summit, at the top of The North Face, he put his freezing hands in his coat pockets and hunched his shoulders against the cold. Staring down at the jagged rocks made him think of summat he'd known since he were a nipper. Nature could be beautiful and dangerous. No mistake. He ran his finger over the ridge on his forehead, left by that cut he'd got on these rocks in the summer of '76. Funny how sometimes it was like it still hurt.

Slipping his hand back in his pocket, he looked at the Fowlbeck Christmas lights and pinpointed Bowers' Family Butchers. A fading link in the community. Akin to himself. Well, if the shop went, the part Michael Bowers had been raised to play in life would be lost too, wouldn't it? Was there any point denying it?

Michael gazed at the sheer slope of sharp rocks at his feet. Why had Hargraves gone to such extremes? Perhaps you could just put it down to him being a selfish bugger, like that day beneath this very spot all them years since. Or maybe the last time you worked on the bike with him and told him some home truths had riled him enough to tip him over the edge. Perhaps it's all been your fault. Should have kept your bloody gob shut. But then what did any of it matter anymore? He suddenly felt dizzy and lightheaded, and the rocks below became a blur, losing their sharpness, as if they were nowt but a soft grey pillow.

His shivering wouldn't let up now. He hunched his shoulders tighter against the cold. Best get a grip on reality, lad. Reality is you've run out of choices. Not cottoned it yet? You've let everyone down. You've no choice left. Folk will pity you, but what's the other option? Time to accept it. That's the least you can do. It's all for the best. You've no choice but to do it for Elsa and Bernie. If you really love them, you'll do it. Haven't they suffered enough because of you? Do the right thing by your wife and child. Put them out of their misery. You've no longer a choice. You've got to sell the shop.

Michael looked at The North Face rocks another few moments, then stepped back from the edge. In a kind of daze, he started wandering about the summit, circling the stone cairn, looking out in all directions at his beautiful Yorkshire Dales cloaked in white. Now he'd made his decision, he felt a pain in his heart that he'd not known since his dad died. Akin to a second bereavement, knowing he'd be losing the shop, knowing that the Bowers family's place in this community would now be gone after over a century of graft and toil and pride. He stumbled once or twice as he looked at this world he'd always loved, the ache of loss making him clumsy, weighing on him like a massive slab of rotten meat.

When he at last stopped stumbling about, he stood staring at his village in the dale below, tears turning cold on his face. There's nowt else for it but to go back, lad. You'll just have to face the heartache, the guilt, the humiliation. You've got to do it for Elsa and Bernie.

The light started fading a bit quicker as he headed back toward Fowlbeck, following the footprints he'd made on the way up, the weight of his devastation keeping his pace slow as he hauled himself along. He'd have to ask Mum about selling the shop. She'd be upset, course she would. But, what with Eddie earning, she wasn't desperate for the wages, was she? And she'd understand they had no choice. He'd have to let on to Mark sometime too, mind. When Christmas was over, anyhow. Worked at the shop a long while, hadn't he? Poor bloke would be gutted. He's got a few hours at The Dog and Gun, but hopefully he'll find more work elsewhere. Unemployment were at its highest since '87, though. Perhaps if Kinnock had got in this time he'd have kept his promise of fettling the economy. Oh yes, saved Bowers' Family Butchers too, would he?

For the next half hour or so, despite the growing darkness, Michael could still see his footprints and followed them down the snow-covered Beacon and sloping fields, doing his best to get a shift on so as to warm up. And, all the while, the breeze he reckoned he'd sensed at the summit he knew to be in the air now, touching his face, whispering in his ears. And it were Dad's voice whispering, the way it had done many a time on the breeze since he'd been killed in that crash all them years back. Except it wasn't speaking of butterflies fluttering by anymore, or nature showing miracles. It just kept repeating two little phrases, over and over and over: 'I won't let yer down, Daddy.' 'I know yer won't, Son.' Carrying the deadweight of guilt, the pain of grief, Michael had all on planting one foot in front of the other.

When he eventually passed a couple of dog walkers in the lower fields, his senses seemed to have thawed a bit and he'd given over shivering, but his heart was still breaking. Over and over and over. And what the hell was he going to do when the shop went? He'd no trade other than butchery. What would he do? Work for another butcher? Be a supermarket butcher? Humiliation complete.

By the time he was approaching the river, it had got properly dark and so he used the two orange lights atop the swing bridge to guide him to it. When he at last dragged himself onto the bridge, he could hear the river flowing beneath. He stopped under the first light to look over the rusty-smelling side and watch the brown water sliding by like the end of a dream.

"By gum! What's Michael Bowers doing abandoning ship two days afore Christmas?"

Bloody hell, Beaky Susan. Michael watched her walking her mangy old dog along the bridge from the opposite side, passing under the other light in her long manky coat as she made her way toward him, her wellies squeaking on the snow.

"What you up to, lad?" she said, as she stood next to him, the orange light shining on her beaky nose.

"What can I do for yer, Susan?" said Michael, copping for the smell of dog coming off her and her mutt.

"You don't look reet happy."

"Are you happy, Susan? Pryin' into folks' lives all t' time?"

She smiled at him like she didn't give a toss what he thought, little spasms of frosty breath escaping her wrinkly mouth, as if she were having trouble not laughing.

"Everyone's partial to a bit o' gossip, Michael," said Susan, yanking the dog lead hard to hold back her whining animal, which seemed set on escape. "Why do you think Princess Diana's book's sold in its millions this year, eh? Because she's dishing t' dirt on Charlie-Boy and Camilla, that's why. Have you not read it? By gum, it's a good read!"

"Let me alone, Susan," said Michael.

"No offence intended, eh, lad? But why are you out here looking glum? Thought you'd be celebrating."

"Celebrating? What the hell you on about?"

"Have you not heard? Jack Hargraves is selling his shop."

"Stop takin' t' piss."

"I'm serious," said Susan. "Got it from t' horse's mouth this morning. Him, his mum and sister have agreed to sell to them posers from Leeds, Gary and Vanessa."

"Gary and Vanessa are gonna be butchers?" said Michael, laughing at her. "Yer must reckon me a right barmpot if yer think I'm believin' that one!"

"Oh, they're not keeping it as a butcher's shop."

"What?"

"They're having it to sell hiking gear, camping stuff, that sort o' thing."

"Eh?"

"Gi' o'er catching flies, Michael. It's a dead cert. Heard it off young Jack when I popped across t' road to get a pie for me lunch. Could tell summat had gone on. I got it out of him."

"Are you sure, Susan?"

"As God's me witness," said Susan, making the sign of the cross.

"Flippin' heck."

She seemed chuffed to have been the one to tell him and said she'd keep him informed of owt else about Hargraves' shop from the grapevine. Then she was on her way again, squeaking across the bridge with her dog.

Michael rested his elbows on the side of the bridge, gazed at the river, listened to its quiet murmur. Bloody Nora! But you've always known Jack Hargraves hates working at that shop of his. And now he's got a decent offer. No surprise that's all it took. Because he's always hankered after getting out, hasn't he? Because butchery's never been in his blood, has it? No surprise that's all it took.

CHAPTER TWENTY-SEVEN

Jack had fancied a decent lie in on Christmas Day morning, but his brain had been going ten to the dozen since Tracy agreed to sell and he'd not slept right well. Irritated and bothered, reckoning a walk might do him good, he got up while it was still dark outside, pulled on some Calvin Klein's and Levi's, made a brew, supped the tea in his dormer window that overlooked the top of the High Street. Snow falling among the Fowlbeck festive lights. Perhaps six inch on the ground. Village might be cut off today. Better put wellies on.

About quarter of an hour later, in a long wax coat he'd bought a couple of years since because it put him in mind of a gunslinger, he was walking down the middle of the deserted High Street, dragging on a cigarette, wellies making holes in the soft snow. Houses' curtains shut as yet. Glow of front room lights behind a fair lot of downstairs ones. Greedy nippers doubtless snatching presents from under the tree, ripping them open beside coal fires. You could hear bits of screeching excitement coming from those rooms, smell the sooty air rising from the chimney pots. Jack had a struggle on remembering a happy family Christmas. The kids were welcome to it.

He sensed the sunrise now, cloud-filled sky getting a bit brighter. You could even make out The Beacon, three mile off, if you squinted against that breeze blowing snowflakes in your eyes. As he neared the bottom of the street, he heard a diesel engine behind him. He turned to clock a council wagon coming down the hill, its orange light flashing, its bolted on plough proper slicing through the snow, piling it up on one of the pavements like soil from a trench. He took a final pull on his cig, stepped onto the opposite pavement, watched the wagon rumble past and round the corner where him and Michael Bowers had tipped over that time in Fowlbeck Children's Bogie Race. Nibbling at the little bulge in his bottom lip, he gawped at the spot where Micky lost control back in '76. Fairly freaked out when they'd crashed, hadn't he?

After a moment or two, Jack snapped out of it and looked over his shoulder at what he'd known was there. Right proudly announced in that faded but fine and dandy lettering above the shop window.

'Bowers' Family Butchers – Finest Quality Meats Since 1877.'

Maybe, now Hargraves' Butchers was getting flogged, Michael would have no bother breathing life back into his old place. That would be summat at least.

Setting off again in brightening daylight, through falling snowflakes and deepening snow, Jack headed to the river, crossed the swing bridge, reached the sloping fields. By the time he lifted the iron fastener on the first mossy wooden gate, his mind was going like billio. What the fuck are you playing at out here? Always wanted to escape, haven't you? Maybe, because now you know you'll soon be gone for good, you're after getting a feel for leaving Fowlbeck. The way you used to as a kid. Forever escaping out here, weren't you? Expeditions with Micky to The Beacon. Treks to your secret place, The Waterfall Den. Wonder if the collection's still there? And now he knew where he was off to. The Waterfall Den. He didn't know why, mind. And the wet snowflakes were blowing in his face. But he didn't give a shite about the weather.

Stepping in and out of the deep snow, Jack moved through the fields toward the stream that led to the waterfall. At least he'd made the best of things these past few years, eh? He'd hated being stuck at Hargraves' Butchers, but he'd made a success of it. Deserved some credit for that, didn't he? Making a success of a bad job. Wasn't that heroic? Had to be, didn't it? Well if it wasn't you've been living a lie. Seeing yourself like that has been the only way you've managed to carry on. But what if you've been living a bastard lie?

In the wintry air, he pushed on across the white ground, through more gates with cold iron fasteners, over rickety stiles set in the mottled limestone walls. Excepting when the wind got a strong gust on, it was right quiet out here. Doubtless the white stuff deadening noise. No mooing or bleating farm animals about. Likely huddled up warm in barns. More sense than some fucking idiots. Jack needed to clear his head this morning, though. Not that this walk was doing the trick yet.

When, despite Mum's moaning, Tracy said yes to selling the shop, he'd been as chuffed as owt, hadn't he? Bless her for reassuring him she'd be all right, for telling him she fancied branching out more for herself anyway, for saying she only wanted the best for him. Oh yes, he'd been on a real high at first. Well, course he had. Got what he'd always desired. A proper chance to ride off over the horizon. Same as Clint in his Westerns. Fulfil his destiny and all that. But it had not been long before other thoughts started creeping into this perfect picture. Distorting it, putting cracks in it, tearing it apart. What the hell was he going to do out in the big wide world? Not like he'd covered himself in glory the last couple of times he'd dipped his toe in, was it? What was going to be so different this time? All be fine and dandy now, would it? To think he'd read pieces in The Observer this year about former Soviet Republics gaining independence and freedom, Georgia joining the United Nations, Lithuania creating a constitution, Estonia electing a President, and attached some kind of significance to his own importance in it all! What, because he'd been a link in a human chain at Greenham Common once and they'd done similar in the Baltic states a few years later? Because he'd been on a little march in Leeds to celebrate the Berlin Wall coming down? What was he, an inspiration to millions or summat? When he thought of it now, he laughed at his vanity. Near as damn it narcissistic.

When he reached the fresh water flowing over rocks, he began following it upstream toward The Waterfall Den. Same as he'd done years since, whenever him and Michael walked along the banks of this stream, he made use of a fallen stick and swished through the tangled undergrowth that smelt of decay, striding across the water to the opposite side whenever his path got blocked by snow-covered hedgerow, hawthorn or holly. The bushes and hedges brought on memories of when him and his best mate used to search for objects for their collection among the knobbly branches and prickly leaves. Taken the job right serious too, hadn't they? As if eggshells, quartz, smoothed pieces of broken glass were nowt less than precious jewels. Micky had definitely needed a fantasy to believe in after his dad was killed. There for one another back in those days, weren't you? Jack for Michael. Michael for Jack. As Tracy said a few days since, Micky was the one who was there for you when your dad died. You might not give a flying fuck about The OB these days, now you only remember him for what he was, but you were gutted when he popped his clogs.

Jack carried on upstream, snow on the banks keeping his pace slow, a strengthening wind blowing the falling snowflakes against his long wax coat, his numb face, his closely cropped head. Just a bit of weather. He could have remembered a hat and gloves, mind. Brain all over the shop since Tracy's casting vote. Better put your hood up, continue swapping hands on this swishing stick so you can keep warming both in your coat pockets. This route starting to sink into its ravine a bit now. Waterfall not right far off. Stream sounding lively over those rocks up ahead. Little robin redbreast on that hawthorn branch. But now he couldn't give over thinking about what he'd done to Michael.

How much did you slag off his shop these past three years, eh? Always chipping away at its reputation, using whatever means you fancied. Blackboard signs in your own shop, door-to-door leaflets, articles in The Gazette, gossip over the cabinet Beaky Susan would be proud of. Sneaky little digs and hints and implications. Why did you do it? Why were you forever undermining Michael like that? Because making Hargraves' Butchers successful somehow made you a hero? Because he was the competition you needed to beat to feel good about yourself? Or because he told you some home truths that time when you were working on the Norton which you weren't right fond of hearing? That part of it too, was it? You were the one who started laying into him first anyway, that time in the pub. Telling him he was stuck in history, held back by the generations, trapped in Fowlbeck and he couldn't even see it. What right did you have to say those things to him? Same as trying to destroy the lad's whole identity, that was. Then you get a sulky cob on because he fights back and points out one or two things about you. And he was fucking right in what he said as well. You have done summat and nowt out in the wide world. You did make a pig's ear of the chance you had to be with the one person you've ever fallen in love with.

The ravine got narrower and deeper as Jack moved further upstream and, by the time he heard the rush of the waterfall on the final bend before the den, it was the way he remembered it. Earthy-smelling sides, as steep and tall as buildings, blocking out a fair lot of light and all the wind. And then he was there, standing in the space that opened out into a horseshoe shape, carved from layered limestone rock. The Waterfall Den.

With snow filling the air and covering everything, the place looked proper different to what he recalled the last time he'd traipsed out here with Michael, the day of The OB's funeral nine years back. But not much else had changed. Ivy creeping among the limestone's nooks and crannies, a couple of ash trees shed of leaves, that big slab of rock, near the pool under the waterfall, that they'd used for their blood brother ceremony in '76. The waterfall itself, cascading from thirty foot up, turning white with its force, giving off spray and noise and energy. He stabbed his swishing stick in the snow, sparked a cigarette, gazed at the gushing water a while. Summat about the power of it that drew you in. Near as damn it put you in a trance.

When Jack had finished his smoke, he moved to the edge of the horseshoe and started feeling around in the rough nooks and crannies, smell of wet limestone in his nostrils, searching for objects he remembered from the collection. And, as he worked his way round the wall of grey rock, he found one or two buried deep. Slate arrowhead, purple glass, iron key. He gawped at them on the palm of his hand for a bit. Maybe he should hold on to them for old times' sake, shove them in his pocket, take them back to Fowlbeck. Somehow didn't seem right, that, mind. So he polished them on his Levi's and carefully put them back where they belonged.

Looking up, he squinted through the horseshoe and falling snow. What with that wind whistling fairish among the trees out in the open up there and swirling the snowflakes about, perhaps he'd better set off back. Didn't want his bollocks frozen off in a blizzard. It was only weather, though. Besides, there were a couple of collection objects he wanted to see that he'd not found as yet. Weird that he felt the need to hold them again. Fat chance of remembering where he'd left them nine years on. But hadn't he always put the stuff close to eye level? He carried on moving slowly round the edge of The Waterfall Den, fingers feeling inside the limestone, until he was next to one of the ash trees. Wasn't it near here where he hid those two objects? What was that he could feel deep in the rock? Right smooth, it was. He pulled it out. The seashell. Speckly brown, but, inside, pinkish and curled under like an ear. Listen to it, then. Sea still there. Almost smell its saltiness. Definitely the sea. But sort of hollow sounding. He listened a while longer, then put it back.

What about that other thing? Did you not leave it close to the seashell all those years since? He felt a bit further along the same cranny. Wait on, what's that? Jammed in tight at the back? He got his fingers round it, yanked it out. It was that other thing. The belt buckle. Holding it between his thumbs and forefingers, he stared at it while snowflakes melted on its rust. Then he had a go at rubbing the rust away, tried scratching it off with a thumbnail. But you couldn't get rid that easy, could you? Similar to some memories. You couldn't just rub them out.

"On your bed now, Son... On your back... Pull your pants down... Reet down to your ankles... Now flat on your back... Look at me. Straight in me eyes. Don't move. Just look at me. Any more o' your cheek, lad, and it'll be an extra five cracks o' t' belt next time. Understand? Don't move. Look in me eyes. And next time I'll use t' buckle end again. I swear to God I'll crack you into t' middle o' next week, lad. Give over shakin'. Not cold, is it? Look at me. Don't move until I say... Until I say... Until I say... Now on your front. On your front! There's a good boy... One... Two... Three... Four..."

He could still feel those lashes burning across his arse when he thought of them. Still made him flinch too. He moved to the pool at the bottom of the waterfall and tossed in the buckle. Make a frigging wish, why don't you? And then he was standing over the big slab of rock that him and Michael had used whenever they'd ticked off the collection checklist and carefully polished the objects. Came in handy for that blood brother ceremony too, didn't it? Why did you cut so deep that day? Micky was kakking himself. That what you wanted, was it? More like The OB than you'd care to admit, eh? Always have been. Same then as now. Set your stall out to hurt Michael in whatever way you could these past three years, haven't you? Why? Because you've got this stupid idea in your head that the more success you make of a bad job the more heroic you are. Fancying yourself heroic when you're not isn't heroism, is it, you idiot? More like narcissism. He looked up at the waterfall, listened to its power as if it was a revelation. You *have* been living a lie. You're no hero. You're a fucking narcissist.

Jack decided to head back to Fowlbeck. He'd not put a watch on, but it would doubtless be mid-morning when he got there and he was supposed to be off to Mum's at eleven to help her and Tracy prepare Christmas dinner, open presents, all that bollocks. He left The Waterfall Den, began walking downstream along the beaten track he'd made on the way up, six inches of snow keeping him slow. For a while, the ravine's tall sides shielded him from the wind, but he could still hear it blowing fairish up there, out in the open fields. Snowflakes looked to be getting bigger too.

He carried on beside the stream. Hands, turned pink with cold, out of his long coat's pockets now, hood down so the flakes landed on his closely cropped head and cut to the bone. It was like he'd taken to defying the weather. Didn't give a shite about it. Did he give a shite about anything anymore? Fancying yourself a hero, eh? Is that all you've got left? Fancying yourself? Falling in love with your own reflection? When is narcissism ever heroic? It's nowt but destructive. Setting about destroying Bowers' Butchers so you could love yourself for it. Except you don't love yourself for it, now you've finally seen it for what it is, do you? You hate yourself. Because what were you playing at all along? Setting about destroying Bowers' Butchers meant you were after destroying Michael too, didn't it? As Tracy said, that shop means the world to him. The lad who was your best mate all those years. The lad who was always there for you.

After a while, the stream's ravine didn't cut so deep into the earth and Jack was close enough to the open fields to properly hear how blustery the wind was getting. And then his uncovered head was bobbing up and down at field level. And, each time a gust whipped a load in his face, his eyes took to squinting against the snowflakes again. Then he missed seeing some brambles once or twice and got his raw hands scratched summat rotten. And why had he left his swishing stick at The Waterfall Den? And why the hell had he come out here, anyway? And what the frig was he going to do with his life now he'd run out of excuses not to ride off over the horizon? Because you've already failed twice, haven't you? The second time you were even rejected by the woman you loved. So how are you going to fare this time? What, just because you'll have no obligations in Fowlbeck anymore, just because you'll be carrying a wad of brass in your pocket like a silver bullet, you reckon you'll have no bother finding your place in the world this time round? Most folk would likely give themselves a decent shot under those circumstances. But you've got form, lad. Two failures and a rejection. And how about these past three years, eh? Fancying yourself heroic, but living a lie? If that doesn't show you're still a failure, what does? Oh yes, because that bodes well.

Jack was soon treading downhill across the open fields toward Fowlbeck, stepping in and out of the deepening whiteness, the strengthening wind making a right racket in his ears, blowing big snowflakes against his long gunslinger coat, bare hands, face, head. Proper stinging his skin now, this weather. Putting a shiver in his bones. But he didn't give one. It could fling what it wanted at him. What difference did it make? His mind was fucked up more than his body could ever be. Squinting through the snow-filled air at the High Street Christmas lights as they drew nearer, he carried on toward the village where he'd been stuck for twenty-eight years, not knowing why, wondering if it was even worth the bother. He'd never felt so low. Making use of the rickety stiles and mossy gates, he went through the limestone walls where snowdrifts were starting to form, biting the bulge in his bottom lip like it was a lump of cancer. Diseased. Spreading. Terminal.

CHAPTER TWENTY-EIGHT

It was snowing and windy in Fowlbeck at nine o'clock on Christmas Day morning, but at least it wasn't blowing a blizzard. Ever since he'd opened his presents at six a.m., Bernie had been nattering Michael and Elsa to take him out on the plastic red sledge that Santa had brought him. So now they were messing about by the river, in the sloping field you got to by the swing bridge, wrapped in thick coats, gloves and hats, the snow nearly reaching the top of Bernie's little stripy wellies each time he stepped in it.

"Push me faster this time, Daddy!" he said, beaming, ruddy cheeks aglow, as he pulled his sledge up the last few yards to reach Michael halfway up the field.

"All reet," said Michael. "Hold on tight to that rope, mind. Raced down a hill or two in me time, lad, and you've allus got to hold on tight."

"All reet," said Bernie, hugging Michael's leg, chubby face snuggled against brown corduroy. "Love yer, Daddy."

"Love yer, Son."

Michael held the sledge steady as Bernie sat on it. Getting blustery now, weren't it? Snowflakes bigger too. Bernie gripped the rope and shouted to Elsa, who was about a hundred yards away at the bottom of the hill.

"Ready, Mummy?"

"Ready!" said Elsa, arms outstretched toward him.

"Daddy's pushin' me faster this time, Mummy, so watch out! Go on, Daddy, go on!"

"One... Two... Three... Go!" said Michael, pushing on Bernie's back.

"Here I come, Mummy! Here I come!"

Michael watched his boy gather speed downhill through

the falling snow, gripping the rope right tight, akin to how he used to himself in them bogie races with Jack Hargraves. A proper tyke, Bernie, wasn't he? No mistake. You had to feel flipping lucky when your kid was such a little belter, didn't you? Good that he seemed happy now, after that scene at Sunday dinner a few days since. How could you put him through that? At least there were a bit of hope now. Some relief that things might be turning round. Not that she exactly trusted Jack Hargraves, but Elsa felt it too. And Mum and Eddie had agreed to loan them some brass to tide them over a while. As long as the sale of Hargraves' Butchers goes through, Bowers' Family Butchers has a decent chance of survival, doesn't it? Once the competition's gone, and once them underhand tactics have stopped, surely you can build the place up again. Who knows, so long as you keep selling finest quality meat, maintain the old traditions, maybe you can try one or two new products and ideas as well. But you're not thinking on that today, are you? Today's Christmas Day. Today's for Elsa and Bernie.

The lad was in his mummy's arms at the bottom of the hill now, laughing his head off. And now she'd taken to holding his wrists and spinning him parallel to the ground, his shrieking face toward the low grey sky. Seeing them merry again fairly warmed Michael's heart in the cold day, filled it with love.

"Oy, you two mad alliks!" he said, raising his voice, cupping a gloved hand round his mouth. "Fancy makin' a Christmas snowman?"

"Go on, then, darlin'!" said Elsa. "Just as soon as I've finished wi' this cheeky monster!"

"Faster, Mummy! Faster!" shrieked Bernie.

"Couple o' barmpots," said Michael to himself, smiling as he reached down into the snow, made a snowball, started rolling it downhill.

That wind were properly picking up now. While Michael bent over the growing snowball, he could feel its chilly bite as it blew snowflakes in his face. Brilliant snow for snowmen, this. Not too powdery. Stuck together well. Made a creaking noise when you rolled it. After a minute or so, he stopped for a breather and stretched his back. Bernie and Elsa lobbing snowballs at one another now. The lad's got a blooming good throw on him for three and a half. There goes another missile, arcing through the air against that backdrop of tall, leafless trees along the riverbank. Smack! Right on Elsa's bonce. Nearly knocked her glasses off.

"Sorry," said Bernie, suddenly frozen.

"You little ratbag," said Elsa, straightening her specs, but giggling anyhow. "Ooh, you're for it now, my boy."

"No, Mummy, no!"

By the time Michael got close to them at the bottom of the hill, the snowman's body he was making had grown to the height of his chest.

"Flippin' heck, you two," he said. "Any chance of a push? I'm jiggered."

They stopped snowballing and came to help.

"Flippin' heck, Daddy, it's massive!" said Bernie, between Michael and Elsa, as they all pushed the giant snowball the last few yards to where the field flattened out a bit.

"Grand job, that," said Michael, when they stepped back to look at their handywork.

"Family hug?" said Elsa, arms outstretched again.

And they all went in for a big one.

"Merry Christmas, Mummy and Daddy," came Bernie's muffled voice from in among their coats.

"Merry Christmas, Bernie," said Michael and Elsa, smiling, looking into each other's eyes above their boy's head.

But then Elsa's eyes shifted from Michael's and she were staring past him.

"What's up?" said Michael.

"It's Jack Hargraves."

Michael's heart jumped. He were suddenly riled. But what did he expect? Not as if you could get over the last three years just like that, was it? He came out of the family hug and turned to see Hargraves a couple of hundred yards away, walking across the top of the field.

"Who is it, Daddy?" said Bernie.

"Jack Hargraves."

"Oh aye, it's Mr Hargraves from Hargraves' Butchers. Merry Christmas, Mr Hargraves!"

"Quiet, Bernie!" said Michael.

"Are we mekin' this snowman or what, you two?" said Elsa.

"Summat's not right."

"Forget about him."

"Look at how he's moving."

"Darlin', it's Christmas Day."

"Fairly hunched over, in't he?" said Michael. "Head lollin' a bit an all."

"Sod him," said Elsa.

"Something's not right."

Michael watched Jack walking slowly across the field. He must have seen them. Looked to be in a different world, mind, so maybe not.

"Shall we make the snowman's head, Daddy?" said Bernie, tugging Michael's coat.

"Yer what?"

"Snowman's head."

"Aye... I suppose..."

The two of them rolled a head and stuck it on the body. But Michael kept glancing at Jack moving further away and, when he disappeared through the gate into the next field, he turned to Elsa.

"Summat's up," he said. "I'll not be long."

"You're not goin' after him?" said Elsa.

"I've got to."

"Have you forgotten what he's done to you? To us?"

"He's the best mate I've ever had, darlin'."

But Elsa had been struck dumb. There was nowt but an icy stare in her eyes now.

"Are yer goin' after Mr Hargraves, Daddy?" said Bernie, chin trembling.

"I'll be as quick as I can, Son. I'm sorry."

"But we've not done t' snowman's face."

"Mummy's brilliant at faces, Bernie. I'm sorry. Don't wait for me if this weather gets much worse, you two. Get yourselves off home. But I'll be back afore yer know it."

And then Michael was off up the field, trying to blank out his wife's stare and his boy's crying pleas for him to stay.

....

Jack was glad of it, being out of that field where the Bowers were. Perhaps he should have said hello, especially when the little one wished him Merry Christmas, but he was too ashamed to face them. Jack Hargraves was no hero. He felt frigging knackered now. Given over thinking straight. But he trudged on. Heading downhill toward the river. Somehow seemed drawn to it. What time was it? He'd no idea. Supposed to be at Mum's for eleven. Summat made him want to walk upstream along the riverbank a while, though. Snowflakes getting bigger. Dead blowy now too. Weather could do whatever it fancied. Made fuck all difference to him.

He reached the riverside path, nowt but a yard from the brownish water drifting silently by. The path was overhung with bare, dark branches of sycamores and oaks, its usually exposed tree roots under about eight inch of white. His wellies squeaked in the snow and, excepting the odd whistle from that strong breeze, the brushing of his sleeves against his long wax coat, it was the only sound he could hear. Shielding the Zippo flame from the snowflakes, smelling its fuel, feeling its heat on his palm, somehow tempted to let it lick his cold skin, he lit another cigarette and plodded on. How far to The Surge from here? Twenty minutes?

....

When Michael reached the gate at the top of the field, he saw Jack's footprints in the next field, making a trail downhill. No sign of him, mind. Hold up, there he is. Long coat, dead short hair, moving upstream among the leafless trees along the riverbank. Where's he off to? Best see if you can catch him up.

Turning left by a limestone barn with rotting wooden doors, Michael started walking down toward the river. What the hell's up with Lanky? Hunched over like he's lugging ten ton on his back. You'd have reckoned on him being happy as owt, wouldn't you? What with that sale agreed on his shop and the chance to leave butchery behind. Do summat more suited to him. You'd have thought he'd be lording it over all and sundry now. 'Look at me, I'll be off to save the world soon!' But there was still nobody who knew him like Michael, was there? All that bravado, that ego, covered up a lot, didn't it? When you scratched beneath the surface, that's when you knew how he really felt about himself.

....

For the last few minutes, since soon after The Surge came into his head, Jack had got more of a shift on. Had a strange power, that place. Could draw you in even when all you did was think of it. He was having to squint through the weather again now, blustery wind swirling the falling snow about, whipping it up from where it had drifted at the base of the trees. Not much of a bother to him, though. More important, what must life have been like for Micky these past three years, eh? Having to take all that shite you flung at him and his shop? The lad's a worrier at the best of times. Doubtless you've messed him right up. He'll be loads better off when you're no longer about.

....

When Michael had walked half a mile or so along the riverside path, he were getting jiggered. Hard going, underfoot. Caked up hiking boots properly heavy. That stinging wind coming at his face. Putting shivers in him. Slowing him down. And he kept losing sight of Jack. Why had he got a shift on now? You couldn't see right far in what was starting to look akin to a flipping blizzard, anyhow. And now the lad was hundreds of yards away, barely visible among the creaking trees and snowy air. Where the hell were he off to? Maybe you should shout to him. As if he'd cotton on with this weather in his ears. Elsa and Bernie would no doubt have gone home now. You'd best just go back there. Once you've made sure Lanky's all right. What's up with him? Where's he going?

....

After a while, Jack was close to the bend in the river near The Surge. You'd usually have no bother hearing that rush of white water from here, gushing through its narrow gap. But the wind was making a right swishing noise in the trees now, branches moaning like old fogies. Pointless you moaning anymore. You know what will happen when you leave Fowlbeck, anyway. You'll only make a pig's ear of it. You've got form. You'll only fail again. You'll only fuck it up.

....

By the time Michael was nearing the bend in the river, he kept having to drive himself forward against the snowstorm. Head low, like he used to have it in Rugby River Scrum, eyes scrunched, face flipping freezing. He could follow them footprints right enough, but he had all on glancing ahead every few seconds, making out where he'd got to. That bend's just afore The Surge, isn't it? That's not where Jack's off to, is it? Always had a fascination with that place, hasn't he? But why... Shit... No, don't be daft... But...

....

The wind buffeting his gunslinger coat, Jack stood on the wet rocks near the edge of The Surge. The power, the energy coming off that rolling, spitting torrent was somehow melting the snowflakes in mid-air, before they had chance to settle on the ancient limestone either side of it. You had to be in frigging awe of this place, didn't you? Set your heart going like billio, listening to its hellish racket, gazing into its frothing rapids, its swirling whirlpools. He took a step closer, so he could properly smell its cold freshness, feel its spray on his face, taste it in the air. A right temptress. Could put you in a trance.

....

Michael reached the bend in the river, breathing hard

now from straining to move quicker through the snow. Kept slipping too. As soon as he'd rounded the bend, he nearly fell, but then steadied himself, stopped, peered through the blizzard. There's Jack, nowt but fifty yards off. Looked to be flipping close to the edge of The Surge, didn't he? Too close.

"Jack! Jack!" shouted Michael, suddenly stiff with panic. "Get back from t' edge! This gale's got its dander up! Jack! Lanky!"

But he seemed not to have heard Michael. No wonder, in this howling weather. And The Surge is dead noisy on calm days. What the hell's he thinking? Step back from there, mate! One slip and... One of them gusts... Best get to him... Got to get to him...

....

Jack took a step closer to The Surge, the toes of his wellies overhanging its edge. Power of the thing blew you away, didn't it? Pulling the river in, dragging it under, spewing it out. Had anyone ever survived it? All those stories of folk falling in, finishing up as bloated corpses, washed up on the riverbank somewhere downstream. Maybe it was a load of bollocks, but they reckoned some bodies were still jammed under these rocks. Strange being this close to death.

....

Michael kept yelling at Jack as he scrambled through the blizzard, slipping all the while, on all fours half the time. He were full on fretting now. Lungs and heart fit to burst. Did Lanky want to kill himself? Bloody hell, he's right on the edge!

"Jack! Lanky!"

Then Michael reached the rocks at the side of The Surge, where the snow hadn't settled. Gasping for breath, that sheer force of water loud in his ears, spitting spray in his face, he gently put a sodden gloved hand on Jack's shoulder. Jack turned to him, stared at him a moment.

"All reet, Micky?"

"All reet, Lanky?"

"You're shiverin', lad."

"It is a bit parky."

Jack smiled.

"Could say that."

Michael were about to ask Jack to step back from the brink. But he was near as damn it on the edge too. And a big gust of wind caught him unawares. And he'd not had chance to steady himself like Jack. And he slipped on the wet rocks. And he were falling before he knew it. And then he was in The Surge, underwater, getting sucked down.

Paralysed, Jack stared into the bubbling, swirling water.

"Oh fuck, oh fuck, oh fuck! He's gone! He's dead! He's fucking dead!"

Why didn't you catch him? It all happened so quick. The Surge had you in a trance. You were too slow. And now it's taken him. He's dead! He's fucking dead! But, ripping off his wellies and gunslinger coat, Jack jumped in after him.

The freezing water put shock in Jack. He was getting tossed about like a mouse at a tiger's mercy. He was in the jaws of a monster. The currents were so strong that he kept being dragged down every time he managed to get his head up to gasp for air. But he had to keep going under to find Michael. He couldn't see a fucking thing in this underwater storm, though. All he could do was grope around in the hope he'd grab him. Got to find him! Frigging hell, Micky, where are you? Where the hell are you? But Jack was already starting to feel exhausted and he'd only been in a few seconds. Muscles getting weaker, heart going like billio, lungs fit to burst. And now he didn't have the strength to get his head above water anymore. And the monster was sucking him right under. Deeper and deeper down. And he was proper weak. And he felt like he was about to pass out. Where are you, Micky? Where are you? Got to find him. And Jack's arms were flailing about in the storm of water. And they were getting weaker. Then he touched summat like cloth. A coat? He grabbed it. Micky! He somehow managed to pull him in close, hug him tight. And now they were in a whirlpool the likes of which Superman couldn't escape! Spinning, spinning, spinning. But hadn't Jack read somewhere that the only chance to survive a whirlpool too strong to resist was not to resist at all? To let it take you, in the hope it would suck you through and out the other side? Hadn't he read that somewhere? Perhaps all those dead folk had panicked too much, fought for their lives too much. Hold on tight, Micky! But Michael didn't seem to have any life in him. He didn't seem to have any life in him.

The whirlpool spun them, squeezed them, pulled them. Jack knew it was hopeless, but he didn't resist. He hugged Michael with the last of his strength. He was drowning as well now. They would die together.

Jack was about to pass out when they were suddenly getting dragged in a different direction. Not downstream, was it? So disorientated he had no clue, but they'd definitely changed direction. And now they seemed to be heading upwards. And was the water calmer now? And what was that, light above the water? And then they were near the surface. And the water was calmer. And then Jack had no bother standing on the riverbed. And then they had their heads above water and they were nowt but waist deep. They'd emerged downstream! They'd survived! Jack gasped for air a few moments. They'd survived! But Michael's not gasping, is he? He's limp and lifeless in your arms, his face blue.

"Wake up, Micky!" said Jack, laying him horizontal on the surface, putting a knee under his back.

Pinching Michael's nose with one hand, pulling on his chin to keep his mouth open with the other, Jack tried to breathe life into him.

Nothing.

"Come on, Micky! Come on!"

He tried again.

Nothing.

"Come on, lad! Come on!"

He tried again.

Nothing.

He tried again.

Nothing.

"Come on, Micky!"

Then Michael spluttered, coughed up a load of river water and opened his eyes.